Jon Holland: The Shadow Self

Jon Holland

The Shadow Self

by
Donald Germain

Beech River Books
Center Ossipee, New Hampshire

BℝB

Beech River Books

P.O. Box 62, Center Ossipee, N.H. 03814
1-603-539-3537
www.beechriverbooks.com

LIBRARY OF CONGRESS CATALOGING-IN-PUBLICATION DATA

Names: Germain, Donald, author.
Title: Jon Holland : the shadow self / by Donald Germain.
Description: Center Ossipee, New Hampshire : Beech River Books, 2018.
Identifiers: LCCN 2017053736 | ISBN 9781930149045 (pbk. : alk. paper)
Classification: LCC PS3607.E7625 J66 2018 | DDC 813/.6--dc23
LC record available at https://lccn.loc.gov/2017053736

Summary: "A novel set in the time periods of the Civil War and one hundred
years earlier in the French and English Colonies. The interwoven stories of
the two main protagonists reveals a spiritual alliance that links them forever
to a destiny that is bound by common values and common causes"--Provided
by publisher.

Cover art and design by Ethan Marion

Printed in the United States of America

To Diana, Cody, and Bryce
who bring meaning to my life,
inspiration to my heart,
and peace to my soul.

Acknowledgments

To those people who have blazed the trail of freedom, championed the battle for human rights, and relentlessly pursued the cause of preserving the sanctity of our planet, I salute you. It is your stories that have inspired this work and sustained the hope that human resolve can relentlessly triumph over the evils of human suffering.

And to my family and friends, I bear the indelible mark of your presence, for it has guided me along the undulating path of an uncertain life.

Finally, to Rick and Diane who labored hard and long to help me find the honest truth in my writing.

*   *   *

This is a work of fiction. Although the novel takes place in a historical setting, names, characters, business, events and incidents are often the products of the author's imagination. Any resemblance to actual persons, living or dead, or actual events is purely coincidental.

Contents

"Suffer the pains of scrutiny and you shall discover the soul of the Shadow Self. Only then you will live within the sacred space and walk within the circle between the light and the dark."

Chapter 1

Suppressing the Insurrection

The day's light faded over the mirror-like surface of the dark river that ran along the western border of the Holland homestead. Shannon O'Reilly, a feisty twenty-year-old Irish-American blacksmith ran at a full tilt down the River Road. He vaulted the white picket fence, coursed his way through the slop in the yard, and rounded the corner of the two-story red barn to approach the careworn colonial farmhouse. He smiled pleasantly at the three farmers who relaxed on the rickety porch after a long day of exhausting chores.

Jon Holland leaned against a knurled post on the stoop. He pulled his hat up from over his eyes, sipped a ladle of cool, well water, and polished off a crisp Macintosh. The lanky eighteen-year-old with long blond hair was verbally accosted by Shannon.

"Have you seen it, Jonny?" He shook a copy of a torn government proviso.

Grandad Michael Holland and his son Riordán, Jon's father, both sat up in their rockers. The men stopped their game of checkers, anxiously awaiting the news that Shannon carried.

Jon straightened his back against the post. "Seen what, Shannon?"

The brawny smithy wiped his brow on the soiled sleeve of his blue shirt. "We're going to war, Jonny. It says so right here." He held the placard over his head.

Jon taunted him, "How do you know what it says, when you can't read a bloody lick?"

"Domine Van Dorn ciphered it for all of the lads in the village. President Lincoln is calling for 75,000 troops to lay waste to the Southern insurrection. Are you mustering in, Jonny?"

Shannon's enthusiasm took Jon by surprise. He had not been a person to get excited about much of anything, except maybe a good pint of ale or a bare-knuckled brawl.

Riordán's concern about the threat of civil war was etched upon on his robust face. He had suffered through the insurrection in Ireland before he came to America back in 1850. He was convinced that wars seldom settled anything and laid the land to physical and emotional waste.

Michael yelled at Shannon, "Get your lardy arse up here and give me that dearned bill so I can cogitate over it." The lad bounded up the creaking stairs and relinquished the document. Michael lowered his wire spectacles onto the end of his nose and painstakingly read the notice.

Grandpa Holland was a crotchety Irishman who suffered from his own trials in life. He had left the Holland's homestead as a teen, defying his father's will to work the land. He sailed to Clonakilty, Ireland and took up residence on the abandoned Cork County croft, but was never satisfied with the agrarian way of life he was destined to live. He spoke to Riordán. "I am hard pressed to make head or tail of this drivel. Why don't they write in plain language for us common folk?"

Jon was a strapping, muscular young man with soft blue eyes like his mother's. He was concerned by the edict's demands, for he never remotely considered going off to war. He watched Shannon turn a jig, giddy at the prospect of fighting. He had always been the reflective one and Shannon the muscle. The pair was inseparable ever since they were young boys. Their destitute families had immigrated to America ten years before, living for a time in the ghettos of New York City, before moving to Michael's aging, but precious homestead.

Michael had inherited a portion of the farm at the base of the Adirondack Mountains from his father, despite the rebellious ways of his youth. These rolling bottomlands had been in the family since the time of the Revolutionary War. Now, as war loomed again on the horizon, it would become the source of controversy for Jon, the next heir. He had been bonded to the homestead by a legacy, but longed for something or someone to alter the course of his sheltered life.

"So, are you going, Jonny?" was Shannon's challenge as he slapped him hard on the back.

Jon glanced up at his father, who rocked quietly in his ancient Comb-Windsor. He gave his take on the matter, "A man has an obligation to defend this country and the freedoms that are afforded to him by the promises of the Constitution. Your relatives fought in the Great War for Independence, but on the contrary side to their birthright because they devoutly believed in the newly formed principles of the opposing cause. It ain't easy taking sides on matters of principle."

Riordán looked toward the river as a flock of geese swooped in and unsettled the placid water. "This war will pit brothers under the swathe of one flag against each other. The insurrectionists choose to scoff at the treatises that bind us together. You should understand the reasons why you are fighting before you put yourself in harm's way." He paused. "Shannon here is a brawler like his father, Jimmy, always fixing for a good fight and not caring much for the principles behind it. You are always ciphering, Jon. Only when your mind is made up for certain do you step in."

Jon had never cared much for fighting when he had lived in the rough-and-tumble hovels of the City, only weighing in during a brawl when compromise had failed to resolve a matter. Riordán reminded him about that misery. "If you didn't man up, then the bloody gangs would have swallowed you up. It was all about survival in the ghetto and it is all about survival now."

Shannon boasted, "Defining the principles of the war will only serve to confuse me. I'm signing up tomorrow at the county seat. All of the lads are going at the crack of dawn. Hell, we'll be back here in ninety days. Mr. Lincoln said so." He grabbed the proviso. "It's all written right here."

"Do you know what you are fighting for, boy-o?" Michael bellowed in a heavy Irish brogue. "You'll get yourself killed, breaking the sullen heart of your precious mum. You don't know a damned thing about the cause you represent." He spit on the ground. "If I told you to pick that up, Paddy Boy, for a chance to get into a brawl, you wouldn't think twice about it. It is loud mouth blokes like you that cause wars and never have the gumption to finish them."

Michael had his fill of fighting back in the old country. He felt that trivial wars of stubborn wills only succeeded in dividing countries further. He had lost his friends and family to senseless battles, fought for glorious causes. He valued his freedom, but he was not about to give his life for something that had been conjured up by a group of bar leaning, big mouth braggarts.

"Begging your pardon, Mr. Holland, but I am fighting for freedom."

Michael scoffed, "Whose freedom, boy-o? Freedom is an arbitrary concept that no one fully understands. As long as you are beholden to the will of other people, you have no freedom. You had better get that through your thick, Irish skull before you go and get yourself all shot up."

Shannon retorted, "Well, come to think of it, I don't rightly know much about freedom, sir, but as long as there is a cause to fight for, I'll be the first to stand up for it."

Michael frowned. "I'll bet you a pint of ale, boy-o, that Mr. Lincoln could not tell you the exacting causes of the pending war. You see, the country is divided over petty things and a century's worth of war ain't going to change that. Single-minded folks are set in their ways and it takes a powerful, brave man to alter thinking on such matters."

Riordán looked across the newly plowed fields. "Our personal history is steeped in the deepest recesses of human suffering. The ground we till is a tribute to the ideals that allowed us to overcome oppression and uphold our sovereignty and identity as a race. I suspect that if a man came and tried to take it from you; you would fight to the death to preserve it."

Michael bantered with the lads. "The Domine preaches about the evils of greed and tyranny. He believes this uprising is about states' rights, religious sectionalism, political power, and economic graft. Those causes have been festering in America since its inception, when men like John Randolph and the Old Republicans led a movement of states' autonomy to bolster their own power. Now the Rebs in South Carolina weigh in with blasphemous rhetoric and armed resistance or the New York Tammany Hall politicians use a hard hand to enforce their own brand of corruption. We need to return to a sovereign life that was beholden to no government. We are people of the land, bound together by the natural instincts of survival, nothing more."

Riordán nodded. "Contemplate this: by going off to war will your lives here in the Valley change as a result of it? Is it worth the risk of getting killed to preserve your heritage? Other men stood up for lesser things simply because those trifling trials would significantly alter the way they carried out their independent lives. You can sit here and hope that nothing personal will change. Or, you can pitch in and try to alter the course of the war to your liking."

Jon had heard enough. "I don't care much about what happens in the Southern States so long as I can uphold the bequest of our people. We have the right to live freely and work the land without fear of oppression. We have fought hard as a family to safeguard that birthright. I will fight to the death to not have it taken away. Will this brewing conflict affect me living a thousand miles away? For that, I cannot be sure. So, like my ancestors, I must take up arms so that there is no doubt about the preservation of my way of life or at least die, desperately fighting to preserve it."

Riordán lifted his head off of his chest. "You have my blessing, Jon. If I were not so old, I would stand at your side and battle toe to toe with them Southern fellers. Some things are worth giving your life for." He took a sip of warm ale. "I fear, though, that you will have a bloody devil of a time swaying your mother's opinions about war. She is a rationale woman and can see the good in a cause if you present it to her with the right conviction. This farm and the legacy of our family mean everything to her, so approach it carefully and she will embrace your enthusiasm."

At the supper table, when the conversation began to wane, Jon appealed to his mother's loyalty to family and country. He had trepidations about marching off into the unknown, a fear welling up in him that he had never experienced before, but his convictions to his personal values trumped his fears. "Mama, I am fixing to enlist. It is something I need to do as a man."

Draighean Holland looked at him across the table. With no visible sign of emotion, she grabbed the last potato roll from a wicker basket. "Do you care to eat the last roll, Shannon?"

"I am stuffed to the gills with your good home cooking, Mrs. Holland. Give it to Jonny. He needs to be fattened up like a Christmas turkey before we ship him off to war."

Draighean's blue eyes glinted in the candlelight as she brushed her strawberry-blond curls from her face. "So, give me a good reason, Jonny darling, why I should embrace this half-cocked notion of sending my only boy off to be killed in an obscure place, fighting a hapless war?"

Jon tried to avoid his mother's questioning glare. "You see, mama; I need to help preserve the heritage of our family and the land we are bound to." Guilt immediately welled up in his heart. "I'll take the last roll. Chasing that Hereford gave me a fierce appetite."

His patriotic fervor aside, Jon could not muster the courage to tell them the real reason he had decided to enlist. He treasured and respected the cultivation of the land, but it was time for him to move on. Times were changing and so was he. The war provided him with an opportunity to face challenges away from the grinding predictability of farm life.

"You are not beholden to us on this matter, Jon, but you need to understand that we share a grave concern for your well-being." Draighean declared firmly, "Your father and I respect your right as a young man to follow your conscience. But please understand that war is a ghastly thing and no mother openly wills her son to step out into harm's way."

Jon felt much like the ancient woodsman that permeated his grandfather's stories. That wayward man had overcome tremendous adversity to see the light of his own calling. He, along with his Mohawk wife, became the foundation upon which their family was built, but that came at a hefty cost. It took years of trials and heartache to create that bond. If the woodsman could overcome his afflictions, then Jon wondered why he could not do the same. He embraced the guarded blessing of his parents, although he felt guilty about making his mother cry. At the break of dawn on the next day, he headed off with Shannon to muster into the infantry.

It was an unusually cold day in April, 1861 as the two men began their walk toward the recruiting camp. The air was crisp and the trees were beginning to bud under the frosty mantle that covered them on this uncertain morn. They passed Jon's dad in the upper field, out long before sunup to herd the cattle with a willow switch toward the barn for the morning milking.

Riordán waved his cap, "Take care, lads. The glory of the nation rests in your hearts."

They doffed their caps before turning the corner at the wood line to head east. Other men joined them as they made the nine-mile trip to the county seat. The recruits lined up in front of a table on the courthouse steps, the Ionic columns of the building posing as a backdrop for the officers dressed in blue that greeted them. Each volunteer penned his mark on the muster role, as commanded by the scribe, and placed their fate in the hands of the fledgling Union Army.

Jon and Shannon were assigned to Infantry Company A with about 100 other men. They would train under the watchful eyes of crusty Mexican War veterans Irish Master Sergeant James Gilhooly and Sergeant Hezekiah Woodley. Gilhooly led company formation and manual arms drills for an hour each day before turning the lads over to the regimental officers to learn more complex maneuvers. In a few weeks, the awkward, raw recruits had been licked into fighting trim.

The rigorous training was easy for the lads who were strong by nature and used to grueling labor. But they were free spirits, not tolerant of the harsh discipline that army life demanded. The wily sergeants made sure that they tempered the men's independence, but did not suppress their will to fight, as they relentlessly prepared them for the uncertain trials of battle.

"Get on with you lads and increase your rate of fire. This is not a turkey shoot in your upper forty." Gilhooly taunted them, aware that they had no idea what the horrors of combat would be like. "That country bluster will cease when the blood of your brothers is spilled upon your blouse."

The lads were given a furlough before boarding the train in Albany that would take them to Washington where the Army of the Potomac was mustering. The entire town turned out to honor the regiment at a raucous barn dance held on the Holland farm. The lads drank heavily, danced to the spirited fiddling of James O'Reilly, and swanked about heroic deeds. As the sun set over the river, they found themselves frightfully alone, perched on Jon's porch, contemplating their fate.

Shannon bragged, "I am coming back a hero with a mess of ribbons plastered to my chest and a fine woman cradled under each arm. We will make quick work of the Rebel rabble."

Jon chastised Shannon, "I am afraid that the drink is doing your talking. You had better not be too confident about that conquering hero harangue or you may be coming home in a pine box."

"That is nonsense. Those ramshackle Southern boys will be putty in our hands. Look at these fine uniforms and new rifles they have given us. Do you think that an underdressed, countrified Reb shooting a squirrel gun will be any match for the likes of the soldiers of our majestic army?"

Jon furrowed his brow in disgust. "Overconfidence has gotten you into more than one scrape and it seems that I am the one who always has to bail you out. I am afraid that I am not going to stop a bullet for the likes of you, Shannon O'Reilly, no matter how dear you are to me."

The two bantering cronies were interrupted by Jon's parents, who had just sent the last guests home from the boisterous merrymaking. Riordán spoke, "We need a moment, if you please."

Shannon took his leave. "I'll see you at first light to march off to catch the war train, Johnny."

Draighean coaxed, "Shannon, darling, we harbor no secrets from you. Please stay."

Shannon tipped his kepi. "Thank you, Mrs. Holland. That is most kind of you."

Draighean spoke gravely, "Jon, we want to give you a treasure. It has been passed down through the generations of Holland men. Your father is keeping the tradition alive by presenting it to you."

Riordán removed a gold pocket watch from his vest and polished it on his linen sleeve. "Jon, this watch represents a precious legacy of our family. It is a true representation of what we stand for and it is only fitting that you carry it off to a war that will serve to preserve that legacy or eventually destroy it. It will provide you with the strength you need to survive by the sheer magnitude of its spiritual power. Call upon it when things are most dire, for it will subtly remind you of the supremacy of the human spirit and man's exacting will to overcome adversity. It has sustained our family for over one hundred years. Through debilitating wars, the purge of our ancestral people from their sacred land, and the throes of the Great Famine, it represents our fervent resolve and our strong will, bound together by a bond of trust."

Jon never understood nor cared about the watches' aura. "You speak about the watch as if it possesses human qualities, Papa. What are you trying to reveal to me about its legacy?"

"The watch is not magical, son, it is inspirational. The mystery of the watch will be revealed to you at another time, in another place. You can discover its true power by meeting life's challenges face to face. You will be shepherded by the legacy of its past and driven by the spirit of the people who carried it long before you. Their bequest is its guiding light. This legacy will steer you along a path of understanding when despair reigns down up you and all hope seems to be lost."

Jon was surprised to hear his pragmatic father speaking in riddles about an inanimate object like a watch, as if it had a persona. He examined the scratched cover, wondering about the initials JPB inscribed upon it. He opened it to reveal the slightly bent second hand under the glass careening around its face, precisely marking time as it had for over a century. He rubbed his finger over the beautifully inlaid image on the inside and then closed it abruptly. "I am not worthy of this gift. You keep it until the war is over. It is too precious of an heirloom for me to carry into battle where it could be lost or destroyed."

Draighean hugged him. "It is fitting that you take the watch at a time of uncertainly, a time when your doggedness will be truly tested. It will be a desperate struggle, but you will soon discover the power that the watch holds over us. The secrets to revealing the truth to its birthright can only be discovered at the hands of controversy and personal affliction. The challenges of the war will bring that all to light. Please take it. It will make us very proud."

Jon placed the watch in the pocket inside of his frockcoat, under his heart. The precious heirloom would continue to reside there as he faced the dangers and vagaries of war. He leaned back against the porch railing and closed his eyes, overcome by a vast array of emotions. One of his grandfather's stories came back to him, as they often did when his skittering soul was troubled. He wondered if he was up to the task of upholding the rich legacy that a fiery wilderness woodsman and an Indian princess with mystical leaning had created.

The four uncertain souls sat silently under the porches canopy, cradled beneath the April sky laden with brilliant stars that illuminated the land. Soon the dawn would break over the river and the tiny beacons of light would be obscured by the ambiguity of a new day.

Chapter 2

Le Loon

The red, two-wheeled dray bumped haphazardly over the rutted path. Its glowing whale oil lantern, hanging from a spindle, swayed with the undulating rhythm of the road. Upon its splintered bench sat a diminutive woman, her body concealed under a tattered, hooded cape.

A glint of sun peeked over the escarpment, as the woman shivered from the biting cold of a brisk wind bowing off of the river. Its rays inched across the landscape and revealed the distinguished walled city of Quebec. The fortress loomed precipitously ahead, a forebodingly dark icon against the intensifying tangerine sky. It was the year 1752 and war was lingering over the horizon.

The woman called out in a meek voice to a frail boy who tugged on the ox's tether, "Put the whip to him, René. We need to get along promptly so we can get back to the homestead before sundown. Your papa will be arriving homewards from the hunt. As sure as the Lord graces our presence, he will be vexed if his vittles are not on the table when he arrives."

The lad was confident. "There is no need to beat the beast, mama. He will mind me."

The rickety cart crested the hill, passing under a cover of thick hardwoods onto an expanse of ground known as the Plains of Abraham. The sun's rays illuminated the plateau, its emerald sea of grass split in two by a thread of road. It was a short distance to the massive stone archway known as the Saint Louis Gate, the main portal into the city and the Citadel that protected it.

As the two weary travelers approached the fortress, they were confronted by soldiers of the Gardes-Francaises. A hardened Captain of the Guard held up his hand to stop René, while his two cronies sidled around the cart. "State your business, madam!" the Captain gargled.

Angelique Dubois pulled back her hood, careful not to look into the man's eyes. "We come to barter for domestic staples that we cannot procure from the gifts that God provides."

The officer walked to the rear of the cart. "What have you hidden under this sailcloth?"

Angelique turned around. "It is imperative that we complete our business before sundown, sir."

The soldier pulled back the tattered canvas to reveal a small cask of grain, a stack of cordwood, and a festering cache of beaver pelts. "What do expect to fetch for this meager batch of goods? These pelts are moth ridden and no trader will risk his return on this lot of waste."

"We are simple folk, sir. We do not require much in return." Pleading her case, she became agitated, "I beseech you sir, please let us pass."

The guard looked up into Angelique's deep blue, piercing, and persuasive eyes. "You are a pretty thing, madam, although I'd say that your mister does not appreciate you like I do. Did he lay those bruises upon you, about your eyes and nose?"

Angelique lowered her head in shame and pulled the hood up to conceal the purple-green marks. "I appreciate your concern, sir, but I am a resolved woman. Can we pass?"

The officer put his arm around René's shoulder. "Does your papa wail on your mother, son?"

René was a tall, malnourished boy of nearly ten years. His disheveled clothes fit poorly. The sleeves of his russet sailcloth coat were too short. He wore a tattered red-and-white gingham shirt. His tight leather breeches, held up by leather suspenders, clung to his skin. His feet were bare and dirty. He wore a broad brimmed hat made from black felt. Long, dark hair streamed down his back.

"I asked you a question, boy. I expect a prompt answer in return."

René looked to his mother. She shook her head to indicate that he should let the subject lie.

"Cat got your tongue, boy? Well, your silence tells me a thousand tales. At the very least, I believe that you should reveal to me your papa's name, for future reference of course."

René could smell the reeking sweat emanating from the soldier's soiled white uniform and feel the man's hot tobacco breath upon his cheek. He peered deeply into the man's eyes. They were dark, but he could sense that a gentle spirit resided within their depths. He decided that no harm could come from a response. "My papa answers to the name Henri Dubois, sir."

The Captain and his comrades spontaneously laughed. He lit his clay pipe and blew smoke into René's face. The boy coughed, attempting to move away, but the soldier collared him by the back of his ruffled coat. He exhaled a guttural laugh, "So your mama is married to The Loon? That lunatic has spent more time in my jails than any other man in this city."

Tears pooled slowly in René's eyes. He was embarrassed for he knew that the officer's presumptions about his father's worth were to the mark.

Angelique tried to intercede. "Can we please make our way into the city, sir?" Tension was evident in her voice. "We must complete our trade in a timely manner."

The officer's rough deportment changed. "If you should ever need my intervention with Henri, madam, I stand here most days guarding this gate and I would be happy to oblige you. A fair lady should not be subjected to the outlandish antics of a madman the likes of Henri Dubois. You would do well to sidle up to a more refined man." He stepped aside to let the dray pass.

René got the ox moving before he changed his mind. Reluctantly, the cart inched forward and crept under the grey, stone arches of the gate. The Captain of the Guard called out to him, "Mind me, boy. You had best look after your mother. She is a first-rate woman, too fine to be in the company of a barmy man the likes of The Loon. Heed my warning. Henri Dubois will leave you lingering on the brink of insanity if he does not attempt to strike you down before then."

Chapter 3

Satan's Waltz

The brightness of the dawning day gave way to a miserable; misting evening, making cart ride back to their wilderness homestead long and arduous. Angelique sat on the seat of the dray, the rain dripping off of her hood. She did not seem to notice, too caught up in profound thought and solemn prayer. Her chin rested on her chest as she contemplated the disorderly nature of her life. She had committed to a vile marriage, trapped in a humdrum existence of violence and hatred. It hadn't always been that way, but now it seemed almost too much to bear. The beleaguered matron glanced up to watch her son diligently guiding the cart over a hill.

René was a good boy, obedient and industrious, but strangely introspective. Angelique wondered how he had managed to keep a sense of balance in his life as chaos reigned around him. Concerned about her son's welfare, she yelled out, "How are you faring, boy?"

Without looking up, the boy responded, "No need for concern, mama. I enjoy walking. It brings me closer to natural things. I find the solitude peaceful."

"You pay no mind to that soldier. Your father need not be bothered with such trivial things."

"Yes mama, but papa beats you without cause. He wails on both of us if his mind is set to it."

"We are servants of the Lord. We must be obedient to his will and the will of your father."

"It don't seem right to me, mama."

"You pay that no mind. Through the guidance of the Holy Father, peace will be our destiny."

René did not understand either of his parents or the circumstances under which they lived. His father was an irascible man who bore the scars of managing diverse personalities, each one bent on suppressing the will of those around him. René feared him, not knowing from minute to minute, which Henri Dubois would materialize. The lad felt a deep sense of hatred for the man. He had rightfully earned the nickname that the soldiers had placed upon him, The Loon.

Angelique felt alone, clinging to the word of the Lord for comfort. She had looked for a fresh start in Quebec City when she made the arduous journey from France in her early teen years. She lived for a time as an Ursuline nun at Three Rivers, fulfilling her vows of devout servitude to the Catholic Church. While cloistered there, she tended to the spiritual needs of God's flock and nursed the ailing colonists back to health. It was rewarding work, but as all young girls do, she became restless, wanting, and distracted. She longed for something more fulfilling in her life, to dance again, laugh, and even bear children. She realized that the convent was not to her liking. Even though her love for the Lord had not waned, her marriage to his duty had many voids.

"Are you ok, mama?"

"Yes son, just feeling a little under the weather is all."

Angelique had not entered the Ursuline convent by choice. The untimely death of her bourgeois, Catholic parents in a horrific carriage accident had dramatically altered her future. A life of exposure to higher education, social dignity, and Parisian refinement was suddenly lost. Once a ravishing beauty who frolicked in a lacey dress down the Boulevard de Capucines, she now found herself mired in poverty deep within the uncivilized backcountry of New France.

Angelique enjoyed the trips to the Quebec City, for they exposed her to some refined living. The street markets inside of the walled fortress, although simple by Parisian standards, offered a menagerie of fine trade goods such as silk handkerchiefs or lavender sachets. She could pick up a sachet and hold it against her nose for a long time before reluctantly placing it back in the merchant's basket. She wished she could scrape up a little extra money to spoil herself just one time, but Henri would not allow her to possess precious baubles of frivolous pleasure.

The ox slowed to a mere crawl as it navigated a sharp turn that angled down a steep hill. Angelique gripped the iron handles on the seat of the dray. The strain was evident in her face as she struggled to hold on. The ground soon flattened, the ox reestablishing its methodical gait. The sullen maiden was finally able to relax her grip and resume her melancholy.

The bond between Henri Dubois and Angelique Papineau was a happenstance of fate. Henri sought the comfort of a doting wife. Angelique yearned to be a part of a family and escape the bondage of her cloisters. It was a mutual agreement to satisfy their selfish desires. They both questioned the decision in hindsight, but at the time it seemed like the sensible thing to do.

Angelique spoke. "You will have a better life than I. Truth tells that requited love and loyalty transcends all else. Heed the word of the Lord and everything will be resolved to your liking."

The boy was too young to understand the highbrow provisos his mother preached daily. His life was measured by fear, nothing more, despite her persistent coaxing to think that it could be translated into better terms. He did not share her devotion or understand the nature of a supreme being. To him, discipline and faith were measured by the strike of his father's capricious hand. Truth was devoured by the pain of each sadistic moment of torture he endured. Living and survival for him was simplified into these terms: do whatever it takes to see the sun rise on the next day.

The rest of the journey seemed tedious. They were late because the weather was foul and they had struggled to trade their wares. They finally turned south onto the overgrown path that led toward their homestead. They could see the rickety, hickory cottage looming in the distance.

The one-room shack was built by Henri out of hand-hewed logs. The grey chinking of wattle and daub was carelessly slapped into the spaces between the logs. A small porch covered a squat entry portal. A few small rifle slits carved randomly into the crevices of the mortar served as windows. The roof, thatched with peat, supported a cobblestone chimney.

As the two travelers approached the dwelling, Angelique noticed deep black smoke pouring from the stack, a sure sign that René's impatient father had arrived home before them. He always stoked the blaze with wet peat, too lazy to fetch dry kindling. There would be hell to pay.

"I will bed down the ox for the night, mama," René volunteered to avoid the inevitable rage of his father. "Do you want me to see you in and tend to that later?"

"I'll be alright, son. You serve the needs of the animal. He has done well by us on this day."

The aging matron climbed down from the seat of the dray as her son held the ox in place. She adjusted her cloak about her shoulders and then raised her hood over her head. She gathered up her meager cache of belongings from the rear of the cart and reluctantly headed toward the cottage. At the stoop, she paused to muster the strength to enter the hut. She reached for the latch on the portal, but stopped abruptly as the creaking flap swung violently open.

"Angelique, my precious darling, it is so good to be back in the comfort of my home with my family. I have stoked a warm fire and shot a few plump squirrels for our evening meal."

Angelique was taken aback by Henri's jovial mood. She forced a smile, entering the hut as he held the door open for her. It was warm inside, but rather smoky. She squinted as her eyes adjusted to the dim light. Everything seemed in order, just as she had left it.

Henri politely took her packages and placed them upon the small wooden table. She draped her cloak over a hobnail tacked to the backside of the door. She shuffled over the creaking pine boards toward the hearth and sat down in her rocker, adjusting her greying frock. It was worn, the mends holding it precariously in place upon her frail shoulders. She unconsciously brushed herself off, as if it mattered and then closed her eyes to revel in the peace of the moment.

Henri interrupted. "Where is the boy?"

Angelique answered in a whisper, "He is tending to the stock."

"You had best fetch him for me. I need him to skin these squirrels."

Before Angelique honored Henri's wishes, she glanced about the room. There were no immediate signs that her husband had been drinking, but that did not mean that he wasn't intoxicated, the tavern being but a stone's throw back on the King's Highway.

The hovel was sparsely decorated. A Dutch fireplace and hearth consumed the back wall. A small rope bed with a soiled straw mattress settled in one corner of the room, a table and two chairs in another. Herbs and drying game hung from the shallow rafters, the remains of their lifeblood staining the wooden floor below. A tin wash basin and pitcher sat on a teetering pinewood stand by the door. A narrow ladder rose up from the corner of the room, disappearing into a small loft.

Angelique savored the brief moment of respite. She turned toward the hearth to warm herself, facing a hand-carved wooden cross that hung above it. The wood was stained from water that leaked from the roof and the smoke of the constant fires that burned below it. She prayed to an imaginary image of Jesus before succumbing to the will of her duties as an obedient wife. She carefully sidled around Henri who stared down upon her. He rubbed the curious indentation on the side of his head as she passed. She crossed the room, pulled hard on the sticky latch to open the flap, and called out into the night for her son, "René, come quickly to help your mama."

The boy appeared around the corner of the house. He could sense that something was amiss. He did not question his mother, aware that his father was lingering just inside.

Delaying the inevitable, Angelique said, "Fetch a bucket of water from the well, dear boy."

The boy obeyed without question. He lowered the wooden bucket into the dark abyss, extracting the chilly liquid from its depths. He quaffed a drink then waddled off toward the house, the bucket dangling between his legs. His father greeted him, "How do you fare, René?"

The boy answered promptly, "Fare thee well, Papa." He was careful not to spill the water, but the cracks in the wooden vessel made drips inevitable.

His father admonished him. "If I have taught you nothing else, lad, it is to respect your father. Clean up that muddle. When that is done, skin those creatures lying on the table. We will sup on squirrel stew this evening, if your mother ever gets around to preparing it."

René tried to understand what drove his father to distraction. It could be a simple thing, like a bit of the water on the floor or something far more complex, like a rampaging wolf killing the livestock. He cleaned up the spill and gazed momentarily at the man hovering over him.

Henri resembled a tall, gangly, and undernourished scarecrow dressed in buckskin. He wore freshly blackened Hessians on his feet, their broad tops folded down about his ankles. On his deformed head rested a white thrum cap, its tasseled top draped to one side. His dark hair was rumpled under the cap. His black beard and mustache, home to a variety of small objects, and sun bronzed skin shrouded his turbulent interior. Those who did not know him would say that he had a kind face dotted with gentle hazel eyes. The pupils dilated as his fickle mood swung to and fro.

René had learned to read his father's fickle oval orbs. When the green-grey iris consumed them, it was a time of inner peace. When the pupil raged a darkened glow, brutality was afoot.

René whispered to his mother as he passed by her, "Are you ailing, mama?"

She shooed him away. "Mind your papa, René. We have vittles to fix."

The boy hustled off to the table. He grabbed the knife that his father had left lying there and immediately began the laborious process of skinning the stout foragers.

Henri was known to be exuberant at times, only to suddenly turn jocularity into rage. "How was your trip to the city, René? Did you see any curious fellows while you were there?"

The boy wanted to avoid the conversation that took place with the soldiers. "The ox had a mind of his own today, papa. He possessed the will of the devil, but I made him obey."

"Fine son, I am pleased that you managed him well." Henri became distracted. He began to hum a tune, barely audible at first, then louder so Angelique and René could hear it clearly. They exchanged surreptitious glances. This is how the violence often began.

Henri waltzed over to Angelique, as if dancing with an imaginary partner. He grabbed his wife about the waist. "I suspect that it is time that we take a turn at the dance, mother."

Before Angelique could protest, Henri whisked her away from the fire, reeling her about in a macabre waltz. The gawky woodsman hummed a ditty, but when it changed, so did the steps of the dance. She followed compliantly and secretly enjoyed these moments. They reminded her of the days when she danced with the ballet. But Henri soon tired of the game. His steps became quicker and he thrashed her about like a rag doll.

René watched his father's pupils dilate. The boy called out, "Papa, can you help me with these squirrels? I fear they are giving me a devil of a time." It was too late.

Henri threw Angelique viciously across the room. She stumbled on the rocker and struck her head on the bluestone hearth, a trickle of blood ran down her forehead and chin. He grabbed his head in both of his hands, his eyes fueled with rage. "How dare you neglect my supper, you useless woman. Do you not understand that my needs are to be first and foremost? There is no time for the foolish pleasures of mindless frolic. Get on with you woman before I thrash you."

Angelique lay motionless, too delirious to respond.

Henri digressed, "Where have you been off to, wench? There is no supper in the pot and my bed is cold. Make haste or I shall lash you until you bleed." He grabbed Angelique and hauled her up off of the floor. A sadistic punch to her ribs made her buckle over in pain, her breath taken away. She refused to cry out, however, for it was a sign of weakness. "Get up woman."

Angelique prayed for forgiveness while she brushed her hair from her face. She was still a stunning woman, despite the bruises that darkened her eyes. Her round, cherubic features and piercing blue eyes glowed in the firelight. Her disheveled blond hair, once vibrant, scattered about her shoulders. With great difficulty, she rose, using the rocker as a crutch to right herself.

Henri paced the floor, hands clutching his head as he muttered nonsensical phrases.

René cringed under the table. He always kowtowed to his father, but today was different. He remembered what the soldier had said to him. *You had best look after your mother, boy.*

Angelique did not respond rapidly enough for Henri. He lurched at her and grabbed her by the hair. He lifted her up so that her feet dangled above the floor.

René could no longer stand idly by. In a fury, he grabbed the knife and leapt upon his father's back, thrusting the small blade into the meat of the woodsman's shoulder.

Henri cried out in anguish, but managed to throw René to the floor. He reached across his body, quickly removed the knife from his shoulder, and tossed it aside. The blood from the wound flowed down his back to create a dark stain on his tunic. He clamored after the boy, who cowered under the table. He threw the table aside. It tumbled recklessly, scattering the squirrels and other foodstuffs across the planked decking. One of the table legs broke clean off. Henri scooped it up as he approached René. "You ungrateful troll. I have sacrificed for you and this is how you thank me? You will pay dearly for your misguided loyalty, boy."

Henri seized René by the ear and dragged him toward the hearth. The boy cried out as Henri stuck the table leg into the fire. "I will mark you for life, you ingrate," He raised the torch over the boy's cheek. Before he could brand his son, a weak, but determined Angelique desperately threw herself at him, gouging fiercely at his eyes. He screamed in anguish and confronted his wife. Unparalleled rage masked his contorted, scratched, and bleeding face. "I'll deal with you later, boy. As for you, you miserable excuse for a woman…"

Angelique cried out, "Run René. Run deep into the forest and save yourself."

Henri dropped the smoldering table leg and struck Angelique across the face. As suddenly as a lightning strike, all went black for the scorned woman.

René seized the opportunity to escape. He opened the door with one nimble pull on the latch, and was poised to rush out onto the porch. The knife sailed by his ear and struck the door jamb with a crack, falling harmlessly at his feet. He stared in horror at his father, who stood triumphantly over his mother. For an instant the boy was torn. He should help his mother, but that would mean a certain rendezvous with his own death. René slammed the door and bolted off of the porch. He bound through the overgrown grass and weeds until he reached the relative safety of the forest. He ducked in and out of the brush and entered a thick grove of ash, poplar, and sycamore saplings. Beyond this point lay the deeper recesses of the wilderness where he would be out of harm's way.

Chapter 4

The Harvesting of the Corn

Jon's regiment spent most of '61 on provost duty. Their fighting had been limited to regimental squabbles and the quelling of mob unrest in Baltimore, which had been dubbed Mob Town due to the propensity of its people to bring their sentiments into the streets.

The savage glory the men had hoped for had eluded them. They were anxious to pitch in where others were dying. Many, like Shannon, became disgruntled by army life. "Move on, you slacker, before I run you through." Shannon shoved a young boy who had taunted him. "Damned mess we are in, Jonny, wasting away playing wet nurse to some sniveling civilians."

"Don't be too hasty to get yourself into combat, my friend. From what I hear from the passing troops, it is not as glorious as we make it out to be."

"They are a bunch of cowards. Send me to the front and they will see how a real man fights."

By August of 1862, the Union Army had suffered a series of humiliating defeats against the aggressive Army of Northern Virginia. Battle attrition had decimated the ranks and the government was forced to call up reinforcements. The ninety-day war had passed into a grueling battle of wills blanketing the nation in a shadow of misery.

Jon's regiment left Baltimore and moved to Centreville where the scattered corps had concentrated to move against General Robert E. Lee's offensive thrust into Maryland. The farm boys were about to get their first taste of combat, but in a way they never could have imagined.

It had been two days since the regiment's first fight at Turner's Gap, a bloody affair to secure passage over the Blue Ridge at South Mountain. The battered Rebs had withdrawn in the cover of darkness and left the position in the hands of the exuberant Yankee corp. Victories were bittersweet for these churlish chaps, as they suffered through close combat for the first time.

"Now what do you think of battle, Shannon?"

"It ain't what I expected, for sure, but I am satisfied just the same."

Jon was shaken to the bone by what he saw and felt. The carnage marked his soul, but his heartless friend, Shannon, could not begin to understand his duress.

The fall landscape started to take form as the massive army descended the Blue Ridge in long, snaking columns. The existence of a supreme being was never more apparent than on this day, as the sun warmed the valley floor and heightened the spirits of the men.

General Lee's infamous *Special Order 191* fell unsuspectingly into Union hands, giving Major General George McClellan a tactical advantage. But as sporadic resistance was swept aside by his advanced guard, there seemed to be no urgency to pursue the Rebs.

Federal flags fluttered in the gentle breeze over the shops and homes of the quaint village of Boonsboro. Demonstrative cheering and rousing songs seemed to heighten the soldiers' mood as the people of the town came out to greet the Union troops. The blue clad soldiers flirted with the young ladies who hand out Johnny cakes and cool drinks of mountain spring water.

"This is a fine reception we are receiving, Jonny. Do you think they could spare a pint of ale for a weary soldier?" was Shannon's inquiry.

Jon looked up at O'Reilly. "You are insufferable at times with this propensity to drink. Settle yourself by quaffing some sweet Maryland water and eating some of that lovely Johnny cake."

Shannon took his advice. He left the rank and accosted a pretty young girl standing by the wayside. The smithy relieved her of the entire basket of cakes and shared them with his friends as he ran back to the column. He then callously tossed the empty basket by the side of the road.

The sweet Maryland maiden, too fearful to confront Shannon, wept uncontrollably.

Gilhooly ran up from his position at the rear of the unit. The feisty noncom was not more than five foot six inches in height, but he managed to grab the private by his collar and pull his face down toward his. "You have made that generous maiden cry, you big oaf. If you leave the rank again, I will have you drawn and quartered like they did in the old country, ripping you from limb to limb. Step lively and be smart about it." Shannon was not about to challenge him. To make sure, the Master Sergeant marched by his side for the better part of the day, berating him at every wrong turn.

The word soon spread that the Rebs had drawn up on the hills outside of the small village of Sharpsburg, Maryland. The tiny hamlet was situated on the northeast bank of the Potomac River, nestled between the river and Antietam Creek, just a few miles beyond Boonsboro.

After a short rest along the National Road, the column turned south toward Sharpsburg and posted on the right of the developing line. Corps commanders defiantly voiced their displeasure with McClellan for his failure to engage the enemy. He would not be moved to battle on this day, nor the next, giving the Rebels time to bring scattered corps in from their points of bivouac. One of the greatest opportunities of the war was lost as "Little Napoleon" strategized. Although he was an outstanding organizer and inspirational leader, he was not up to commanding an army in the field. His hesitation would lead this army directly into the teeth of the lion.

Hookers' Corps was ordered to cross the arched stone Upper Bridge over the Antietam Creek, and deploy between the East and North Woods. Rickett's Division, which contained Jon's regiment, was posted near a cornfield on the extreme left of the First Corp's line across the Smoketown Road. They rested on their arms and were treated to an insufferable night long bombardment. Just before dawn, a lull in the firefight finally occurred.

"Company A, get your fat asses off of the ground and form up immediately on my mark," Gilhooly's deep voice broke the eerie silence.

Jon shouldered his pack and rifle. He encouraged Shannon to move. "Ain't you coming?"

"You won't need that pack where we're going, Holland. Maybe you will be fit enough later to come back and fetch it." The angry Sergeant Major drew a line in the soil with his sword and then sauntered over toward Shannon. He was too tired to suffer through another lecture. He gathered his weapon and accoutrements and took his place in line. "Forty rounds per man, am I clear? You heard me right you bloody beggars, forty rounds. You will thank me later."

The soldiers retreated to their packs and filled their ammo boxes. They had been resupplied in Boonsboro, complaining about carrying the extra weight. The reality of the order shocked them.

As Shannon filled his cap box, he made light of the moment, but there was tension in his voice. "Well, Jonny, we sure as hell ain't going squirrel hunting. Forty rounds are our limit."

The company was deployed in a line of skirmish at the edge of a cornfield. With the Potomac River at their back and one hundred thousand Federals pressing them, Jon thought that the Rebs were trapped like a fox in a hollow by a pack of dogs. But he knew that they would fight like wolverines, in unconventional ways, to turn the tables on them if they were not careful.

Shannon was agitated. "Why is it that we always draw picket duty? I was planning on a hot meal and a nap. Now, I have to lay here waiting for some Reb to sneak up and lop my head off."

Gilhooly was fed up with Shannon. "Stop your bellyaching, O'Reilly. I swear, you moan louder than a cheap English whore, you bloody Mick. Do your duty, you bleeding malcontent."

Shannon answered defiantly, "If you expect me to probe blindly through that corn for some grey-back bushwhacker, you have another thing coming, Master Sergeant. They don't pay me enough to take a Burton bullet for those lads back in the woods fixing coffee."

Gilhooly removed his revolver from its holster, cocked the hammer, and placed barrel at the back of Shannon's head. "I'll solve that problem for you right here and right now, shirker. Before you can spit again, I'll spread what there is of your meager brain all over Maryland."

Shannon wanted to get up and thrash the Master Sergeant, but thought better of it.

"I see that we have an understanding. Now turn to, you bloody fool, and remain vigilant."

The picket line moved out fifty yards ahead of the regiment. The men spread out ten paces apart to cover the expanse of ground at the edge of Miller's cornfield. The field reminded Jon of home. He loathed agrarian life, but now it seemed a damned sight better than being in harm's way. He questioned his decision to fight. Was it for slavery, states' rights, or to preserve the Union his ancestors had fought so hard to create? Was it for selfish greed? After all, wasn't war exciting? After the lead began to fly, war and its underlying causes did not seem as glorious as they implied.

An officer astride a magnificent black stallion appeared out of the mist. He stopped where the pickets where kneeling and garnered their attention with his unshakable presence. The flags carried by his escort snapped and cracked to break the eerie silence that hovered over the field.

Brigadier General Abram Duryea was in charge of General Rickett's lead brigade. The staunch, well respected New York City native steadied the combatants. He was a handsome man with curly black hair, large sideburns cut sharply across his cheeks, and a firm jaw. Before the war, he had been a wealthy merchant who dealt in commodities and the sale of mahogany. The General was well liked by the troops. He had rapidly risen from the lowly world of a private to a respected brigadier. A fierce fighter, like his men, Duryea would never refuse to put himself in harm's way.

"When the fight comes to our quarter, give them hell boys for the glory of the regiment...for your mothers and sweethearts...and for the nation that cradles you in her bosom."

Chapter 5

Death's Shroud

The September morning mist clung to Jon's uniform like a death shroud. He could smell the fear and sense the trepidation. He could see the boyish faces of his friends peering into the haze. Some shivered from the uncertainty. Some prayed. Some reveled in the thrill of the hunt.

Jon was convinced that there would be another harrowing day of bloodshed. He reached into his breast pocket and pulled out his watch. He glanced at the marred cover that was a reflection of his first few months of military service. He opened the face. It was 5:30 A.M..

Shannon's voice fractured the eerie silence. "What is ailing you this morning, Jonny?"

Jon spoke quietly, "I was just thinking about Turner's Gap. You know our first brush with death and all? Do you think the Rebs will put up less of a fight today?"

"I must admit that I was frightened, but I'm over that," Shannon reminisced. "I thought I could take to killing, but when they drew blood it was more horrible than I could imagine."

"Keep your powder dry lads or it will be hell to pay," Sergeant Woodley's voice rang out.

The Turner Gap fight seemed like a bad dream. The action that evening had been fierce as the brigade struggled to take the pass. Dusk was gathering over the field and a light rain fell. The regiment was called forward to refuse the right of the Federal line. At the double quick, they moved into position behind a fieldstone wall, only to be met by a horrific volley. It was the first encounter they would have with the seemingly invincible rabble Bobby Lee called an army.

A marked bullet struck Sylvester Van Antwerp in the chest. It broke a rib before lodging in his lung. He staggered, convulsed, and dropped his weapon to clutch at his chest. Blood gurgled in his lungs as he uttered the name of his sweetheart, "Lottie". He grabbed Jon's arm and fell to the ground. His blank stare revealed his lingering pain as he expired.

The blood from the ragged wound spattered Jon's face. He stood awkwardly over Sylvester's lifeless form, too overcome by emotion to properly load and fire. He breathed hard, as he tried to overcome the urge to run. His knees began to melt as the horror of the battle raged around him.

Gilhooly heard the slap of the bullet upon Van Antwerp's chest. He directed his attention toward that portion of the line and smacked Jon hard on the buttocks with the flat of his sword. "Steady boys; steady! We need only to return the fire and we'll have them on the run."

The regiment loosed a devastating volley that, for an instant, illuminated the landscape and revealed the silhouettes of the Rebel ghost regiment just a few rods to the front.

Jon was shocked back into action, shivering like a dog in the rain. He repeatedly loaded and fired his rifled musket at an enemy he could barely see. He watched the muzzle blast of a Rebel gun and then shot back into the blackened void it left behind. The carnage he witnessed in the decimated Rebel line at dawn confirmed that his marksmanship had been painfully true.

The firing slackened and a grand "huzzah" rose up from the Rebel line and echoed through the valley below the Gap. The mystical cheer put an end to the fighting on this disheartening day.

Jon crouched on the ground, only to stare with horror into Sylvester's fixed eyes. He was unable to stomach the grief in his glare. The touch of Sylvester's skin was cold as he closed the lids. He was stricken by the horror of battle, so gruesome and so loathsome that it defied description. Now, a few days later, he relived the terror of *seeing the elephant,* a term depicting the horrific emotion of engaging in combat. He remembered that his body quaked with fear, reduced to a mindless killing machine. He had overcome the stomach sickness and the urge to run away, pumping lead into men he did not know or understand, but who had callously taken his friend's life.

Mysterious voices ran unchecked through his head. *The land is your sacred gift. Cherish it beyond all else, for it is your Mother and your keeper.* They summoned him. *Venture forth into the intimidating shadows and infuse them with mystical life.* He closed his eyes to exorcise the demons. His breathing was short, his mind wandered. *If only he could have helped him.*

Van Antwerp was a Dutchman whose roots could be traced back to the first settlers of the Hudson River trading community of Beverwijck. Some believed that he was related to a sailor from the Half Moon, but there was no definitive proof. The family moved to a land patent along the Mohawk River outside of the wilderness village of Schenectady. Their sleek bateaux opened up lucrative inland trade routes and solidified strong relations with the Iroquois tribes.

Jon thought about men like Sylvester's ancestors who broke ground for a new way of life. *What possessed them to fight for tiny plots of land? Were they drawn by greed or was its inherent value in the freedom it afforded them?* Before long the tiny cornfield to his front would be soaked with the blood of thousands of combatants, to what end?

Jon thought he saw a solitary figure dash across his sightlines. He raised his weapon, taking a bead. A tattooed warrior peered through the corn. Long dark hair flowed behind him in the wind and a frightful scar coursed across his bronzed cheek. Jon froze, his sweating palms grasped tightly around his weapon. The warrior's mouth did not move. And yet, within his befuddled mind, Jon could hear him speak. *Your legacy is bound to matters of the heart. Within its rhythmic calling lie the answers you seek.* The warrior placed his hand over his heart and disappeared into the shadows.

Shannon sensed Jon's anxiety. "What is it, Jonny?"

Jon lowered his weapon and shivered. "It was nothing, just fear playing tricks on my mind." *Realize the power of a natural life, for peace resides within its bosom.*

Jon opened the watch, barely able to make out the figure of a horse, lightning bolts inlaid upon its body. He could distinctly hear the tick, tick, tick, of its second hand as it wound its endless path around the face, pausing as it stuck at the top for a brief whisper, before careening headlong down the other side. He strained to see the time. Five forty-five A.M., September 17, 1862.

Shannon snapped, "That watch has possessed you to a point of distraction, Jonny!"

Jon replied, "The watch intrigues me, nothing more. There is no telling what magic can be conjured up from this vessel of time, but who am I to dispute the stories that have manifested themselves over the course of its history. Grandpa says this watch has mystical powers, but I think that those are nothing more than rants that an old man conjures up to pass the time."

"Be careful what you say, for your negativity may wake the dead. He tells the stories with such conviction that it is like he was there when they occurred. How could they not be true?"

"Believe what you will, Shannon. You have not heard those tales a million times like I have. Just the same, I am most grateful to have such a precious heirloom in my possession."

"If you ask me, Jonny, there is something powerful emanating from that image. Whoever carved that representation of a horse had the skilled hand of an artisan. It has a supernatural quality about it. This watch is a cradle of love, loyalty, and devotion. You had best respect it."

Jon placed the watch back into its refuge under his heart. The image of a tall, stately woman flashed across his sightline. A fearsome warrior, she drew her bow and set her sights on an imaginary foe. He rubbed his eyes and wiped the cold sweat from his brow.

The sudden flash of a signal gun broke the silence. Jon and Shannon looked up to follow the blazing shell as it arched over their heads. They instinctively covered their ears to await the blast in the rear. The desperate Battle of Antietam had finally exploded all around them.

Chapter 6

The Voice of the Songbird

René rested in the grove of trees, suspecting that his father was hot on his trail. He breathed hard, but did not linger. His father's mood was so foul that he may resort to anything, so he needed to give Henri Dubois time to quell the beasts raging in his soul.

The lad turned south toward the brush line. He parted the brambles, the thorns raking his exposed skin, but he hardly noticed. He surmised he could mask the trace of his trail in the forgiving water of the stream. He looked over his shoulder to see if he had been followed. His father was a crafty tracker and could spring upon him in an instant from the blind. He entered the beck and ran until he dropped. He lay on the soft ground panting like an overheated hound.

René heard nothing except the rush of water and saw nothing except towering trees. He relived the incident with vivid clarity, wishing that his father would succumb to his spells. But he felt guilty, consumed by the violence and distraught over his mother's inability to cope or at least walk away and take him with her. He drew his knees to his chest and began to cry as the sharp knife of emotion stabbed at his heart. Up until today, he too had done nothing to stand up to that monstrous man. The plunge of the small knife into his father was nothing more than a feeble, bungled gesture of hatred. The rage and mind-numbing remorse was too much for a boy his age to endure. He wanted to run far away, but he was bound to his family, if only to serve the basic needs of his own survival. His father had taught him how to live in the wilderness, but he realized that he was too young to take on that challenge alone. So, despite it all, he must find the courage to return.

You had best look after your mother, boy. The words of the soldier echoed through René's head. He was worried about his mother and fretted over his own wellbeing. *Should he help the beleaguered woman or keep running?* The answers to these questions eluded him as exhaustion consumed him. He nestled down between two imposing granite slabs and was soon lulled to sleep.

René was aroused by a ferocious splash upstream. He opened his eyes and sat up abruptly. He thought that he was dreaming. He craned his ear and heard the noise again, as if the waters of the stream were boiling. He peered over the rocks and saw a man standing waist deep in a pool. He surmised that he was an Anishinabe warrior by his markings. They were a relatively peaceful people, but he did not want to take any chances.

The Anishinabe wore only a loin cloth. It flowed freely in the current, away from his sculpted form. A choker made of wolf and bear teeth dangled about his neck and bracelets clung to his biceps. Eagle feathers, bound to his scalp lock with leather thongs, draped down his back. His burly frame was tattooed with strange images. He stood motionless, peering into the dark waters. He thrust his hands downward to haul in a large steelhead. The fish writhed in his powerful arms, but he easily tossed it among others onto a beach. He resumed his vigilant posture over the pool.

Huddled in the shadow of the boulders, René's heart pounded. He cracked a small sapling, disturbing the peace of the hollow and breathed deeply, too anxious to move. Finally, he summoned the courage to take another glance. The man was gone. He breathed a sigh of relief, gathered himself, and stood up. As he turned around, he was confronted by the towering warrior. He let out a scream, frightened by the macabre nature of the man's appearance.

The brave's oval face was stern and regal. It was painted a vibrant scarlet color, as if ablaze with fire. Black and white stripes separated the flames into fingers that licked at his mouth. His presence was terrifying. He squatted down, looked René in the eyes, and then placed his hands firmly on his shoulders. In English, then in French, he said, "I mean you no harm."

René was petrified. He looked into the warrior's dilated eyes. He mistook this for anger and struggled to get away. The warrior tightened his grip to calm him, but it only heightened his fears. He studied the man. His chest was tattooed with the image of a baying wolf. He was muscular and well proportioned. Escape seemed impossible. René's demeanor changed from fear to awe. He blurted out, "My name is René Dubois and I run from the lash of a madman."

The warrior was stunned by this honest admission. "Well then, René Dubois, I see that you have the voice of a songbird…quite pleasant and not yet tainted by the devil's discourse.

René was puzzled by the mysterious parable. He was used to hearing direct commands.

The warrior shaded his eyes from the sun. "How is it that you are alone in the wilderness?"

René did not answer honestly, "I have lost my way, sir. I live along the King's Highway toward the great city. Somehow I misplaced the path that leads to my home."

"Then I shall make it my business to see you back to that humble place. A boy of your age should not be out here alone. It is a dangerous and unnatural thing."

The boy was somewhat relieved, although he still feared the worst. The presence of this warrior in his home might set his father off, for he did not take kindly to people of other races.

"I sense that you are running from something. Follow me to the King's Road and I will return you to your mother." The warrior picked up his weapon and the string of fish and gave the boy a strap of venison to chew on. He put his arm around the lad's shoulder and guided him away from the stream, cutting a path through the thick brush toward the northeast.

As they walked, the Anishinabe broke the awkward silence. "I am called Three-Legged-Wolf, after the beast that commands the packs on the plain where I live. On this day, it pleases the spirits that I have had the chance to meet you, René Dubois."

Chapter 7

St. Bartholomew's Day

"Angelique Papineau Dubois, you have been anointed by a tainted God. Have you not learned a thing from being cloistered amongst the dogged nuns at Three Rivers? My God woman, your benevolent Catholic preaching has taken my son from me, disrupted our paltry lives, and consumed me with blind rage. From this day forth he shall be lifted up by the teachings of John Calvin."

Angelique tread lightly. "You are blinded by the rage of your families' persecutions, Henri. We are living in an era of enlightenment, yet you cling to the treatises of the ancient ones. You must find peace, for we can no longer live these lies. Let me help you overcome your afflictions."

Henri's kin were devout Huguenots living in the French countryside outside of Paris more than two centuries before. Many of them were brutally murdered during the St. Bartholomew's Day Massacres, when Roman Catholic zealots purged the land of the inflammatory Huguenot faithful. Henri's family survived the eradication. They made their exodus to the Netherlands and then secreted across the Channel to England. Their flight eventually brought them to Scotland where Henri's father Sébastien was born. This century's long path of migration continued during the Lowland Clearances, which forced the family out of Scotland and onto the shores of New France.

For a time, Acadia had been a haven of hope for the family. They lived on secluded Sable Island, farmed the sea, and were free from religious persecution. Isolated on the sparsely populated, rocky shores of the island sanctuary, the Dubois family gave birth to their son Henri.

Angelique pressed on, "My dear husband, if you would only seek council in the Lord, the demons would be shed from your soul. Let us pray together to exorcise the evil from your heart."

"The only demons that haunt me woman," Henri interrupted, "are those that you have cast upon me through this marriage. You have shackled me to a life of poverty and shame. They mock me for marrying a former mistress of the Catholic Church, a woman with no dowry, a woman who has lived a cloistered life." Henri rubbed the side of his head and winced.

"I see you are experiencing the infirmity of the head again. I could nurse you to better health, as I did for so many others at the Cloisters, if you would only let me."

"I do not need your sympathy, wench."

The gaunt woodsman slumped into the rocker and put his head in his hands. The episodes were more frequent now. The purple, festering mark from the hoof of a mule was still visible upon his brow. He was not more than René's age, a jovial lad with considerable promise when it happened. While his father was teaching him to shoe the mule, the sudden sting of a horsefly changed Henri's life forever. The mule's swift kick struck the boy on the side of his head, knocking him senseless. Up until that point, his intellect had been sharp and his spirit unrelenting, then it abruptly ended.

Sébastien observed alterations in Henri's moods, so his mother, Marie Bourbon Dubois took him to the vicar to exorcise what she perceived to be demons. It proved to all be for naught. Henri continued to deteriorate until it was intolerable for anyone to be around him. He blamed his abhorrent behaviors on others and in time, abandoned his family to settle in Quebec City, where he lived in squalor. The people of the street mocked him and took advantage of him. His irrational behaviors often resulted in incarceration, where the guards treated him poorly. He finally decided to live a more secluded life, thinking that it would be practical to take a wife to share his misery. Angelique, whether by design or providence, fatefully stepped into his lair to fill that void.

The door creaked open and a disheveled, but spirited René peered into the room. "René, my darling, we had given up hope of finding you." Angelique rushed across the room to hug her child.

Henri glanced up at the boy. "Keep your distance, lad. I'll have none of you right now. You damn near killed me. How dare you return to my home and expect sanctuary and forgiveness?"

René held back the tears and glared menacingly at his father. He would do it all over again if the right opportunity presented itself, but the next time he would finish it.

Angelique looked over René's shoulder toward the open door. Abruptly, she let out a blood-curdling scream and instinctively pulled him behind her.

Three-Legged-Wolf stood calmly in the breach; the dark pools in his eyes were serene. He waited to be challenged by Henri, only then would he be forced to react in kind.

Henri rose quickly from the chair. He grabbed his fowling piece and raised it to his waist.

"Stop, father. This warrior has saved my life. He means you no harm."

Henri raised the piece, pointing it directly at the Anishinabe's exposed chest. "You can never trust these savages, boy. The fire on his face is a sign of evil. You can plainly see that the devil's preacher resides within him. Move your mother out of harm's way so I can shoot him dead."

"He has been kind to me, Papa." Rather than engage his father in a debate, René walked to the door and led the warrior into the room by the hand. "This man's name is Three-Legged-Wolf. He resides in the Anishinabe village up river a piece. We should repay him for his unselfish kindness."

The warrior was shocked by the stark living conditions and utter squalor of the hovel. These people were destitute. He sensed a tension in the room, not of his doing, but was not one to judge others. Maybe they preferred the simple life, just as he did.

The bruises on Angelique's face told a thousand-shameful tales about her misery.

Henri's demeanor bespoke of anger, abuse, and the over-indulgence of alcohol. "You are not welcome in my house, savage." He spoke harshly to Angelique, "Give him a trinket and send him on his way before we are subject to reprisals from his people."

Angelique went to the cupboard to fetch a small loaf of moldy bread. She approached the brave cautiously and presented it to him. She backed away, putting distance between them.

The brave spoke gently to her, "I found the boy huddled among the rocks by the river. I have returned him to you so he can be cared for properly. I am pleased by your gift, a token of your respect. In turn, I offer you these fish." He passed the stringer of trout to René's hand.

René blurted out, "Will you visit us again, sir?"

Three-Legged-Wolf glanced at Henri and then looked down at René. "It is the better man who walks away." He bounded off of the step and headed toward the southwest.

Henri watched the warrior through the doorway, his gun to bear. "Mind you boy, if you take to me with a knife again I will have you hog collared and eviscerated. Now get off with you to the barn to serve your punishment. I will fetch you back when the spirit moves me."

The boy lingered for a moment, fighting back tears. He looked at his mother for intervention, but she simply turned away to dress the fish. He brushed by his father in the doorway, banishing himself to the dank, dark barn without as much as a spot of drink or morsel of supper.

Henri returned to the rocker and cradled his throbbing head. He spoke angrily, "I am possessed by the devil's brood, Angelique. Fetch me some spirits so I can ease the pain of my afflictions."

Chapter 8

For the Glory of the Union

A blinding flash of a thousand rifles belched out fire, smoke, and ball. The men on the picket line ducked for cover, as small arms ordinance thumped into bodies. The air was hot with lead as a lively cannonade blanketed the field with a shroud of smoke, the putrid taste of black powder, and the burning scent of sulfur. The Battle of Antietam had kicked off with a devastating fury.

General Duryea rode anxiously up and down the line, waiting for the regiments on his right to become fully engaged. He would then send his brigade forward in echelon to envelope the exposed flank of the Rebel line. He was not too rash, as many officers would be in the heat of the battle, for timing was everything when it came to the matters of waging effective warfare.

The General's frenzied horse reared at the strike of a nearby shell, almost spilling its rider into the mud. Duryea tried to calm the usually stalwart warhorse as it turned frantically in circles.

Jon sensed that the General was losing control of the animal. He calmly braved the barrage of bullets to grab the halter. The beast's dilated eyes gazed out in fear as he snorted in distrust of the approaching soldier. Jon pulled his head down, stroked his nose, and spoke in a whisper. The animal miraculously regained his composure. Confident that the situation had resolved itself, Jon doffed his cap at the General and returned to his place in the line of battle.

Shot and shell exploded violently around them, throwing up the earth, sending shrapnel through the air, and making even the most resolute men cower under the strain. The wait was excruciating, as each man marked his fate and quietly made peace with his maker.

Duryea commanded over the roar of battle, "Bring in the pickets and close the ranks, gentlemen, bayonets fixed to the front. Now at the quick step, march." The regiments moved out at the 110 paces per minute, as required by the manual of arms. "Guide toward the center and rally on Old Glory when things get hot." Duryea shouted, "Give them hell, boys, for the glory of the Union."

Explosions, rapid cracks of rifle fire, deafening volleys, whistling shells, screams, drums, bugles, smoke…blood…the acrid smell of death as it lingered at every turn…

Jon stepped off, shoulder to shoulder with his comrades. He daydreamed about life on his peaceful farm, trying to overcome his fear. The lightening-strike of a whirling projectile plowed the earth in front of him, showering dirt upon his uniform and scattering shrapnel in every direction. He instinctively ducked, but the spent object had already passed without harm.

The gentle voice of a woman challenged him. *Press on, Jonny. Fear is a contrived consequence of human frailty, nothing more. Command your weakness.* He squeezed his tense finger around the trigger. *Will I ever see my parents, return to the home of my blood brothers, or have my guts spilled in this God forsaken place to forever rest among the withering corn…*

Chapter 9

Closing the Lid of the Coffin

The boom of massed cannon from Thompson's and Matthew's Pennsylvania batteries concussed the men's ears as they stepped off. The 1100 men of the brigade made up of regiments from New York and Pennsylvania marched with uncertainty through the corn as the distinct voices of the noncoms guided their ranks. The inevitable Rebel volley was moments away, death lingered at their doorstep. But they forged ahead with conviction despite trepidations and fears.

Jon crouched slightly as he moved, hoping to avoid the foreseeable onslaught of minie balls fracturing his frail skin. Gazing with the keen intensity of a hunting eagle, he looked for some sign of the ghostly enemy. He mulled over the battle scenarios, the endless drilling, the complex maneuvers, and the confusing orders. He prayed, as if some miracle was about to extract him from the horror he was about to face. The sweat poured down his brow to sting his eyes and blind his vision. The uncertainty was too much to bear. *How much further must we go?*

The Rebs, lying prone behind a rail fence and stone wall, watched intently as the Yankees advanced. They could to see the bayonets of the blue bellies, as the rising sun glinted off of their cold blades. The grey-coats capped their muskets by command and waited patiently.

The Yankee brigade moved relentlessly into the breach, as if on parade. Their muskets rested on their hips, bayonets fixed to the front. They emerged from the corn into a lea that adjoined a narrow, fenced-in farm road. Posed defiantly in front of them was the entire Confederate Army, spread in a long line across a series of low hills facing north and east. Their artillery batteries, lined up hub to hub on a hill, loaded frantically and sent grapeshot into the ranks of wavering blue lines off to the right. The sudden appearance of this new brigade caused some of them to change front. Their smoking muzzles stared defiantly down at the bold soldiers advancing to contest the ground.

Jon wanted to run toward the guns and stop the inevitable massacre, but Gilhooly's calm voice held him fast. "Steady boys, steady. Halt and dress your ranks. Charge bayonets to the front."

It appeared that the Rebel infantry in this quarter had withdrawn under the heavy fire of the Union artillery and the pressure from the troops on the right. It appeared like the grey-coats flank could be turned with a bold dash. But in an instant, General Lawton's Georgia Brigade rose up from behind the stone wall, as if they had been resurrected from the dead. They poured a deadly volley into the Union ranks. The men in the first line fell, as if engaged in a ghastly dance of death. The line wavered, some men running for the rear, despite the commands to hold the line. The more stalwart men stood their ground and returned fire, pouring a devastating volley into Lawton's men.

At two hundred and fifty paces, the two lines defied each other over open ground. Blue-black smoke filled the void between them, stinging the eyes and scratching the throat. Neither line moved, standing toe to toe like two Irish bare-knuckled street brawlers to slug it out.

Jon nestled in a plowed trough, lying in a pool of warm blood. He loaded and fired from a prone position behind the body of a gut shot comrade. Nausea consumed him, but he continued fight with a vengeance. Mysterious images ran through his head as he rammed the lead down the barrel of the Enfield and then blindly fired it through the wall of smoke. An ancient Indian sang macabre tunes. An antediluvian woodsman loaded and fired in synchronization to his. He somehow blocked out the cacophony of screams and the pandemonium of senseless butchery. He found peace in the routine of his nine-step firing drill: load, handle cartridge, tear cartridge, charge cartridge, draw ramrod, ram cartridge, return rammer, prime, ready, aim, fire.

Gilhooly braved the fire to offer words of encouragement or sharp reprimands. As he ran passed Jon, he spoke, but the farmer could not hear him over the din. He pressed his ear closer when a Rebel solid shot removed Gilhooly's head. Blood and brains covered Jon's blouse, as Gilhooly's lifeless body slumped onto the soil next to him. He buried his face in his hands and screamed, as whizzing lead rained in around him. He felt his heart racing and wanted to run away, but something held him in his place. The whisper of a woman's voice called to him. *Step out of the shadow into the light to free yourself from the trepidations that you cradle in your bosom.*

General Duryea's brigade was decimated. The Rebs began to out-flank them on the left and counterattack. Fearing that they may be overrun without the reinforcements he expected from Hartstuff's and Christian's Brigades, the Brigadier ordered a methodical with-drawal back through the cornfield, relinquishing the precious ground they had fought so desperately to take.

Shannon collared Jon and pulled him off the ground. They retreated to the edge of the field, where they stopped to fire a defiant volley. After just thirty minutes of ruthless carnage, the field was strewn with blue and grey bodies lying in the maze of broken corn. Writhing men under the haze of smoke made the earth crawl like slithering snakes. It was too much for any man to bear.

Jon thought that he heard a voice. He looked about, but every-one else was caught up in the chaos. He heard it again. *I am Pashk-wadjash. Do not look for the answers to the questions you seek in that which you see. Seek the answers to those elusive riddles in that which you don't see.* He reeled and found the Reaper casting his pall: mangled bodies, faceless comrades, pools of lifeblood staining the black earth. The anguished screams of the wounded unnerved him. He uncon-sciously knelt down behind a low stone wall to shake the fog from his befuddled brain.

The man next to him cried out as Jon left himself dangerously exposed, "Stop daydreaming, boy. Get down you damned fool before those Secesh overrun us."

Jon was thrown violently to the ground by the slap of a minie ball upon his chest. The pain was excruciating. He rolled to his side, his face immersed in the mud and blood of the field. He gasped for air.

I'm killed. But the pain began to subside and he wondered if the Lord was bringing him to a tranquil place. Perhaps it was the work of the mystical Indians that haunted him. *Was there peace in death, as Domine Van Dorn had preached so insufferably during Sunday sermon?* He was never a religious man, but found himself praying while everything around him whirled in a nonsensical haze. He looked up toward the heavens, obscured by grey and black smoke. His mind began to clear and he could see faceless beings, hear melodic voices. *Angels!*

"I tried to warn the dearned fool, but the arrogant Mick thinks he is invincible."

"Close up your bloody yap, boy." was the riposte from Sergeant Woodley. "Get down behind the wall, you blighter, and fight on like you are possessed by the devil.

Jon regained a semblance of consciousness. He struggled with the debilitating pain in his chest, but was able to raise himself up on his elbows. He shoved the now recognizable face of Addie Jones in the mud. "I'm far from dead, as it may please you, and you are the damned fool."

A ferocious Rebel volley sent the blue-clad soldiers diving head-long for cover as the merciless projectiles ricocheted off of the wall. A Southern voice from across the divide mocked them, "Git yourself back to your womenfolk, you cowardly Yanks. Y'all run along now like your brothers at Manassas, cause we're coming over there to git you, Billy boy."

Jon was shaken to the bone by his brush with death. The ball had miraculously ricocheted off of his watch, but never pierced the skin. He glanced into "Pappy" Woodley's chromatic eyes, as he spoke to him, "You look like one of them plantation darkies. Johnny's bullet can be a merciless thing, but it seems like this was not your day to die. Now get up and close up the line. The fighting is far from over in this quarter and we need every able-bodied man to stem the Rebel tide."

Holland watched him disappear into a smoke-filled void some-where off toward the eastern end of the line. He could see the grit in the hardened Sergeant's green eyes. He could smell the tobacco of his pipe and the coarse touch of a stoneworker's hands. He hardly knew the man, but he admired him. He surmised that his grandfather would like Woodley. They were both crotchety men who would surely lift a pint and shout out raucous tales until the drink put them to sleep.

To everyone's relief, another brigade flanked the Rebs and drove them back across the cornfield. As the men of Jon's regiment huddled together behind the cold grey wall, they assessed the bloody carnage that had completely altered their simple lives.

Private Holland winced with pain as he put his finger into the hole in his frockcoat. A spent minie ball fell harmlessly into the palm of his hand. He squinted to see its deformed shape and then placed it in his vest pocket as a reminder of what might have been. He pushed through the pain to load his weapon and rest it upon the wall. His ears were ringing and his temples throbbed. The ghostly voices of his fallen comrades and the eerie whispers of his mystical demons echoed in his head, as he suffered from a lack of food and water. The rumble of fighting moved off to the left, but nothing could alleviate the trauma of the horrific experience he had just endured.

It was 10:00 A.M., but in the few hours that the armies had battled for possession of the cornfield, only 250 by 400 yards, 13,000 thousand men had fallen. Their blood intermingled to stain the hallowed earth. The tiny field of maze had exchanged hands no less than fifteen times during the desperate combat. Off in the distance, the chilling sound of bugles seemed to play a morose march. Death's shroud now blanketed the men in arms, bringing peace to the ravaged landscape.

Chapter 10

The Bloodiest Day in Hell

The battle of Antietam raged on throughout the day, moving from the right flank aggressively toward the left. At the Bloody Lane, a sunken wagon road which ran between the lines, Union troops broke though the hard-pressed Rebel forces. They had to withdraw, however, when an entire corps slated to come to their aid wallowed in reserve across the creek.

On the far left, General Burnside took the stone bridge that spanned the Antietam. He could not make good his gains and was driven back late in the day by the timely arrival of AP Hill's Confederate Corp, as the war's bloodiest day drew to a somber close.

General McClellan claimed that he had won a rousing victory when General Lee reluctantly withdrew his army back across the Potomac to Southern soil. It was a hollow triumph, but it raised the spirits of the fickle Union populace and removed, for a time, the threat of further invasion.

The families of the 22,000 casualties in the campaign were devastated by the carnage. For the first time in history, newspapers displayed sickening pictures of the gruesome battlefields. This telling new technology brought the war into people's homes, once a sanctuary from the macabre disposition of combat. As 1862 drew to a close, there appeared to be no end to the brutality.

On the morning of September 18, black buzzards circled over the field. The stony silence was broken by the clink of the spade and crunch of the shovel in the downtrodden soil. The burning carcasses of a thousand mounts ripped the air with foul black smoke, a slaughterhouse of roasting flesh. As far as the eye could see, horribly maimed and bloated bodies still lay in repose.

Under the muzzles of the sinister artillery, the burial parties from both armies mingled beneath a flag of truce. They labored to dig long, shallow trenches to bury their fallen comrades. They exchanged conversation, coffee, and tobacco, always respectful of each other's place in life.

Jon sat in the West Woods, poking at the first fire he had managed in days. The scent of freshly brewed coffee, crisp fatback, and roasted corn soothed him. He fondled his swollen chest to feel his cracked rib. It was not debilitating enough to send him to the rear, but served as a reminder of how precarious life could be. He rubbed the indentation on the cover of his watch. It seemed like providence, the timepiece intercepting the projectile that measured him for death.

Shannon tossed his cap into the trampled grass and rested against the battle-blackened stone wall. "Brutal day, hey Jonny? I thought that I had bought the farm on the first volley." He poked his finger through a large hole in his sleeve. "That ball went clean through my frock and struck Reginald Jenkins right in the abdomen. He's in the field hospital in the Dunker Church, but he ain't going to make it, gut shot you know." He sighed heavily. "That could have been me."

"The Reb fire was like the buzzing of a thousand angry bees. I have never felt so afraid in my life." He tossed the remains of his coffee into the fire and wiped out his cup. "The only thing saving me from this ball was my watch. Why have we committed to this maddening undertaking?"

"I don't have much to say on that matter, Jonny, but we are here now and we are going to see it to the end. We owe it to our families and to those lads lying out there in the mud."

"Something puzzles me, Shannon. You had a chance to sign on with the cavalry as a smithy. Why have you chosen to enlist in the infantry and put yourself in harm's way?"

Shannon held out his tin cup for more coffee. "I promised your mamma that I would look after you. Shoot, I can get into a brawl every day, either with those stubborn Rebs or with my mates in the ranks. The army has fulfilled my fondest dreams." Shannon spit and acquired a third round of the muddy liquid. "Confounded coffee grounds are like eating dirt. I could ask you the same question, owing to your specialized work with horses. Look how you handled the General's stallion. You calmed the nerves of that horse like he was a newborn child. You have a gift.

"Don't know about that. I came here to find an elusive dream, but all I have gained is a hardened heart. The war is turning me into a coldblooded killer." He reluctantly continued, "I see these images while I am fighting. They haunt me to the point of distraction and drive me insane."

"It's just your imagination playing tricks upon you. My pap told me that he took part in the Young Ireland Movement back in '48. They would get into brawls with the British Bobbies and he would lose his wits, see things, and do things he never did before. He told me that the hooligans would fight to a raging frenzy, possessed by the devil himself. Facing rocks and bottles ain't like standing up to a bullet though, but I imagine that you are experiencing similar visions."

Jon smiled at Shannon's analogy. "Those senseless fisticuffs got them absolutely nowhere. The rebellion fizzled out, the famine continued, and now we find ourselves in America still brawling."

"Well, brawling is in my blood and I fancy it." He puffed his chest with pride.

"It still does not explain the demons, the curious nature of the watch, or my escape from death."

A large contingent of men on horseback approached the camp. The flags of the general staff fluttered in the breeze as they road slowly through the maze of resting men. General Duryea stopped at each bivouac to honor them for their bravery and comfort those who suffered. He stopped at the wall where Jon and Shannon were sitting and spoke to an aide, who pointed at Jon. The General reached into his pocket and removed a locket. He leaned over and handed it to Jon.

"Please see to it that this is returned to its owner. I believe you will find her picture inside."

Jon was puzzled by the personal attention he was receiving from the stalwart General.

Looking out over the field of carnage, Duryea digressed. "Bloody awful day filled with senseless killing. What possesses a man to commit such atrocities and stand up in the face of such horror, day after day after day?" He did not wait for an answer. "Woodley tells me you were struck by a ball yesterday, below the heart. How is it that you survived?"

Jon removed his kepi before speaking, "Luck of the Irish, sir. My ancestors' pocket watch snatched the ball clean out of the air, like magic." He forced a smile.

Duryea laughed, "You damned Irishmen have a way of getting around the mischief. Well, you are blessed, private. Others have not been so fortunate." The General's mood changed. "The locket belonged to Gilhooly. He told me that you would take care of his personnel effects. He must have had a premonition about losing his life, so he sought a private audience with me to put his house in order. This locket is the only thing of value he owned, so take good care of it, son."

Jon reached over the wall and accepted the locket. "I will do right by him, sir."

The General smiled, "I expect you will. He spoke highly of you. Holland's the name?"

Jon nodded. "Private Jon Holland, sir."

"It's Sergeant Holland now. Gilhooly told me that you had some spunk. The way you handled my horse confirmed it for me. I didn't get a chance to thank you during the battle, but I am indebted to you." He turned to his adjutant, "Orderly, make sure this man gets his stripes. If we are going to carry on this mindless slaughter, then we need good men leading our troops."

The General rode off, the paths of the two men never to cross again. Duryea was so affected by the gruesome nature of the battle and the effects of his wound that he took a thirty-day leave. When he was ready to return to do his duty to the country he loved, he was stunned to find that his command had been given to Brigadier General John Gibbon, his junior in rank. Disgruntled by the whole affair, he resigned his commission to sit out the remainder of the war.

Jon opened the locket to reveal the faded portrait of a dowdy young girl. Her eyes sparkled, much like Gilhooly's. Jon guessed that she was the Sergeant Major's daughter or a long-lost lover. He gently closed the tarnished cover and wrapped it in a kerchief to place in his gunny sack for safekeeping. The image of Gilhooly losing his head weighed heavily upon his heart.

"I told you. Nothing but good can come out this war. You take a bullet, live through it, and then get promoted, all in the matter of two days. God is watching over you and that bloody watch is twisting the capricious fortune of your life." Shannon slapped him so hard that his bruised ribs flared with pain. "Don't think for one minute that you are going to order me about."

Jon loathed the thought of taking the command, for the rabble of the regiment would press him for favors. He faithfully did his duty, but once again, somebody else had determined his fate and forced him to play by their rules. So as autumn faded into winter, the strains of being a non-commissioned officer turned him into a hardened veteran whose blood ran cold with resentment. He scoffed at death and heartlessly killed men he did not know or understand. He patently comprehended the brutal realities of combat and drilled the troopers relentlessly. He tried to remove variables that could alter the outcome of a fight and help them survive. His motivation was to save every soul, but he would only succeed in driving himself and the men into a merciless hell.

He berated them for the simplest mistakes, "Close that line grunt or the Rebs will drive a wedge through it and kill you all."

Shannon would try to temper him. "Ease up on the lads, Jonny. They will go to Hades and back for you. You don't need to push them so hard."

"Mind yourself, Shannon. I press them so they stand a chance of living for another day. There is no room for cowardice or doubt when you face a line of Rebs hellbent on destroying you. Hardened men do extraordinary things. Hardened, disciplined men can defy death."

Shannon agreed with Jon, but the plain fact of the matter was that his single-minded approach to discipline was wearing thin. "All I am saying, Jonny, is give them a break once in a while."

"And what will I say to their mothers and sweethearts when they are laying face up to the sun, the breath of life draining from their soul?"

"You will tell them that they died with honor, face to the enemy, giving their lives for their country." Shannon put his arm around his friend and walked with him across the barren plain that made up their winter quarters above the fall line of the Rappahannock. "Let's put our feet in the river and see if we can catch us some fish. We can leave the fighting for another day."

As the two men walked toward the river, Jon contemplated the course of his life. *Men and women who have come before you have lit the lamp that will guide you toward your providence. Search for the truth in the lore. It will be revealed to you through the people who blazed the trail before you. Look to Tekeni Karahkwa and Pashkwadjash for the wisdom that you seek.*

Chapter 11

The Devil's Deal

Things did not improve much for René over the next few months as his father admonished him for his aloof behavior and his frightened mother did nothing to stave off the unrest between them. Hatred festered, so he would wander off by himself to enjoy the peace of the wilderness.

One lazy spring afternoon, Henri left the homestead after he finished the planting. He would frequently disappear for days, but this time he was gone for a full cycle of the moon. René was more at ease in his absence, but still spent much of his time alone. His mother gave up trying to cajole him and turned her attentions to her voluminous chores and her bible. She surmised that René no longer cared about them or had lost interest in their way of life. He was a cold-hearted lad. She blamed Henri for the failure, but did not have the courage to confront him.

Henri returned to the farmhouse on a sweltering evening. He stopped on the porch to wipe sweat from his brow and then proceeded to throw up on his boots. He was drunk again. He threw open the door, so violently, that it knocked over the milk can that sat on the wooden pedestal.

Angelique rushed over from the hearth to right the can. "What ails you man? Are you drunk again? You have wasted our meager milk supply. What shall I feed the boy now?"

"Never mind that, wench. You should know that I have completed the finest transaction that could ever be imagined. We will now be rich beyond our dreams and quite comfortable I might add. You can buy all the milk that you like or even purchase a new cow for that matter."

"What kind of devil's deal have you made, Henri? We have little of worth to give in trade."

"That is where you are mistaken, my dear wife. I have sold René's services to some high browed, but underhanded military officers, and I have made a fine profit from it to boot."

Angelique, dumbfounded by Henri's revelation, dropped immediately to the floor. She spoke to him defiantly, rage written on her tearful face, "Have you lost what little mind you have left?"

Henri staggered across the room and plopped down in his rocker. Spittle from his vomit lingered in his beard. "Some soldiers at a tavern have paid me handsomely for his adoption. I told them that René was a fine lad with a strong will and the potential for great physical prowess. It took some masterful coaxing, but they agreed to take him lock, stock, and barrel."

"You sold our precious son, Henri, to a pack of vile soldiers?"

"They gave me a fair penny." Henri spread sovereigns on the floor. "I had more, but my thirst was fierce and the soldiers expected a round for their generosity. After all, they have relieved us of a mighty burden." He paused to let her absorb the magnificence of his deal. "I was possessed to gamble, which did not prove to be profitable. All in all, it was an advantageous undertaking."

Angelique wept uncontrollably, too overcome to accept the truth. "You have made a slave of our son? How dare you take such liberties with that boy's life and sell him into bondage?"

Henri showed no remorse. "I knew this would strike a chord in you, woman. But just the same, it is done. Those soldiers carved out a hard bargain, but I told them that if they wanted a lad as fine as René, then they would have to pay handsomely." He headed for the door. "Where is the heathen, woman? I need to shuffle him off before sunrise. Prepare to say your goodbyes."

René was seated on a fence rail in the waning shade behind the barn. He ignored his father as he crossed the yard and continued to whittle a bird out of a piece of wood.

"Pack up you kit, boy. You and I are off to frolic in the walled city," Henry lied.

"I do not want to go to the city with you. I am staying right here," René said defiantly.

"You will do as I say and like it, boy, or I will take the switch to you." He grabbed his son.

René dropped his bird in the commotion and tried to retrieve it, but his father would have none of that. It wallowed there in the dust; its one carved eye looked up at the wispy clouds.

"Mind yourself, lad." Henri dragged René across the yard by his collar, up the creaking porch steps through his vomit, and into the house. "Say your fare-thee-wells to your mother, boy."

The boy screamed as he was dragged back into the yard, his mother clinging desperately to his legs. He kicked and squirmed, but his father's grip was too firm.

"Don't cross me on this, wench. I shall have my way and you will like it. This boy has been defiant and unruly. He is going to live with the savages. They will break him or he will die."

Henry kicked Angelique and she lost her grip on the boy. He lifted René onto the horse tethered to the porch. He lashed his hands to the saddle pommel, threw his grieving wife to the ground, and mounted behind the boy. He spurred the horse, causing it to bolt headlong down the path. Ducking under a branch of an oak, he disappeared. At the crossroads of the lane and the King's Highway, a small, seedy detachment of cavalry from the French Provincial Guard waited. Henri stopped his horse abruptly, untied René, and handed him over to the officer in charge.

The squalid officer spoke, "If those savages can't subdue him, sir, then no one can."

Henri glanced defiantly at René and then turned his horse about and rode off.

"Settle yourself, boy. Defying me will do you no good. We have deceived the Anishinabe into thinking that they are adopting wayward children. They are not party to the fact that we have profited from this affair." He spit on the ground. "You are about to become a warrior, boy. You had best act like one. The Anishinabe expect their men to be strong, heartless, brave, and cunning."

Chapter 12

Reborn

The trip to the Anishinabe village was arduous, as the horses and men struggled along the narrow footpaths that led toward the compound. The hollowed-out trails coursed through a canopy of heavily wooded backcountry and worked their way toward the southwest. The uncertainty of the passage frustrated the soldiers and heightened the anxiety of the boys they held in captivity.

René peeked through the morning fog as he scanned the lush landscape. Tall pines interspersed with hardwoods sheltered the travelers. Streams coursed through the dense undergrowth to gradually descend into the river basin. The path opened into diminutive meadows and then slipped again into fern-filled hollows. He sensed that he been in this place while hunting with his father, but to a boy with an untrained eye, much of the wilderness looked the same.

It was dark under the forest canopy, even though the sun shone brightly. The cool air attracted the black flies and mosquitoes. Their persistent buzzing was almost too much to bear. The scent of hemlock provided a pleasant distraction from the annoyances of the pestering gadflies.

The soldiers informed the boys that this was the land of the Anishinabe and the shaman-warrior Three-Legged-Wolf. René felt relieved by his circumstances. But even the promise of living with the warrior who had saved his life could not alter his adverse feelings on the matter. He listened intently, trying to garner every bit of information that he could about what he was getting himself into. As nearly as he could figure, these unscrupulous soldiers had cut a deal with disgruntled or destitute parents to buy young provincial boys and then immerse them into Native tribes, for profit.

The soldier heading up the expedition spoke openly about their mission, "I have built subtle alliances with the savages to adopt these boys. I have influenced them with surreptitious manipulation and commanded their allegiance. In turn, I have made a fine yield from the trade."

Another soldier tried to clarify what he had just heard. "So, you have deceived the Indians into thinking that they are helping these boys, when in reality we are profiting from their bondage?"

"If we play our cards right, we can build an enterprise from the immersion of these boys. They will beholden to us as we manage their assimilation and benefit from their relentless work." He paused. "But heed a warning. The Crown will not tolerate our little endeavor. We must hold this secret close to our vests and play our cards with utmost care or be remanded to the gallows.

The squad leader tried to intimidate René, "You know, son, your father is a hearty wag. For a small fee, we have absconded with you. You see, you are now a slave to the whims of me and my mates. Mark my words boy; we will be coming to collect from you and the fool-hardy Indians. You had best do right by me or you will pay with your life."

René did not understand the corruption that measured these men nor did he care. He was René Dubois. It mattered little to him about family, God, or country. He vowed that he would escape this imprisonment and bear no allegiance to anyone. He feared nothing and kowtowed to no one.

On the last evening of travel, the journeymen settled into camp in a meadow. René convinced one of the guards to free him. "If you please, sir, I would like to cleanse myself in that cool spring."

The soldier balked. "What makes you think that I can trust you, boy?"

René baited him. "Where am I to go, sir? I have no horse and I do not know these woods. It would be reckless for me to venture out alone. I would soon become prey to the wolves."

The soldier relented. "I will cut you free, but mind me, boy, if you run, I will shoot you dead."

René smiled as the soldier cut the ropes binding his wrists. He rubbed them briskly. "I will make quick work of my cleansing and return to you before the meal is cooked to your liking. The soldier shooed him away a flick of his hand, glancing up every so often to watch him. He walked the short distance across the field to the edge of the pond and removed his reeking tunic to bare his scrawny chest to the wind. He glanced about momentarily to see what the soldier was up to. The man nodded at him and then picked up his musket as a sign of intimidation. The boy turned away and then plunged head first into the dark, refreshing water.

"You let that wild boy loose, soldier?" the officer berated the man.

"I could see no harm in it. He is a mere boy. What kind of mischief could he get into?"

"I have ridden with him for the better part of two days and he has caused me nothing but grief." The officer exposed his forearm. "He has bitten me, see here? He has kicked me in the shins and every time I let him loose he runs. I fear that I made a devil's deal with Henri Dubois."

"You told him, sir, that he was beholden to you as long as you see fit."

"I have changed my mind on that matter. The Loon was not as crazy as he might have seemed when he sold us that child. The lad is as barmy as his father."

The men's conversation was all the distraction René needed to slink away from the meadow. As they commiserated over his ill-begotten behaviors, he slipped out of the water and secreted himself in the reeds and cattails. It only took a moment for him to elude them.

The officer gazed across the meadow. He waited for a moment, expecting the rippling surface of the water to boil up and reveal the boy's whereabouts. He admonished the soldier, "You see, turn your back for a minute and he is gone. Go after him. Shoot him if you have to. Do whatever it takes to bring him back. I have too much invested in him to lose him now."

The soldier saluted and raced toward the pond. Not knowing where the boy had gotten off to, he stopped momentarily by the spot where René had entered the water. His hesitation gave the boy enough time to slither away, creeping like a cat along the bank and then crawling on his belly toward the woods just a few feet beyond. As soon as he was hidden amongst the trees, he began to run. He quickly weaved in and out of the vegetation and did not look back, for fear of reprisal.

The soldier, hearing a rustling in the brush beyond the pond, let off a random shot in the direction of the noise. The ball remarkably avoided any of the obstacles, whizzed by René's head, and struck a tree. As the ball passed, he instinctively ducked in reaction to the buzzing it made in his ear. He sat for a moment under the tree breathing heavily. He looked up at the fresh mark scored by the round in the bark just above his head. Sighing deeply, he resumed his flight.

It wasn't long before the soldiers tracked René down. He had given them a good run, but proved to be no match. They hogged tied him to a tree with a sturdy rope and deprived him of any sustenance. He sulked throughout the night about the unfortunate turn of events in his life.

Early the next morning, the squad of soldiers crested a small rise and came into view of a magnificent valley. A meandering river snaked its way toward the horizon, cutting a deep ravine in the bottom land. It harbored a complex Anishinabe community. Smoke rose from the compound and filled the voids in the canopy of trees with a grey cloud. A ramshackle palisade surrounded an array of buildings. It seemed as if the carefree attitude of its residents translated into a mismatch of dwellings configured by the whim of the builders. European style homes made of clapboard were intermingled with ancient huts, longhouses, and wigwams, all in some state of disrepair.

As the squad approached the fortified village, they were greeted at the stockade gate by an aging warrior who was plainly dressed in a tunic and leggings. He bowed his head and then motioned with his hand for the riders to enter. The guests dismounted and allowed their horses to run free so they could graze and take water from the river.

René sensed that these people were extremely poor. He noticed that the animals roamed freely. Dogs barked at rooting pigs, chickens skittered about looking for seeds and grain, and a gaggle of geese harassed the new guests. He thought that it was a disorderly, chaotic place, not unlike the home he had just left. He sensed that the people who lived under these conditions were not going to be any different from those that he had encountered in his life, thus far.

After the matter of restitution was tended to, the soldiers handed over the boys to the tribe. Of the five boys to be assimilated, René was the youngest. The others were in their early-teens, ready to face the challenges and rigors of a warrior's way of life. He was stronger willed, however, hardened and carelessly courageous because of his delicate, personal circumstances. He already possessed certain unattainable skills that a boy of his age could only hope to realize. He had developed these skills so he could survive the daily ordeal he was put through by his father. Because of his hardened heart, he was more prepared than the teens to undergo the rigors of a wilderness existence, but he would still have to prove himself in the contrary tribal culture.

Each lad was parceled off to an Anishinabe brave to be trained in subtleties of the warrior world. The four other boys were selected quickly, being larger in stature and more mature than René. No one wanted to take charge of him, so he was left standing alone and dejected.

The trooper who cared for him informed the chief of René's unique situation. "This one is as wild as a boar. I suspect that you will have a difficult time taming him. He took a knife to his father and has a knack for running away as it suits him. He challenges the will of the most patient man. If you can master his spirit, then I suspect that you can accomplish just about anything."

Feeling closed in, René pushed the chief's hand off of his shoulder and stood alone.

The soldier responded to this action, "You see, he bears no allegiance to anyone. Mind yourself boy or I will have to take the horsewhip to you."

The chief spoke privately to a young warrior and he ran off. After a few moments, he returned with an impressive man following him. Three-Legged-Wolf smiled as he approached the group. "I believe this young fellow is called René Dubois. I present salutations to you, my friend."

René recognized him immediately; his fiery, painted red face glowed in the sunlight. He was relieved that he remembered him. "I have been sent to live amongst your people, sir."

"Well then, René Dubois, you shall live and learn with me. The chief informs me that you are quite a handful, but I welcome you into my home without reservation." The warrior escorted the boy to the far side of the compound where a small, square log structure with a round roof stood.

René crawled on his hands and knees through the opening to enter the hovel. It was smoky inside, permeated with the sweet smell of aging herbs, root plants, and game. A river cobblestone fire pit was situated in the center of the room underneath a gaping hole in the roof. A fire burned briskly within the pit and warmed the steamy edifice. A wolf's skin hung upside down on the wall, its eyes staring directly into René's. He moved to the other side of the room, but the eyes watched him wherever he went. He turned his back upon the wolf to avoid its unnerving glare.

Three-Legged-Wolf pointed toward a small reed basket along one wall and said, "You can make up your bed there and store your belongings in the basket."

René had a small satchel that contained a fresh shirt and a small, black Calvinist bible, nothing more. He looked into the basket. Assured that no harm would come to him, he put the canvas satchel in the vessel. Then he sat down on the bearskin robe that served as his bedding.

The warrior began to teach the boy. "If you are to live among us, then you are to be one with us. You will learn our language and hunt and fight with our warriors. You will till the fields with the women and care for the children." He handed René a piece of dried venison. "I have lived among your people to better understand their lifestyle. We are different in many ways, but we have many things in common. It is those commonalities that will bind us and transform you into a man."

René was confused by the parables because he was only listening half-heartedly.

Three-Legged-Wolf admonished him, "I sense that there is something troubling you. Your eyes run cold with fear and hatred, but I suspect that it is because you have been taken from your loved ones against your will. There is a hollow darkness in your soul. Your transformation will not be easy, but you can trust that I shall be by your side throughout the entire ordeal."

René felt that the warrior was somehow different, more spiritual than any man he had ever met. His painted face and flowery language mesmerized him, but he would not be swayed by idle talk. His mind was made up. Freedom from oppression was his only alternative for a better life.

The Algonquin interrupted his thoughts, "Your eyes and ears are the window to your mind and soul, the vessels of absolute truth. You are distracted by the circumstances of your life. Rage saps your strength and clouds your vision. You must temper your anger and quell your desire to seek revenge upon those who have wronged you. The wiser man will win the day."

René thought that this stranger could not possibly understand the pain he was feeling. He could not have experienced the heartache that ran cold inside of him. He could never be fully healed, for if he did not love or show allegiance, he could not be hurt again.

Three-Legged-Wolf sensed that the boy was putting up a wall. "I have studied your language. The wisdom that I garner from it makes me stronger." A frown crossed his brow. "Because of this, I know you better than you may think. It has been revealed to me that your name is the signature of your fate. Your name, René, can be translated as *reborn* in your language. On this day, you shall be given a rebirth to a new life. What you make of this opportunity is of your own doing."

The reflective warrior removed a glistening turquoise bracelet from his arm and handed it to the boy. "Take this gift from me as a sign of your rebirth. Wear it proudly as a reminder of this day, a symbol of your baptism into a new life. It is my legacy to you."

The boy studied the bracelet before placing it over his bicep. He had never received a gift of this magnitude, so he was ashamed that he did not know how to respond to this unselfish gesture.

The warrior spoke again, "It is the custom among our people to honor a gift with a gift. What is it that you shall present to me?"

René wondered. *How can I even begin to match the value of the gift that I have just received with one as meager as I possess?*

"Do not be ashamed by the size or worth of the gift. Its quality is not measured in its magnitude. It is measured in the spirit of giving of oneself to one you respect and trust."

René reached under his shirt and removed a diminutive chain which his mother had given him from about his neck. A tarnished Christian cross dangled on it. He kissed it, as he had been taught to do, and then handed it to his new mentor.

The warrior accepted it with a nod of his head. He proudly attached it to his lance, just above the black-and-white eagles' feathers that were interwoven upon its shaft. "This is a fine gift that you have given me, René Dubois. I have displayed it in a place of honor upon my lance. I will cherish it as I cherish my own life. We are now brothers in the eyes of the spirit that joins us." He searched for some further wisdom. "Now that you have been resurrected, you shall be blessed with a meaningful name. While you live among us, René Dubois, you shall be known as Pashkwadjash, The Wolf. Let the spirit and wisdom of that great beast guide you and keep you."

Chapter 13

Carpet Bagging Shyster

Following the Antietam Campaign, the Union generals postured with Marse Lee, but were unable to bring on the coup-de-grâce of the war. As the hostilities slogged into their third year, the opposing armies thrust and parried like great swordsmen, but neither could gain the upper hand. Winter approached and the grunts in the trenches settled into their dreary camps.

The Army of the Potomac camp sprawled for miles over the low hills that formed the northern bank of the Rappahannock River near the city of Fredericksburg, Virginia. The sea of men and material gathered there transformed this quiet little valley into a bustling metropolis.

Jon's regiment was posted above the winding fall line of the river by the village of Falmouth. The opposite hills were occupied by the Confederate Army. Save for a few artillery duels, some ill-advised assaults, and some pesky sniping, winter camp in 1862-63 was monotonous and dull.

Shannon chastised his friend. "Why do you work us to the bone, Jonny?"

"You know what the Bible says about idle hands, Shannon."

"I swear, Jonny, if you continue to drive the men they will rise up and strike you down."

"Stop your bellyaching, O'Reilly. I will do whatever it takes to keep these men from getting killed, even if it means digging shit-holes." Jon was distracted by the voices. *Your destiny is to lead, but take great care not to let your heart be vanquished by your mind.*

Bloodier battles were still to be waged and many men would fall.

As Jon prepared them for these uncertainties, he wondered about his own fate. *Would the next bullet whizzing toward him suddenly end his life in some obscure, nameless place?* Haunting voices taunted him into action that he hesitated to take. *Shallow roots will cause the mightiest of oaks to topple, uncontested to the ground in a storm. Life is fraught with the challenge of facing many storms. Spread your roots, Jon, and tend to them so that their fingers touch many lives and alter many fates.*

The troops tested Jon, but they appreciated his leadership and respected his courage. They swore they would follow him into the depths of hell if the Rebel Army marched there, but lately, they were questioning their resolve and challenging his relentless pursuit of perfection.

Jon struggled with the vagaries of the war. Why had he survived while others fell? Why the uncertainty, something or someone choosing who shall live and who shall die? Why was he taunted by the voices and visions when others seemed to have no spiritual direction? His understanding of these complex questions was muddled. The blind faith of others could not console him. He sought the advice of his commander on these matters, but little had come of it.

The regiment's commander was a stern preacher named Joshua Phelps, who made it his mission to resurrect the souls of his soldiers. "God wills men to do extraordinary things. Believe in the word of the Lord and he will guide you to a path of freedom."

Colonel Phelps rode among the formations on an enormous, white stallion. He was profane to a fault, but justified it as God's will to move men to do extraordinary things. He would lecture his lieutenants and read scripture during the drill. He would rather that you miss formation than a moment of reflection in God's house. The punishment was severe if you did. In battle, Phelps would quote verse from the Holy Book over the roar of cannon and the screams of the dying.

Jon's religion was a metaphor of life. He sometimes attended a staunch Dutch Reformed Church, but often felt that was a mask for his families' true feelings on spirituality. They professed to a life bound in part by a natural existence; similar to the one adhered to by New Englanders like Emerson. These Transcendentalists believed strongly that divinity was pervasive throughout nature and life and therefore should be treated as such. They celebrated a pious life by working the land, not at the preacher's calling in the confines of a cloistered church.

To Jon, the order of life was driven by human resolve, not by divine intervention. As he struggled with those nebulous concepts, particularly in light of the visions and voices that taunted him, he surrendered to the reasoning that he did not personally control every aspect of his own existence. He respected the convictions of others and understood that it was their faith that bound them together. Without something to cling to, these men would revert to their savage instincts, shirk their duties, and become an unruly mob. A brotherly bond to survive and harsh discipline were all that kept them from mutiny.

On a relatively warm December day, while the men cooked a midday meal, the typical camp followers were allowed to linger longer than usual to ply their trade. Pay call had just occurred and many of the men had script burning a hole in their pockets. Some sauntered off to private places with the charlatans who frequented the camps. Some squandered their money on frivolous card games, while others sent it home to help their families. No matter how the men chose to distribute their funds, by the end of the day their pockets were as empty as when they had started.

A slick young man sauntered up to Shannon's hut where he and several other soldiers had just polished off a pot of gruel. The man, a curious sort, sported an ankle length coat with large lapels. It was drawn up over a freshly laundered shirt and pleated pants. He wore a top hat that set back on his head. From the hat's silk band protruded a black and white eagle's feather. As he approached the men, his smile revealed four gold teeth in the middle of his sizeable mouth.

"Good day, fellers. The name's Seamus McGuilicutty, speculator and land baron. I am about to propose a deal that you will not be able to refuse."

Shannon questioned the man, "What could you possibly offer us on this frightful day that would make our lives any better?" He had been party to this type of speculation as a boy in Hell's Kitchen. He was wary about the motives of this city slicker.

McGuilicutty patronized him. "What is your name, son?"

"My name is of no matter to you or others of your kind, you carpet-bagging shyster."

"How dare you judge me, soldier, when you know nothing about me? Do not let appearances deceive you, for I am not what I seem to be. My nature is to help those less fortunate than I. Since you have chosen to speak for the others, in a most demanding way, I will generously offer you the first crack at my bounty. It will cost you nothing, mind you, to play my little game of chance. Are you up to a wager or are you just a loudmouthed braggart?"

The crafty shyster opened his carpetbag and removed a felt cloth, a piece of wood, three walnut shells, and a lead pea. As he spread the cloth upon the frozen ground, he spoke to Shannon, "All you have to do is guess which shell the pea is under, a childlike task, and one acre of prime land west of the Mississippi will be yours. What do you say, soldier? Are you a gambler or a coward?"

"Are you barmy, mate? You think you can lure me into your scam?"

The swindler was not swayed by Shannon's threats. He had met tougher marks than this boisterous Irishman. He suspected that he would be putty in his hands in a short while. "I'll tell you what, Irish, since you are so skeptical, I will throw in nine more acres if you can best me."

"And what will it cost me if I don't?"

"You will owe me no debt, my friend, but I will not offer this lucrative deal again."

Shannon could not resist the temptation, although he knew that he was probably being duped. "I'll take you up on your offer, but know this, if you try to deceive me in any way, I will twist your head from your body and remove your shiny gold teeth as my reward. Are we understood?"

McGuilicutty smiled. "You drive a hard bargain, soldier. I dare to say that I would not want to confront you on the field of battle." He laid out the three shells on the board and rolled the pea across the felt for Shannon to examine.

Satisfied that everything was aboveboard, Shannon tossed the sphere back to the man. He removed his kepi and knelt down on the cloth, his dilated eyes affixed upon the shells.

The smartly dressed conman knelt across from him. He hid the pea under the middle shell, exposed it for Shannon to see, and then rapidly shuffled the shells across the surface of the board, as he tried to distract the Irishman with incessant babble. "Which shell will it be, soldier?"

Shannon studied the shells for a long time, while the other soldiers randomly yelled out their choices. He turned around and scowled at them before he decided which one to pick. With his large hand, he quickly grabbed the middle shell and tossed it aside. The pea rolled across the board toward him and he smiled. "Where's the deed to my land, McGuilicutty?"

"You have bested me, soldier. I see that you are the better man when it comes to the matters of gaming." McGuilicutty opened his coat and removed a document printed on letterhead that was embossed on top with the symbols of two crossed pickaxes and inscribed with fancy letters.

Shannon quickly grabbed the deed to examine it contents.

"Not so fast, my friend. Care to double your wager?"

"What are you offering if I should beat you again?"

The shyster feigned a dilemma. "It seems to me that you have me over a barrel. I have a thousand acres of prime prairie land in the Oklahoma territory, free from rampaging Indians. I'll wager that land against your whole allotment of army pay. Care to take me up on the matter?"

Shannon studied the document, but could not make heads or tails of its content. Not able to read, he pretended to understand the paper's contents. "This here paper looks official to me. I think I'll keep my ten acres and be done with you, but I can't speak for the other fellers."

"You are passing up a great bargain, but I can see that you want to generously defer to others. Step forward young bucks and get rich. It will only cost you a day's wages to best me."

The commotion at the far end of the street stirred up Colonel Phelps' ire. "Holland, get your weapon and follow me to that company of rabble that you command. I suspect that something is amiss." He brushed aside an orderly and lit out toward Company A's bivouac as if his life depended on it. He plunged through the crowd of hangers on and let out a string of profanity, "What kind of damned mischief have you gotten into, O'Reilly? Speak up boy, this very instant."

O'Reilly was seated on the edge of the blanket and held a large wad of greenbacks and pay vouchers in his right hand. He immediately saluted Colonel Phelps. "Come to attention, mates."

"Good day, Colonel. Would you care to join us for some harmless gaming?" McGuilicutty smiled and extended his hand to Phelps who ignored him.

"O'Reilly, make sure that money gets back to the rightful owners and disperse this mob. I will not tolerate the evils of gambling among my troops."

McGuilicutty objected, "That money belongs to me, fair and square. What right do you have to abscond with it without good cause?"

"Sir, you have fouled the air of my camp with your evil preaching. The sanctity of these poor boys' souls has been violated and I, for one, will not stand for it. Take up your blanket and your shallow wares and be gone." Phelps pushed McGuilicutty. "Holland, escort this man to the edge of camp and if he tries to return, shoot him."

Jon saluted and then exposed his bayonet to McGuilicutty's abdomen. "Move along, you huckleberry, or I will be best served to run you through."

McGuilicutty fumed. "You are making a grave mistake, Colonel. I know people in high places who will not take this dismissal lightly. You are the one who is shackling these men, not I."

"Men like you who prey upon the weak will be shunned by the Lord, struck down by a bolt of lightning when the judgment day arrives. Get him out of my sight, Holland. He sickens me."

The shyster grudgingly placed his belongings back in his bag. He grabbed the land contract from Shannon, who protested his insolence, and then moved on at the point of Jon's bayonet. As the two men descended the hill that led toward the river, McGuilicutty spoke, "That Colonel misunderstands my intentions. I just wanted to bring some sport to those weary soldiers. Hell, what harm have I caused? I get a few greenbacks and they are entertained, which takes their minds off of the certainty of death they are about to face. I provide a valuable service to those men. I lift their spirits so they can go to their Maker with a song in their hearts."

"Get on with you, sir. Stop trying to convince me that what you do sways these men toward something good. You have robbed them of their pride and taken food out of their children's mouths. Do you still think that what you offer is honorable?"

"You see this eagle's feather in my hat? It represents what I used to be. I was a shaman, a righteous man who preached about the sanctity of a clean life and the precious nature of the hereafter. Day in and day out I would see men who were broken by the realities of their existence, the mundane routines of finding their next meal, or the insanity of the meaningless things that would press upon them, like this war. Surely you can understand that?"

Jon was intrigued by the man's line of thinking, but was still convinced that he was conning him, just like he had conned the troopers.

McGuilicutty continued, "I would speak to those men about a virtuous way of life, but in the end, little changed. So, I abandoned my mystical calling. I stopped trying to alter the men on a cerebral level and started giving them what they wanted, a distraction, if you will." He paused by the pontoon bridge to light a cigar. "You see, we only live a short while on the back of our Mother. Why not live that life doing things that we love to do and not what other men would have us do? After all, are we not sovereign beings beholden only to our own will?"

Jon had heard this speech before in the shadows of his grandfather's stories. He looked into the man's eyes where he hoped to find the answers to the questions that had eluded him. Those mysterious, shadowy orbs seemed to twinkle.

McGuilicutty looked across the river. "You know soldier, I ain't up much on military affairs like you are, but it seems to me that Napoleon once said: *A man does not have himself killed for half-pence a day or for a petty distinction. You must speak to the soul in order to electrify him.*"

He exposed his gold teeth with a crafty grin. "You think those Rebs over there would enjoy my little game, Yank?" The shaman-turned-shyster looked into Jon's boyish face. "Your eyes are the window to your soul, soldier. You might try a little mischief yourself, Sergeant Major, to ease your own troubled heart. Let the Great Eagle guide you on your path toward a different life and then you may understand what it is I am trying to tell you." McGuilicutty picked up his carpetbag, tipped his cap, and sauntered across the bridge.

Jon leaned on his rifle and watched the bizarre young man vanish between the buildings of the sleepy little town, as if whisked away by something supernatural. He wondered what this chance meeting really meant in the greater scheme of his troubled life. The regimental bugles sounded call to quarters and he was summoned back to the realities of his own existence and the horrors of the civil war that ravaged the once Promised Land. *Maybe McGuilicutty was right.*

Chapter 14

Bilge Rat

On a blustery day, Jon decided that he wanted to speak to the souls of his men as McGuilicutty had suggested, so he visited the regimental quartermaster. The surly snit was an uppity Bostonian, graduated from Harvard, and enlisted on the privilege of his daddy's Brahmin heritage, preparing him for a life as a politician after the war. The troopers called him Boston Charlie or King Charles, due to his illustrious birthright, but he was nothing more than a conniving twit.

Charles Winthrop Pritchard was short and burly with a round face and a long, dark mustache that curled down his cheeks past his chin. He dressed impeccably, his uniform laundered daily. He chewed on imported cigars, but seldom lit them. He sipped posh French wine from a flask, but was never opposed to trading it for a stiff shot of single-malt Irish whiskey. The Captain avoided the horror of battle by delegating the supply distribution to a gaggle of orderlies he ruled with an iron hand. He was exacting in his methods to procure and distribute the lifeline of provisions, but always extracted a high price. He would soon be a valuable ally to Jon for some winter chicanery.

Jon approached the bilge rat with a proposition, "Captain, I have a proposal for you that could be quite profitable, if you will hear me out."

Pritchard detested Jon. "I cannot imagine how I could benefit from a scheme you have devised. You are the consummate company man, never straying from your chosen path. Surely you don't think that I would be party to anything you have concocted?"

Jon masked his anger. "I need a favor, sir. Could you procure some spirits for my men so they can pass the Christmas holiday in joy and peace, as it should be?"

"What is in this for me, Holland? Surely, you don't expect me to do this for gratis?"

Jon swallowed his pride and fought desperately against the urge to wail on Pritchard. "I have nothing of value to offer, but I will owe you a debt if you can see fit to carry this out for me."

Pritchard examined Jon with a smirk on his face. "I have been watching you, Holland, and I thought you showed great promise. But I have found that you are nothing more than a sniveling fool, just like the rest of the farmers." He rolled the stub of his cigar in his mouth. "You know what your problem is? You are a man with God-given talent, but you are mired in a box of mediocrity, always taking the low road. How is it that you can be so commonplace?"

Jon pushed his chair back and stood up. "Begging your pardon, sir, but are you saying that I should have been born of privilege, doing everything possible to circumvent the system as you have? If you recall, it was farmers that gave you that license during the Revolution. They are the ones who left their families, fought the battles, and ultimately died so aristocrats like you could profit. You have never lifted a hand to procure the prominence you now wallow in. Brahmin blood or not, I think you owe those men a debt. If you expect any of them to vote for you after this wretched war, then you had better treat them with dignity, despite their lineage."

Pritchard was incensed. "I am an officer and a gentleman, Holland. You, Master Sergeant, will honor me with respect; although I must say that I do admire your spunk."

There were men dying every day and people like Pritchard were profiting. Jon had seen the bloodshed and felt the pain of battle while Boston Charlie lingered safely in the rear. "Putting rank and privilege aside, go down there and live in their shoes for a day. You will be a better man by rubbing elbows with us commoners. You need to understand the pluck that drives them."

Pritchard would not be talked down to. "It is none of your affair why I fight, but if you want to make something of your own life, you need to take some risks, challenge the ordinary, and climb out of that vessel that binds you to tilling the soil." Pritchard placed his hands firmly on the table. "Men like you who waste their potential thinking of grander things and not acting on them are the lowliest form of being. You too can learn some valuable lessons from the forefathers."

He spit his cigar in the dirt and removed a fresh one from his coat. "You bloody Irishmen are all alike. You talk a good game, but do not have the gumption to back it up. On the surface, you are a tough Mick, but deep down inside you are nothing more than a sniveling, lazy coward."

Jon backed off. "So, what is it that you would have me do?"

"You seek me out after the war and I will set you straight on how to become landed gentry. You can forget the whiskey unless you can come up with a plan by which we both can profit. If you want to help your men, then show me the determination from which you say you are made."

Jon's motivation was not to profit, but rather to give his hard-driving troopers a break from the calling of the sword. He was unwilling to let the scheme drop just because Pritchard was not keen on the idea. He had played his hand and now he needed to face up to Pritchard's challenge.

Pritchard interjected, "What is it that you want to accomplish, Holland? I am party to any man's wicked enterprise so long as there is something in it for me."

Jon explained the scheme to the Captain who simply laughed at him. "You have proven my point. You have devised a crafty conspiracy, but your thinking is too ordinary. Let me tantalize you with a more grandiose plot." Pritchard conjured up an idea. "In exchange for my help you will set me up in a lucrative brewing business, let's say to supplement the moral needs of all of the regiments. A distraction as you put it. Once the plan is in place, I will be able to sustain a secret and lucrative whiskey exchange. Can you see the wisdom in my entrepreneurship?"

King Charlie's plan was simple, but Jon's counterproposal was sheer genius. And so, the two men who hated, mistrusted, and despised one another, set aside their differences and conjured up a devilish partnership to make money and help the troopers. They met over the next few weeks to finalize the details and when each was satisfied, they sealed the deal with a pint of brandy.

Pritchard boasted, "You are a good student, Holland. I salute you for a most cunning plot. We would make profitable partners after the war. Consider a transfer to my commissary unit. I can make it happen for the right price and then we can both be better served."

Pritchard's arrogance blinded him to the fact that Jon had bested him at his own game, but the Master Sergeant chose to let a dead man lie. "You have set me straight on matters of the world, Captain Pritchard, and for that I am grateful."

The two soldiers set their plan in motion. In short order, they had transformed the contents of a little-used Conestoga wagon into a traveling tavern, stocked with bartered brew, some lagers procured from Charlie's Boston breweries, and some local rotgut, bastardized white lightening.

Jon felt guilty about his deviousness, but his obligation to help his men trumped his need to remain within the confines of a chosen path. Its secretive, dishonest disposition weighed heavily upon his heart. He put aside his abject feelings and decided to help the troopers that were wallowing in self-pity over the miseries of war, their souls scarred by melancholy. He thought of McGuilicutty's words. *Your eyes are the window to your soul, soldier. You might try a little mischief yourself, Sergeant Major, to ease your own troubled heart. Let the Great Eagle guide you on your path toward a different life and then you may understand what it is I am trying to tell you.*

Chapter 15

Rounders

The regiment licked its wounds after battles that marked some of the darkest days of the war. Many of their brothers had fallen on the plains above Fredericksburg in ill-advised frontal assaults on a sunken road situated behind a chest high wall on sloping Maryes' Heights. General Burnside insisted on attacking this impregnable position, only to have his regiments slaughtered after each desperate try. Despite the advice of his generals, Burnside believed that he could break the center of Lee's formidable lines. The result was irreparable carnage as the demoralized combatants had to lie prone on their arms in the snow throughout a frigid night.

Jon's regiment avoided the brunt of the fight while they watched the devastating assaults from their position as a provost guard. As the army retraced their steps back across the river on the swaying pontoon bridges, they settled back into a cold and gloomy routine of camp life.

Shannon was on the verge of mutiny as the oppressive cold, a bout with dysentery, and the slaughter took a toll on his nerves. "We have had enough of your all in for the Union attitude. A lot of good it does when we get mowed down like hay under the hand of a sharp scythe."

Jon agreed, "I am sick to death of wallowing in reserve while our brothers fall in our stead."

"Get off of your high horse. You've been preaching to me since we were kids and what has come of it?" A frustrated O'Reilly pushed passed Jon and ducked out of the door of the hut.

On Christmas Eve of '62, Holland and Pritchard decided that it was time to break out their barrels of spirited concoctions. Each member of the regiment would be given a complimentary cup of malt. If the fellows wanted more, they would have to pay a slight fee to their suppliers. The rest of the brew would be sold off to the officers of other regiments.

Pritchard anticipated a lucrative haul. "My share of the profits will go toward funding my post-war campaign for the Senate, Holland. You should consider doing the same."

Jon decided to donate what he earned to the families of killed or wounded soldiers in the Valley. He was confident that it would not be much, but assumed that every bit would help.

The two unlikely business partners went to great lengths to insure the secrecy of the affair. The high command was at a raucous corps party. Their flamboyant music and rambunctious behavior could be heard throughout the valley. A Confederate attack would catch the army with its pants down, but the icy river, screeching wind, and holiday season deterred the notion.

Pritchard hitched up a mule team to the wagon that housed the tavern and slowly maneuvered it through the snow and mud into the camp behind the makeshift huts the soldiers called home.

Sergeant Major Holland called out the troopers for daily drill. As they left their huts, they grumbled loudly. Jon could sense the dissension. After all, it was Christmas, the most holy of days.

Shannon threw his rifle down on the ground in disgust. "What ails you, Jonny? My mother would not let me go out on such a terrible day. Do you realize it is Christmas, laddie?"

Jon quieted the troops by drawing his revolver and cocking the hammer. "Get in line and stop your bellyaching. Did you see how those Rebs slaughtered our boys? They may look like a lot of rabble, but they fight with the vengeance of a wolverine."

Shannon mouthed off. "Tell you what, Jonny, I will wager that I can lick you. If I win, we all go back to our warm huts. If you win, we will do as you say and like it" Shannon removed his coat and rolled up his sleeves. He was an imposing man, strong and virile with bulging muscles from shaping the iron. He made most men cower, but Jon knew how to best him.

In his best brogue, Jon questioned Shannon's courage. "Do you really want to be doing this, Shannon? Through that bravado, you are nothing more than a sniveling coward."

Shannon breathed some foul air into Jon's face. "Well there, Sergeant Major Jonny, I really do not want to be doing anything. You see, I've been sitting on the latrine all day, shite coming out me arse until it aches, and I do not have the gumption to be marching or fighting. But if you insist on making me stand here in the bloody cold, then I insist on kicking the snot out of you."

"Is that so, Shannon?" said Jon. "And what makes you think that you can kick me arse? You damned well couldn't do it when we were kids and you sure as hell can't do it today." Jon referenced a not-so-pleasant experience that Shannon endured when he worked in the Brooklyn breweries. "With a name like Shannon, you haven't got the lant in your pants to clean me boots."

Jon sensed that things might get out of hand. Before he could bring things back under control, Shannon's bearlike fist came into view. He instinctively ducked. The force of the swing caused Shannon to lose his balance. He fell head over teakettle and landed with a flop in the quagmire. Jon seized the moment and planted his boot on Shannon's chest. He leaned over the prostrate giant and placed the barrel of his cocked revolver on his temple.

"Now Shannon, if you insist on spoiling my day, then I may have to shoot you. Blowing your brains across the drill field would be a waste of good lead. So, get up out of that slop, Mr. O'Reilly, stop acting like a Neanderthal, and join me in celebrating the season with a pint of hooch."

Shannon's responded, "Did you say something about a spot of ale?"

"I may have mentioned a pint or maybe two, but you must cease with this ruckus and fall into rank like an obedient soldier." Jon had restored order so he secured his pistol. "By the left flank march. Be smart and step lively lads for the eyes of the Republic are upon you. We are going out for a lovely stroll, as the good Lord would will it, on such a glorious Christmas day."

The troopers, all showing glimpses of their assorted configuration of teeth, readily stepped off to his command. Jon led them down the company rows, right shoulder arms, slopping in the mud as they proudly held their heads up high. At the regimental head-quarters, he saluted the Officer of the Day. "Eyes left." The troopers cocked their heads and dipped the national colors to honor him.

"Snappy looking group you have there, Mr. Holland."

"Thank you, sir. We're just setting out for a sprightly jaunt. Would you care to join us?"

"Thank you, Mr. Holland, but I think I'll return to the comforts of my hut, seeing that you have everything in good order. Carry on good fellows and have a Merry Christmas!"

"And a very good Christmas to you, sir," said Jon as he tossed him a carrot of tobacco.

The company made their way toward the end of the regimental street. As Jon had expected, the weather deterred the OD from staying outside. He smartly turned the regiment by the left flank and called them to a halt in front of the quartermaster, as the flag bearers cased the colors.

Boston Charlie leaned on the Conestoga. He eyed his pocket watch and puffed nervously on his cigar. He barked at Jon, "What the bloody hell took you so long? I've been waiting a wicked long time in the blessed cold. I never should have trusted you to do anything without my guidance." He harrumphed, "Did you bring half of the bleeding army with you?"

Jon appealed to his vanity. "I told them that you had a Christmas present for them. You are a saint for patiently passing the time as we sorted ourselves out. Merry Christmas to you, Captain"

Pritchard was temporarily appeased. "I haven't got all day, Holland. Get these boys up here for a bit of Christmas spirit before I change my mind. The ruckus they have made coming over here probably aroused the interest of the provost guard and the Rebs on yonder hill."

The regiment stacked their arms and formed a line of battle. Shannon brushed aside a green recruit with a heavy elbow to the jaw. "Move out of my way, you blackguard."

The soldiers got their fill of the grog and then reached deep into their pockets to procure a more from the gloating quartermaster. Pritchard could not have anticipated the potency of the mix and soon discovered its ill effects on the thirsty, malnourished troopers.

Addie Jones was the first to exploit the courage he found at the bottom of the cask. He confronted Shannon, but not wanting to take a swipe at his monolithic nemesis, he craftily employed a different tactic. He gathered his bunk mates and moved off to a small, treeless hill. Using the soft snow, they built a breastwork. When their preparations were ready, Addie fired the first salvo of what would soon be an impressive barrage of snowballs.

Shannon was oblivious to the goings on around him until a well-placed shot caught him on the back of the head. He stumbled forward and spilled what was left of his drink.

Jones had proven to be a prolific Rounders, or Town Ball player. The skills acquired in that game sharpened his snow throwing accuracy. The artillery officers would have been proud of such a well-placed ball. He immediately went to the ground in a frenzy of laughter.

Shannon hurled himself up the slope in hot pursuit. The defenders unleashed a barrage of snowballs that stopped him cold in his tracks. He turned tail and retreated down the hill to regroup, as the attackers called his courage into question with profane barbs. By this time, others had gathered. They built an arsenal of snowballs and huddled to develop a strategy to take the works.

The troopers on the hill taunted them, shouting out a grand "Huzzah"!

Shannon spread his legions along the base of the hill for a renewed assault. With a mock Rebel yell, they flanked the works and divided the defending force. Shannon and a few other brave souls attacked the center of the fortifications. In a few moments, a hail of snow projectiles consumed both sides. The two armies came together and fisticuffs ensued. The melee was on.

Jon and Charlie watched as their well-intentioned work had turned into a fracas. They did nothing to stop the free-for-all. It was good for the morale and they were enjoying the revelry.

The provost guard emerged from behind the huts, following the OD who brandished a saber. He issued commands and then hit a large patch of black ice. He fought to keep his balance, but lost everything in a kilter as he went to ground. His sword took a roundabout path to the same place. Just in the nick of time, the officer rolled over and watched the blade stick harmlessly in the ground next to him. He laid there for a moment and hoped that no one had seen.

The regiment scattered to the four points of the compass and wound their way back to their own huts to escape the grasp of the rampaging marshals.

Boston Charlie quickly mounted the seat of the Conestoga and coaxed the mules with a string of profanity that would have disbanded him from his illustrious New England Anglican Church. A slap on the lead mule's backside by a fleeing trooper sent the entourage pell-mell down the road toward the river. Charlie tried to keep the mules from running amuck. He fell back in the seat, but managed to right himself long enough to see the braying mules hurl themselves over an embankment. He suddenly became airborne and landed harmlessly in a bank of snow. The wagon continued to careen toward the river and disappeared over a hill. Charlie collapsed back into the snow to mull over the destruction of his enterprise and the future of his political career.

Jon watched the episode with a smile. *Had these men ever had such a wonderful Christmas?*

After a few days, the whole affair was sorted out by the investigating officers. The regimental commander and his superiors, in the Christmas spirit, were lenient with the offenders.

Jon took the brunt of the blame, drawing extra duty. It was worth it to stand the guard for the good of the regiment. He had finally reached into their souls as McGuilicutty had prophesized.

Pritchard turned coat on Jon, avoided his superiors, and bribed his way out of any punishment.

By New Year's Day of 1863, the entire affair had been forgotten. The regiment prepared for what would later be known as the infamous Mud March, another failed debacle in a long string of disasters for the hapless Army of the Potomac.

Jon had received correspondence from his Uncle Joe Holland who had chosen to take to the sea like many of the Holland men in the old country had done before they had immigrated to America. He had pulled duty as a gunner's mate on Admiral Farragut's flagship, the *Hartford*, but was recently discharged after he lost his hand in a fight with a Confederate blockade runner. Joe claimed that things were going well back at home, but with most of the menfolk gone or disabled, it was hard to keep up with the work. The letter prompted Jon's own literary escapade. He managed to craft a down-to-earth letter to his parents, with the help of one of his more literate friends.

Jon reflected on the lives of the men and the families they had left behind. There was some sadness in his thoughts, but his hardened soul soon gave way to the realities of the war. He shivered a bit from the cold, stoked the fire at his feet, and pulled the blue, wool army-issue blanket around his shoulders to shelter himself from the mordacious winter wind. It was almost midnight. He surmised that the spirits had left his timepiece to find a more comfortable place, away from the harsh elements that raged outside. A distracting growl wandered on the wind from a distance behind the hut. *Were the spirits trying to summon him?* He realized that he had been deceived, broke into a sheepish farm boy's grin, and called out to Shannon, "Happy New Year, grunt!"

Chapter 16

Hornet's Nest

The seasons passed quickly in the peaceful Anishinabe camp. The orphans were immersed into the Indian culture and endured excruciating rituals that measured their ability to survive on their own; care for one another's needs, and thrive in the unpredictable wilderness. They also competed in *The Creator's Game,* which the French referred to as lacrosse. Each of these matches measured their courage and helped build a collegial tribal order.

As René entered his fifteenth year, the land was ravaged by war, as the French and British wrestled for control of North America. His clan had isolated themselves from the fighting, while the two sides postured to bring the Indians into the conflict. But it would be another year, in 1758, before the Natives, by treaty, would agree to fight.

René's immersion into a life of rigorous living made him a formidable man, even at this young age. He was muscular and virile, towering over the other men. They were rarely his equal in tests of physical prowess, although they could usually best him due to his emotional frailty and rash behaviors. He bore hardened, dark features. He wanted to leave the tribe, but did not have the gumption to venture forth, even though he openly bragged about his independence.

Three-Legged-Wolf sought to temper the teen's anger and defiance. But the warrior struggled to bring the young man to a rational mental state where he could utilize his extraordinary gifts effectively.

René was up to the challenge of conquering most tasks, but there were times when his imprudent behavior alienated him or subjected him to ridicule. His inability to control his inner spirit left him vulnerable and prone to outbursts of unconventional conduct and anger.

One cool fall day, as the trees were beginning to turn, Three-Legged-Wolf led a party of warriors on a mission to confront a band of renegades from a neighboring tribe. They had been stealing the livestock. René and the other orphans were asked to help recover the animals.

Most of the day proved to be uneventful as the two war parties thrust and parried with each other in the defiles of a wooded coulee. As the confrontation became more heated, the orphans were asked to stay behind to guard the rear of the war party from any flanking action.

Three-Legged-Wolf warned them, "You are to hold this ground at all costs. Under no circumstances are you to relinquish it. Spread yourselves out along the crest of this ridge. Should our enemies attack; it will be your responsibility to delay them. Am I understood?"

At the base of ridge in a swampy hollow, the two tribes were engaged in open conflict. The rear guard could not see much through the smoke, but the screams of the wounded, the crack of sporadic musketry, or the howls of the warriors gave them an idea that it was a hot fight.

René situated himself behind a large oak log that had fallen across a path. He loaded his musket and rested it over the trunk. He was itching to get into a fight and was angry that he had to sit idly by, like a spoiled child being punished, while the other warriors got all of the glory. He did not understand the importance of his role. It was a test of his will and courage. But he decided to take matters into his own hands, suddenly heading down the hill toward the sounds of battle.

One of the other men called after him, "Where are you off to, Pashkwadjash?" You are going to get us all killed if you leave that ground exposed." René ignored him and headed deeper into the forest. "Where is Pashkwadjash going? Should we follow?"

Another angered warrior berated him, "Leave him to his own devices. He will only serve to get you killed. We were commanded to remain here and that is what we shall do."

Two other men left their positions on the ridge to follow René, which left only two men to guard the entire rear of the battle line. "Pashkwadjash, wait for us."

René stopped long enough for the others to catch up before he led them onto the right flank where sporadic fighting was taking place. He rushed in, clubbing an enemy warrior with the butt of his musket. The three men were suddenly overwhelmed by rival braves who dashed out from the blind. One was immediately struck down by a ball to the head. The other ran for his life back up the hill. His mouth was agape with terror as he was tracked down and swiftly lost his scalp.

René fought with a vengeance and was soon joined by other warriors. They managed to extricate themselves from the fray, but the damage had been done. His misguided courage had turned the tide of the battle. Having no other alternative, the Anishinabe warriors retreated up the ridge. When they reached the top, they found that their rear was fully exposed. The organized retreat became a riotous rout. The bloodied, defeated warriors skulked into camp as the sun set.

René soon joined them, but was ostracized. Two of the other orphans had been killed and one wounded because of his rash behavior. The battle had been lost and the neighboring tribe now held the upper hand in the valley. It was a day that the other warriors would not let him forget.

Three-Legged-Wolf was beside himself with anger and grief. His friends lay dead, mutilated by their attackers who committed vile acts of depredation upon their bodies to block their souls from rising to the heavens. The shaman-warrior waited several days to quell his wrath and then mustered the fortitude to speak to René. He found him in a makeshift lean-to, skinning a beaver.

"I do not wish to speak with you Three-Legged-Wolf. What's done is done and quite frankly I would do it all over again if the opportunity presented itself to me."

The warrior was calm, "Have you no remorse for what you have caused, Pashkwadjash?"

René spoke quietly, "I have simply acted on my instincts, like you have taught me. If the others had not skulked cowardly behind the cover of the boulders, we would have won the day."

Three-Legged-Wolf spoke harshly, "You are a misguided, rash, and foolish young man. You display no penitence for my friends, your brothers, who lie dead by your hand."

"I have slain no one save the warriors who foolishly crossed my path. Have you not heard the biblical saying, an eye for an eye?" René looked up at the brave defiantly.

"I will not succumb to your baiting, young wolf. You will learn that you are not an island unto yourself. The other warriors want you killed like a raging bear, but I have convinced them that you are worth saving. Your fate lies within your soul, so search it carefully to find the truth."

Three-Legged-Wolf turned his back on the woodsman and headed back to camp, hoping that he would follow. His strong will had been tested by this lad, but he would not give up on him as others had. He saw something in the René that reminded him of himself at a younger age. He thought that if he could crack the hard shell of his emotions, he could make a man out of him.

René had trouble dealing with the fallout from his bungled attempt to become a hero. He would return to camp, but when he was pushed too far, he would escape by running away.

The great warrior would often tag along after him. "You surmise that you can elude me, but I am bound by a covenant to keep you on a straight path. You will gain your freedom when you confront your demons, not when you run from them. Do not be deceived by the state of your being, for you are not invincible. When you unlock the dark cavern of your soul, you will recognize the truth and then you can run uninhibited like the deer."

René defiantly challenged him, "What right do you have to shackle me to your way of life?"

"I honor a promise, a lesson you would be best served to learn."

The brash young man answered insolently, "It is of my choosing to live as I do. Solitude and independence are what I desire. Neither you nor my estranged father shall keep me from that destiny."

"Then tell me what it is that forces you to return to me after you have run? Surely you are not afraid of the secrets that the wilderness harbors for you?"

René screwed up his face as he failed to comprehend the many unanswered questions.

The warrior pressed him, "The man who has no kindred or country shall be doomed to a life of loneliness. Your name will be but a breath of air upon a howling wind."

The game of cat and mouse continued. René would run and the persistent warrior would pursue. It became a match of skill and daring. The warrior embraced the challenge, for he hoped that it would lead to a revelation for the woebegone teen. During one episode, the lad lured the warrior into his lair. His pursuer took the bait and he sprung the trap. A woven rope of vines snared the Algonquin's leg and lifted him above the forest floor. Try as he may, he was unable to free himself.

"I have taught you well, Pashkwadjash. Now release me and be done with this charade."

René looked up and smiled. "I shall not release you until you have assured me that I am your equal and I do not have to succumb to the pressures of your tutelage anymore."

"You may have won the day, young wolf, but you have much more to learn before you are my equal. I shall not pretend that it is so, nor shall I give you false hope or promise. I will hang here until the passing of the moon rather than let you live a lie. I will hunt you to the ends of the earth, for I am dedicated to set you straight. I see in you a light of hope that needs to be kindled."

"So be it. Then you shall hang there until you die. The next time we meet it will be in the house of the Great Spirit where you will be kneeling before me to pay homage." René felt invincible. He now believed that he possessed the skills and courage to settle the scores of personal revenge.

Chapter 17

Tormenting Beasts

Several months had passed since René had left the Anishinabe village. He began to understand the complexities of living a life of solitude, but he felt that it was a far sight better than the heartache he experienced when he was in the company of others. He built a shelter fashioned from hides in the wilderness along a meandering stream. The refuge was nestled in a grove of pines under the shadow of an escarpment. It was a simple, but satisfying dwelling.

René reveled in his independence. Much of his time was spent hunting and trapping. He obsessively immersed himself in his trade so he did not have to think about his troubles. Independent living quelled the tragedy that he harbored in his soul, but he remained conflicted. As he sat cooking a small meal, he seethed about the myriad of perceived injustices that haunted him.

It was late fall and a hint of winter wafted over his face. He looked across the stream toward a meadow. It was placid, unlike the turmoil that raged within him. He reflected on time spent with the Anishinabe. He regretted his harsh behavior toward Three-Legged-Wolf who had been a wise teacher. His hatred for his father, lack of respect for his mother, and his forced refuge among the indigenous people strengthened his will, but left him emotionally shallow. He was determined to exact some measure of revenge upon people who wronged him, so he plotted and schemed. He soon decided to take action. He left his haven and headed north. He coursed his way through dark hollows and heavy forests as he approached the civilization he loathed. He happened upon isolated farms and scattered villages. He did not stop except to sleep and nourish himself.

After a few days, René had worked his way back to the King's Highway. He was driven by a mysterious inner-demon moving him toward revenge. He began to run along the rutted road. His long, loping strides carried him swiftly across the dusty terrain. He soon came upon a broken-down hay wagon. Its rear axle was in shambles, one wheel lay in the ditch. Its driver was hobbled.

The farmer tried to flag him down. "I beg for your assistance, sir. I have injured my leg in the fall and cannot repair my wagon on my own. Would you be so kind, stranger, to stop and help?"

René paused for a moment in front of the man who leaned on the wagon to take the pressure off of his swollen leg. He was moved for a moment by the old man's plight, but in an instant, he questioned his fleeting impulse to help the man. *Had anyone shown pity toward me in a time of need?* When it was all said and done, he callously ignored the farmer and moved on.

The feeble farmer called after him, the pain of his injury evident in his anguished voice, "May the devil strike you down for your insolence, you laggard."

As he ran, René reflected on his childhood, now just a blur of painful experiences. He neared his father's homestead. Increasing his speed, he deftly moved his musket to the ready across his chest. When he reached the farmhouse, he paused momentarily in the barnyard to survey the scene. A few chickens clucked in rebuke at the sudden disturbance, but nothing had changed since he was last there. It was smaller and more dilapidated than he had remembered. He bounded up the steps, grabbed the ax that lay on top of the wood pile, and threw open the door.

The one lone room of his former home was empty. It was dark inside and smelled musty, much like he had remembered it. The table that his father had broken had been replaced with a newer one, but everything else was much the same. He did not linger to reminisce. He headed back out of the door, leapt off of the steps, and sped toward the outbuildings. As he scattered the chickens, he alerted the two people who were working inside of the barn.

Angelique came out to see what the commotion was and screamed. "René, my dear, I would recognize you anywhere, boy. Come to your mama and give me a hug."

The woodsman towered over his mother. He was developing into a handsome and powerful man. He was chiseled, with bronze skin and the same mysterious eyes that she had remembered from his childhood. There was pain written upon his face, his blank stare telling a thousand tales.

Angelique's face was scarred and swollen from the incessant beatings. Her hair was cropped short, as it had been when she wore the habit of a nun. She was so frail that he suspected that a strong wind could break her in two. Tears welled up in her hollow, but beautiful blue eyes.

René did not let his gaze linger there for fear of stirring up deep emotions. "Where is he?"

"If you are referring to your father, he is in the barn tending to the cow. She gave birth…"

René tossed his mother callously aside, as he had seen his father do. She fell to the ground. "Get out of my way, wench." He heard his father's voice resonating from the far stall.

"Is that you, woman? Who has come-a-calling?" Henri was squatting over a new calf, cleaning the embryonic fluid from its nostrils. He turned away from the animal as it tried to stand on its own accord, wobbled on unstable legs, and then fell back down beside its mother.

René walked deliberately to the stall, lit by sunlight filtering through the cracked siding.

"My God, René, is that you, boy?"

Before anymore could be said, René raised the ax over his head.

Henri reacted quickly. The ax fell upon him as he turned away, glancing off his arm, but causing no serious harm. "What ails you, boy? Henri shouted. "It will be the hangman's noose if you kill your father. If you persist with this violence I shall be forced to hang you myself."

René raised the ax once again. "No one has ever had the courage to stand up to you. You have abused mother and sent me off into the wilderness to live among strangers. I have come here to exact my revenge upon you so that those who have suffered for so long by your hand can finally find some peace. Look into these eyes, Henri Dubois. The anger that resides within is of your doing. Take my pain to the grave with you, sir. May your soul rot forever in the depths of hell."

A pleading voice from behind him caused him to hesitate. "Don't do it, René. You will be no better than he if you succumb to this violence. Leave it be, son, you hear me? You will only live to regret this day. Remember the Commandments, son, and let them guide your course."

René could not believe that she was so brazen to interfere. He thought, *How is it that she is suddenly finding the courage to stand up to someone?* "An eye for an eye, mother?"

While René was distracted, his father attempted to attack him, but the woodsman planted his moccasin-clad foot on his chest and pinned him to the floor. Henri looked gaunt; the abuse of drink had made the hollows of his eyes dark. His hair was grey, pulled back and tied behind his head with a thong of leather. He was haggard, as if the life was being sapped from him. The hideous purple hoof print upon his brow posed a stark contrast to his bronzed skin.

"Do not preach to me about righteousness, mother. There is no pity to mete out, for you are as much to blame as he is. You have failed to take any action upon him and condoned his violence with your meek, feeble acceptance of his bidding."

Henri managed to free himself from the pressure of René's foot and rose to his knees. "Have mercy on us, boy. What have those savages done to make you so angry, so aggressive towards me and your mother? Has the Lord vacated your soul while you lived amongst those heathens?"

"Unlike you, father, they have turned me into a man. They measure life by different values, lessons you could not begin to comprehend, but would be best suited to learn."

René thrust the ax into a beam. He could hear Three-Legged-Wolf. *It is the wiser man who walks away.* The warrior had been more of a father figure to him than the pariah at his feet. Henri was a coward who was now reduced to a pathetic wimp, begging for his life.

The woodsman stuck his fingers into a bucket of wagon axle grease. He wiped it across his brow and nose to paint two jagged lines resembling lightning bolts diagonally across his face. "Mark my words, Henri Dubois, upon the rising of three moons you will reside forever in your grave, tormented by the demons of hell." He spit upon his father's face. "If I hear so much as a whisper that you have harmed my mother, I will return to strike you down dead."

His mother's blank stare left him unsure if she respected his courage or was horrified by his display of bitter hatred. Too consumed by emotion, he pushed her aside and ran back up the lane.

Angelique called after him, "René, my darling boy, do not leave us. The three of us can sort this all out. The Lord will guide us with the wisdom to make it right."

The woodsman did not even glance back. He increased his pace and ran until exhaustion gripped him. Too shaken to proceed, he lay prostrate in a haystack alongside of the road. The demons of conflict soon possessed him, as emotional storms brewed in his heart and head. His violent confrontation with his parents had changed nothing. *Will I never be free from the tormenting beasts that reside within me?*

Chapter 18

Resurrection

René awoke to a stirring in the rushes outside of his wilderness shelter. It was a cool morning and mist clung to his exhausted body. Brushing a cricket from his chest, he sat up and listened. The rustle in the bushes was now behind him, growing nearer.

Recent discord had disrupted the land as the French and British engaged in a series of global military and political conflicts which resulted in the Guerre de la Conquête or French and Indian War. Bloodshed spilled into the American Provinces where the severely outnumbered French tried to ally themselves with the Indian tribes to stem the tide of British aggression.

René was acutely aware of the turmoil, but avoided entering the war and evaded any collusion with the opposing governments. Hidden in the woods, he hoped to ride out the storm in relative obscurity. If he was discovered, he would be branded a shirker, banished to some obscure prison; or worse yet, some desolate, outpost on the frontier. He took care to avoid the patrols and minimize contact with other people. *Had they discovered him?*

Before René could conceal himself, the imposing figure of Three-Legged-Wolf appeared, arms folded across his bare chest. The sun filtered through the clouds and cloaked the warrior in a fiery glow of luminescence. The woodsman was startled. It was as if the devil had appeared to punish him for the heinous act of patricide he had tried to commit.

"You have done well to elude me for near three moons, my son," the warrior said. "I was beginning to believe that the Earth's creatures had swallowed you up."

René cupped his hands and scooped up a refreshing drink, ignoring Three-Legged-Wolf. He had proven himself to be a formidable man, so the warrior could bloody well wait.

Three-Legged-Wolf would not tolerate the disrespect. "You can choose to treat me with disdain or you can share your misery with me. The furrows of your face reveal your troubles."

"It angers me that I have become my father's seed, acting like a raging wolf and committing callous acts. I have shamed myself in the eyes of my mother."

"You puzzle me, Pashkwadjash. You possess the cunning of the wolf, the vision of the eagle, and the power of the bear. You run like the deer or hide in plain sight like the ghost insects. You are a calculating trader and a shrewd tracker. Yet you have the heart of the wolverine; cold, defiant, and intolerant, filled with shameless hatred."

René challenged his mentor, "What you say may be true, but I will not be beholden to the feeble manipulations of the so-called civilized man. You preach of solitude and inner peace, but when it suits you, you mark those words with battle-hardened hatred. I do not seek to live as other men live. I care solely for my own needs and am free to do as I please."

"I fear that you have only sought to venture down one path. If you take another, you will know that life's twists and turns will lead you toward the truth. Sit with me upon this log."

The two men sat on the shell of a fallen oak covered with the grey-green lichen.

"This forest is ablaze with the fire of life. It appears to be serene, but if you look and listen you will see that it is a symbiotic community of energy, each component dependent on the other for survival. Tell me exactly what you have learned from your communion with nature."

"I have seen the bee extract the pollen from the womb of the flower. The flower has grown from a seed nurtured by the grace of the fallen tree. The bee weaves the nectar into honey to nurture the queen and her young and then the cycle begins all over again." René forced a smile. "I suspect that the bear cub on yon rise will get his snout full of that honey, much to the chagrin of the bees."

"If any one of those things wavers, the entire string of life is broken. We are so naturally bound to one another by this chain of survival that we often take it for granted. Our greed, hatred, and misunderstanding become our undoing. If you choose to be independent, you will falter, for you need the comfort and support of others to survive and surely they will need you."

The brave grabbed a handful of dirt. "You understand that a delicate balance binds all living things. But you have not spoken about that which you do not see. They are the intangibles that fill your spirit with sanctity. Because you do not see them, does not mean that you should not value them. They are as much a part of the circle as the things that are clearly visible to you."

René thought, *Why doesn't he just come out and say what it is he wants me to know.*

The warrior handed his calumet to René. "Take this blade and strike a blow to the hollow of this log. What is it that you discover?"

René raised the finely-honed ax and made easy work of the wood. It shattered to reveal a large nest of swarming ants. They spilled out onto the men's legs, causing them to abruptly vacate the log. "I have discovered that I am not too fond of these creatures randomly biting me."

"Would you have known that they were there had they not been revealed to you? They would be still at peace inside the shelter of the log and you would not have had them lash out at you so violently in retaliation for your aggression, an instinct of their survival."

"I suspect that they and I would be better off if we left well enough alone."

"You must realize that they are as important to the balance of life as the bee that flies visibly before you? So, what lesson is derived from the plight of the ant whose home you have invaded?"

René surmised, "You have taught me well and for that I am grateful. What is evident on the surface of our lives is only the shell of our existence. It is those things that we do not see, nor fully understand that make us wiser and more humane; or weaken us to a point of destruction."

Three-Legged-Wolf put his arm around René's shoulder and encouraged him, "Let us walk in silence toward our home and your eyes will reveal to your soul some hidden wisdom."

The men reached the swale that led to the disheveled Anishinabe compound. René stopped at the top of the rise. "I cannot return there. The warriors despise me and the women shun me. I will only bring discontent to your people, while they question the trust they have placed in you."

"You will not dishonor me by returning to our home. My people have forgiven you for the lack of wisdom you showed as a child. It is right for you to absolve them of their indifference."

Three-Legged-Wolf was greeted by a throng of children who cradled his legs or climbed upon his back. The warrior gave each child their due and then summoned René, "Come with me. We shall spend the evening in the sweat shack. Its fires will cleanse our souls and free our minds."

René followed the warrior to an isolated hut on the outskirts of the camp. The two men entered the stark hotbox, disrobing inside. They sat quietly with blankets draped over their heads. The young woodsman found it hard to breathe, but withstood the ordeal so as not to offend the warrior.

The brave whispered to him, "Let the spirits freely enter your soul and then you shall be liberated. In the end, a light will emanate before you and your path shall be cleared."

René breathed in the misty smoke and closed his eyes. Sweat poured from his bronzed skin and mysterious images goaded him. An eagle swooped down, hovered briefly, and then disappeared into a dark void. A jovial Frenchman taunted him with felonious pranks. A shadowy warrior with a black hand plastered across his mouth chastised him. A faceless squaw curled a finger in a gesture of calling. A child laughed as she chased a butterfly about a mysterious hollow. A horrific serpent lashed out. War, carnage, murder, massacre, shame, and misery…enlightenment.

René cried out, "Leave me be you sullen beasts of the Underworld." Then he awoke.

Three-Legged-Wolf removed the blanket from his head. The red salve painted upon his face dripped onto his chest, like blood emanating from a gaping wound. He rose to his knees and cupped his sweating hands about René's face. Visibly weakened by the trial, he whispered, "I have had a vision. The spirit of a diabolical serpent resides within you. He rises up from the Underworld to toil master-fully upon your heart. A bird of prey has tried to enter your soul to cleanse you." He seemed to be in a trance. "The corridor that leads to your soul is a dark maze of confusion and guilt. The light to guide him to the truth has been extinguished by the serpent and must be rekindled." The warrior slumped over in a catatonic state.

René threw off the blankets and escaped into the night. He inhaled the cool evening air and felt its veil freshen his sweating skin. Three-Legged-Wolf had led him to the path and he under-stood now that he must follow it. He must enter the underbelly of civilization to battle the beasts within him, cleanse his soul, and unearth the truth. He must tread in the shoes of other men. So, as the sun crested the eastern horizon, he threw his satchel and mus-ket over his shoulder, said sorrowful goodbyes to his mentor, and headed away from the mounting light. Something in its yellow-orange glow made it clear to him that this time Three-Legged-Wolf would not pursue him.

Chapter 19

The Whispering Winds

René passed a short time in the wilderness as he began his personal transformation. He needed to make sense of his thoughts and formulate a plan that would drive his quest. He understood that he needed to move away from the places that had harbored the seeds of his burdens. With a cleared conscience, he surmised that he could discover the true meaning of the questions that the warrior Three-Legged-Wolf had placed before him.

At first, he made sure that the encumbrances of living in the wilderness were not a burden or distraction. As his confidence grew, he found that the Indians had taught him well, for he felt as if he were one with the forest. He was invigorated by the freedom, but a vacant shelf remained within the deep hollows of his heart. He was impatient, not willing to let life run its course. Through deep reflection, he surmised that he had to return to the homestead to confront his parents on a more visceral level. He must put aside his anger and retrace the steps of his roots. Only when the ghosts of his past had been exorcised could he fulfill his dreams.

The walk to the homestead was a few days in length. He took his time, enjoying the rolling landscape. He stopped in a village to trade some furs for gold. Its carefully groomed white buildings appealed to him. They were picturesque against the background of green and grey hills. The church in the center of the cluster had a tall spire that drew his eyes toward the heavens.

He found it easy to barter with people and suspected that his size had something to do with it. The shopkeeper was impressed with the quality of his furs and paid him a large sum for his cache. He treated himself to a stick of licorice root, a luxury that had eluded him as a child.

On the road to the homestead, he crossed a covered bridge spanning a swiftly running creek. He descended the steep bank to refresh himself in the water. He threw his pack and weapon on the shore and immersed himself in a muddy pool. A call from downstream drew his attention.

"You there, good sir, can I call upon you to assist me?"

René squatted to look under the timbers of the bridge. A few yards downstream he could see an old man trying to coax a cow out of the mud. He recognized the man. It was the injured farmer whose wagon he had refused to fix. He lowered his head, almost ashamed to see him.

The frail old man limped up the bank to get a better look at the stranger. He adjusted his blue coveralls and shook the mud off of his feet. He called, "I suspect that I have met you before stranger, but I cannot recall where that may have been. I am in dire need of your assistance. If the current breaks her legs, I will have no recourse but to shoot her. She is the only cow that I have."

René waded downstream and ducked under the bridge to approach the farmer. "If you tug on that tether, I can free her legs." He waded along the bank, careful not to be consumed by the muck and mire. He placed his long arms around the cow's girth and interlocked his fingers to secure a firm grip. "Give her a good heave ho. I think I can manage on this end."

The old man jerked the tether. Slowly, with the woodsman's powerful assistance, the cow was extricated from the mud. The farmer doffed his cap and reached out his hand to help the woodsman. "You, sir, have been my savior on this day. How can I ever thank you?"

René pulled his hair back. "You owe me nothing, sir. I am the one who owes you a debt."

The farmer still felt obligated. "Just the same, I want to repay you for your generosity."

René smiled. "I have to be moving on, for I have some important business to complete."

The farmer replied, "That is my house up the lane." He pointed to a small white farmhouse just down the road from the bridge. "Gather up your belongings and follow me. Mother will fix you a hearty meal. It's on your way, traveler, so don't give me any sass about this."

The woodsman did not argue. He moved back upstream to gather up his belongings and then followed as the farmer slowly limped toward the house, the muddy cow in tow behind him.

The farmhouse was a white, two story dwelling. Flowers grew in front of a porch. The door was painted red. A black cast-iron knocker clung to the middle of the portal. To the left of the door were two tall etched glass windows with lace curtains hanging inside.

The old man joined René by the stoop. "Not much to look at, but rather quaint I would say. Well, don't just stand there. Go on in. I can smell the cakes baking and the chicken stewing."

The farmer was British and had lived the better part of his life in this countryside. He was a stout man of mid-height, who wore blue coveralls over a red gingham shirt. He had a small thrum cap on his melon-shaped head. His grey hair was pulled back in a ponytail. His face was always consumed by a proper grin. The twinkle in his eyes revealed his propensity for humor.

René felt awkward, but did what the man asked. He opened the door to enter a hallway that led to the back of the house. To the left was a parlor with a large fireplace. It was decorated with several comfortable chairs and a beautiful, handcrafted cherry sideboard. Next to the parlor doorway, a steep, narrow stairwell led up to a second-floor landing which was dark and quiet.

"Go on into the parlor and have a seat. I'll let mother know we have a guest."

The woodsman entered the cozy room. The waning light filtered through the two windows on the front wall to illuminate the space. He did not sit down for fear of soiling the furniture, so he stood awkwardly in the center of the room, dripping mud on the rag rug.

The farmer returned with his dowdy wife on his arm. She was a frumpy woman dressed in a green housecoat. "This is my wife, Martha and my name is Silas. This lad helped me get Lucy out of the muck." The farmer pressed the woodsman for information. "Who might you be, lad?"

"My name is René Dubois, sir, but I prefer to be called Pashk-wadjash."

"That is an unusual name, lad. What would its origin be?"

René did not answer, for the Natives were not often respected in these parts.

The farmer toyed with René. "We don't often have French visitors, due to the war and all, but you have helped us on this day. So, let's make amends and set that disagreement aside."

The woodsman did not want to be drawn into a political debate. He was anxious to get back on the road. "I really must be on my way, sir. I do have important business to attend to."

"Mother and I don't want to keep you from your appointments, but we insist that you take some food along with you. It won't be more than a moment. Martha, fetch the vittles."

"Can I offer you a glass of honey mead, son?" René waved him off, as the farmer poured a small glass of the golden liquid from a decanter sitting on the sideboard. "Cheers mate!"

The farmer shared news about the war. "I heard tell of a siege at Fort William Henry by eight thousand French Irregular Troops and a band of Indians down in Provincial New York. They bombarded the fort forcing the 35th British Foot and 60th Royal American Foot to surrender the works." He hesitated for effect. "You know those uncouth savages massacred many of the Brits and some of the civilians on the march back to Fort Edward for parole. Damn shame as I see it." Silas lied to protect his own reputation. "When I fought as a young man for King George II in Father Rale's War against the Wabanaki back in '24, we fought with honor and gave men quarter as gentlemen would have it. There was still a measure of chivalry back then. Now it seems that men have all become rogues who rape and pillage as they see fit without care or cause."

He paused to sip his honey wine. "Have you had any cause to fight in this war, young sir?"

"It is none of my affair. I pay no allegiance to country or cause. It is an unnatural thing to be beholden to men who exact their will upon you. We are all equal in the eyes of nature."

The farmer smiled. "You are a damned sight wiser than the lot of them, boy."

Martha returned to the parlor. She carried a tin pail by its handle. She handed the bucket to her husband, afraid of the woodsman. He in turn handed it to René. "It ain't much, son, hardly more than a pittance for a man of your stature, but it should satisfy you just the same."

The woodsman took the bucket from the man and lifted the lid. A roasted chicken sat in a rich broth covered with a variety of vegetables. On top of the chicken was a wheat biscuit, honey drizzled over it. His broad grin indicated that he was pleased.

"Let me show you to the door, Frenchie. We are grateful for your help today."

René stood on the porch, doffed his cap, and quietly spoke, "Thank you for your generosity. It is the custom where I come from to honor a gift with a gift. I would like you to have this pelt in return for the morsel of food you have provided for me." He handed the farmer a beaver pelt, one of several he had left in his pack. He bounded off of the porch and started back down the lane.

The farmer called after him, "I don't take kindly to the French, but you have changed my thinking on the matter. Your charity is appreciated, despite the fact that you left me by the roadside, injured and insolvent. I harbor no ill will toward those who have found their way."

René was pleased that the man held no grudge, a lesson he could not bring himself to learn. René's unselfish act had brought him a simple, but satisfying reward. But the closer he got to his place of birth, the more the torment of his life welled up again in him like a raging storm.

The woodsman approached his parent's ramshackle farm. He stopped long enough to load his piece before he entered the southwestern field. He noticed it was overgrown during the prime planting season. His father had never neglected this particular field. Something was amiss.

René reached the outer perimeter of fence line. The rails were lying on the ground or rotting where they stood. There were no livestock. He suspected that they had wandered off or were taken by the wolves. He stepped through the sprung gate and picked his way among the scattered farm implements. It was eerily quiet, but he could see wisps of white smoke emanating from the cobbled chimney of the house. He threw open the door and entered the dark and dank hovel.

The rocker by the hearth moved slowly to and fro. "Is that you, Giselle? Put the gruel upon the table. I'll fetch it later when the mood suits me. I'll not be in need anything else today." There was no answer, so the woman peered around the side of the chair. Sensing that there was no danger, she turned back to the flames and then continued to say her rosary. "Come and sit by me, René. We have a lot of catching up to do. There is no need for that piece here."

As if he were a child, René did as his mother had directed. He sat on the hearth. His mother's once beautiful azure eyes were now covered by a milky film. "Are you blind mother?"

"I no longer see life as you do. I only see good now, the flowers in a sunlit meadow or the face of my long-lost son. The Lord has restored my vision in a new, enlightening way. I have never seen life more clearly than I do on this day."

"How did you know it was me in the room, or for that matter, that I carried a weapon?"

"My senses are keen, René. I recognize your gait as if you were a child bounding across the floor. It is a firm, but lively step, like that of the joyful lad I once knew. I can smell your essence, as I could on the day you were born. You are not a mystery to me, son, as you may surmise."

"And what of the gun, mother?"

"I could smell the powder, feel the tension. There is no need for that wretched thing here."

"Speaking of wretches, mother, where is he? I have a score to settle with him."

"There will be no need for that, dear boy. The Lord himself has seen to it. He lies yonder on the hill behind the barn; too much drink and too little kindness made him a marked man."

The woodsman was somewhat relieved by the revelation of his father's death, if for nothing more than the fact that his mother would no longer have to suffer at his hand.

Angelique's frail body showed the compromises of years of hard labor and incessant beatings. The liability she bore left its marks on her drawn, but still beautiful face. She no longer saw the world through a clear lens, but her once vibrant eyes gleamed as she looked into the darkness.

"Let me see you, son." She moved her hands up his tall frame and then slowly over his face. "My, my, you have grown into a handsome man. Your papa was handsome too when I first met him, despite that horrific scar, but the drink transformed him. I sense that there is great tension in you. You are fragile and broken. Have we done this to you, son?"

He pulled away from her. "I am leaving this wretched plateau. I must fulfill a destiny that closes the void in my heart. I cannot do that in a place where remorse and hatred prevail."

His mother stared through him, as if looking for a mystical sign. "You must face the realities of an uncertain world to find your moral compass. I know that kindness and decency has eluded you. I suspect that you will find a civil calling, one that fulfills the dreams of others, and creates a legacy of hope for future generations. You can undo the hatred that we have served upon you."

For the moment, her words eased his deep pain. For the first time in his life he felt a bond with his mother. She didn't seem as cold or as distant as she had been in the past. She had been guarded because of Henri's abusive behavior, but now she was revealing to be a more compassionate, intuitive, educated, and refined woman than he had ever known.

She whispered, "What will you do now, my son?"

"Hard to tell, mother, but I find comfort in the wilderness with the creatures of the forest. I am troubled by a sedentary life, for my roots are shallow and have failed to stand firm. I must venture forth so that I can benefit from time spent with other people." Rare tears welled up in his eyes. "Three-Legged-Wolf told me that I am like the whispering wind, drifting without direction or cause. I imagine that I need to shackle those winds. I'll never know who I really am or what I can fully achieve unless I explore life beyond these highlands."

Angelique rose carefully from the chair and walked effortlessly to the window, as she had done a thousand times before. "Where will you go, René?"

"I thought that I would head west toward Montreal. I have saved a fair amount of gold. I am a simple man with simple desires, so some of the coins I have set aside for you."

The imposing woodsman reached into a leather pouch and drew out a handful of sovereigns. He walked to the window. One board creaked as he passed over it. It was stained with blood. There were countless times he meant to fix it, but found it too menial a task. He carefully wrapped his mother's red shawl about her shoulders. It barely covered her frail body for it, too, was old and worn. He slipped the coins back into the pouch and placed it gently into her housecoat pocket.

Angelique felt his strength and the warmth in this final hug. She moved his hands away and turned to reach and clasp his cheeks. She began to weep uncontrollably.

He had never seen her cry like this before and the pain of leaving welled up in him.

Angelique eased his anxiety, "You take care now. You hear? The Lord will guide you in all things, so listen to His calling. He will bring you peace." She wiped the tears from her cheek and scolded him, "And for land's sake, trim up that frightful hair. You must look like a ragged Injun."

She ushered him out of the door. "I am proud of you, son. My heart will follow you as you venture off on a quest to unearth your soul. I will go to my grave knowing that you will undo the burden that your father and I have so grievously placed upon you." Angelique blessed herself with the sign of the cross. She closed the door abruptly, so as not to prolong his departure.

Three months later, Angelique Papineau Dubois died in her sleep, a peaceful but lonely death, clutching her rosary and the satchel of coins her son had given her. She was buried at her husband's side upon the hill above the house under granite cross that marked her place in time.

René placed his hand upon the door, as if to transmit some spiritual message into the cabin. He pulled his coat up about his neck and wondered how the unusually cold weather had appeared so suddenly on this fateful summer's eve. *It must surely be a sign of things to come.*

Instead taking the lane toward the King's Highway, he chose to ascend the hill behind the barn. He reached the top where a granite stone wall surrounded a small graveyard. There, lying partially hidden in the dirt was the carved bird he had dropped in the soil on the day he was whisked away to the Anishinabe. He passed through the stone gate and approached a marker that honored a young child. It was simply inscribed, *Boy Dubois*. He assumed that lying beneath the stone was a nameless brother who had died in childbirth. Further up the hill was a larger wooden cross, roughly carved by a callous hand. He brushed the dirt from the inscription, *Henri Dubois—The Loon.*

The woodsman began a eulogy, "Henri Dubois, the Maker has seen to it that you have suffered the fate that you fully deserve. I spit upon your grave and remove all allegiance that I have to you. Be it known from the depths of hell that I am no longer the seed of your loins." He picked up the carving and placed it on top of the cross, its one sculpted eye keeping watch.

"I have concluded that René Dubois has died along with his father. In the presence of all natural things, I hereby declare, Henri Dubois, that your crimes to man and womankind shall be transcended by my integrity. I rise up, upon the grave of my disconsolate father, in honor of my mother, to fully resolve that I shall be known to the world from this day forth as Papineau."

Chapter 20

We Will Stay and Fight

As spring approached, Jon and his lads trudged out of camp. It was April 27, 1863 and the new Union commander, General Joseph Hooker had devised an ingenious flanking maneuver designed to envelope the Confederates, but its cautious deployment and faulty execution left the Army of the Potomac wallowing in another humiliating defeat.

Jon's regiment was in the thick of the fighting at a crossroad called Chancellorsville. The army was overrun and mauled by General Jackson's foot cavalry. Forced to retreat across the Rappahannock, they limped back into camp, badly shaken from the experience.

Jon was angry. "Why do we train so hard and fight so bravely when our generals maneuver us so poorly? We were caught with our pants down by Stonewall's Brigades. Our regiment is decimated." He ate a handful of stale, crumbled cake his mother had mailed. *Tread lightly upon the thawing river, for it may suddenly swallow you up into its cold depths.* "Stop!" He shouted.

Shannon, grazed by a Rebel ball, tended to the wound. "Who in blazes are you talking to?"

"Sorry, Shannon, it's the demons again."

"You had best settle yourself or they are going to send you to the nuthouse. I am going over to see a surgeon. Hell, I have been hurt worse in the smithy, but I ain't taking any chances."

Jon was left alone to mull over his legacy. *Was he truly blessed with a mystical gift, or was his grandfather simply building in him the will to overcome adversity by telling him that? What good would a gift of that magnitude be if he did not understand it or could not use it?*

After the beating at Chancellorsville, the regiment licked its wounds, but was soon on the move again. They campaigned all spring, but saw limited action. While the others fought and died, Jon and his men were assigned to tasks that sustained the army's infrastructure. Reorganization soon sent them back to the First Corps. General John Reynolds was given command of these vaunted brigades, placed at the vanguard of the march. This elite Corps contained the infamous Black Hat Boys, the Iron Brigade, who were known for their unwavering courage and ruthless fighting. Jon's regiment was in the Second Brigade, to mop up what the Iron Men started and often finished.

The march took them north as scuttlebutt raged like a wildfire through the ranks. They trudged through Virginia into Maryland, as they had done in '62, but it did not end there. They soon were heading toward Pennsylvania, deep in Federal territory and closer to their families.

The Corp rested in Jefferson, Maryland on the 26th of June of '63 and then followed the ridge line of the Catoctin Range until they were at Middletown, opposite Turner's Gap again. Jon remembered his first exposure with death in that Gap. That scrap seemed so long ago, a distant reminder of the horrors of his first campaign when he was afraid, lonely, and uncertain.

The cavalry screens had indicated that Confederate forces had penetrated as far north as the Susquehanna River around the city of Harrisburg. Instead of turning west to meet the enemy, as expected, the column turned east at Middletown and crossed the Catoctin Range. By the 29th they had reached Emmitsburg, Maryland. They entered Pennsylvania the next day following the Emmitsburg Road, headed toward a small village of 2,400 souls called Gettysburg.

Dawn broke on July 1 with feverish frenzy. Couriers rapidly came and went, brigades scrambled to make ready, and the line of march was formed. The distinctive echoes of large and small arms fire could be heard from the north. The pesky Rebels had been found.

There was a sense of urgency as the long blue columns scurried at the quick step through the rich Pennsylvania countryside. The sound of firing grew heavier and the hardened troopers pressed the march. There would be no Johnny Cakes or spring water on this restless morning.

The Iron Brigade left the pike to deploy near Herbst's Woods and McPherson's Farm. They immediately came under fire as they relieved the troopers from Buford's Cavalry Brigade. Those 2,500 men had effectively held the field against a greater force as they pleaded for reinforcements. Their crafty deployment on the ridges and their smart use of Sharps carbines, *Beecher's Bibles,* and other breech-loading weapons bottled up the Rebs until the First Corp's timely arrival.

The conflict was hot, but the Iron Men and their comrades held the ground below the town and drove the Rebs temporarily from the field. The Second Brigade came up and was deployed in the neighborhood of Willis Woods and the Lutheran Seminary to support the Black Hat Boys.

Bugles and drums, the fluttering of flags and the shouts of desperate commanders marked the arrival of the Union 11th Corps in the early afternoon. The fighting spread to the hills to the north and east as the 11th deployed. But with little support and ammunition running low, the Federals soon gave way to the Rebel onslaught. The arrival of Ewell's Confederate Corp on the right flank doomed the army to a full retrograde movement toward Cemetery Ridge just south of the village.

Portions of the army were routed, but some units did not succumb to the Confederate blitz. They fought their way through the town and redeployed in a defensive perimeter on the ridge. Generals Howard and Hancock managed the posting. Probing attacks by the Confederates on the Union defensive line soon fizzled out as the day closed and darkness consumed the field.

Jon's regiment had been engaged in minor scrapes and were threatened by capture during the retreat through the village where order was lost and confusion reigned. They narrowly escaped and were posted at the center of the line. Fighting broke out on the flanks in the afternoon of the second day and their position became threatened as the Rebs tried a furious breakthrough to their left. The timely intervention of Union reserves staved off the disaster and the breech was closed.

On the evening of July 2, Jon hunkered down behind a stone wall. He was restless, pulling his coat up over his ears to block out the screams of the wounded. *What cause could be so valued that we have to sacrifice the lives of young men to preserve it?* He got up, grabbed his canteen, and started to walk toward the rear.

"Where are you headed?" Shannon questioned. "If you leave your post they will shoot you."

"I am escaping this misery for a while. There is too much death here for my liking. Can't a guy get a drink of water and a little peace once in a while, Shannon?"

"Do you want some company, laddie?"

"Thanks, but if it just the same to you, I would like to be alone."

Jon found that it was impossible to find any solitude. The Union line was in a state of frenzy, as the general staff redeployed troops in preparation for renewed fighting. He wandered over the ridge and came upon a farmhouse that was being used as a hospital. Wayward soldiers from other regiments lingered there. Wounded, dead, and dying littered the yard as orderlies worked frantically to bring some order to the pandemonium. *How could these men so callously disregard their fallen comrades?* He grabbed an orderly under the arm and asked, "Can I pitch in?"

"Take your pick of the litter, Master Sergeant. They could all use a little comfort." The man loosed his arm from Jon's grip and quickly ran off.

Jon looked around, distraught over the gloom that pervaded the place. He knelt down over a man who leaned against a fence and spoke to him, "Can I give you some assistance soldier?"

The man opened his eyes and looked up at Jon. His piercing orbs glimmered in the soft light of the bonfire that burned in the yard. He weakly coughed up a reply, "I am mortally wounded...gut shot..." He lifted his bloodstained hands off of his stomach to reveal a gaping wound in his abdomen. "Don't have much time, but a little cool water would be soothing."

Jon uncorked his canteen and poured some water into the palm of his dirty, calloused hands. He knew that he should not give sustenance to a gut shot man, but he relented.

The private breathed heavily and sporadically as the life slowly drained from his body. "My mother is surely going to fret over this…Death is so cold…so dark…"

Jon sat down and put his arm around the man's shoulder. He cradled him tightly and tried to stave off the chilling clench of death that was consuming him. "What is your name, son?"

The man turned his head, but he could not speak. He slowly raised a bloodied hand and fondled a small piece of paper pinned to the collar of his frockcoat.

Jon examined the paper, but struggled in the dim light to read the scrawled words etched upon it. He mouthed them out loud, "Barker Lloyd, 125th New York…"

Lloyd nodded and then gasped, as blood trickled slowly from the corner of his mouth.

"Ease yourself, son. My grandpa tells me a tale of hope. When things seem most dire and darkness seems to be consuming every fiber of your being, a glorious light will shine down upon you. Cling to the hope that you will soon be bathed by the effervescent light of a new life, as your old one is being extinguished. A wise, ancient Indian matriarch once professed, *Let the eagle guide you on a path to a new life."* He whispered. "Go in peace, for a better life awaits you."

Lloyd squeezed Jon's hand. He breathed a last defiant breath. His head tilted to the side, eyes still open, to rest on Jon's shoulder. A faint, but peaceful smile coursed over his lips.

Jon held onto Lloyd for a long time. This personal brush with death moved him to tears as he struggled with the insanity that seemed to slowly move in a macabre dance around him.

An orderly shook Jon back to his senses. "Sir, let him go. We need to inter him."

Jon looked into the eyes of the spectacled man in a white duster that was covered with blood. He reluctantly removed his arm from around Lloyd's shoulder as two faceless soldiers lifted the body and callously tossed it onto a cart. He was shaken by their heartless treatment of Lloyd's remains. He gathered himself, filled his canteen, and headed back to the wall.

Shannon grilled him. "Where have you been, Jonny? I thought that you may have deserted."

"Leave it be, Shannon. I have been closer to death than I ever wanted to be and it disturbs me to distraction. Someday, if I survive this God-awful war, I am going to change the way men treat each other. I am going to stop the insanity created by vile human behavior."

Jon rested against the wall, his kepi pulled down tightly on his head. He opened up the face of his watch. In the dim light of the small fire at his feet he could barely see the time, 3:15 A.M.. As he was closing the face, the image of the inlaid horse twinkled in the firelight and a vision of an Indian woman entered his mind. She was smiling, reaching out to him with two hands extended before her, as if calling him into her embrace. He soon succumbed to a fitful slumber.

The horse shall be emblazoned with bolts of lightning prominently displayed across his neck and torso. You shall ride upon the horse, through history, with others of our family, influencing how it evolves, as a faithful reminder of what we will forever stand for; how we have transformed ourselves, the lives of others, and history itself.

Troops continued to arrive throughout the night and redeploy along the ridges and surrounding hills of the fishhook shaped Union line. The Union commanders held a Council of War in the Lydia Leister farmhouse situated behind the center of the line. The generals squeezed into the smoky, cramped space to strategize with commander, Major General George Meade.

Major General Hancock spoke frankly, "We have formed a formidable defensive line, Meade, and should challenge the Rebel force on this ground. To retreat again would only serve to demoralize our men and further press our ability to safeguard the Capital."

Meade considered a retrograde movement to the more defensible line at Pipe Creek. Most of the generals embraced the Gettysburg line. As Cavalry, General John Buford had emphasized in his communiqués', *"This is good ground."* Meade announced, *"We will stay and fight."* With those fateful words, he sealed the destiny of the army and altered the course of a nation's history

Chapter 21

High Water Mark

The summer weather had been harsh for the entire campaign. July 3, 1863 proved to be no exception. With temperatures hovering around 90 degrees and with distressing humidity, the fateful morning arrived with unbearable discomfort. The two giants jousted on the flanks for the better part of the day, with little change in the possession of the contested land.

The pristine landscape was now scarred by the ravages of conflict. The stench of war curdled the senses with putrid tastes and overbearing odors, waking Jon from his sleep. He peered over the fieldstones to gaze across the open expanse of ground. He could see the fence-lined Emmitsburg Road a few rods from his position and Seminary Ridge about a mile to the west. He watched a company of Union soldiers battle for a large barn with a company of jousting Rebs. The edifice was finally burned to the ground which ended the senseless skirmish.

Jon settled back under the safety of the wall, propped his back up against its warm stone, and pulled his cap down over his eyes. He soon was asleep, despite commotion. He began to dream. A voice called out to him in a language he did not know, but understood. *I am Pashkwadjash. I am the Shadow Self who has followed you to this fateful place. Call upon me, Jon, when all hope seems to be lost. Call upon me to guide you through the darkness and into the light of a new day.*

About 1:00 P.M., a signal gun fired from the woods on Seminary Ridge. A whisper of silence followed the report of the gun and then a solitary, whistling shell drifted harmlessly over Jon's head to explode violently in the rear. A horrific bombardment followed. It rocked the land and awakened the spirit of the dead as the shells rained down upon the Union position. They dismantled trees, plowed the earth, and shook the ground like a massive earthquake. After an hour of unrelenting confusion, the bombardment abruptly ended, followed by an eerie, deafening silence.

Jon peered cautiously over the wall, rubbing his aching ears. In the distance, he could see an array of Southern Crosses defiantly fluttering in the breeze along a mile-long front. The roll of distant drums and the resounding blare of bugles signaled the advance, as the Rebel brigades stepped off. They marched as if on parade, impressively reforming after every swale in the undulating terrain. The battle line soon disappeared into a defile, as if swallowed up by the earth. It slowly reappeared, flags first, then bayonets, and then the heads and bodies of the vaunted troops.

Addie Jones yelled out in admiration, "It's the goddamned devil's brigade rising up from the bowels of the earth. My God, it's a glorious sight."

The Yankee artillery laid down a barrage of shot and shell on the advancing Confederates, mowing them down by the score. The determined Rebs closed ranks and proceeded into the hail of iron. As they reached the Emmitsburg Road, small arms fire rattled them and the big guns switched to double canister with devastating effect. The assault became bogged down by the well-built fences that slinked their way off into the distance on either side of the byway. The Rebs continued to close ranks, but the intermingling of units created confusion and hampered the commanders' ability to keep them in any conceivable fighting trim. Still they came on.

Trapped between the fences, many of the Rebs chose to lie prone in the sunken road to escape the carnage, too shocked to advance, too bottled up to retreat. On their left, the concentration of flanking fire from the 8th Ohio, began to destroy all sense of order. Some Rebs retreated. Some reformed and advanced. Some just melted away into history, never to be heard from again.

Batteries of cannons belched canister over the Jon's head. He yelled out a command to load, waiting until the Rebs came into range before they loosed a devastating volley upon them. His mind drifted back to the stories of his oppressed ancestors. *How can one man intrude on the sovereignty of another, callously casting him aside because he was somehow different?*

The Master Sergeant looked out at the Rebs approaching his position. They didn't look any different than he did, yet they had arrived here determined to turn free soil into a den of slavery. Bondage and oppression had followed his family throughout the course of history. His Indian relatives were swallowed up by a horde of land grabbers. His Irish countrymen were imprisoned under British totalitarian rule or ostracized in America just because they were bloody Irish. It seemed that they always had to dig out from under a shadow of tyranny. *Surely these crusty, disheveled Rebs had experienced the same oppression as they struggled to assimilate into the Antebellum American landscape and make their uncertain way in life?*

Jon understood that most of them did not own slaves, but fought to suppress them when their own lives hung in the balance. *Why harbor such deep hatred? Why fight for a cause they did not live by? Why not turn on the landed gentry that suppressed them?* He raised his rifle in rage, not accepting the madness that put him in harm's way. Screaming, he pulled the trigger and released the ball. As if transformed, he followed the projectile as it crossed the plain. His aim was true; the shot plunged through the chaos to strike a Rebel officer between the eyes and knocked him off of the fence, dead before he hit the ground. *What evil possesses you, Jonny?* He reloaded. *I shall not be party to oppression and will fight to the death to preserve my land and my freedom. Let this be the high-water mark of freedom for all men or let us all wallow together in the depths of hell.*

The Confederate regiments on the right moved progressively to the left in echelon, combining with those in the center. Rifled cannon fire from the Round Tops ripped their flanks and slowed their advance. The center became congested and chaotic. The numbers of able-bodied men dwindled into nothing more than a defiant mob as they approached the copse of trees. Stannard's Vermonters flanked these Rebs and poured a relentless fire into them. Still, they still came on.

Jon loaded and fired as fast as he could. It was like a backyard turkey shoot. He was feeling invigorated by the power of the moment. His wits were keen and revenge welled up in his heart, as he wanted to avenge the death of men like Sylvester Van Antwerp and Barker Lloyd. Images raced through his head as he mechanically loaded and fired his weapon.

A screaming Mohawk warrior, a lance protruding from his side, raised his war ax high in the air and then lopped off the head of a devil-faced shaman kneeling before him.

A young British officer, his face horribly scarred, mocked a powerless citizen as he dangled helplessly by the neck from the Dule Tree.

A grieving widow cradled her starving son to her bosom as he desperately clung to life.

An ancient Indian warrior, lying face up to a relentless sun, spoke in parables as his lifeblood flowed from a gaping wound in his chest. He clung to a handful of rich, black soil.

You can climb upon the back of my Mother and strike me down with the wrath of the Underworld, but you can never take away my freedom. My spirit will fly over the land upon the back of an eagle and my life's dreams will be fulfilled through the valor of my offspring.

A bullet grazed off of the stone wall to nick Jon's cheek. It shook him back to the reality of the conflagration raging around him. A century old fight by his family for freedom and sovereignty was held in the balance on this oppressive summer day in Pennsylvania.

The Union line bent with the pressure of a final charge led by Confederate General Armistead. With his hat on the tip of his sword, he moved defiantly through the firing artillery and tried to rally the troops. Just after crossing the wall, the fearless General was wounded three times. The Confederate attack stalled and the timely arrival of the Union reserves destroyed all hope for the future of the Rebel cause. Most of the beleaguered Rebs were easily captured. The rest sullenly trailed their arms across the Pennsylvania landscape toward a grieving General Lee.

Jon rose up from behind the cover of the wall to a crescendo of mocking cheers all along the Union line. "Fredericksburg! Fredericksburg! Fredericksburg!" He scanned the rolling landscape. A thousand lay dead and scores more suffered from horrific wounds. He wrestled with contrary emotions, devastated to the point of sickness, but elated that they had finally prevailed.

Addie patted Jon on the back. "Let's go git 'em!" He leaped over the wall to pursue to the fleeing enemy, only to be recalled by the blare of a regimental bugle. He was disappointed that they were not allowed to end the madness. He turned back to see Jon perched on top of the wall. He was aiming his rifle at chastising Reb posed contemptuously on the fence lining the road.

Jon got the insolent Reb in his sights. *This would be just like shooting squirrels.* He held his breath and began to squeeze the trigger. He hesitated. *The better man walks away.* He raised his rifle over his head, taunting the man. He smiled as he looked down upon his jubilant comrades and suddenly, anguish and fear marked his twisted, boyish face.

Jon turned a pirouette on the wall and released his weapon. The fall seemed slow and agonizing as he tried to grasp the magnitude of what had just happened. The rock under his foot slid forward to accelerate his decent and place him on his back, face up to the unrelenting sun. A dark, red stain formed on the dusty hardscrabble. The fine dirt rose up around his prone form and then settled haphazardly back down onto his uniform. He tried to regain his feet, but slumped back to the earth.

The vision of a woman called out in a prophetic, soft voice. *When you are troubled, be still and wait. When your doubt has been lifted from you, then go forward with courage. So long as the mists encircle you, be still. When the sunlight pours through your soul and dispels the mists, as it surely will, then act with conviction, for your true calling has yet to reveal itself to you.*

Shannon was the first to reach Jon, blood spewing like a fountain from his shoulder. The smithy leaped over the wall and knelt down next to his friend. He applied pressure on the wound to arrest the blood flow. "You'll not be dying on me this day, you ugly Mick!" he yelled. "You'll not be dying on any day, if I have anything to say about it." Shannon then looked up at Addie and gave him an order, "Stop gawking and go to fetch the surgeon, you buffoon."

Jones hurdled over the wall and headed for the field hospital. The artillery batteries were still firing from the hill's crest, as he ran past them. He found a surgeon attending to General Hancock's wounds. A bullet had struck the pommel of his saddle and entered his right thigh, along with wood fragments, and a bent nail. When Addie inquired where to find assistance, he was met with a bewildered stare from the physician tending to the General.

"I need to tend to the General first and then the hundreds of others that lay between here and your sergeant. You tell me, boy, which man should I sacrifice so another may live?"

Jones' face streamed with dust-stained tears. "But he's not just my sergeant, sir, he's my friend. He needs help now or he will surely die."

General Hancock sensed the distress. "Go with him, Doc. Tend to the needs of the other men."

The doctor protested. "Sir, if I do not shore up this wound, you could bleed to death."

"Nonsense, my aides have applied a tourniquet and I have removed the nail in the wound." He commanded, "Orderly, escort the doctor to the front and make sure he completes his rounds."

Jones doffed his cap, "Thank you, sir. Your kindness will long be remembered." He led the surgeon to the wall, dragging him along by the arm as he tried to assist other wounded men.

The physician hastily examined Jon and callously remarked, "Let him go in peace and give up this false hope of reviving him." As he spoke, a revolver was cocked behind his head.

Much to everyone's surprise, it was Boston Charlie. The troopers were amazed that he was close to the vicinity of the fighting. When the call for ammunition came, he complied, under great duress, and found himself smack dab in front of the wall where Jon's company was posted.

"He is stubborn Irishman who is not going to die today." Pritchard challenged the surgeon. "Get to work or I will not hesitate to spill your blood on this sacred ground."

The surgeon questioned, "Are you threatening me? I am the ranking officer here and will place you on report, Captain. There are hundreds of other men that I can actually save. Let me do my service to them." He turned to the General's orderly. "Have this man arrested."

The orderly balked. "I have no authority here, sir. General Hancock ordered you to this place. With all due respect, I suggest that you obey his order, sir."

Charlie pressed his revolver to the surgeon's temple. "Time is wasting, sir!"

"I service this man against my will. I will have you court-martialed when this is over, Captain."

Pritchard was unfazed by the man's threats. "So be it. Now give this man your full attention."

The surgeon worked feverishly to close the holes in the Jon's chest. He fumbled with his instruments, the weight of the moment wreaked havoc with his nerves. It was easier working on the General than this non-com, whose comrades hovered over him with rifles to bear. He began to realize that Shannon's pressure had given him some hope that he could possibly save Jon.

The surgeon looked up at Charlie, who had relaxed the pistol pressure on his head. "It's in God's hands now. Take him to the field hospital and ask for Dr. Zacharias. He has lost a substantial amount of blood and I cannot guarantee that he will live past sunset."

Colonel Phelps appeared, barking an order, "You have had your fun for the day, gentlemen. Return to your duty stations. The Rebs will surely come back, more vengeful than when they left."

Shannon fashioned a rudimentary litter from a broken artillery caisson. He loaded Jon's limp body onto it and dragged it to the rear. He stopped an orderly and asked for Dr. Zacharias.

"He is in the barn performing surgery. He cannot help you."

Shannon, in his deep Irish brogue, replied, "Then we will wait."

"Look around you, soldier. You will be waiting a long time," the orderly rushed away.

And Shannon waited. For two days, the smithy sat by his friend and cared for him as best he could. He never saw the doctor and barely had contact with anyone with medical experience.

A young lady from York redressed Jon's wound and dusted it with moss to check infection. He had not regained consciousness and his breathing was shallow, as he fought for his life.

Heavy rains hampered operations, as the Yanks barked at the heels of the frantic Rebs who retreated into Virginia. The victory at Gettysburg and the capture of Vicksburg by Grant's Western Army made people believe that the tide of war had finally begun to turn.

Chapter 22

Sacred Space

Jon tossed in a stupor as the pain of his wound and the power of the opiates clouded his mind. He drifted in and out of consciousness, unable to distinguish between reality and fantasy. He clung to life by a thread. *The shadow of doubt passes over the land as it follows the sun toward the horizon. There it mingles with the darkness to become one with the night.* In his brief moments of lucidity, he tried to decipher the intricate riddles. One particular dream haunted him to distraction.

It was the blackest of nights. He was mounted on a large stallion, his arms wrapped around the horse's neck. The charger bolted up a narrow, winding mountain path toward a speck of light. A violent storm raged. The rider trembled as deadly lightning, pelting rain, and a slick path kept his life in the balance. He sensed that the will of the horse was greater than his, so he leaned forward and coaxed the steed to press on. The stalwart mount's dilated eyes flashed with a fire. He snorted with anger then dropped his head against his chest to fight his way through the tempest.

The beacon began to intensify, as if opening up a portal that summoned them. Faces appeared out of the darkness. They screamed for help or called out with a message of hope. The storm began to subside and the valiant horse began to slow. Jon recognized the faces with a clarity that frightened him. They asked him to put aside personal endeavors to heal them or comfort those whom they loved. *Barker Lloyd, James Gilhooly, Sylvester Van Antwerp, all dead...Shannon O'Reilly, Michael Holland, Seamus McGuilicutty, men who struggled with personal demons...*

And then there were those people who lingered in the shadows, their faces unfamiliar, ghostly images from the past or perhaps an uncertain future. *Guide us toward the light of peace...*

It had been two weeks since the battle and Jon lived on the precipice of death. He lay on a small canvas cot in a sweltering tent. The lesion on his shoulder oozed a pink, opaque liquid as it drained. He was fortunate that gangrene had not attacked the wound or he would be buried in an open trench with others; their bones intermingled for eternity, doomed to anonymity.

The York maiden, Gretchen Jung, had the presence of mind to redress the wound and stave off the nefarious disease. She grew up in a Palatine family that had immigrated to the Colonies in the 1700s. They settled in the borough of Germantown outside of Philadelphia. The staunch Anabaptists, or Plain Dutch, referring to their simple, spiritual existence, moved to York when Gretchen was young. Her father set up a small ministry on the outskirts of the thriving White Rose City. When the Rebels occupied York, Gretchen pitched in to comfort the sick and wounded. She traveled to Gettysburg with other emissaries of mercy from her father's church as the battle raged.

The fair-skinned seventeen-year old Pennsylvania Dutch maiden was petite. She had long blond hair that was gathered tightly in a nest under a white coif. She wore a simple black waist coat and petticoat under a plain, white apron. Around her neck, she wore a lace shift, which draped slightly over her shoulders. Although rather ordinary in appearance, she was well educated, had an uncanny intellect, a pleasant smile, and seductive opal eyes.

Jon was haunted by a ghostly Indian. His face was hidden beneath a hooded robe. The headdress looked like wolf with keen yellow eyes. He chanted. *See more than the spirit can tell. Understand more than you can see.* Jon stuttered the word Pashkwadjash in his sleep. *I am the healer. I am the light. Live within the Sacred Space, walking in balance between the light and the dark.*

"Wake up, Jon." Gretchen never tried to exorcise the demons, as her father would. She waited for Jon to extract himself from his stupor and help him to decipher the bizarre meaning of the tales.

Jon whispered in a shallow and hoarse voice, "He haunts me so, Gretchen, never letting me rest. He has a hideous scar on his face that glows with the power of the sun. It contrasts against his dark features and transforms me with its mystical power. He summons a will in me that is enlightening, a spirit of such magnificence that it almost resurrects me."

He collapsed back onto his pillow. "I often see the image of an Indian princess. She seldom speaks, but within the depths of her eyes I see a light of hope as the moon passes in front of the sun. It is as if the disease that burdens me is absorbed into her soul. Her healing power courses through my veins. She calls upon me to comfort those who suffer more than I."

"Dear Jon, you must rest. These struggles will only serve to weaken you." Gretchen fed him some soup and redressed his wound before she pulled the blankets over him. "I must go now, but I will return in the morning." She brushed his hair from his eyes and blew out the candle next to his bed. He was thrust him back into the darkness that he had come to loathe and fear.

Chapter 23

The Wolves Within

The large Sibley Tent was dark as the sultry August evening turned into an oppressive August night. Jon lay on his cot, sweat soaking his clothing and linens, and looked up at the conical peak of the tent's roof. It was like a symbol calling to him, but he fought the urge to succumb to the malaise. He wanted to go outside, smell the fresh air, and run his fingers through the soil again.

The flap of the tent opened and Gretchen entered, carrying a pot of hot tea. She stopped to talk to the orderly and then poured a cup for a soldier from the 69th New York, the Irish Brigade. She then pulled up a chair by Jon's cot. "It is nice to see that you are up. I was beginning to fear that you were succumbing to the wound. How do you fare, you know, with the demons and all?"

Jon did not want to speak about the dreams, but this girl had given her soul to him. He at least owed her the courtesy of a civil conversation. "I am still burdened by their haunting."

"Tell me one of the stories, Jon, so I can understand as you do."

"I would only serve bore you. I do not have the knack for story-telling like Grandpa."

"Just the same, I like to hear them. Folklore is the essence of our heritage. You should not be ashamed of your lineage." Gretchen propped Jon up on his pillow. "My, my, you are nothing but skin and bones. You should forego the soup and eat something of more sub-stance, if tolerable."

Jon began to tell her an intriguing tale. Soon, other wounded sol-diers gathered around his bedside, happy for the entertainment and mesmerized by his unusual gift. After an hour, with everyone hanging on his every word, Jon finished the yarn, "...and so, the marriage of these two unlikely suitors began the legacy of the Holland clan. They fulfilled the prophecy of an ancient chief and built a heritage bound to the land. They became healers who gave their lives so that others may be free from tyranny."

The unworldly sway of the story revealed the unbelievable power of the human spirit. The soldiers contemplated their own pedigree. They had descended from many countries, many religions, and many diverse races; Germans, Dutch, English, Irish, French, Protestants, Catholics, Jews...They were all fighting to preserve the birthright that made them strong individuals, but bonded them together as one nation with common ideals.

The soldier from the 69th spoke, "So tell me, Jon, how did these wilderness people know that the bond that they formed would be so vital, especially when it defied all logic?"

"My Grandpa puts his hands over his heart when he finishes this tale. We often take pilgrimages to the wilderness hollow where they lived. It is a harsh and secretive place where only a few footprints have disturbed the peace of the soil. It is called the Black Bottom, high up in the Falcon's Trace by the most holy of places, the Eagle's Nest. It is a haven where the doggedness of the human spirit is keenly measured."

Gretchen could see that Jon was exhausted. So as not to insult the other men, she intervened. "I think it is time for each of you to return to the comfort of your cots. Off you go to get some rest so you can return to your homes with stories to tell your own children."

Jon confided in Gretchen just before he nodded off, "I had another terrifying dream last night. I did not want to reveal it to you in front of the other men for fear that they would think that I was battle fatigued. They call it the *Soldier's Heart* and I worry that I might be stricken by it."

Gretchen listened while she tucked a newly laundered sheet under Jon's freshly shaven chin.

"I was in a cave deep in the bowels of the Earth. The light was dim and it was totally void of sound. A mist rose from the steamy embers of some burning coals. Suddenly, I was accosted by a bald eagle. He hovered over my head; talons posed to rip open my exposed flesh. He spoke in a forgotten tongue. At first his words were gibberish, but then, I began to understand them." Jon looked into Gretchen's eyes. "He mocked me and challenged me to climb upon his back, but no matter how hard I tried, I could not lift myself off of the ground to appease him. He revealed himself to me. He had the powerful body of an eagle and the fiery face of a man possessed by the devil. He spoke a parable and then vanished, leaving me to wallow in the dark."

"What did he say, Jon?"

Jon caressed her pale cheek. *"Man cannot discover new oceans unless he has the courage to leave the shore.* According to legend, the eagle is our guiding light, keeping vigilant watch over us. This deviled face eagle was possessed by two beings wrestling to take one another's soul."

"Focus on the message, Jon, not the messenger. You struggle with the reality of whom you are and who you wish to become. You are besieged by the uncertainties of life and death." She sensed Jon's anxiety. "You told me a tale while you were in a delirious state. I thought your rant was brought on by the opiates, but as time went on, the story seemed to make perfect sense."

"So, to what story do you refer?"

"You spoke about the *Tale of Two Wolves* or *The Wolves Within.* Legend foretells that each of us has two wolves that battle for our soul. The passive wolf keeps accord. The aggressive wolf undoes the balance of life. As long as you keep the harmony between them, your life will remain as it is. The answer lies within the legend's prophecy: Feed the wolf that you want to win."

Gretchen, in a few short minutes, had revealed to Jon the simple essence of his dreams. The dreams urged him to follow a path of salvation and service. The reverie about the horse began to make sense. *I am the Shadow Self, the Pathfinder to your life. Heed my words, fair soldier of fortune, for within them lies the secrets to your legacy.*

Chapter 24

The Shadow Self

Papineau squatted by a rushing brook, consumed by the spiritual revelations of his recent experiences. He drank heartily from the brisk mountain runoff. He had hiked a long way, leaving his homestead to head toward Montreal, far off toward the west. Along the way, he had rescued a massive wolf entangled in a lair. Instead of euthanizing the beast as he would have done in the past, he chose to bind its injured leg and release him back into the wild.

The woodsman glanced at his reflection in the water. He was pleased with what he saw, a stronger more invincible man. His heart pulsated with rejuvenated confidence. René Dubois was gone and the woodsman Papineau had emerged in his place. But had he really changed?

Papineau's senses were alive. He was consumed by nature as he rested his back upon the moss-covered ground. He decided that this would be a day of contemplation. He would do nothing more than prepare for the next. As he dozed off, he failed to notice a disturbance in the water upstream, for the pleasant cascade of a spilling waterfall masked the eminent danger.

A large bear appeared above the crest of the falls. Lumbering across a rock ledge, he glared intently into a dark pool of water. His reddish-brown fur glistened in the reflected light. With a violent swipe of his paw, he scooped a salmon from the depths of the pool. The fish landed on the bank, where he pounced upon it and ravenously devoured it. But a shift on the wind brought a new scent to the bear's undulating nostrils, more appealing than the odiferous fish. He sniffed violently, leaped off the ledge, and loped downstream toward his new prey.

An angry eagle swooped down over the bear. Its screech aroused Papineau. He removed his cap from his face and sat up, only to be abruptly bowled over by the onrushing animal. Before he could unsheathe his knife, he was toppled onto his back, half in and half out of the water. The bear's enormous paw swiped across his cheek as he struggled to free himself. Blood gushed from the deep wound, as the bear pinned him to the ground. He fought back, but the bear thrashed him about like his father did to his mother. He was no match for this misfit of nature.

Just when all seemed lost, a large wolf flashed out of the blind, landing squarely upon the unsuspecting bear's back. The raging creature fought to throw the wolf aside, but its claws were firmly entrenched in its thick skin. The wolf gnawed at the bear's throat to get the upper hand.

With the bear's grip relaxed, Papineau rolled out from under his crushing weight. Too weak to escape, he lay prostrate on the ground, helplessly awaiting his fate. As chance would have it, the frustrated bear gave up the fight, stood on its hind legs, and roared in defiance. It loped upstream to lick its wounds, as the wolf tilted back its head and howled at the sun.

Papineau, in a stupor, could barely make out the form of the wolf. Its yellow eyes were dilated with anger, much like his father's. He interpreted the bloodcurdling yelp as a sign of aggression. His instinct was to fight back, but his injuries were too severe. The bright landscape around him soon faded into darkness, as he passed out from the loss of blood and sheer exhaustion.

When Papineau awoke, his body ached from the festering wounds, lack of nourishment, and the harsh manipulation of the elements. He began to come to his senses and felt a strange warmth against his side. He raised his head, barely able to make out the form of the wolf lying next to him.

The cunning wolf, its grey and black fur bristling, perked its ears. He sensed that the woodsman had awakened and leapt up to move off. He barred his teeth and growled. He flared his nostrils and puffed his cheeks. Eventually, he sat down, but never took his eyes off of the wounded man.

Papineau sat up, his head in a fog. He gazed into the placid stream to assess his wounds. His cheek had been laid open. The wound looked like the lightning bolt he had drawn upon himself on the day he confronted his father. He suspected that the scar would mark his fate for the rest of his life. It was a harsh injury, but not life threatening. The determined woodsman dressed the lesion and examined himself further. His tunic was torn and large gashes covered his arms and chest.

The wolf cocked his head to one side as he assessed the curious routine the woodsman was going through. He continued to snarl at the man every time he sent a glance his way, but sensed his weakness and ran off into the brush downstream.

Papineau tried to stand up, but tumbled back down. He realized that his recovery would be a long and arduous process, so he hunkered down as best he could to weather the storm. He was not as invincible as he had imagined. He loaded his fowling piece and vowed that he would never be caught off guard again. As the dusk began to engulf him, he sat vigil over his own life.

Two glistening eyes appeared out of the darkness. The woodsman lowered his weapon and tightened his finger around the trigger, but something made him wait. It was the wiser choice. The feral wolf appeared, a hare clenched in its jaws. He approached Papineau guardedly, limping as he came on and dropped the hare at the man's feet. The woodsman noticed that his leg was bound in a soiled cloth. He soon realized that this was the wolf he had rescued from the snare. He studied his markings. The black mask around the wolf's eyes and his distinct grey-black fur easily identified him. He suspected that the creature was paying off his debt.

"Thank you, my friend. If not for your bravery and cunning, I would have been the feast of that rampaging bear. And to think, you accomplished this feat on three legs. I applaud you, sir, for your courage. The warrior, Three-Legged-Wolf, told me that you would appear to me as the Shadow Self, the pathfinder of my life. He dreamt that you would arrive in the first phase of my adventure to balance my independence, offer me wisdom, and guide me spiritually." The woodsman threw the rabbit on the fire. "The sage's medicine is strong and I sense his life-force within you. My personal resolve has been strengthened; Shadow Self, so move on to save another soul."

Papineau lopped off a leg of the roasted rabbit and tossed it to the wolf. The crafty alpha sniffed it then quickly devoured it, never taking his eyes off of the woodsman. He licked his chops with satisfaction, cleaned himself, and disappeared into the gloomy night.

Eventually, the woodsman was able to continue his quest, despite his suffering. He had survived a rigorous trial, but his destiny had been altered by the encounters with the wolf. He was too self-absorbed to realize that survival in the wilderness hung on a thread. To survive, he would have to learn that he would have to place more value upon the relationships he entrusted to others.

The wolf limped along, shadowing Papineau from afar. He would move in close at night, secreting in the brush, then move off at daylight to keep his vigil. Papineau summoned him. "Why do you dog me, Shadow Self? Do you not trust that I am capable of acting on my own accord? Mark my words teacher: I am Papineau, neither the elements, man, nor beast shall be my undoing."

Chapter 25

Lobsterbacks and Lemons

Papineau moved west through more civilized country. His wounds were healing and he was eager to intermingle with other people. He soon became disgruntled, meeting Provincials who tried to sway him from his chosen path or take advantage of his backwoods naiveté. He was not quite sure what marked a man as a savage or a gentleman, but he would soon begin to sort it all out.

Papineau came upon a curious English peddler coaxing a cocking cart up a steep hill. His bright orange, horse-drawn dray reflected his peculiar persona, for it was full of strange wares that had been scavenged, bartered for, or stolen. The comedy of the man was evident in his physical appearance: a red bulbous nose, a rotund build, and fiery crimson hair. He wore ostentatious yellow knickers and red stockings. Linen gloves covered his stubby hands, the fingers lopped off so he could firmly grasp the lapels of a brown waistcoat. Under his arm, he carried a riding crop and upon his head he wore a green, plumed chapeau. The man repeatedly snorted snuff.

The woodsman decided to barter for a new blade, for it was a staple of his trade. As he began to look over the cart, he was accosted by the man who spoke in a high pitched, nasal voice. He tried to ignore him, but from his diatribe, Papineau had learned that the fellow had fought in three wars, had procured the services of four wives, and had sired at least twenty children.

The peddler, "Thomas Lewis Thompson the Third", scolded Papineau as if he were a child, "Mind what you are touching, trapper. Some of those pieces are priceless."

Hidden deep amongst the wares, Papineau found an appealing

mocotaugan or crooked knife commonly used by the Algonquin. It had a carved elk antler handle toned in ashen and taupe. The blade was made of fine steel, honed by a skilled artisan.

"That is a jolly good piece of steel, my good fellow." The peddler boasted, "It was taken from a rebellious chief in the last Indian war and used by an English nobleman to abscond with the scoundrel's scalp. I have the infamous locks in the cart to prove it." The peddler rummaged through in a blood stained, oilcloth gunny sack and withdrew a long Huron scalp-lock.

"How much do I have to part with so I can procure the mocotaugan, Thompson?"

"Well, seeing that this fine piece of cutlery comes from the house of a great nobleman…"

Papineau was growing impatient, "Forgo the stories, Thompson, and give me a fair price."

"For you, my friend, I will reluctantly relinquish it for ten gold sovereigns."

"That is highway robbery," Papineau put the knife back on the cart and turned to walk away.

"Don't be hasty, Frenchman. You are lucky that I am willing to trade with you at all considering the nature of the relationship between our people, with the war and all. It is made from Sheffield steel and will fetch me a good price in the city beyond the river." He snorted back some snuff. "I can offer you a bargain, inspired by my benevolence. I'll even throw in the scalp."

Protracted negotiations, among other things, were what made men like Thompson so detestable. "I will find a knife elsewhere at a better bargain, my friend, and gladly be rid of you."

Thompson had met many a man who drove a tough bargain, but this stranger was different. He had a gleam in his eye and a way about him that was like a wolf: cunning, sly, and cagey. The hideous lightning-shaped scar on his face and his disheveled appearance accentuated his aura. The peddler had enough savvy to understand that he was not someone to trifle with.

"Tell you what," he carefully considered his proposal, "I will trade you that crooked knife for your old sticker, two of your finest pelts, and that beaver slouch hat that rests upon your head."

"Throw in that gorget, Thompson, and we have a fair deal. You can keep the scalp."

The peddler was reluctant to part with the ornate Spanish silver gorget, but he coveted the beaver hat. He feared that the Frenchman might take what he desired and he would be helpless to stop him. Better to lose a little in trade than have his head lopped off by a crazed trapper. Thompson grabbed the hat, pelts, and knife from Papineau's hands, not wanting to chance a change of mind. He felt the fine the soft beaver lining and closed the deal with a deep bow.

The remainder of Papineau's journey took him through beautiful country. Carefully cultivated fields, herds of livestock, and picturesque orchards replaced stands of hardwood and pines. The weather remained cool as the he glided over the well-worn road. There were few passersby to share his thoughts with, although he was the type that would rather contemplate things. He liked the anonymity and cared little if he saw another human being for the rest of the day.

As the daylight waned, the woodsman came upon a sprawling lodge situated at the crossroads of two worn thoroughfares. He preferred the outdoors over a confining shelter, but he longed for a hot meal and a bath, something he had not had in several weeks. He had never seen such a magnificent dwelling and paused on the doorstep to study it. He admired the craftsmanship of the sign over the door, but could barely read the words. The carved picture of a black coach with a raised red and gold crest of a lion on its door helped him to decode the letters below. The Black Coach Inn was a palace of such a grand stature that it took him several moments to take it all in.

The two-story structure had an ornate wraparound porch. Its ship-lapped siding was freshly painted in shades of black, red, and grey. Hand-carved scrollwork adorned its window and door frames. Lace window dressings covered the imported glass. The red-and-grey slate roof was carefully cut into overlapping octagons. Tall stone chimneys rose from each end spewing smoke.

The blackened oak door swung open. A footman, dressed in fine English livery invited Papineau inside, "Won't you join us, sir. We will be serving tea and scones with strawberry jam in the drawing room. I believe it is a fine Devonshire cream tea today, if it pleases you, sir."

Papineau was distracted by a disturbance in the forest. He heard the anguished cry of a wolf. At first, he thought that he had been deceived, but when the distressed howl echoed again, a surge in the beat of his heart convinced him that something foul was afoot. Without acknowledging the footman's invitation, he dashed off around the main house and headed toward the stables. A shot rang out, and then, an instant later, one last howl of deep pain stabbed at his soul.

Four British military officers emerged from behind the stables, engaged in an animated conversation. They were cloaked in brilliant red coats with white lapels and cuffs. The brass, pewter, or ivory buttons that secured them identified their rank. Each man carried a pistol in his belt and a saber at his side that clanked in harmony with each step. Their black riding boots had been polished to sheen, but were spotted with barnyard excrement. The men's heads were adorned with blue tricorn hats, topping well-groomed powdered wigs that nested upon them.

The first officer to round the corner was tall and muscular. Unlike the others, his uniform was covered in gold braid. He carried white gauntlets in his right hand, incessantly beating them against his left. He sucked on the rind of a lemon. He appeared to be the nervous type, always fidgeting.

Papineau noticed that his skin was covered with white powder, his lips and cheeks painted rouge. He looked like the marionette he had seen at the puppet show in Quebec City as a child.

The officer's dark eyes were piercing and cold, a stark contrast to his artificial skin. His jaw was set in such a firm manner that his cheeks puffed out as he breathed. He had a pug nose, which he carried with an arrogant flair. His long strides were confident as he led the other officers toward the front of the Inn. They marked each step with attention to the details of his every word. Their brash demeanor exuded careless confidence and a propensity toward rash or foolish behavior.

Papineau quickly ascertained that these men were not the type that he would have any favor with. Their conversation waned when they began to approach the towering giant who blocked their path.

He put a hooked finger to his hat to acknowledge them as they sidestepped by.

As Captain Ezra Merritt, the supercilious leader of the band brushed by the woodsman, he gathered a whiff of the pungent odor that emanated freely from his body. In a bourgeois British accent, he addressed Papineau, "My good fellow, the pigs are kept in the sty behind the stable. I do believe it will be very much to your liking." He chuckled, as he pointed toward the barns.

The others got a hearty guffaw at Papineau's expense, but he ignored them and stepped back to let them pass. As he did so, he carelessly bumped into a young lieutenant named Cameron James. He was carrying a recently-fired Long Land Patterned Musket affectionately known as a Brown Bess. Grey smoke emanated slowly from it barrel. The derivative of the curious name for the popular weapon was in question. Some said it was named in honor of the Queen Elizabeth I. Others indicated that it came from the German term *braun buss,* meaning strong weapon. Either way, its use on this day was about to become a matter of scrutiny.

Papineau questioned, "What mischief have you conceived with that fowling piece, sir?"

James was a swaggering fool who had more bark than brains. "What business is it of yours, woodsman, what I may do with my weapon? But quite frankly, I dare say that I had some good sport with it. In yonder wood a prowling wolf was rousing mischief with the horses. I made quick work of the beast, one shot to bring him down, the second, with dead aim mind you, to finish him off. Would you say at about one hundred paces, Carlton?"

Papineau was incensed by the revelation, "Did this wolf have distinctive black-and-grey markings about its eyes, sir, like a Native death mask?"

"For that matter, I believe it did. What concern is it to you, sir?"

Papineau grabbed James by the lapels and lifted him off of the ground. "That wolf was a messenger from the spirits. He saved me from a certain death. You have callously shot him."

James spit in Papineau's face. "If you know what is good for you, you will unhand me."

Papineau placed James on the ground. He was a powerful man, but no match against four well-trained, well-armed military officers. He did not want to trifle with them and headed for the woodlot to find the wolf. He was struck a blow to the skull by the butt of James' musket. The gargoyle-like figure on the stock drew a trickle of blood. He wiped the blood away and faced his provocateur. His stabbing azure eyes glared and his lightning bolt scar glowed a fiery red.

James barked, "How dare you touch an officer of the King, you French son of a whore?"

Papineau restrained himself. "You will have to answer to me if you have harmed that wolf."

James took Papineau's restraint as a sign of weakness. "I give no quarter to French vagabonds, you wretch. I demand satisfaction for your insolence, sir."

Merritt seemed to enjoy the fracas, along with the last few measures of his lemon. He removed the rind from his mouth and tossed it over his shoulder. "Leave it lie, Cameron. His loyalty to the wolf is refreshing. Your rash behavior, however, has become intolerable. If you are to remain a respected officer of the King, then you need to curb your impulsivity. I have paid a handsome commission to support your advancement, but if you insist on taking matters into your own hands, then I will withdraw my support of your grade. Is that understood?"

James appeared to back down to appease Merritt, but his anger got the best of him. He handed his musket to Lieutenant John James Cook, removed his cape, and draped it over Cook's arm. Without provocation, he tried to strike a blow to Papineau's face.

The woodsman anticipated the rash move and caught James' fist in direct flight toward his exposed chin. He stared menacingly at the startled Anglican, as he squeezed the officer's hand until he bent at the waist in submission. He quipped, "If you wish to pursue this folly, sir, I am afraid that you will dearly regret its outcome and suffer at my hand."

The other officers attempted to jump in, but were stopped by Merritt. "We need not bother this good fellow. Leave his rotting corpse to the cold and the wolves."

Papineau pushed James to the ground. He stepped over the prostrate officer and left the Inn.

Merritt berated James, "You are indeed a hearty fool, sir. If you were of lesser lineage, I would have let that man thrash you. Mind yourself, sir, for you are beholden to me for any future favors."

Papineau had measured up to his first serious challenge from men who represented a contrary way of life. He glanced back, wondering what it might have been like had he entered the black oak door. But he felt obligated to avenge the foul play against the wolf. Lighting out around the stable, he disappeared into the wooded cloak in search of the celebrated animal. His exploration would unexpectedly carry him further west, as he continued to wrestle with his resolve.

Chapter 26

Sorghum and Stew

The city of Montreal lingered on the horizon across the Fleuve Saint-Laurent. Papineau could see wispy smoke rising up to kiss the cold Canadian sky and then disappear into the cerulean heaven. It looked inviting to him from this lofty distance, but he had been fooled before.

The woodsman had searched in vain to find the wolf, but his blood trail had gone cold. He felt that he had owed the wily beast that much for saving him. He surmised that the creature did not want to be found; or had succumbed to the will of the elements. Either way, it was disheartening.

A menacing fortress of drab stone, its deep crevices interspersed with moss and vines, encapsulated part of the city by the waterfront. The Union Jack fluttered defiantly over it in a stiff breeze, but it had not always been that way. Adverse ideologies had embroiled the French and British in political and military conflicts all over the globe. After desperate fighting in the North American Provinces that included posturing Provincials and Indians, the Brits had secured most of the region under their rule. By the Articles of Capitulation of Montreal in 1760, the French ceded the city to their rivals. But it took three more years of fighting to settle the whole affair.

Papineau's encounter with the British officers had tainted his trust. *This is a sprawling continent. Surely, I can avoid being drawn into relations with people that I do not have confidence in.* On the brighter side, he had found the farmer and his wife to be accommodating. He was discovering that he should not get caught up in the judgment of others, lest they judge him.

The woodsman made his descent to the river along a sloping byway. He observed a boatman drawing a rope ferry up to a newly constructed landing. He called out to the fellow, "You there, boatman, can you be so good as to convey me to the other side before the sun sets?"

The sinewy little man acknowledged his call with a wave and pointed to a shanty up the bank.

Papineau tipped his hat and headed toward the boatman's hut which seemed older than the city itself. It was roughly hewn from chestnut logs, loosely stacked. Waddle and daub of grey silt from the river bottom filled the gaps. The structure leaned precariously toward the river, as if it were about to topple over. Its roof was thatched. A curiously crooked stove pipe protruded from the peak and poured out black smoke. The woodsman smiled at the appearance of this strange haven.

The boatman yelled, tying up his craft, "We do not stand on formality. Go in and seek comfort."

Papineau pulled on the leather thong and the door swung inward to reveal a great expanse of darkness and pungent smells. He reached up and turned the cock on the whale oil lamp to bring up the flame. He felt like a kid again as he explored the boatman's accumulated menagerie of objects.

The boatman's boots crunched on the tundra, as he entered the hovel. He was a delightful man, weather-worn, but strong from the hard work he had put in pulling the rope ferry to and from Montreal. He extended a sinewy hand, "Jean-Pierre Balmond, at your service, sir."

Papineau measured the man. The top of Balmond's head barely reaching his chest. He had a pleasant, round face and a broad, toothless smile. His long nose extended well beyond his parched lips and curled under into a curious point. His small round ears twitched as he puffed on his pipe.

Jean-Pierre grabbed Papineau's hand. "I must say, mate, you are a rather hearty fellow."

Papineau spoke to the river sailor with a deep and firm voice, "It is a pleasure to meet you, sir. Papineau is the name." Before Balmond could ask he added, "Just Papineau."

"Well, Monsieur Papineau, what is the cause for such an unusual name?"

Papineau was unusually frank. "I have given up my surname in deference to my father's ill-suited ways. I have gone by many names to avoid prosecution or persecution, but rather than bastardize it again, I took my mother's maiden name, Papineau. I have recently acquired a newfound respect for her and a deep-seated hatred for my father. I am a changed man."

Balmond had heard it all before as he navigated his raft. He responded to him politely, "Then I suspect, sir, that the name suits you well, for there is no other like it."

The boatman poured a dark, syrupy liquid from a brown, clay jug and studied Papineau. He appeared to be nearly twenty hands high. A buckskin tunic and breeches, stained with blood, tightly covered his sculpted frame. His dark hair flowed in a great mane down his back, some braided with chewed red leather. His face was worn, but still rather boyish. His bright blue eyes emanated intelligence, but masked mysterious secrets. They seemed out of place, glowing like the sun amidst his other dark features. The boatman instantly connected with him and motioned for him to sit.

Papineau was not much for drink, because of his experiences with his father, but decided that he would sample the liquid, since it was offered in the spirit of friendship.

Balmond proudly highlighted his brewing prowess as he raised his glass to drink to their health. "I distilled it myself from my own sorghum and flavored it with the blackberries that grow on the moor. Best thing for what ails you after a long day on the river."

The drink was thick like molasses and tasted of burnt blackberries. It seared Papineau's throat as it went down, but warmed his stomach. It soon took the chill out of his tired body.

Balmond handed him a slab of bread. "It tends to rot your gut if you do not eat something. This batch is particularly potent." The boatman swirled his mug. "I suspect that you want passage to the city? If you're expecting that I get back out on the river tonight; then you will be sorely mistaking. I've been running that boat near fourteen hours. My bones are aching, my hands are raw, and there ain't anything, but an act of God that would stir me. Sides, you look like you could use a hot meal and you smell like you could use a bath. Hell, for a couple of shillings, I'll take care of you like your mamma. Then, if the spirit moves me, ferry you across at dawn."

Papineau did not have to think twice. "Sounds like a deal a man can't ignore."

Balmond refilled their glasses. "Done!" He told Papineau to help himself to the chromatic, oily concoction simmering in a black cast iron kettle hovering over the fire.

Papineau lifted the lid of the caldron. He could smell the delightful odor of a hunter's stew: herbs, root vegetables, and game meats simmering in the rich broth. He dipped the ladle and drew out great chunks of hogs' jowls, fatback, and wild boar's snout from the depths. He filled and emptied the mug four times before he realized that he might be overstepping his welcome.

Balmond was delighted by the voracious appetite of this regal woodsman. He smiled as he sat down in his rocker and placed his clay pipe between his lips.

Papineau cleaned the bottom of the cup with the last remnants of bread and leaned back in his chair. *Would the meal at the lodge have been any better than the one he had just consumed?* He always marveled at the way things seemed to turn out: an incident of disappointment would often lead to one of pleasure or the other way around. He would soon discover that this quirky balance between all things was the guiding force to life itself and would dramatically alter his future.

Papineau sized up Balmond as he peacefully rocked with his eyes closed. The boatman wore a white, but excessively soiled duster. It was open enough to reveal a heavy blue woolen sweater with a large collar that covered his neck. He wore stained leather breaches that were tucked into his knee-high black boots. Precariously perched on his head was a knitted red seaman's cap.

Balmond sensed the woodsman's stare. "I'm quite a sight for you, hey? The weather is harsh in these parts." He took a puff on his pipe. "In my younger days, I had to fight off the wenches." He yawned and summoned Papineau to a room that was hardly bigger than an Indian sweat hut.

The woodsman ducked under a crossbeam and stood hunched over in the confined space. In front of him lay a tin tub full to the

brim with scalding water. He was not one to bathe that often, however, he was crawling with annoying vermin. He stripped down to his
underwear; full of so many holes that it barely covered him. He
immersed himself into the tub and rested his arms on the rim. The
soothing water immediately brought back memories of the days
when the Indian squaws would bathe him in the hot springs, endlessly squawking about having to care for the wild, white child. He
secretly loved the attention, except when they took a coarse sow's ear
to his skin. He try to escape, only to be beaten back by the switch of
a cat-o-nine tails on his buttocks.

While Papineau bathed, Balmond boiled his clothes and then
fixed a bedroll in the corner of the main room. He stoked the fire and
rummaged through his belongings until he found a musty buffalo
robe. He retired to his rocker and took comfort from the jug of
sorghum. He began to snore rhythmically as he rocked in his chair
while Papineau completed his constitutional.

"Was it to your liking woodsman?" Balmond quipped as he
stirred from his catnap.

"It was as fine an ending to a contentious day as I could expect."

"So, tell me, dear sir, what brings you to these parts in such a foul
state?"

Papineau was not one to haphazardly reveal his thoughts, but the
drink had loosened his tongue. "I make my way to this fair city to
seek my fortune and learn about its people."

"By the looks of you, you have been in a few scrapes of late. I suspect that if you cross that river on the morrow you will have your fill of
mischief on the other side. They are a rowdy lot just beyond those walls
that don't take too kindly to the likes of people of your persuasion."

Papineau was insulted at Balmond's frankness. "And you refer to
me, sir, as a miscreant?"

"I have measured men like you every day. You are all of the same.
You come in from the backcountry and hope to find something that
doesn't exist. You will see that the fortune that you seek will elude
you. Your heartless, fierce independence will be your undoing. It
always is."

"How can you pretend to know me so well, boatman when we
have just met?"

"Why, it's written all over you. You are ragged and unkempt, you bear the scars of recent battles, and your mannerisms are unrefined. I fear that we are not so different on those fronts, but I have learned to make peace with my faults. You harbor deep-seeded secrets, masked by false trust. I'll bet my stock in yonder ferry that you are not seeking fortune, but running away."

The bluntness of this stranger took Papineau by surprise, but his unflappable nature was cause to stand up to this buffoon. "What do you know of these things, boatman?"

"I have learned many things navigating that craft, for I have met an array of strangers, each one harboring a new lesson about people and life. I am not as shallow as I may appear." Balmond hesitated to reveal more. "I too have crosses to bear: dark secrets that haunt me from my past, but I refuse to allow them to consume my will. I am as independent as you, but I have made a bond with the river and the people whose needs are entrusted to me. Those things distract me from my burdens and give me something wholesome to cling to. Even though it is a hard life, it fulfills me, for I loyally go back out there every day. What is it that you cling to, sir?"

Nobody except Three-Legged-Wolf had ever challenged Papineau's motivations. "If I am to survive the hardships of life in a god-forsaken world, then I cannot be burdened with the trifles of wavering emotions. It is not for you to judge me on this, for only I can know what inner spirit drives me. I will not be bothered with frivolous affairs or undue burdens that shackle me. I shall always find solace in nature and independence, for I need nothing more."

Balmond continued to press him. "And who will you grow old with, my friend?"

"You, Balmond, speak like the snake, with a forked tongue. It matters not what you imply, for I shall live my life from the dawn to the dusk and then I will start afresh on a new day."

Balmond loved to play games of deception. This awkward woodsman was proving to be a formidable opponent. He was crafty and cunning, but had many flaws. If the hour were not so late, he would press him hard to reveal his secrets, even at the risk of exposing himself for what he truly was. He withdrew his gold watch from its place of harbor around his neck. "I fear that our bantering shall have to wait. As the sun sheds the light of a new day, we will part ways, never fully understanding what deep enigmas we each conceal."

"That is a fine timepiece. How did you come by it?"

"That tale is for another day, sir. If I am to have the will to pull you across the divide, then I need my sleep. I am to take leave of you now for we rise early in these parts."

Papineau took one last swig of sorghum and retired to the makeshift bed where he experienced a restless slumber. The little man of the river had made his journey's end a pleasant one, but he did not understand the depth to which the boatman had challenged his personal convictions.

Chapter 27

Death on the Landing

The last few hours of Papineau's slumber had been restless. An awful dream continued to haunt him. A battle raged, two armies of faceless men, one in blue and the other in grey, senelessly slaughtered each other. It always ended the same way. Upon a pedestal, high above the conflagration stood a single warrior. He raised his weapon triumphantly over his head and then, in an instant, fell into a sea of humanity and violence. *What did it all mean?*

A clamor of noise at the landing aroused the woodsman. He looked out of the distorted glass and saw Balmond engaged in a heated argument with some red-cloaked soldiers. It was Merritt and his three cronies from the Inn. He briefly contemplated the situation and then decided to intervene. Unable to find his fowling piece, he discovered an ancient blunderbuss nested above the door. He doubted its worth, but under the circumstances it would have to do.

The woodsman watched the officers knock Balmond into the water. He surveyed the ground leading to the landing and found no cover to conceal his movements. He decided to trust his fate to the blunderbuss and its questionable accoutrements. The distance between him and the Lobsterbacks was considerable, but it was his only option. He loaded the flintlock with powder and shot, secured the crooked knife about his waist, and cracked opened the door.

Papineau boldly figured that he could take two men down with the shot, if his aim was true and they remained in close proximity to one another. The remainder he would have to subdue with the blade. He would need help from the unsuspecting Balmond and a considerable amount of good fortune to carry out his loosely crafted coup.

He let the barrel of the weapon protrude from the opening. He cocked and primed the antediluvian gun. He assumed deliberate aim and waited for the horsemen to come into a tight group. They obliged him most directly.

The woodsman held his breath and squeezed off a round. The blunderbuss hesitated as the primer took and then belched out the buck and ball in a cacophony of flame and smoke. He fell back against the door jamb, jarred by the kick of the primitive weapon. The shot took off at great velocity, but he was not sure if the weapon was up to the distance and could not tell through the smoke and flame. Without hesitating, he rushed from the doorway. His long strides carried him swiftly over the ground like a gazelle. He pulled his mocotaugan from his belt and brandished it above his head in small circles as he approached the landing.

Lieutenant Cook was holding his face, blood pouring through his fingers as he writhed in pain.

Lieutenant Carlton's horse dragged him up the byway at break-neck speed. The officer's foot was caught in the stirrup. He fought desperately to get free before being dashed upon the rocks.

Balmond portrayed the image of Charon, the mythical ferry-man from Greek folklore, striking out at the dead who lingered at the gates of Hell. He had the presence of mind to beat James about the head and neck with a boat pole, rendering him uncon-scious.

Captain Merritt, aroused by the blast, drew his saber, spurred his warhorse, and charged the woodsman. The blade glanced off Pap-ineau's arm and tore away at his exposed flesh. He quickly recovered, only to find Merritt bearing down again. He had to react immedi-ately or he would be dead on the next pass. Out of the corner of his eye, he spied a large flat rock that sloped up and away from the river. He ran furiously toward it. His long strides carried him up the rock just as Merritt's saber headed for its mark. This time Papineau had the presence of mind to leap and narrowly avoid the crack of the blade upon the back of his legs. The trajectory of his descent carried him directly into Merritt's path. He landed awkwardly upon the horseman's back. Both rider and runner tumbled to the ground as the horse veered off toward the river.

The ferocity of the blow stunned Merritt and gave Papineau a momentary advantage. He raised his mocotaugan as the two combatants rolled in a macabre embrace. One furious thrust of the sharp, curved blade split the Englishman's breast. He gasped as the Sheffield steel cut deeply into his lung and grazed his heart. Papineau twisted the knife and finished the kill.

Merritt looked up into Papineau's eyes, pain etched upon his anguished face. Blood spewed from his mouth and with his dying breaths he gurgled a taunt of admonition to his murderer. "Know this, you bloody French son of a bitch: your path through life shall be haunted by my ghost until sweet revenge has been served upon your soul and the souls of your loved ones."

Chapter 28

The Headwaters Beckon

Papineau withdrew the blade and rushed toward Balmond who shouted, "I had been waiting for the time when I could bring these brigands to justice. I had surmised that revenge would be sweet, but it has sickened me, resurrecting the memories of another violent day from my youth."

Papineau was curious to know how a man so jovial could be pushed beyond the bounds of his good nature. The macabre panorama provided an answer. Cook was mortally wounded and James lie in a senseless stupor. On a rise, Carlton's horse nibbled on blades of clover. To the south, Merritt's body lay motionless in the windblown grass. The circumstances were grave. Other riders would soon arrive and bear witness to this repugnant scene.

Balmond shook James. "Wake up you senseless bastard. You shall not die on my watch."

Papineau questioned his actions. *Am I no better than my father, cruelly subduing anyone who challenges my convictions?* He composed himself. "Fetch me that rider on the hill. Leave no witness to the massacre we have brought forth upon this place."

Balmond balked. "Why should I be left to clean up your dirty work, woodsman?"

Papineau threatened, "If you fail to do as I ask, Balmond, our heads will hang from a noose."

Balmond imagined his lifeless body dangling from the end of an executioner's rope, something he was very familiar with from his sketchy past.

Papineau went about the task of dragging the bodies across the plain and placing them in the hut. James was alive, which put the woodsman in a quandary. Should he be killed, or should he be revived, at the risk that he could be their undoing in the future? He chose the latter, for he never once doubted that it was the right thing to do. He carefully placed him on the bed in the hovel.

Suddenly, the door burst open. Papineau prepared to disarm the intruder, stopping just short of removing Balmond's head with a poker. "I am sorry, sir. I don't know what has overcome me."

A grim Balmond took the sorghum jug and collapsed in his rocker in the corner. In a stupor, he contemplated how his life had been altered by the stranger who sat across from him.

James began to regain consciousness. He reached for a pistol concealed beneath his waistcoat, but fumbled to cock and load it. He was gently relieved of his grip on the weapon by the woodsman who casually flipped it, exposing its metal encased butt. With a swift flick of his wrist, he struck the officer in the center of his forehead and knocked him senseless.

Balmond realized that his years at the helm of his ferry were frittering away in moment of misguided hatred. He had his share of spats with the drunks and braggarts, uppity socialites, and politicians, but never before had it come to blows. He always held the trump card, which made him a powerful man. By a twist of instantaneous fate, that authority had been snatched from him. There was only one thing to do. He stood up and walked across the room. He picked up the pistol and finding it loaded, cocked it to fire. He rested the piece against his temple and twisted his head to absorb the blow of the ball. But before Papineau could react to this maniacal scene, Balmond turned the gun on the delirious James and let off a round. His hand twitched on the recoil of the weapon and the ball glanced off of the Lieutenant's temple, ripping away his ear.

Papineau wrestled the pistol from Balmond and shook him violently. "Get a hold on yourself, man. This is no time for foolish and rash behaviors."

Balmond looked up at him in disbelief. "You dare preach to me about foolish behaviors? It is because of your impulsiveness, woodsman, that we wallow in a bath of blood. Before you intervened, I had situation well in hand. Now we are vexed with a conundrum that can only be resolved in the dungeons of the fortress across the way, or worse yet, by the hangman's noose."

Papineau knew what to do. "There is always another way to resolve a dilemma of this magnitude. I have learned that much from the Indians. I have been told about a river to the south, in the land of the Man-eaters, where the game is plentiful and the wilderness is a haven to peaceful living. Join me on this journey and you shall be free from the oppression that you suffer."

Balmond was too set in his ways to tramp off into the wilderness and he could not place his life in the hands of this assassin. "You ask me to abandon all that I know and place my trust in you, a man who has demonstrated to me that he is a heartless, callous murderer."

"Have you an alternative, Balmond?"

"I will plead innocence to any wrongdoing. I was defending myself from the aggressive actions of the King's Dragoons. My reputation as an honest citizen will resolve any ill-will that festers from this matter. You will see, woodsman, that justice will prevail on my behalf."

"So, Frenchman, do you think that the British will show favor to you after killing the King's Guard? You, sir, are a dead man. Stay if you will, but I am taking my leave of this godforsaken place." Papineau headed for the door. "Where have you hidden my fowling piece?"

Balmond pointed to the far corner of the room behind the door. There, hidden under some hides, was the weapon. "I suspected that you may use it against me in my sleep."

"I do not need this firearm to lay you to waste, boatman. You had best take care of how you handle my personal items. Because of your fears, I was forced to use that ancient blunderbuss. I suspect that if that weapon had failed me, it would be you lying dead on the landing." The woodsman exited the hut. He called back to warn Balmond, "A carriage is cresting the rise. I suspect that they will want passage over the river. What should I tell them of your fate?"

Balmond was now in a state of panic. He looked down at the bodies strewn around his cabin. He would be held accountable, despite his notions, as the woodsman got away scot free. He rationalized that the only thing to do was to eliminate the evidence and flee. He gathered himself, bent over to remove a floor board, and unmask a small, musty cavern. He resurrected a modest bag from the breach. Nestled inside were a cache of gold sovereigns and a locket. He had no personal attachment to the rest of the wares strewn about his disheveled home.

The boatman yelled to Papineau, who was spurring Merritt's horse toward the tree line, "Wait for me, woodsman. You have left me no other alternative than flight." He mounted and spurred a horse to strike out across the plain at breakneck speed, heading south away from the city.

Papineau waited for Balmond in the pine barren and then lingered among the trees to make sure that they weren't followed. He watched as a regal black London-Farringdon coach with white wheels drawn by four magnificent horses began to ease up to the abandoned landing. It was accompanied by a guard of uniformed horsemen. The woodsman made a hasty retreat and caught up to Balmond. He looked back one last time. Large volumes of black smoke billowed from Balmond's hovel. It was soon engulfed by a rush of flame that licked the darkening sky.

Chapter 29

Last Full Measure of Devotion

Summer passed into the fall of 1863 and Jon began to regain his strength. He sat outside of the hospital tent in a rickety folding chair given to him by Dr. Zacharias. He enjoyed the cool breezes, the sweet smell of the turning leaves, and the autumn colors. The battlefield was now quiet, too surreal to be imagined. Passing militia were encouraged by news from the front. The Federals held the tactical advantage and pressed the Rebs all over the continent. Jon suspected that his regiment reveled in the aggressive strategy, but he had not heard from any of them.

Jon was consumed by the messages in his dreams. They had served to strengthen his stubborn will, despite his fragile physical and mental state. He was determined to follow the path where the voices led him, valuing the kinship that he had with other people. They sought his advice or ask forgiveness under his comforting hand. His ancestral Indian grandmother would have likened it to the power of a shaman. They possessed a spiritual and mental acumen that enabled them to lead where others could not. She was one of them and he suspected that he too had the gift.

The young men around Jon were free-spirited, possessing a unique combination of fortitude and determination. Their personal independence was anchored by a doctrine of loyalty, love, and devotion. But the Holland cause went beyond that. They valued a heritage manifested in the land and nature. Possessing the land was a way to cling to their fragile freedom. It was about preserving nature in its undisturbed state. It was about an unbroken circle of harmony, Immrama, as Grandpa Michael would preach.

It took the shocking thump of a Reb bullet to help Jon find that in his soul.

Late one evening, Jon fumbled in the dark to find his watch on the nightstand. It was not there. He searched the floor and then panicked at the realization that the timepiece was gone. With an uncommon anger, he summoned the orderly, "Orderly, I command you to come here this instant."

The young man put down a bed pan and rushed across the tent to Jon's bedside.

"My watch was on this table and now it is gone. Would you know where it has gotten off to?"

The orderly fumbled with his words, "No sir, I have been busy tending to the pots. I'll get the doctor, sir." He rushed from the tent in search of a physician.

Jon tipped over the night table. He lay down on the bed and placed his hands over his face. Tears seeped through his fingers, as he saw the disappointment of his failures written in the furrows of his grandfather's Irish brow. *How could I be so foolish?* A tap on his hip aroused him.

"Are you alright, son?" It was Dr. Zacharias.

Jon rolled over to look into the bespectacled eyes of the stoic surgeon, the sleeves of his linen coat still faintly stained with blood. "I am fine, sir. There was no need for you to fret."

"Just the same, let me look at that wound." The surgeon undressed the wound and probed at it with his long, almost feminine fingers. "It looks very good, but I suspect that it will give you trouble for the rest of your life: stiffness and some pain, you know. The salves seem to help and that Jung girl worked a miracle with the mosses. What's this I hear about your watch?"

"My heirloom watch is missing. It would mean a great deal if you could make some inquiries."

"Gretchen tells me that you believe that the watch has some mystical power. Is that so?"

"Well, sir, my grandfather believes it, but I am skeptical, although every time I carry it something extraordinary happens. If you could get it back I would be indebted to you. It is an irreplaceable part of my family lore and its loss would serve to put my granddad in his grave."

"I'll see what I can do, son. Now you go ahead and rest."

"I have had too much rest, sir. It is time to get out of this god-forsaken bed and move on."

"Then I will sign your release orders and get you on a train back home by next week, if that suits you. You are healed sufficiently well to carry on without further medical assistance."

"I would be most obliged if I could return my unit at the front, sir."

"You will have you marching orders in a few days, but are you sure that you want to rejoin the war effort? You have earned the right to go home, son."

"Yes sir. I have a score to settle with my conscience."

Three days later, Jon was visited by Gretchen. He was preparing his kit for the march. "I have missed you a great deal, Gretchen. Where have you been off to?"

"I had to go to York to help my father with a church function. Are you going somewhere?"

"I will get my orders to return to my unit in a few days. I need to see this war to its bitter end."

The disappointment was written all over Gretchen's face. "Then you will be in need of this." She reached into her apron pocket and pulled out Jon's freshly polished watch.

"How did you come by this?" Jon was elated.

"It is a long story, but Dr. Zacharias told me that the orderly who tended to you stole it right out from under your nose. He got a little drunk one night and tried to sell it to a wounded soldier from the 20th Maine. Zacharias just happened to walk in and witness the exchange." She handed the watch to Jon, who hugged her in return. "The orderly has been arrested."

"Thank you, Gretchen. You will never know how much this means to me. Tell Dr. Zacharias not to prosecute the man. War does curious things to a man's soul. The man has comforted me. It is time I return the favor. Forgiveness is a powerful thing."

"I was hoping that you would say that. The orderly will be trans-formed by your mercy."

One late fall day, as Jon awaited his errant orders, he and Gretchen strolled along the wall that represented the highwater mark of the war. He paused where he was wounded to look out over the now desolate field, squatting to pick up a handful of dirt. "You have provided me with the strength and will to carry on when everything seemed to be lost." He took her hand, noticing a faint blood stain on the rocks where he had fallen. "I owe you a great debt."

Jon removed a silver Gaelic knot bound on a leather chord from about his neck. "When my great, great grandfather Conlan met the Mohawk woman Nadié, he gave this to her as a token of his love. It has been passed down through generations of Holland men and woman. I wear it as a symbol of power of their eternal bond. I want you to have it."

"I cannot take this, Jon. It is a precious heirloom that should remain in your family."

He interrupted. "It is meant to be. You have given me back my life. It would mean the world to me if you were to wear it. It represents the Trinity, bound by the power of human resolve."

"My father would not approve, Jon. He only knows you from my stories and he would perceive this as a pagan idol, not worthy of the Lord's contemplation. If he could meet you, he would understand the grace by which you present this gift to me."

"I do not wish to offend anyone, Gretchen. We have always considered this symbol to be a representation of God's power and the sanctity of the human spirit. It is only fitting that you have it. You have revived the light of life in my soul. For that, I am eternally grateful."

Gretchen wept as she embraced the tall, lanky soldier. She wiped away the tears and tied the locket about her neck where it dangled over her heart. She then cuffed Jon on his shoulder.

The soldier looked dumbfounded. "What did you go and do that for?"

"You had better not go and get yourself killed, Jon Holland. On the day that the war is over, I will meet you in this very spot to resume our friendship. It is fitting that we end the war in the place where fate has brought us together." The two young souls walked hand in hand, silently contemplating the day when they would return to this hallowed ground.

Jon spent his last hours in the sleepy Pennsylvania town with Gretchen. It was November and the leaves had left the trees to fall harmlessly upon the new graves of reinterred Federal soldiers on Cemetery Ridge. They walked arm in arm to the Evergreen Cemetery where a crowd had gathered. A Marine Band played while they waited to hear a speech from orator Edward Everett. He would open the ceremonies to dedicate the new National Military Cemetery. Jon paused by every stone and tried to decipher the name emblazoned upon it.

"Who are you searching for, Jon?"

"I am looking for my regiment. I need to pay my respects before I go. I can cipher the Bible some, but when it comes to reading anything else, I suffer mightily."

"Not to worry, Jon. When you come back to me from the war I will teach you how to read."

Jon and Gretchen wandered through the perfectly aligned rows of 3500 graves, as the band finished the song and Everett began his profound, but laborious two-hour speech. They listened half-heartedly to his words as they finally came upon the markers of his fallen comrades.

Jon stood quietly over the gravestones. He squatted down and touched the stone of his cousin, Color Sergeant Ezra Holland, while Gretchen gently placed her hands on his broad shoulders. The freshly shaped words still cradled the dust of the stonecutter's work as Jon lingered there.

Everett finished his speech and the crowd politely applauded before listening to a hymn. Then President Lincoln, who sat among the dignitaries, slowly stood up to speak. He looked frail, the heartache of the war, the loss of his son Willie, the trials he endured managing his inconsolable wife, and the discomfort of a nagging cold were pasted upon his pale and drawn face. His presence hushed the crowd, as he removed his stovepipe hat and fumbled with bits of paper. Soon, his high-pitched, nasal voice resonated over the throng with an inspiring tribute to those who had sacrificed. Although barely two minutes in length, his carefully crafted oratory was timeless.

Jon turned to Gretchen, who was deeply moved by the President's word. Tears streamed down her pale cheeks. He pressed close to her and squeezed her arm in his. He did not speak. He did not have to. There were some things in life that were more powerful when left unsaid.

Chapter 30

Root Hog or Die

Jon threw his pack onto the ordinance crates destined for the armies at the front and climbed up onto the massive Conestoga. He reached down to grasp Gretchen's hand before seating himself next to the aging wagon master, who nodded. He cradled his musket across his lap and pulled up his collar to stave off the biting cold. He tipped his cap. "Don't fret, for I'll be back lickety-split."

It was late November of '63 and the realization of a harsh winter was in the nipping air that whipped along the Emmitsburg Road. The wagoner's melodic baritone voice echoed over the wind, coaxing the mules. "Get on with you, oh mules so strong, the boys in battle gonna hear my song. Praise the Lord that Billy Yank fight, gonna have my freedom before the dead of night..."

The wagon bobbed and weaved under the weight of its shifting load. It moved at a snail's pace, snaking its way along the rutted roads as a part of a supply train that was miles long. Its wagoner drove the team with precision, gently encouraging the stubborn mules with a lash to the ear.

Jon interrupted the wagoner in mid-chorus. "If we are going to ride together, then I suspect that we ought to get to know one another. Sergeant Major Jon Holland, at your service, sir."

The teamster kept his eyes on the mules. He pulled up the collar of his worn grey sack coat and snatched the brim of his hat down over his eyes. "Josias Weed, Boss, at your service."

"It is a pleasure to meet you, Josias. Where do you hail from?"

"I come by way of the Hampton Point Plantation on St. Simons

Island in Georgia. It is a gruesome place, sir, for the coffles, you know, us slave folk, but I is obliged that you asked."

Jon looked at the careworn man sitting next to him. He was of medium build, with a full grey beard and a hint of grey hair protruding from under his slouch hat. His skin was dark, but his eyes shed the light of a newborn day. "So how is it that you are driving a team in Uncle Sam's Army?"

"By the grace of God, Boss, and the kindness of a saint. Miss Fannie and her Philadelphia Abolitionist friends helped me to escape that oppressive place. It was during the *Weeping Time*. I slipped away in the dead of the night on a small boat. You see, the plantation overseers were selling off my brothers and sisters to pay their debts, so I up and left. I ran like the devil through the Carolinas and ended up at the Dobbin House right here in Gettysburg, all with the help of them Underground Railroad folk. Shoot, it was as if the Lord had placed me there himself, just waiting for the great battle to begin." He revealed his sparse, rotting teeth. "Got me this here job from Billy Yank 'cause I been driving the teams back in Hampton Point since I could remember."

Jon interrupted Josias. The former slave was not able to stop talking once he got started. "That is magnificent tale, Josias. You must be a proud man. Who is Miss Fannie?"

"Shoot, that fine white woman is Fanny Kemble, Boss. You heard of her I expect, the famous British actress? She done married the plantation owner Boss Pierce Mease Butler, but did not take too kindly to his extraordinary ways, you know, with the coffles and all. She didn't care much for Southern life and the oppressive islands didn't suit her fair disposition. Well, shut my mouth, she up and left one day. That whole mess of contrary people got under my skin like a pesky chigger."

Jon was entertained by the quirky teamster, but was a bit naive. "So, what is slavery like?"

Josias sat in a hunched over position, his arms resting on his thighs as he managed the mules. He looked at Jon, his smiling face changing to one of scorn. "May I speak freely, Boss?"

"You will receive no retribution from me for speaking your mind, Josias."

"There are folk in the North that harbor ill-will toward us dark-ies and I can get too free with the tongue. Care for a drink soldier?" Josias took a wooden flask out of his sack coat pocket and popped the brass cork. "Ain't much, just some honey cider, but it will warm your innards."

Jon took the flask and wiped the opening with the sleeve of his frockcoat. He took a small sip of the sweet liquid and then handed the flask back to the teamster.

"Mighty fine cider, ain't it, Master Sergeant Jon? I save it for special occasions." He took a drink from the flask and corked it. "I've been fighting all my life to be free. As a young man, I was a willful fellow on the plantation, bound to the land, but I tried to escape its bondage every day."

Jon began to recognize a familiar theme in Josias' story.

"Mr. Butler was sometimes good to me, at the coaxin of Miss Fannie, but the field bosses took the lash to me like I was some kind of animal. One day, I lashed back. Well, they tied me to a tree, ripped off my clothes, and beat me until I fainted dead away. If not for the grace of God, I would be pushing up roots. It took near five weeks to recover from the ills of the lash." He placed the reins in his mouth and lifted up his sack coat so Jon could see his back. "See here? This is what they done to me." Josias' back was crosshatched with ugly, raised scars, too numerous to count.

Jon was appalled.

"I stopped my contrary ways, but that did not stop the beatings. They were hellbent to leather on making an example of me. Then, in March of '59, they took my family. They shackled 400 coffles, put them on the boats, and shipped the lot off to Ten Broeck Racetrack in Savannah. They sold them outright to the highest bidders to pay their mounting debts. That was the *Weeping Time*."

Jon hesitated, but asked, "Why didn't they take you? What happened to your family?"

Josias chastised the mules. "Get on with you, you ornery beasts." He wiped away a tear. "Nobody wanted me on account of my defiance. Hear tell that my missus is in Charleston, a house slave in a fine mansion beside the sea. She was a delicate flower who did well tending to the young white mistresses. Don't know where the children are. My boy Esau, he was a brute of a man. I'll bet they bid high for him, having good teeth and all. Jenny Lynn, she was a frail, sickly child. She bring nothing at auction, excepting for some plaything for them backwater trashy white Crackers."

Jon was shocked by the misery this man had to suffer and the abysmal nature of his existence.

"I suspect I'll never see any of them again, but I be free. Mr. Lincoln said so. Someday, when you Yanks win the war, I'm heading south to find them. In the meantime, I'll drive this wagon to help the war effort, seeing as they won't let me fight."

"You took a great risk running away, Josias. If they caught you, they would have killed you."

"The way I look at it, it was worth the risk, for I was already dead. Gad night living, ain't nothing that the boss man could do to make things worse. Dying and going to heaven would be a damned sight better than living the hell of plantation life."

Jon was amazed by the resilience, courage, and wisdom of the man. He had no formal schooling, but had acquired an acute perspective on life. He had been shackled to the land by its owners, but through desperate determination, had managed to escape his bondage. Jon contemplated his own life, shackled to the soil by his heritage, but he did not have the courage to step into the unknown like Josias. It took a national war to prod him away from the homestead.

"So, what did you do, before soldiering and all, Sergeant Major?"

"I was a farmer, much the same as you, in upstate New York. It is a pretty place along a magnificent river, not more than 125 acres or so, but fertile as any land in America."

"Begging your pardon, but I doubt that our lives were similar. It sounds nice, all of the same."

"I did not mean to offend you. My family has had its share of struggles. Our Native land was taken from us after the Great War for Independence. We nearly starved to death during the Irish famine. We were abused in the slums of New York. You know something, the Irish are the lowest form of human fodder in that city of sin. Even the Negro folk garner more respect in most quarters."

He paused to adjust his seat on the hard wagon bench. "We may not have suffered the trials that you have, but we understand how cruel one man can be to another. It ain't right, Josias, and that is why I am fighting. I have tasted freedom and will fight to the death to preserve it for everyone. I am bound to help others when this war is over so that this rash of oppression ends."

"Well, you are a noble man. No man should live in bondage. Each should live as he sees fit, so long as it does not encroach on the lives of others. You go off and fight your war and in the end, we will see if anything changes. You need to root hog or die, Master Sergeant Jonny."

Jon was amused by the quirky phrase. "I do not believe that I have heard that phrase before."

The Wagoner scratched his scalp. "It is a simple Southern locution that means you need to pursue your dreams with a vengeance or roll over and die. It has become a credo for me."

Jon began to realize that the encounters he had since entering the war were pushing him toward a new understanding of life. He was being challenged to do something extraordinary. He was being exposed to the good and evil that could disrupt the harmonic circle of existence. The fickle hand of fate had presented these diverse people to him to test his will and question his convictions.

Josias was still talking. "So, what will you do after the war, assuming some Reb doesn't cut you down?" He digressed before Jon could answer. "You know those Reb boys can shoot the eyes out of a needle at one hundred paces. I've never seen anything like it. I suspect you know that by the looks of your uniform. If I was you, Boss, I'd be on the next train back to my mama."

Jon half-heartedly jested, "The red-faced devil is driving me back to the front."

"Then I am going to pray for you, for the Lord knows me well and watches over my soul."

Jon fetched his pack and drew out a few sandwiches. "Care for something to eat? Gretchen packed me some leavened bread and smoked ham. You will savor her country cooking."

They did not speak again for some time, as Josias had fallen asleep after the meal. The ornery mules, relaxed of Josias' deft hand, put their heads down and followed along behind the others. As if spiritually commanded to do so, they never strayed from the path that led back to the front.

After a long journey, the wagon train approached the Union camp sprawled along the Rapidan River. Jon and Josias had delved deeply into each other's personal lives. Surprisingly, they were very much alike, even though they came from vastly different backgrounds. To the average man, they were separated by the distinct color of their skin. Jon didn't really much care about that, for he knew that a man's soul ran much deeper than the face value of his race, color, or creed.

Josias halted the team. "If you don't mind me, Daisy, I am going to send you to the meat factory so these soldier boys can eat." The lead mule looked over its shoulder and brayed in defiance.

Jon gathered his accouterments and then jumped down from the seat.

The teamster cursed up a storm to steady the strident beasts. "You seem real anxious to get back to the business of fighting. Are you sure I can't change your mind?"

Jon kicked the dust off of his brogans. "A wee bit of insanity on my part, I presume, but it is something I am driven to do."

"You were given the red badge, why come back?"

The lad replied, "I am a lot like you, Josias. I have a strong inspiration to fulfill a personal promise. I suspect that most people would not understand that, but I know now that you do."

The teamster touched his hat and yelled at the braying mules, "Git up and git along you mangy critters!" The wagon slowly moved off toward the commissary. "You take good care, Sergeant Major. You look me up when this is all said and done and we'll make those dreams come true."

Jon turned to take in the vision of the sprawling camp nestled on a plateau. It stretched for miles, larger than most American cities of the time. Thousands of blue-clad soldiers had made it their home, anxious to cross the Rapidan one last time and end the war, keeping the great American dream alive for everyone and that now included men like Josias Weed.

Chapter 31

The Owl and the Rabbit

After their altercation with Redcoats, Papineau and Balmond trudged through the muck and mire of vermin infested swamps and backwaters, heading south. They took great care to avoid the common thoroughfares, survived off of the land, and traded sparingly to keep up their subsistence, but otherwise kept a low profile. The two men bartered away one of the cavalry horses for sundries, leaving them with three. No one questioned how these magnificent warhorses came into their possession because that was the way of the woods: one man's secrets were another man's profit.

The two travelers stopped outside of a small trading village known as Saint-Jean-sur-Richelieu. The hamlet was nestled along the banks of a tranquil river. Colorful shops, private homes, and quaint taverns sat in neat rows along narrow tree-lined streets. Papineau stayed in the trees, while the non-descript Balmond entered the village to haggle for supplies and information. He admired the peaceful nature of the place, but it seemed out of place in the rough wilderness. He made quick work of his business, but his keen eye detected chaos around the *Chemin des Patriotes* where the military traffic was unusually heavy. He inquired subtly about the commotion from a passing purveyor. The peddler's hasty reply came in muddled Scotch-English, ranting about the massacre of four British officers. The boatman understood and beat a hasty retreat back across the river.

Papineau could not be found, so Balmond became suspicious. *Maybe that fickle woodsman had seen fit to abandon me?* As he wandered down the pike, he was suddenly hoisted over a fieldstone wall and placed swiftly on his back. Before he could protest; a hand was placed over his mouth by Papineau as a company of Dragoons galloped by. They were fortunate to go undetected.

The Richelieu River continued to course south, emptying into a large body of water called the Champlain. Traveling by water would be quicker and less risky, ultimately leading them to the potential safety of the mountain ranges. That area was rich with game and home to multiple indigenous tribes they could befriend; living for a time in obscurity. So, the two fugitives decided to procure a boat, the horses being a liability. They would travel by night to pass undetected by the fortresses, trading posts, villages, and naval vessels that could be found in and along these waters.

At nightfall, they made their way back toward the river. Balmond was reveling in the time away from the hardships of his ferry trade. "I feared that you were going to drag me off into a life of uncertainty. My senses have been awakened and a different way of living has been revealed to me. Quite frankly, I am invigorated by the whole experience, despite the pursuit of the patrols. I do not like secreting in the hollows, but I must admit that the intrigue and adventure is rejuvenating."

Papineau had a different perspective. "Take heed, for those who live carefree suffer at the hand of those who fight to survive. This scar on my cheek is a measure of my own complacency, for all things are not as they seem in the fickle wilderness. I will teach you to read the signs of the wood and you will teach me about the pitfalls concealed in the deep recesses of the dark waters."

Balmond understood the complexities of life on the water; the hidden obstructions or the fickle nature of opposing currents. "The waters present to you a peaceful surface, only to sweep you away in an underpinning of deadly currents. Surely the forest is not as secretive as the devilish recesses of the briny sea or the treacherous dashing runs of a swiftly coursing stream?"

"I fear, Balmond, that I am not one to comment on the fatality that the waters hold within them, but I assure you that the forest is a living, breathing entity that measures your every move. It seeks to find in each of us our weaknesses and then pounces upon those frailties to expose us for what we really are. Measure each step well, sir, or doom will certainly measure you."

A well-worn footpath along the water's edge provided them with easier passage, but it was fraught with uncertainty, as its cloistered confines enveloped them in a shroud of darkness. The boatman observed. "I fear that the blackness of this night harbors a bad omen for our future, sir."

Papineau glanced back, barely able to see his dwarfish form in the darkness. He questioned his logic, "Take heed, sir, for the blackness of this night, my friend, may be our salvation."

Laughter and then a drone of incessant arguing cut the cool night air, bringing them to a sudden halt. Both men instinctively squatted near a hedgerow and caressed the horses to keep them still. As a light rain began to fall, Papineau tied his horses off to a tree and moved stealthily on his haunches to get a better view. He could smell the stench on the wind of the unkempt men huddled together around a fire, fully engrossed in a cask of swill. He held up three fingers to inform Balmond that there were three men. He could quickly discern by his cropped hair and ornate markings that the man closest to him was a Huron. He had crossed paths with these prodigious warriors when he lived with the Anishinabe. He respected them and had no quarrel with them.

The Huron had a strong presence in the Canadian provinces, forming a fragile alliance with the French. The name Huron was derived from the French language meaning wild boar. The French often altered the names of the tribes to better identify them. Those names had a tendency to stick among the European people. The dwindling Wyandot or Wendat tribes were given this moniker for their unusual Mohawk-style hair cropping that looked like the bristled pelt of a wild boar.

This warrior was caped in a scarlet robe made of broadcloth. A leather thong dangled around his neck, strung together with beaver's and bear's teeth. He was covered with blue tattoos. A lavish headdress adorned with eagle's feather covered his scalp lock. He cradled a war ax with an ornately carved handle and a shiny brass head in his arms as he hoisted the jug of malt with zeal.

Facing the lake was a man with bulging forearms, humongous hands, and an ample midriff. He had an oozing scar on his face. He wore the soiled and bloodstained powder-blue greatcoat of a French military officer. His booming voice was in a tongue Papineau did not recognize. He glanced over his shoulder to gain a sense of whether Balmond understood the tongue.

Balmond identified the language in a whisper, "German, Palatinate or Pfalz region, as they would prefer."

Papineau, stunned by Balmond's knowledge, turned back to continue to survey the scene.

Across the chest of the boisterous one lay a musket. At his waist was a glistening French saber. Blood had coagulated on the blade that twinkled in the light of the fire. The overbearing man fondled the hilt with one hand and then reached for the jug with the other. The Huron instinctively pulled away, but when the German raised the sword to his throat it affectively changed his course.

Papineau knew that the Hurons were aggressive and subservient to no man. He was sure of that the warrior's act of compliance was temporary and that he would exact a suitable revenge in time.

The third man sat quietly, slowly turning a spit that cradled a wild boar piglet. Papineau watched this routine, noticing a vessel resting on the shore behind the man. The storm driven winds raised the canoe's stern in a rhythmic dance as the waves lapped against it. The stranger systematically reached back to make sure that it did not drift away. As he did so, Papineau was able to get a glance at his face. His skin was dark, his eyes piercing. The woodsman had heard as a boy that people with skin as dark as the gloomiest night resided across the sea. *Could this weathered young man be the stuff of those legends?* He focused his attention on the boat and pointed it out to Balmond.

While Papineau and Balmond decided how to handle the situation, a rabbit skittered across their path, pursued closely by a great white owl on the wing. The rabbit weaved through the chaotic camp, where it managed to evade the pursuing bird of prey and the grasp of the frenzied trappers.

In the excitement, the German fell backward off of a log and discharged his weapon into a small sapling. The slim plantlet toppled from the strike of the ball and landed smack on the head of the freedman. He was knocked into the water, which allowed the boat to drift freely with the current.

The Huron leaped to his feet and dropped the jug into the flames. Embers flared and the wood alcohol exploded. His cape caught fire, which he frantically attempted to extinguish in the river.

Papineau sensed an opportunity. He slipped into the cold river and swam swiftly toward the runaway boat, a finely crafted Indian canoe about twenty feet in length. He maneuvered himself into its path and directed it downstream. He skillfully guided the canoe up a small stream and then dragged it upon a sandy inlet to conceal it in the brush. He discovered a satchel of supplies and a cache of beaver pelts in the boat's bottom. But for now, he needed to pluck his friend out of danger.

The three men were disoriented. Each blamed the other for the loss of the boat. The freedman, still rubbing his head, tried to be the voice of reason, "We need to make haste and fetch the craft.

"You dimwitted fool, you have caused us this dilemma," the German chastised the freedman.

"It was your insistence on loading our weapons that has led to our demise. If you want to place blame, then look no further than yourself," the freedman chastised.

The German pushed the freedman into the river and then placed the point of his saber on the warrior's throat. "What are you gawking at, you useless Indian? Redeem yourself and get after the vessel before it drifts too far and we cannot retrieve it"

The reluctant brave grumbled and then stumbled down the path in pursuit of the canoe.

The trappers' confusion presented Balmond with an opportunity. He figured that he was no match for the remaining men, so he devised a ruse to lure them away from the camp. *The blackness of the night is our savior.* He quickly removed their belongings from the horses. He slung them over his shoulder and slapped each horse on the hindquarter. They careened through the trappers' camp, the surprisingly deft of foot Balmond following after them. He hoped that the commotion would draw one or more of the men away from his path so he could move toward Papineau.

The horses scattered the trappers long enough to give Balmond the opening he needed. They left the clearing in pursuit of the horses, which would be quite a prize if they could to catch them. Then

Balmond scampered across the divide and entered a coulee. Assured that he was out of harm's way, he ran through the clearing to scoop up the French saber sticking out of a stump. He ran out of the south side of the camp toward an anticipated meeting with his companion.

Papineau heard the ruckus and moved toward Balmond. He came face to face with the drunken Huron staggering along the path. He assessed his options and slipped sideways into the brush. As the warrior passed, he swept his feet from under him and struck a blow to his head.

The Huron adeptly rolled on his shoulder and regained his feet. The rain washed a trickle of blood from his split scalp, as he lunged at the woodsman with the fury of a rampaging bull and thrashed at him in a fit of rage.

Papineau fought back with a vengeance, but the hefty warrior sitting upon his chest thwarted his ability to counter the blows. The Huron raised his war club and let out a bloodcurdling scream. Before he could crush Papineau's skull with the hefty weapon, his eyes rolled back in his head and blood spurted from his mouth. He turned belly up, dead before he hit the ground.

Papineau wiped the blood from his eyes while he lay on the forest floor recovering.

Balmond stood triumphantly over the brave, bloodied saber in hand. "Get up. That German feller will figure out what has happened and will be hot on our trail. Where is the canoe?"

Papineau sat up, a bit woozy, and pointed down the path into the underbrush.

"I'll make her ready. You gather yourself and join me when you are able, but don't tarry." Balmond rushed off and found the canoe in the underbrush. He stowed his gear and then slid the sleek craft into the water. He did not have to wait long for Papineau's arrival.

The woodsman loped over the rise, followed closely by the hefty German on horseback. "Shove off boatman and be smart about it."

Balmond feathered the canoe away from the shore as Papineau entered the river and pushed on the bow to hasten the retreat. He climbed over the gunnels while the boatman paddled away.

The German reached the shoreline just in time to see the two comrades disappear into the mist. He dismounted the Dragoon's horse, desperately trying to load and fire his weapon. It was a futile gesture. He threw the weapon on the ground and cursed the thieves as they escaped.

Papineau tried to make light of the affair. "Well Balmond, it appears to me that you have lost our fine English horses. What do you have to say for yourself?"

Balmond mistook his intent and grunted an answer. "Have you nothing to say to me other than berate me for mismanaging the horses?"

Papineau responded quickly, "I expected that the horses would be sacrificed so that we could procure this fine canoe. I was merely jesting."

"Have you not noticed that I saved you from certain death? If not for my timely arrival, sir, you would be lying dead, the Huron eviscerating your bowels and relieving you of your scalp."

"As I have mentioned, Balmond, there is a balance of all things in nature. I offered you a new life on the landing; you have responded in kind to me today. There is nothing more to it."

"Your arrogance is insufferable, dragging me into one mishap after another. You have proven that you are not invincible, as you may believe and have frailties that you cannot begin to imagine."

Papineau countered, "You speak in parables, Balmond, the mark of a man who thinks too much about life. What is it about killing for survival that angers you so?"

"I was unwilling thrust into an unscrupulous livelihood before my time on the river. When I finally escaped the injustices that I was forced to serve, I became a more introspective man. You will have to earn my trust if you want me to take you deeper into my hell. For now, I suggest you explore your own life, for I fear that you harbor too much hatred and not enough remorse." Balmond guided the vessel around a large rock. The sleek craft tracked effortlessly along the western shore toward the opening at the southern end of the river that led to the lake. Silhouetted against a rising moon, the two men, bound together by providence, drifted out of the storm.

Chapter 32

A Chance Encounter

Both men enjoyed the pristine scenery of a stimulating morning, lofty mountain ranges, abundant waterfowl, and glistening water, as they looked for a suitable place to make camp so they could avoid detection. On this particular day, they had to move farther down the lake than anticipated because the steep cliffs prevented a landing. Signs of spring were everywhere, but it was still cold. Buds formed on the trees and a few robins could be detected skittering about on the rocky shoreline. Except for an occasional ice flow, the lake was open for travel over its full length.

Papineau was sullen, not able to see the act of saving his life as an extraordinary thing. To him, Balmond's intervention was a small part of a natural sequence of events that maintained the balance of life. But the jovial boatman, unable to hold a grudge, saw life in a different vain. "So, has the devil taken your tongue? You are so possessed by your own cares that you fail to recognize the worth of others. I refuse to succumb to your pretentious ways by altering my own state of mind. If you are going to travel with me, then you had better share your thoughts and reveal your secrets."

The woodsman looked over his shoulder and glared at him. "You treat me like a child and I will not allow it. I am twice the man you are and will remain so until I am put into my grave."

"That may be so Papineau; or is it René, or Pashkwadjash, as it may suit you? Changing your name will not alter your soul. Your life courses like a rudderless ship. A real man recognizes his weaknesses and does not use them as a crutch to mask his frailties or cover up his failures."

An infuriated Papineau revealed some dark secrets. "Know this, boatman, I was cruelly beaten as a child and it has hardened my heart, made me virile, and filled me with resolve. I was abandoned by my parents, left to fester in an Anishinabe camp like a stinking savage. I dare to say that you have not had as hard a life as I. I have overcome my challenges by personal defiance."

Balmond's secrets were darker than the depths of hell and too painful to be exposed. "You have done well by yourself, but you must understand that it is your soul that will ultimately define you, not your physical presence." He took several strokes of the paddle and then let the canoe drift. "I will not let you ruin this glorious day by drawing me into a senseless debate about the arbitrary nature of life. We had better get off this lake before the sun makes its mark upon us."

A few leagues to the south, the two travelers happened upon an inlet that led to a swiftly flowing stream. The runoff, fueled by the melting snow from the high peaks, rushed from the narrow opening and then calmed as it intermingled with the placid lake water. Papineau whispered to Balmond and pointed toward the underbrush just off of the beach that lay by the mouth of the stream, "Did you see it? Someone is hiding in the rushes."

Balmond dipped his paddle and backstroked, slowing the craft considerably, while turning it so he could get a better look at the shoreline. "Your eyes have deceived you. It is nothing but a few wood ducks. See, they are crossing the beach to enter the water by that large rock."

Papineau cocked his head to one side and squinted. "I swear that I saw a man watching us. I am afraid that lack of sleep and my unsettled mind have played some tricks on me."

Balmond suggested. "Let's paddle up to the base of those falls and then portage onto that bluff. We can rest above the rapids and then take to the lake again when the sun begins to set."

The two men eased the craft into the rapidly rushing stream, stroking hard to resist the current. They navigated through a few rifts before running the craft aground. Papineau leaped onto the shore and with a hefty tug on the bow beached it under a sycamore. He helped Balmond maneuver the robust vessel through the undergrowth and up a narrow path that led to the top of the falls. The ascent was easily managed and in a few minutes, they stood on an overlook above the lake.

Balmond did not waste any time climbing over the gunnels and lying down amongst the packs. He looked up at Papineau and winked. "Slumber is what I need and slumber is what I shall have." He pulled his blanket over his head and was soon sound asleep, snoring loudly.

Papineau grabbed his musket and headed deep into the forest to hunt for food. The crack of some branches caused him to squat. He listened carefully and watched intently. He heard the noise again, this time louder and closer. He saw the antlers of a buck protruding over a bush, so he brought his weapon bear, ready to crack off a shot. The antlers did not move, so he waited.

Suddenly, a screaming warrior charged out of the brush. He knocked the woodsman to the ground and caused him to discharge his weapon toward the sky. The two men wrestled feverishly for control of the tomahawk the attacker brandished. Another warrior soon joined the fray and helped his comrade subdue the feisty Papineau. The woodsman struggled to free himself from their grasp, but a blow to the head with the handle of the tomahawk soon laid him to rest.

Papineau awoke to find himself tied to a tree. Standing over him were two Huron warriors. The first was short and wiry, his face painted with black markings that trailed down his cheeks like tears. He wore a roach cap on his head. The antlers of a small deer protruded from its sides. The second warrior was disfigured, his face marked with scars left there by a fire. His deformity created a facade that looked much like the stark features found on an Indian death mask.

Papineau spoke to the warriors in their Native tongue, "Why have you accosted me here in the deepest recesses of the forest, away from the comfort of your village?"

The shorter of the two men answered him, "You have killed our brother and taken our canoe. Before we lay you to rest, we want you to look into our eyes and see our pain. It is that misery that you shall take with you to your grave as the spirits devour your soul."

Papineau squinted into the sunlight that filtered through the cover of pines. He surmised that these warriors must have been away from the camp on the evening when he stole the canoe.

The disfigured warrior grabbed Papineau by the hair. He forced the woodsman to his knees and put his arm around his throat. As he squeezed Papineau's windpipe, the Huron pulled his knife and prepared to remove his scalp. Without warning, an arrow swooshed by Papineau's ear and stuck the Huron in the throat. The warrior placed his hands on the shaft. He tried desperately to remove it, but his lifeblood gushed from the wound and he fell to the ground with a groan.

The other Huron frantically turned his head from side to side, astonished by the sudden turn of events. He instinctively concealed himself, the fear of being accosted shone in his dilated eyes.

Papineau seized the opportunity and kicked the man hard enough to disable him. He found his musket in the brush. As he readied the piece, another arrow passed by his head, striking the tree behind him. As the shaft of the arrow vibrated in the trunk, the woodsman bent over to place his weapon on the ground. He raised his hands in acquiescence to an unknown nemesis.

Much to Papineau's surprise, a regal Indian woman warrior emerged from the brush, followed by three Mohawk braves. She carried a finely crafted bow. A full quiver of arrows lay across her waist in easy reach. She brushed by Papineau to pull the arrow out of the tree, then placed her foot on the Huron's chest and heartlessly extracted the arrow from his throat. She spoke as she placed the arrows back into her quiver, "The arrow should never be wasted on frivolous killing."

As the sultry Mohawk squaw gathered her arrows, the other braves killed the second Huron by slitting his throat from ear-to-ear. They ceremoniously placed dirt in each of the Wendats' mouths. This symbol of retribution was a reminder to others who came upon them that the land upon which they lay was sacred, not to be violated by those who were not its rightful servants.

Papineau was stunned by the cold-blooded actions of the warriors, but grateful. "I am indebted to you, my friends. How can I repay you for your merciful intervention?"

A stocky, powerfully built warrior shoved Papineau with his musket. His face was painted white with the image of a large black hand emblazoned across his mouth and chin. A single black and white eagle's feather protruded from his carefully braided scalp lock "My name is Standing Waters and you have ventured into our sacred hunting grounds. You are never to return to these forests. We have spared your life on this day, but will not be so benevolent in the future."

"Why have you killed these men?" was Papineau's curt reply.

"It is of no concern to you why we feud with the Wendat or any of the allies of the withering French cause. Be grateful that our quarrel is not with you."

As Papineau picked up his weapon and turned to leave, he bumped into the squaw. She was tall, but he still towered over her. Her features were dark; bronzed skin, raven-like hair, and mysterious eyes set in the hollows of her high cheek bones. He tipped his cap to excuse himself.

The young squaw furrowed her round face in an act of defiance. "My name is Tekeni Karahkwa, Two Suns, and you have intruded upon the sacred home of the Wolf Clan. The errant flight of my arrow has spared you on this day, allowing you to live for another. Cherish each breath that you breathe, woodsman, for each is as precious as life itself. Once it is lost, it shall never return to you again." She pushed him aside, not intimidated in the least by his massive presence, and summoned the warriors to follow her with a wave of her bow.

Papineau watched them disappear into the brush and quickly retraced his steps back to the falls. He shook Balmond. "Get up boatman. We need to leave this place."

Balmond sat up and rubbed his eyes. "That was the best sleep I have had in years. I feel rejuvenated and am ready to venture forth." He checked his watch and then looked at the sun, a bit startled. "Something is amiss with my timepiece. It's telling me that it is noon...and by golly the sun agrees. Why have you awakened me and why in God's name are you covered in blood?"

"There is no time to explain. Gather your belongings. We need to get back onto the lake."

The two men put the boat back into the water and paddled out into the deeper part of the lake. Papineau studied the shoreline to make sure they had not been followed.

Balmond began to question his mate, "What ghost has spooked you, my friend? I have never seen you beat a path of retreat so fast, as I have on this day."

"You know that Huron you killed with the saber? Well, his brothers came a calling to remove my scalp. They must have been tracking us this whole time, waiting for the right moment to exact their revenge. Needless to say, I managed to elude them. I told you I saw someone moving on the shoreline, but you refused to believe me. In the future, you should not doubt my word."

"So where are these warriors now?"

"I have left them on the trail beyond the portage. I don't suspect that they will be following us, but I need to be sure that there aren't others lurking in the blind."

"I suspect that you may have stirred up a hornet's nest. The last thing I want is to have my scalp hanging from a Huron's belt." Balmond removed his red sailor's cap and rubbed his balding head. "Let's push further south and hole up on an island tonight to be sure."

The two men happened upon a small islet. They ran the canoe aground upon the rocky shore and hid it in the brush. After a meal of fresh fish, they both succumbed to a restless sleep. But the chance encounter on the bluff was about to alter their lives and challenge their convictions.

Chapter 33

The Pathfinder

The two careworn travelers, mulling over their uncommon partnership at the divine hands of fate, continued to travel at night along the Champlain water highway. Papineau would not reveal the particulars about the encounter with the Mohawk and Huron war parties. He deduced that they were best left unspoken. And so, the men remained at odds over their diverse views about life.

Three days after that deadly encounter, a tradesman navigating a sailing bateau appeared along the shoreline. Feeling a need for company other than Balmond's, Papineau asked him ashore. "You there, good man, come join us for a morsel." Papineau helped navigate the boat into the cove and tie it off on a fallen oak. "The name is Papineau, trapper by trade. Who might you be, sir?"

In a Scottish brogue, the man answered, "Caleb Graham, at your service: tradesman, trapper, tracker, and tinkerer. The Mohawk tribe up in the Trace calls me Yakohsa:tens, The Horse."

Graham was a curious fellow of medium height and build. He had unkempt, fiery red hair and beard which he braided to manage it in the harsh elements. He had small gold rings pierced into his ear lobes. He wore a tam o'shanter made in his clan's or-and-sable colors. A brocade of ribbons was pinned to the brim, cradling a laurel leaf cluster. He was simply dressed in a hand sewn tunic and a kilt, in defiance to the British law of the time. His feet were bare.

"Balmond and I have little to offer, but what is ours is yours. Is duck to your liking?"

Graham grinned, clearly pleased to have anything in his stomach. "Waterfowl will do just fine."

The three men sat around the fire and ate their fill of several plump mallards. Graham spoke incessantly, crafting yarns that piqued Balmond's interest. He suspected that Graham was a bit of a loner though. "Where do you hail from, trader?"

For Graham, no conversation took the direct route. "I hail from Dundaff, Scotland, landed at Dorchester Heights, went over the hill to the Hampshire Grants through Dummerston, took a trek sideways to Vergennes, and then up the lake. I am a free spirit, going where the wind takes me. Today, I fancy that fine boat, tomorrow it may be a cozy Mohawk wigwam."

"You seem to be a man of the world. What have you discovered in your recent travels?"

Graham leaned in and told a gruesome story, "Scuttlebutt has it that a relentless manhunt is in underway. Truth be told, two fellas killed some Brit soldiers near Montreal. I suspect that the two of you could pass as their equals. Now you wouldn't be those fugitives, would you?"

Papineau deflected. "The only crime we have committed is the slaying of these fine ducks."

"Well then, woodsman, I suspect that you will be acquitted on all counts."

Balmond was relieved that this stranger did not care to stir up the pot of controversy. He suspected that Graham understood the code of the forest, leave a dead man lie where he lay.

Graham was full of tales about Scottish nobles, Indian princesses, and encounters with magnificent beasts of the woodlands. He had a tendency to embellish, but you could always find some truth in his stories. He tantalized their interest with a macabre tale. "I hear tell that a battle was fought not more than a few moons passing. Rumor has it that the Iroquois alliance, led by a legendary Mohawk chief, massacred the people in a village of Anishinabe Algonquin. It is whispered that they killed the lot of them, but no one has revealed the exacting truth to me."

He brushed duck scraps out of his beard. "It appears that the Algonquin were given no quarter. Pray tell, by all accounts, it was a gruesome affair." He stopped to light his pipe, sharing his tobacco with Balmond. "I got that plug from a Tuscarora woman. Curious to me, but the whole lot of them came north from the Carolinas to join the Iroquois Confederation."

Papineau fidgeted, uneasy and distracted.

Graham sensed his discomfort. "What ails you? Do you have a burr up your hindquarter?"

"Finish the story, Graham. Do you know what clan was invaded, who was killed, and why?"

"I trade with a Mohawk Clan, the Wolf People up on yonder mountain. I'm only privy to what they tell me. They have a fine squaw there whom I fancy, but she pays me no mind."

Papineau's was angry. "Do you ever finish a tale without interjecting something else of unworthy contemplation? Get on with it man."

Graham looked disgusted. "As near as I can figure, the Iroquois came on to the Algonquian out of the west, when the sun's setting rays blinded them. The blighters crossed the shallows whooping up a storm. Before the Algonquin knew what hit them, it was over." He grabbed a stick and drew a map in the sand, highlighting how the attack had occurred. "Some tell that a brave called Stanley Two Toes and a mystical warrior with fire flowing from his face fought with a vengeance while the others fled. Blimey Mohawks are secretive, though. They just give me enough information to coax another drink. I have to cut them off or they will drink themselves into a raucous stupor."

Papineau grabbed Graham by the collar and chastised him, "Were they all killed, Graham?"

Graham brushed the woodsman's hands off of his tunic. "If you want me to tell you more and not run you through, then you had best not touch me again." He spit in the lake. "Standing Waters tells me that their souls are now a breath on the wind, but I measure his words carefully."

"Does the warrior Standing Waters have the print of a hand marking his face?"

Graham was astonished. "How do you know that, woodsman?"

Papineau did not play his hand. "So, you do not really know the fate of the Anishinabe?"

"No sir, but the Mohawks are known to be an honest and straightforward people."

Even if Graham's tale was filled with half-truths, then Papineau felt that he must take action on the behalf of his adopted Anishinabe brothers. He made up his mind and nothing would alter his course on the matter. He stood up and grabbed his pack and weapon.

Graham looked up at him. "Have I somehow offended you, sir?"

Papineau spoke bluntly, "Although I have enjoyed your passing company, sir, I fear that your tale has disturbed me. I must take my leave of you to heed the call of my fallen brothers."

The boatman was stunned. "Sit down, woodsman. If you think that you can resolve this affair by traveling back to their homeland, then you are mistaken. It would be a grave undertaking to assume that they are still alive and you could somehow intercede on their behalf. Do you actually think that you could alter the course of events now? Move forward with your life, as you have been commanded to do. Revenge will only serve to be your undoing."

Papineau was distraught. "You speak out of turn, Balmond. Your rhetoric is masked in cowardice, fearing retribution from the British. It benefits you to keep fleeing, for you have nothing of value to return to. You pretend to know all things, yet you hide within the shadow of your own fears, as I wrestle openly with mine. Do as you please, but I am bound to serve a greater cause."

Graham offered a compromise. "It is none of my affair, but the way I see it, there is a greater weight pressing upon the both of you. The truth to this tale lies within the deep hollows of that mountain. You can reverse your course, as your passion desires, or you can seek the truth up there." He pointed to the large peaks looming over them. "The path to answering your questions lays a few leagues away. I can guide you there so that you may seek the wisdom that eludes you, or you can fall back upon the path from which you came, to relive what is already a certainty."

Balmond agreed. "The Scotsman speaks wisely. The path behind us is fraught with suffering; not to mention our certain demise. The path ahead is unclear, but it holds the keys to dispelling all doubt. You convinced me to enter into your trust, suggesting that those mountains held the keys to a new life. Now you seek to avenge a myth that cannot be corroborated."

Papineau gritted his teeth. "I do this out of necessity, Balmond, nothing more. An eye for an eye, as my father incessantly preached to me from his blasted Calvinistic Bible."

Balmond disagreed, "Was it not you who suggested that the wiser man walks away? You speak out of both sides of your mouth. I fear that you misunderstand what the honorable path in life is. You can choose to right your wrongs, or you can continue on the path of self-destruction. For me, it is a simple choice, despite the uncertainty. I will accompany Graham."

Graham spoke, "It seems to me that you need time to mull over this affair. I will hole up with you for the night and then move on as the day breaks anew. You will choose my course. Should you decline my offer, I will sail north to finish my affairs. Should you accept, I will retrace my steps to the south, leading you to the path of insight. Now, if you'll excuse me, it has been a trying day navigating that boat against the wind. Let the dawn shed its light upon the path of reason."

Chapter 34

Crossing the Rapidan

The battle-hardened soldier brushed the dust off his light blue Master Sergeant's stripes and proudly walked down the regimental street. As the dawn broke, tents came down, weapons were cleaned, and rations were prepared; three days' worth. The army would cross the Rapidan.

Jon's journey back to his combat unit took many paths, as he served in many capacities until he could be reassigned. He had been left to mire in bureaucratic red tape for the better part of four months, while the high command tried to sort out his muddled orders. He got frustrated and received permission to go to the Army of the Potomac headquarters to see what could be done.

"The manifest states that you died at Gettysburg, at the copse of trees, and your remains were reinterred in the National Cemetery. *Color Sergeant Ezra Holland killed in action, Gettysburg, 3 July, 1863,*" an overwhelmed adjutant told him. "The books don't lie."

Jon was incensed. "You can see for yourself, my good fellow, that I am a Sergeant Major, not a Color Sergeant. My name is Jon Holland, not Ezra Holland. He is my cousin. I paid my respects over the gravestone which bears his name. I am as alive as General Meade himself!"

"I can only go by what the paper says, son, and it says that you are dead."

"Well, then tear up the paper and write me a new one if it is that simple to foul things up. Are you going to make this right or do I have to go over your head?"

"I can't falsify records. Going over my head would only succeed in raising the ire of the officers. They don't have time for trivial matters with the spring campaign gearing up and all."

"There is nothing trivial about this, you buffoon. You can't falsify the record when I stand here in the flesh. Furthermore, if you notified my mother that I am dead, there will be hell to pay."

Jon was finally given his orders to return to his regiment, only because one of the officers at headquarters vouched for him. He did not hang around long enough for them to change their minds, beating a quick path back to the camp, just in time for the spring campaign.

The regimental headquarters was located at the end of an unkempt street. National, corps, and unit flags flew on poles above a tent to mark its location. Couriers galloped in, received orders, and then quickly left. The bevy of activity meant that the army was going on the offensive.

Jon approached the orderly at the tent entrance. The soldier saluted, withdrawing his hand sheepishly. He could not have been any older than sixteen. He must have lied about his age or maybe the recruiters were so desperate to get him into the ranks that they turned a blind eye to it.

Jon, the wise veteran of twenty-one years, scoped out the sentry's appearance. Everything was strictly regulation. His bonnie blues were spotless, the buckles and buttons impeccably polished. He was naïve, never seeing combat and anxious to engage the Rebs. The boy's makeup was in sharp contrast to Jon's tattered, ragtag appearance, threadbare uniform and brogans that had not been replaced in a year. He remembered when he was mustered in. That innocence was now gone.

"How many days have you been here?" Jon questioned the lad.

"I've been here a week, sir. I'm not used to the protocols yet, sorry."

"Where do you hail from, lad?" was Jon's reply.

"I live on a farm up in the Cherry Valley, in New York just along the Mohawk River."

"The Cherry Valley is a lovely place. I traveled there to deliver some horses to a smithy. Can you please pay my respects to the Colonel and tell him that I am here to report for duty?"

"And who should I be announcing to him, sir?"

"Sergeant Major Jon Holland returning from medical leave and anxious to get into the fight."

The orderly's eyes lit up. He stuttered, "It is an honor, you know, to meet you. You are a legend amongst the rank and file. Why, they have told me stories—"

Jon held up his hand to stop him and remind him of his orders. "The Colonel, if you please."

The orderly was summoned into the tent and waited for the Colonel to recognize him. The Bible-thumping officer, who was pouring over maps, looked up and let out a barrage of expletives, causing the young soldier to stutter. "Permission to speak, sir?"

"Confound it. What is it, son? Can't you see we are bloody busy carrying out a war here?"

"Sir, Sergeant Major Holland asks for permission to enter and speak with you."

"Well, what are you waiting for? See him in."

Jon entered the dour space. He removed his cap and waited for permission to approach. The officers were pleased to have him back. The efficiency of his company had dropped off in his absence. They were defiant brawlers, unfit for battle. He would discipline and motivate them.

Boston Charlie stood at the foot of the table with his quartermaster's charts and orders of march under his arm. He greeted Jon in his thick New England accent. "Welcome back, Jon."

"I am grateful for your timely intervention at the wall. It kept me from bleeding to death."

"It was nothing," Charlie replied. "You would have done the same for me, but you need to thank O'Reilly. That flaming Mick put his hands over the bullet holes to quell the blood flow. He knelt over you near twenty minutes, Jon. Not once did he relinquish the pressure."

The Colonel finished a few notes he was scribing on the map and turned his attention to Jon. "Well, look at what we have here. Mr. Holland, it is indeed a pleasure." Phelps was all about the business at hand, though. "As much as I would like to take a moment to get reacquainted, there is no time for small talk now, son. We march on the hour by order of the new General in Chief." The Colonel addressed the entourage of officers, "Gentlemen, we are crossing the Rapidan."

They had crossed the Rapidan several times before only to be driven back. But General U.S. Grant, the new commander, had a reputation as an aggressive brawler. His imaginative leadership could light a fire under the complacent eastern command so that this crossing would be the last.

The Colonel dismissed Jon. "Report to your company and prepare that rabble for the march. Tell O'Reilly to step aside. If that arrogant Mick gives you any of his Irish guff, shoot him."

Shannon had earned his Sergeant's stripes, despite numerous trips to the brig, because he was a relentless, fearless combatant. Jon understood why the company had been lacking discipline. O'Reilly could not discipline himself, let alone the one hundred men he helped to command.

"Get that company in good order, Holland, or there will be hell to pay. Am I understood?"

"Yes sir, I'll do my best." Jon saluted. "Permission to leave, sir?" Jon picked up his gear as the commanding officer flippantly waved and went back to his maps. The Sergeant Major patted the sentry on the shoulder. "Point me in the direction of Company A, son."

"It's the one surrounded by the provost guard. They are under house arrest."

Things must really be bad! Jon knew he would have to immediately enter the fight, but did not suspect that the scuffle would be with his own men. He sighed and loaded his pistol. As he sauntered down the company street, he was accosted by the sentry.

"Sir, sir, please wait!"

The Master Sergeant tried to get him to relax. "What is your name, son?"

The young man panted, "Cayle Johannsen, sir. Begging your pardon, but I have an order for the provost commander. It relieves him of his duties. I know, shouldn't have read it."

"You had better learn your place, young man," was Jon's harsh reprimand.

The lad cowered. "I am sorry, sir."

"Make it so, and stop calling me sir." Jon fumbled with the note. "Be gone with you, lad, before I have to teach you a stern lesson. Hey! Straighten that uniform, soldier." Pausing briefly, "And for God's sake, be careful." He surmised that the boy was too much like him in a younger day.

The company street was a reflection of the disorderly state of affairs. Garbage was strewn everywhere, the huts were falling down, and the men were unkempt. They sat idly by playing cards and gambling over cockfights. They were not prepared for battle. One of the bravest and most decorated companies of the regiment had deteriorated into nothing more than a mob. As Jon mulled over how he would intercede, he noticed an envelope lying in the mud. He picked it up and placed it in his breast pocket, not bothering to examine it. He had bigger things to worry about.

A trooper on horseback pointed a carbine at Jon's head. "State your business, Sergeant Major."

"I have written order from Colonel Phelps to report to this company for assignment."

The trooper removed his gauntlet and bent down to glance at the order. "Follow me to provost headquarters. You'll find Colonel Monroe inside. Don't stand on formality. Go right in."

Jon lingered at the opening to watch the trooper berate a malingerer. He did not recognize the man, but acknowledged his kind: a bummer or malcontent. As he entered the tent, he was overcome by the stench of cigar smoke and whiskey. Several cavalry officers sitting at a table, laughed at a foul joke they had played on an orderly. They stopped their banter to see who had entered.

A brash Colonel sat in the corner of the room with his feet propped up on a saddle cradled. He took a puff on his cigar and then placed his feet on the floor. He pushed his Hardy hat back on his head and spoke to Holland, "What brings you to this ragtag company of malcontents, boy?"

Jon answered, "I have a written order from Colonel Phelps to rejoin this company, sir."

"Phelps is a Bible preaching madman. Why would he order anyone to join this outfit?"

"Begging your pardon sir, but—" Jon was interrupted in mid-sentence.

"Spare me the speech, boy, and bring me the order."

Jon complied, stumbling over the boots of a soldier who lay on the dirt floor behind the Colonel's trunk. A groan emanated from the body. A set of Sergeant's stripes was visible on the sleeve of his waistcoat. Jon could not see the trooper's face, but suspected he was drunk.

The Colonel took a swig of whiskey and laughed, "Kick him aside. That Irishman lives in the bottom of the bottle. He is nothing but a nuisance to me, but I tolerate him out of pity."

O'Reilly! Jon had the urge to roust him, but resisted. He handed the note to the Colonel.

"Shoot, I am more than happy to oblige them. Gentlemen, we have been relieved of our duty by the Bible thumper. I think that calls for a round of drinks."

Jon pressed the Colonel, "Sir, if you could indulge me. With your gracious assistance, I think I can get this mob back into reasonable fighting trim so they can join the march."

The Colonel mocked him, "Gentlemen, this lowly Sergeant Major thinks that he can discipline this horde of unbridled rabble. Are we to assume that you are the savior?"

"Sir, I do not mean to offend you, but I know what makes them tick. You want to join the advance and I can get you there quicker if you will agree to assist me."

"I have been relieved from this duty soldier," was the Colonel's curt remark. "What on earth would make me want to stay for one moment and help you?"

Jon had an instant reply, "If we are going to whoop General Lee, then we need every able-bodied soldier at the front. I will sweeten the pie to your liking with some contraband."

The Colonel was intrigued. "All right, what do you have in mind, mister?"

Jon laid out a simple plan to restore order to the company. The Colonel agreed to assist, but under a few of his own conditions. He and Jon worked out the details and shook hands to seal the deal. "I'll have your troopers in the field by sunrise or I will double our wager."

The Colonel chided him, "We will see about that, Sergeant

Major." Flicking his spent cigar onto the ground, he exhaled smoke into Jon's face. "We will certainly see."

Jon waved off an offer of a drink. "My first order of business is to sober up that sorry excuse for a soldier lying there on the floor. With your permission, sir, I'll take him off of your hands."

Jon's method for sobering up O'Reilly was unconventional; however, it proved immediate and effective. He had one of the troopers tie a rope around Shannon's feet and secure it to the pommel of his saddle. Jon figured that a form of land-bound keelhauling was just what the doctor ordered.

O'Reilly's limp, intoxicated body was dragged out of the Colonel's tent into the morass on the company byway. The trooper's horse galloped briskly, tossing O'Reilly about like a ragdoll. He cursed at the trooper with a string of Gaelic expletives as he futilely tried to free himself. Shannon bounced by the cheering company screaming bloody murder. On the second pass by the headquarters, the trooper turned the corner and headed for the parade ground. The men, amused by O'Reilly's demise, followed closely behind. The more reluctant soldiers were herded at gunpoint, making sure that everyone in Company A was in attendance for the muster.

The trooper cut O'Reilly loose from the saddle, but did not bother to stop the horse. He tumbled at the feet of the members of his command who kicked him and rebuked him as he lay in the mud.

The mounted troopers lined up in front of the ragtag band of men, carbines loaded and at the ready. Monroe commanded the squad to shoot to kill if any of the men got out of line. A groan of protest was quickly quelled with a pistol shot fired over their heads. "This Company has been the bane of my existence. My boys should be fighting the Rebs, instead we are assigned to house sit you hoi polloi. In less than an hour the army will march. I intend to be at the van."

He fidgeted with his Colt Navy revolver. "I have been ordered to restore discipline, using whatever means necessary. Since you have failed to take orders or police your own, you will now be dealt with severely. I think I'll shoot the lot of you." The officer dismounted his horse and etched a line in the Virginia soil with his saber. As he passed O'Reilly, he kicked him aside. "We have provided you with spades to dig a trench along this line. I suggest you have at it."

The members of the company, who might be digging their own graves, protested. To quell them, Colonel Monroe callously shot one of the soldiers in the leg. Extreme breeches of conduct called for extreme measures of discipline in a war zone. "I've been itching to do that for a long time." He cocked his pistol with the palm of his hand. "Anyone else care to challenge me?"

When the trench was done, Shannon tossed his spade at the Colonel's feet. His Irish blood was boiling. "I won't go down without a fight and I will not be treated like a bleeding criminal."

"We will not tolerate mutiny in Father Abraham's army, you bloody Mick," the Colonel chortled. "Make peace with your maker, O'Reilly." He ordered his troopers into action, "On my command! Make ready!" Carbines were cocked and brought to the ready position. "Aim!"

Fifty rifles were lowered into firing position and pointed at the cowering soldiers. Then, a solitary figure emerged from behind the nearest hut, a carbine in one hand and Old Glory fluttering from a staff in the other. The man's appearance momentarily halted the execution.

"Let's not be too hasty, Colonel. Dead soldiers are no good to me, so fall in lads and let me see if we can change the Army's thinking on this matter."

"May God be praised," Shannon uttered, as a grand huzzah rose from the ranks.

Jon forced back a smile. He knew that with a little persuasive coaxing, he would have them in fighting form. "With your permission, Colonel, I would like to address the men."

"Be my guest, Mr. Holland, but if they get out of hand I will be forced to shoot the lot of them and bury them where they lay. Stand down, gentlemen, but be at the ready."

The troopers could see the other commands moving off toward the fords and bridges. Their horses pawed the dirt or snorted their impatience. The men twisted in their saddles and adjusted their accoutrements. They were exhausted by the shenanigans of this company of riffraff. They had been promised a place in the van of the reorganized cavalry. Their new role was not just to screen the flanks, serve as recon forces, or provide escort. Now they would be charged with disruptive operations behind enemy lines and the destruction of Stuart's vaunted Rebel cavalry.

"You can rejoin this distinguished fighting unit, get into combat shape, and accompany the regiment to the front, where we will whoop the Rebs. Or, you can be shot." Jon paused for effect. "Rally with me around the flag to save our union of states. Past indiscretions will be forgotten and we will proudly fight and die beside our brothers, leaving our fate in the hands of God."

Addie enthusiastically fell in behind the flag. He placed an affectionate hand on Jon's shoulder, as others reluctantly followed. The Sergeant Major kept his eyes affixed on Shannon. If he reneged, the deal would be sealed. He knew that Shannon had been humiliated, so he broke the tension. "Stand by my side, Shannon. Together we can restore glory to the regiment."

Shannon wiped the mud from his jaw and turned to spit blood in the trench. He walked slowly toward his lifelong friend, grabbed the flag, and stood at his right shoulder. He appeared disgusted, but in reality, he was relieved. He knew that the company's demise was related to his inability to command respect. Although he could fight with the best of them, he did not have what it takes to make sound leadership decisions. Jon had saved face for him.

In a few minutes, all but five men had rejoined the company. Colonel Monroe turned in his saddle. "And what shall be the fate of the rest, Mr. Holland?"

Jon hoped it would have not come to this. He had underestimated the disdain that the five drafted members of the squad had for the war. The good Lord would have had trouble managing them. He contemplated the situation for a moment and then whispered a reply to Colonel Monroe.

The five malcontents were lined up in the trench. Their hands were bound and eyes blindfolded. A solemn prayer was quoted from a pocket Bible Monroe had in his saddle bag.

"They are good men, Jonny," was Shannon's plea. "Samuel there is from the village not a day's walk from your farm. He joined us while you were gone."

Jon had just about enough. "Enough of your bellyaching, Shannon, so stow it. They have chosen their fate and you have chosen yours. If we are to fight together, then we must be willing to die together."

Monroe glanced over at Jon and a confident nod assured him of his only recourse. At the command, *"Fire"*, a volley was loosed, filling the air with smoke and lead.

The foot soldiers gasped in disbelief. As the smoke cleared, they observed the five men in various states of shock. One had fainted from the anxiety. One was on his knees begging for mercy. The other three stood defiantly. The volley had been fired over their heads and the affair was over. The five malcontents were put under arrest and sent to the brig to await court-marshal.

Jon and Shannon saluted the approaching officers and turned command of the company over to newly Brevetted Captain Greene. He was a recent West Point grad who had just arrived. Due to a shortage of officers, he was raised in rank immediately. He accepted the command with vigor, directing Holland and O'Reilly to get the men and camp cleaned up and ready for drill.

Monroe shook Jon's hand. "Well done, Mr. Holland. I had my doubts, but you know how to inspire confidence. I may be a little rough around the edges, but shooting an entire company is not my idea of how to impose discipline." He looked toward the river as long blue columns of soldiers waded across the fords to invade Southern soil. "Any time you would like to join my outfit, Sergeant Major, with the Colonel's permission of course, you are welcome. We can use good men like you in the Cavalry to help bring this miserable affair to an abrupt end."

"Thank you, sir, but I am fondly attached to these farm boys." Jon turned to Pritchard. "I knew I could count on you, Captain. I assume I will be paying for your generosity for quite some time?"

Pritchard smiled. "Well, Jon, this one is on the U.S. Army, compliments of Colonel Phelps."

The teetotaler, Phelps, interjected, "There are times in life when one must put aside his convictions for the greater good. This is certainly one of them and it has reaped blessed rewards. The good Lord has overlooked my momentary weakness on the matter." Phelps handed Monroe a case of Kentucky Bourbon and a rolled-up copy of a Horace Greeley *New York Tribune,* carefully wrapped around a cache of cigars.

Monroe tied the small wooden crate onto his saddle pommel, carefully cradling it as if it were a newborn baby. He saluted, turned his horse sharply, and galloped off into the twilight.

"Well, Mr. Holland," Phelps said. "God has blessed the regiment. I will make sure that the chaplain remembers this day in his sermon. Your marching orders will be forwarded to you by week's end. I expect this company will be up to handling them with spit and polish."

Jon spoke, "Colonel Phelps, sir, I have one last request. The young orderly, Private Johannsen, can I get him reassigned to this command?"

"What would possess you to put that wet behind the ears young buck in harm's way?"

"That boy has grit, sir. I would like to take him under my wing."

"Consider it done, Sergeant Major. Now, get that rabble into fighting trim."

There was no time for Jon to reminisce with his comrades. He found his battered friend sleeping on a cot in the hut they shared. He drew a blanket up around Shannon's shoulders and settled against his pack to get some sleep. Before he slipped into unconscious repose, he remembered the envelope he had found. He withdrew it and brushed away the red dust. The hallmark in the upper right hand corner was that of the U.S. government, embossed with an eagle. Much to his surprise, it was addressed to him. He turned it over to crack the wax seal.

FIELD HEADQUARTERS–ARMIES OF THE UNITED STATES–ARMY OF THE POTOMAC
LIEUTENANT GENERAL ULYSSES S. GRANT

By order of the Commander in Chief, Sergeant-Major Jon Holland, for his distinguished bravery and leadership under fire, will be commissioned with the brevetted field rank of First Lieutenant, on this day April 25, 1864.

Ulysses S. Grant — Lieutenant General

Chapter 35

Waltzing with Uncle Bobby

The army was gone, but the evidence of their encampment above the Rapidan still lingered. The stench from a thousand latrines tainted the spring air. Hundreds of grave markers memorialized the resting places of those who did not survive the harsh winter. The landscape was austere, raped of its natural resources. There was a deathly silence save for the bark of a lone drill sergeant, the yelp of a dog, or the chirp of a bird who had returned from its winter haven.

The company drilled relentlessly under the youthful Captain Greene. He let Lieutenant Holland and Sergeant O'Reilly handle the brunt of the training. Jon provided the encouragement and Shannon the chiding. When sober, he had proven to be a strong task master. The grunts responded to their tenacious drilling and unforgiving discipline and were soon in fighting trim.

The spring Overland Campaign opened when the Army of the Potomac advanced through the area of the old Chancellorsville battleground. Combat came on unexpectedly on May 5 of '64 as the Army of Northern Virginia, although severely outnumbered, suddenly turned on the Yanks in the thick hardwood groves. The ghastly fighting was brutal in the Wilderness, as the two beleaguered armies fought desperately to control the tactical advantage.

General Grant sat on a stump and whittled for a better part of the first day of the battle, occasionally receiving and giving orders, while profusely smoking several dozen cigars. He trusted the instincts of his field commanders and interfered only when necessary. Many people perceived Grant's command approach as one of complacency, drunken incompetence, or lack of care. Others knew that this was the command style that he had cleverly implemented in the West.

By the end of the first day of battle, both armies found themselves battered. Darkness brought an end to the fighting with sporadic skirmishes breaking out along the lines for the next few days, but this would only be the start of a horrific summer dance of death.

Lee discretely moved off to the right to concentrate his forces, protect his lines of supply, and keep his troops between Grant and Richmond. The Army of the Potomac did not retreat like they had in the past, but sidled to the southeast, as they tried to get between Lee and the Confederate capital. With this shadowing movement, the waltz with Uncle Bobby had begun in earnest.

Grant continued to press the attack. The citizens of the North were appalled by the lengthy casualty lists and callously referring to him as *The Butcher.* President Lincoln supported his strategic plan to attack the South on all fronts, hoping that the war would end by the New Year.

While the Battle of the Wilderness raged, Captain Greene ordered his command to join the reserve regiments, many of them Negro. The march to the front was brisk, but the warm air and the extended exercise invigorated the troops. They laughed and joked as they traversed the country roads toward a place called Spotsylvania Courthouse. This optimistic air of enthusiasm was quickly made somber, as the troopers crossed into the Wilderness. The malodorous scent of burned and rotting flesh brought them swiftly back to the realities of war. No matter how often they had been exposed to it, they never could get used to the gruesome nature of the carnage.

Captain Greene lost his dignity when he came upon the macabre corpse of a soldier who had been burned beyond recognition. The fire had frozen him in a horrified pose, propped up against a charred tree, his arm extended into the air as if reaching out to God. His mouth was open, sculpted there in mid-scream, as he succumbed to the raging inferno.

Addie, and others who were less sensitive, laughed at Greene's inability to cope with the chilling specter. He ignored them, thinking that they were cruel, cold-hearted men.

Shannon knelt next to a wounded soldier, carelessly left by the roadside. The man was worn to a frazzle, but still alive. O'Reilly shared his water with him and then called for a surgeon.

Next to the wounded soldier, lay another man. His bowels were opened to the heavens, festered with crawling vermin. His milky, glazed-over eyes gazed up in a blank stare toward the heavens. He had been hastily buried, but his remains had been uncovered by God's other creatures. Jon covered him with a blanket, while he masked his nose with a kerchief. He thrust the soldier's bayoneted rifle into the Virginia soil to temporarily mark the grave. He nibbled on some hardtack and then ordered the company back into the road to resume the march.

Jon walked next to Captain Greene, who struggled to sustain the air of decorum required by an officer. "It takes a hardened man to accept all of this senseless killing. You can't dwell on it or it will eat you up. I've experienced the insanity that comes from battle malaise, *Soldier's Heart.* It can be worse than death, Captain, so you need to let it go." He paused to think about his own battle with the demons. "I'll bet that they didn't teach you any of this at West Point!"

Grant waltzed with Uncle Bobby for the rest of the year, continuing to use up both armies. He finally drove the Rebs into the siege trenches that surrounded Petersburg and Richmond.

Addie Jones was killed at Spotsylvania, a crack shot from a sharpshooter struck him between the eyes as he climbed over the parapet during the attack on the hotly contested Muleshoe.

Shannon was given the deadly honor of carrying the colors at North Anna. The fearless Color Sergeant met the fate of many of his predecessors when a bounding cannonball severed his right leg below the knee.

Captain Greene was killed at Cold Harbor, as he led a fruitless charge against a fully entrenched enemy. His body lay on the rampart in the hot sun for the better part of two days.

Neither general would concede the field until Grant succumbed and pulled back. Overcome by emotion for his mistakes at Cold Harbor, the General mourned privately with quiet tears.

Jon suffered minor wounds during these brutal engagements and finally settled into a hollow life in the trenches. He had learned that

Josias Weed was wounded in the attack at the Crater, caught with other Colored troops in a fruitless charge across its abyss. He visited Josias in the hospital to give him aid and comfort. "Is there anything I can do to console you, Josias?"

"My, my, if I didn't know better I would think that the ghosts of the netherworld have risen up right here before my very eyes. I am fit as a fiddle, Sergeant Major Holland...begging your pardon, Lieutenant, and suspect that I will be back in the trenches before you can spit."

The doctors told Jon that Weed's wounds were severe. "What possessed you to sign up for the Colored Infantry? You could have lived out the war driving those blasted mules."

"Them recruiters said they weren't going to take me because of my age and all, but I wouldn't take no for an answer. If I am going to have my freedom outright, then I am going to fight for it." He smiled. "I understand them quota-bound fellas. I slipped them a sawbuck and they turned a blind eye to my age. The boys in the regiment elected me as a sergeant just like you, Jonny."

"Can I help you to sit up, Josias?"

"Don't you fret over me. That confounded Reb I was wrestling with in the bottom of that crater ran me through twice. He had the anger of the devil in his eyes. I will never forget the hatred I saw in the deepest hollows of his soul when he plunged that bayonet into me."

"You are a brave and honorable man, Josias, but I am afraid the war is over for you. Just maybe, when we win, some of that racist hatred will go away."

"Shoot, these wounds ain't nothing compared to the scars the Bosses put on me. Give me a few weeks and I'll be fit as a fiddle. I'm going back to make sure it ends to my liking."

Jon did not want to discourage the effervescent teamster, for his conviction to the cause of fighting for his own freedom was inspiring. "I suspect that you will, Josias."

"You look me up when this war is over, Boss Holland, and we will commiserate."

"I would like that, but you needn't call me Boss. You are a freedman and we are equals in the eyes of the Lord." Jon changed the subject. "Have I told you about my herd of horses?"

Josias glanced up at Jon with an inquisitive, but intrigued look.

"They are a carefully bred line of Arabians passed down from generation to generation. Legend says that my Indian ancestor could coax a horse to do anything. And, she could sweet-talk most anyone, or so the story goes. They say I have the same gift. It sounds crazy, but the horses speak to me and I can will them to do extraordinary things. Be that as it may, I could use a helping hand tending to them. You have a masterful way with the four-legged critters, Josias. How about looking me up after the war and we can make a go of raising them together?"

"That is a powerful offer, sir, but I cain't make any promises. I've got to venture back down south and find my family. I am determined to bring them together, even if it kills me. If the spirit moves me I'll sidle up north to look you up. Hear tell, the Hudson Valley is a glorious place."

"It is God's country, Josias." The two men shook hands and then embraced. "It's a deal." Jon checked his watch. "I need to get back to my command."

"That is a mighty fine looking timepiece. I am taken by the image of the horse inside."

Jon sat back down on the bed. "I think I have a moment for a story you would appreciate." And so, Jon began to tell the tale of the fateful watch and the mysterious horse carved inside.

Josias hung on his every word. When Jon began to leave, as the sun was setting over the riverside, he questioned him, "Tell me something, do you believe in all of that hocus pocus?"

"If a man has the right will," Jon replied, "he can do extraordinary things. Driven men can go to great lengths to change the outcomes of life. You and my ancestors have proven that the essence of life lies within our own fiery souls. Sometimes we just take different paths to find it." He took a deep breath. "The people who handed down the watch understood that. It took a war and a number of chance encounters with people from all walks of life to bring me to that place."

Josias understood. "Over the horizon lies a host of dreams that are yet to be fulfilled."

Jon's friends from the regiment were now all gone. His spiritual resolve was challenged by the continued horror of the war and the fear that he was going mad, but he forged ahead.

An otherworldly warrior with a fiery face haunted him in his sleep. *The red and the white serpents will battle for your soul, disfiguring the land and altering the hearts of its people. When the raging vipers have succumbed to each other's will, leaving a wake of destruction in their path, a powerful light will guide you toward a new renaissance of enlightenment.*

Jon had a brush with death at Five Forks when a spent piece of a cannonball rendered him unconscious. He had bent over to help a fallen comrade and miraculously avoided the full fury of the shrapnel. The injury took him out of the fight, but he was back in the ranks at dawn. On that fateful morn, his tour of duty abruptly ended at Saylor's Creek when he received a ghastly saber wound to his knee during desperate hand-to-hand fighting. The defiant stand by the Rebs was a last-ditch effort by General Lee to extricate his army from the Union pincers and join forces with General Johnston in the Carolinas.

Jon had been seriously wounded four times during the war, but was grateful to be alive. Every day he clung to life by fortifying his relationship with the men around him and searching his soul for renewed faith. He was determined not to let the attrition of battle keep him from fulfilling his dreams. He had vowed that if he could see this horrific struggle to the end, he would make it his mission to change the way men valued life. His promised service to his nation was now fulfilled.

Chapter 36

Two Suns Rising

She sat on a bunk in the longhouse and wove a tapestry of beads upon a freshly tanned deer skin. A fire in a shallow pit lit the space with a glow of soft light. She leaned forward to get a look at a horse she had meticulously crafted. A young squaw approached her cautiously.

Katarina Morning Star spoke softly, "I am sorry to disturb you, Two Suns, but I am deeply troubled. I seek your wisdom on the matter of our transformation as a clan."

Two Suns took Katarina's hand. "Come sit by me, child, and tell me what it is that vexes you."

The undernourished woman with dark hair that hung loose about her shoulders pulled up her tunic so she could sit down. "My father is deeply disturbed by our sudden migration into the deep recesses of the forest, away from the comforts our people. He does not want to challenge Chief Ten Hands, for he feels he will lose face. My father is a proud man who believes it to be futile to put up a false charade that we can somehow overcome our oppression."

Two Suns was sympathetic. "I suspect that your desire is to stay with the clan, but you do not want to abandon your family or disrespect your father. Ten Hands has chosen to forge a different path, but will hold no grudge toward those who wish to stray from it. His journey is one that is contrary and I have chosen to follow that course, for it will preserve our heritage and protect our sovereignty. A shadow has passed over our brothers and sisters, obscuring the light that leads them to the truth. Your father may have unknowingly stepped into that shadow."

Katarina was absorbed by Two Suns' words. "My heart guides me to follow my father, but my head leads me to believe that I must stay with the clan. Help me to settle this so that my father will see the light as I do and not be shamed in the eyes of his brothers."

Two Suns brushed Katarina's hair from her face. "Your father is scarred by the troubles of an uncertain future. He has lost hope and refuses to conform to ideas that are new and vibrant."

Katarina began to cry, for the pressure of her decision weighed heavily upon her young soul.

Two Suns wiped the tears from Katarina's gaunt cheek. "You must eradicate the pain in your heart so that you can think with a lucid mind. Will you live in the villages where the white men have altered the face of our nation or here in the wilderness where we live like it has been foretold to us? You are a vibrant woman who can help us mold our future, but I cannot be the one who decides your fate. Whichever path you choose, your father and I will respect you for your courage."

Two Suns handed a bone needle to the young woman. "You must take up bead work, Katarina. It clears your mind so you can reason without fear or reservation. Here, you try it."

Katarina graciously accepted the skin and with some guidance she was soon weaving the beads into a detailed image of a crude bird. She smiled as she transformed the face of the hide.

Two Suns praised her, "You have a gift that should not be left to idle hands. Let us make it a habit to work together so you can learn the skill and I can have someone to converse with."

Katarina sighed. "Although I fear that my father will disown me, it is better that I stay with the clan. I do not respect the white men, for they do not respect me. The spirituality the Great Peacemaker's vision is emblazoned on the sun and I shall follow its path or die defending it."

"You have made a wise choice. Outwardly, your father will renounce you for choosing a different path, but inwardly he will honor you for your courage to step out of the shadows into the light. You must go to him and share your decision. Tell him the story about the Celestial Twins. It will make him understand why you have chosen to take the path less traveled."

Two Suns kissed Katarina on the forehead. "Do not fear, my child, for I will watch over you. Now go, your father awaits. Return to me when the pain in his eyes is too great for you to bear. We will finish the tapestry so your mind will be distracted and your heart will be healed."

Chapter 37

Footprints in the Sand

She was born in the autumn of the year under the veil of a blood-orange harvest moon. It was at the time of the grand solar eclipse. The air was crisp and the smell of wood smoke and fallen leaves mingled with the sweet fragrances of the virgin forest. As the two celestial orbs crossed each other's path, the sky was darkened, and then, as if renewing itself, the ephemeral night that had marked their existence was overshadowed by the revealing rays of resplendent transformation. At that instant, a newborn baby's silken voice rang through the hollows of the forest.

Legend alluded to a mystical child with piercing eyes, bronze skin, and ebony hair, born at the time of the amalgamation of the waning moon and rejuvenating sun. Two Suns, Tekeni Karahkwa, entered the world under a mystifying shroud. As the deity breathed life into her, cries of joy echoed through the heavens for she would lay down footprints in the sand to lead the clan out of darkness.

Two Suns' Mohawks were a resilient people. Their Algonquin rivals feared them so much that they presumed that they were barbarous man-eaters. Legend foretold of fierce Mohawk warriors who ate their kill to celebrate their victories. But in reality, they were a gentle, agrarian people of innate intelligence and imposing stature. Their tribal name was Kanien'keha':ka or People of the Place of the Flint. They were the highly-respected gatekeepers of the eastern boundaries of the Iroquois Nation, holding a place of reverence in the greater order of that profound alliance.

Two Suns was destined to alter the clan's assimilation into a world influenced by migrating Europeans, trying to hold on to their fragile heritage. She was tattooed in the womb with that birthright and others would follow in her footprints on the path to a new tribal order. As she matured, her mother, Hateya, (oddly translated Footprints in the Sand) would craftily teach her.

Hateya was a tall and stately woman whose age masked her once vibrant appearance. High cheek bones, soft dark eyes, a well-formed nose, and a noble chin marked her mysterious face. Her hair was parted down the middle, neatly braided into precise rows wrapped in white leather and decorated with falcon feathers. They framed her face, accentuating her firmly set, square jaw.

Hateya preached, "My daughter, you will be the vessel that transports the chronicles of our tribe. When your flesh has withered, it will be your spirit that will lead through your offspring." She would pause to allow her daughter to absorb what she had said and then questioned her until she could repeat every detail. These sessions were often long and tedious, but they exacted an uncanny determination and a relentless drive in Two Suns to seek knowledge and act wisely.

Hateya continued, "The Mohawk people, under the leadership of the mystical Chief Hiawatha, Ayenwatha, with guidance from the Great Peacemaker, Deganawida, helped to form the Iroquois Confederacy, People of the Longhouse. This bond now consists of six nations living under one code of governance. This circle of trust amongst our brothers and sisters binds us together into an alliance that marshals our laws, controls our trade, and guides our warriors." She paused momentarily to pick up an arrow. "Take this arrow, Two Suns, and break it."

Two Suns questioned her mother, "Mother, why should I destroy the arrow so callously?"

Hateya was patient with the child, "We sacrifice one arrow to teach you many lessons."

The child grasped the arrow firmly and then cracked the wooden shaft across her knee.

"You have easily destroyed the arrow, child, as it stands against you, alone and afraid. Now take from the quiver six arrows and break them in a bundle as you did the first."

"The sacrifice of one for the good of many is understandable, mother, but to destroy six more arrows is a senseless, selfish, and wasteful act."

The squaw just nodded toward the arrows as a command to proceed.

Two Suns gripped the arrows tightly and brought them down hard upon her knee. Try as she might, she could not lay the arrows to waste.

"Tell me what you have learned from this experience, daughter."

The child always contemplated things before answering. "What you are trying to teach is clear. The single arrow stands alone, weakened by its independence. It easily breaks under the pressures of my hand. But the six arrows, although each remarkably different in its own makeup, stand strong when they are bound together. I cannot break them, for they are stalwart and filled with resolve."

Hateya was pleased. "The Haudenosaunee people are stronger when they act in alliance. See here, on this woven Tree of Life, the eagle carries in his talon the arrows of the Six Nations, a symbol of our boundless commitment to each other. So long as we stand together as a family or a nation, we are invincible. You need to heed this lesson, for it holds the key to your future."

The curious child would always challenge her mother. "Will I not first and foremost be a Mohawk, mother, bound to the people who reside under my roof?"

"The people of the Wolf Clan are bound to the heritage of the Mohawk tribes, like those of the Turtle or Bear Clans. Someday you will lead this clan, carrying on the name and traditions that we value. But you will be challenged to put the good of the clan aside for the betterment of all of the people who reside in the circle under the branches of the Tree of Life. As long as your convictions remain true, you shall be guided by the spirits to choose wisely."

The child asked, "And what if those choices impede upon the sanctity of my family or those whom I love? Shall I then break the sacred bond?"

"These are questions that shall remain with you until you grow old. I cannot guide you in matters of the heart. For those answers, you will have to suffer the pains of scrutiny. A mysterious shadow lingers on the horizon, seeking to break our alliance. I fear that the small cracks in the arrows will eventually erode into vast lesions, drawing us apart and breaking our will. The landscape upon which we now live will be altered and your decisions as a woman and a tribal leader will be influenced by factors out of your control."

She looked into her daughter's eyes. "Take heed to remain one step ahead of change, for it is inevitable, like the turning of the seasons. Take heed to be wiser, more cunning, and more astute than your foe. Take heed to craft your own destiny, not allowing others to thrust theirs upon you. It is for you to mold the future to your liking, while protecting the values that have been our foundation. They are the rock upon which you shall always stand."

Two Suns did not fully understand her mother's testimonies. She was content to be a child, to work in the fields, to play, and to learn her craft. She was not fully invested in the power of her purpose, but she would soon learn that she would carry the staff of preservation for her kin.

Chapter 38

Yakohsa:tens

Two Suns began to grow into a woman of immense stature. She garnered respect for her warrior-like leadership, wisdom, and uncanny foresight; moreover, her mystifying personal allure attracted people to her. She was tall, developing her feminine form early on in her teen years. Her mysterious eyes hid her inner fire, as she skillfully controlled her emotions. She had dark, flowing hair, always nestled under a cap or simply bound in a single braid. She possessed her father's rounded face and her mother's high cheek bones, which accentuated her enigmatic eyes. As attractive as she was, it was her intellect and innate savvy that stood her apart from the others.

The braves postured to be her suitor. She fended off their advances with coy or dismissive glances or challenged them with her sharp wit and bravery. She had become a fierce warrior, trained secretly by her father. He would whisk her off to the forest, away from the domestic duties of a squaw to teach her the ways of the warrior world. Alongside of her brother, Yellow Elk, she would be asked to endure the most grueling physical, mental, and emotional challenges.

Hateya would admonish the chief fiercely, "You teach her things that a woman need not know. It is not in her destiny to fight like a brave or think like a man."

"Hateya, you fret too much about things that do not concern you. Our daughter carries a great weight upon her shoulders. If she is to bear that burden, then she has to be privy to all things. Trust me, dear wife, for I believe that she will someday carry within her the strength she garners from both of her parents. This alone will solidify her prominence in the eyes of the world."

Ten Hands had been chosen as the chief by a conclave of the principle women of the tribe. He had proven to be fearless in battle and possessed uncanny prudence that many would argue could alter the future. He was a tall warrior with a rounded face, broad nose, and wise eyes that seemed to speak to people when they looked into them. His salt-and-pepper hair was cropped into a scalp lock that was carefully adorned with ten eagle's feathers aligned in a row. He seldom wore any clothing save for a loin cloth, only donning a robe when the weather was too cold to bear. His chest was pierced with bear claws and his neck was covered by an ornate silver gorget. He was a judicious man whose appearance was imposing and his wisdom intimidating to lesser men.

Ten Hands would teach his daughter. "If you are to lead, then you must understand many things. Only then will you have the savvy and fortitude to overcome the most grueling challenges. It is not enough for you to be the beautiful, wise, and loving bearer of children. You must also possess the strong will and hardened heart of a warrior."

Two Suns resisted his training at first, finding that it was contrary to what other squaws were doing. She soon saw the wisdom in it. She could run like the wind, deftly handle weapons, and live in the forest for weeks with nothing more than the clothing on her back. Her transformation was rapid and she ascended to a status that no other woman had ever achieved.

One day, the quirky, overbearing Scotsman Graham arrived in camp. He was a jovial sort that the braves admired. He would willingly trade trinkets or sparingly delve out whiskey, if the spirit moved him. He fancied Two Suns, but she detested his European lineage and manipulated him.

While he was trading with the chief, Graham mustered up the courage to speak to her, "You are a pretty thing and it behooves me to present you with a gift from my country across the sea." He removed his prized Glengarry Cap and offered it to Two Suns. He had seen her admire it from afar, and now, he hoped that if he gifted it to her he could find a way into her cold heart.

She was overjoyed at the gesture, snatched it from his hand, and then placed it immediately upon her head. It would, for a very short time, be her most prized possession.

Graham expected something in return for his sacrifice, but was shunned by Two Suns (one of the many weaknesses that this young Mohawk leader had yet to overcome). Her selfishness and sense of personal worth would have to be tamed if she were to guide others. He let the incident go, for that was his way, but he continued to chase after a marriage contract for Two Suns' hand.

Ten Hands spoke frankly to Graham, "I do not wish to offend you, but my daughter's marriage will be to one of great physical, mental, and moral stature. He will arrive here harboring a sinister burden, but will be healed by living amongst us. In return, he will give us the gift of transformation. It is not yet revealed who this mysterious stranger is, but it is a certainty that it is not you."

Graham was offended, but understood. He had lived among the tribes long enough to know that they were driven by spiritual guidance. However, this setback did not deter him. So, in a last-ditch effort to buy her love, Graham showed up one blustery day tethering two fine horses. He spoke to a gathering of curious clan members, "I bring to you the most illustrious creatures on the face of the earth. They can carry you great distances, fight loyally with you in battle, and guide your heaviest plow. Let me introduce you, ladies and gentlemen of the wilderness world, to the horse."

Ten Hands was inspired by their presence, but it was Two Suns who immediately had an otherworldly bond with the majestic animals. "Father, it is meant to be that we accept this gift. These animals will bring us prosperity and enhance our might. Doesn't our fabled lore tell us that the horse, Yakohsa:tens, have mystical power? Do they not represent loyalty, love, devotion, and pride? If we are to be a powerful, solvent clan, then we need to possess the horse."

"It is true that the horse has supernatural powers, but is it practical to own such beasts in the deep recesses of the forest? They will only sap our resources and be of little use to us otherwise."

"I see a future where these animals will rule this land and make us a more powerful people. It would be a misstep not to succumb to Graham's generosity."

The chief contemplated the matter. "What will these stallions cost me, Graham?"

Graham's lips curled. "It will cost you your daughter's hand in marriage and nothing more."

"Even if you offered a herd of horses, I could not, would not relinquish her to you."

"Then what is it that you will offer, Chief? I dragged these nags kicking and hollering all of the way up this mountain. I would prefer not to haul them back down, if you catch my drift."

"I will offer you twenty pelts, a French calumet, and your pick of the lot of unwed women."

"You drive a hard bargain, sir. Forget the woman, for she will only be a burden to me. Throw in one of those new British firelocks and we can call this an even trade. Do we have a deal?"

The Iroquois were respected for their penchant to barter, telling mind altering tales to make a point and then skillfully coaxing their suitors into giving up something of value for a favor or a compromise. The negotiations of treaties were often lengthy affairs, drawn out over days or weeks due to the exacting process the Iroquois demanded when they bartered. The Mohawks had mastered the craft to perfection, usually getting the upper hand when the deal was said and done.

Ten Hands thrust his calumet into the earth, burying the hatchet of acceptance.

Graham nodded. "Although I can see that it troubles you, I suspect that you will not regret this deal. Those horses are bred from a rare, but distinct Arabian line. They will serve you well. Your clan and their offspring will beatify you for making such a prolific trade." Graham gathered up his prizes, not one to tarry too long in one place, and headed back down the mountain.

Two Suns called after him, "I shall be forever grateful to you, Yakohsa:tens," a term of endearment that identified him as The Horse, "for bringing to me this numinous treasure."

Graham was besotted by his nickname, but he knew that she would not turn him a blind eye.

Ten Hands presented the stallion to his son and the mare to his daughter. "You shall share the responsibility for the care, breeding, and training of these animals. This gift will foster a bond of trust between you. Do not fail me, for you will see my disappointment in my many tears."

Yellow Elk reluctantly accepted the gift. If he were going to be chief, then he did not have time to trifle with training a horse he could not expect to use in his overgrown, wilderness home.

Ten Hands saw his disappointment. "If you expect the braves to follow you into the teeth of the Underworld, then you must demonstrate an array of skills. Where you see a burden, I see an opportunity. Master the horse and the shadow of distrust that the warriors have will be lifted."

Two Suns, the impetuous one, spoke to the feisty horse in a whisper. A fire raged inside the mare, but she calmed at the sound of the squaw's ethereal voice. Two Suns sensed that she had discovered a unique gift. She was elated and gave her father a peck on the cheek.

"Mind you daughter, this animal represents the first test of your will. The mare will reveal the inner turmoil that you harbor in your heart. She will tempt you with anger, frustrate you with resolve, and motivate you with determination. The stronger of you will lead, the weaker will follow. Look deep into her soul, for there you will find the qualities you must have to make your mark upon this land. This horse is the testament to your future. Measure her passage well."

Two Suns needed little encouragement, for she immediately sensed a bond with the mystical horse. For now, her elation was the good medicine she needed to move forward with her legacy.

Chapter 39

Barkeaters and Maneaters

The dawn broke clear over the fog enshrouded lake, as Papineau rose from a restless sleep. It was brisk; for winter still lingered in the hollows. He breathed the pine-laden air and felt the chill emanating off of the water. He instinctively wrapped his greatcoat about him before carefully removing the vermin from his knotted hair.

The smoke from Balmond's fire wafted upward, tainting the cerulean blue sky. The impatient boatman challenged the woodsman. "I read in my younger days of enlightenment a passage from a poem that may move you to action. It was from a work called the *Divine Comedy. Midway upon the journey of our life, I found myself within a forest dark, for the straightforward pathway had been lost.* So, what shall it be, north toward certain death or south and west toward the truth?"

Papineau looked at Balmond inquisitively, while Graham just smiled.

"You didn't know that I was a scholar or fluent in several languages? There are many things you do not know about me and do not care to inquire about, too caught up in your own affairs."

Papineau was stirred by Balmond's eloquence. "You startle me with new revelations each day. Here I thought that you were a simple man, carefree and liberated. And now, on this of all days, you reveal to me the wisdom of a shaman. Will this folderol never end?"

Balmond inquired. "Care to eat, my friends? I have conjured up a fine bit of toasted trout."

Papineau was anxious to be on his way. "I shall pass. We have a long journey if we are to make the mountains by sundown. I wish to get started immediately."

Balmond smiled and threw the remains of the trout into the flames before he doused them with water. "Time is fleeting, Graham. Lead us toward the pathway of enlightenment."

The three men wasted little time. They boarded their crafts and coursed their way south. They passed under the guns of Fort Amherst at Crown Point, through the narrows, and on toward the masonry fortress at Ticonderoga. They managed to slip by a small fleet of ten-gun frigates quietly at rest in the depths of lake. Nobody on board seemed to take mind of them.

Graham beached his craft in an obscure cove, as Papineau questioned him, "What haven is this, Graham? There is no discernible footpath here."

"Through that undergrowth lays the path to your destiny, woodsman. You simply need to part the obstructive brush to open the door to your providence."

Papineau leapt from the canoe into the shallows and pulled it onto the rocky shoreline. He gathered his gear and then helped Balmond out of the vessel. Graham sat in his bateau, the lowered sail rustling in the breeze, as Balmond summoned him ashore. "Will you be joining us, Graham?"

"For now, I fancy life on the water. Besides, I have had my fill of that squaw who commands the clan up in that hollow. You will realize that she is a harpy who should not be trifled with."

Papineau thanked Graham. "You have served us well. I wish to repay you by offering up the canoe. Do with it as you will, but know this, it is a marked vessel, confiscated from a band of ruffians." He put his fist over his heart. "Until we meet again, I bid thee a noble farewell."

Graham put a bent finger to his cap and motioned for them to part the brush, as he reset his sail.

The men struggled to separate the thicket, tangled with brambles and shrub oaks. Papineau hacked away at the undergrowth with his mocotaugan to clear a suitable portal. The misfit friends ducked into the opening and disappeared from Graham's sight. Before too long, they reached a clearing where a well-worn footpath headed west up the mountain.

Balmond twitched from a bite of cold. "Why have you had a change of heart, woodsman?"

"There was a secretive message on the cold wind, as I awoke this morning. It told me that the answers to all of the questions that have haunted my life lay up there." He pointed to the high peaks that loomed above them. "Who am I to challenge the wisdom of the wind?"

The narrow path ran under a heavy cloak of trees into a hollow filled with wild blueberries, random patches of moss, or luxurious green ferns. The travelers traversed the undulating, rocky terrain in peaceful contemplation. They soon came upon an Indian camp nestled in the bottom of hidden woodland defile along a swiftly rushing stream. The haze from its campfires filled the forest with a surreal radiance, as the sun's beams filtered through the dense canopy of foliage.

From his vantage point on a hill, the woodsmen could see a herd of horses tethered to a picket line in the village. He saw painted symbols on their hind quarters, but nothing to indicate that they belonged to Dragoons. He was relieved, when suddenly, out of the thicket, a sentry appeared, brandishing a musket. Papineau knew he had been shadowing them. He followed the brave down into the defile as other warriors began to gather. He could not put Graham's story out of his mind, wondering if these were the people who had allegedly massacred the Anishinabe.

The Anishinabe, or Algonquin, as named by the French, had a fickle relationship with the Mohawks. At times, they were reluctant trading partners, but more often than not they were at war, struggling to balance their position of authority in the forest world. During the La Guerre de la Conquête or War of Conquest, the Mohawks came desperately close to extinction, less than five hundred strong. Their race was revived, as they built strong alliances with the other tribes of the Iroquois Confederacy and forged their trading relationship with the Dutch and British. These alliances were fragile, as the powerbase shifted in the region, altering the political landscape.

The Mohawks seemed different than the Indians Balmond had confronted in New France, although they did look remarkably like their ancient cousins, the Huron. They appeared to be docile, contrary to the Algonquin moniker, Man-eaters. Most of the warriors doffed the traditional bear grease, crested hair style or scalp lock, usually closely shaven on the sides. Some warriors wore the traditional cap, Kasto:'weh, adorned with three Eagle feathers extending upward and the identifying tribal symbol on the side to indicate their clan of origin. They were simply dressed: breechcloths, moccasins, and leggings covered with a tunic or robe. A few, however, wore attire they had obtained from the Europeans through trade or battle: waistcoats, military garb, knee breeches, and silk stockings. The clothing was decorated with beadwork or ribbon appliqués to enhance its personal aura. Weaponry varied: clubs, battle axes, or bows, but most carried muskets.

The warrior's faces and bodies had been artistically tattooed. These intricate symbols represented the good medicine that defined their beliefs, indicated their stature as warriors, and honored their exploits, kills, or captures. To Balmond, they were fearsome and intimidating

The path of their descent opened up into a clearing where a stockade of roughly hewn hemlock logs had been erected. The men trod over neatly groomed fields which during the summer contained crops like corn, squashes, and herbs. Drying game and fish hung from caches to cure.

A gaggle of gleeful children taunted Balmond, whose peculiar stature and fiery auburn beard were fodder for mockery. A group of teenage warriors, gathered around a campfire honing their weapons, laughed at him. They eyed him with arrogance, overconfidence, and sullen disdain.

At the center of the compound was a magnificent longhouse, approximately sixty feet in length. It was surrounded by several wigwams and log buildings. It was skillfully made of logs, woven branches, and hides, rounded on the top to shed the weather. The dwelling was rustically adorned with symbolic relics, hanging game, drying clothes, and tribal riches.

Papineau estimated that this was a community of about sixty souls. It was curious to him that this clan was isolated away from the principle villages or castles of Canajoharie, Osserneno, and Tionondogue. Those Mohawk River communities were centers of Mohawk tribal life.

The inside of the main dwelling was dark and smoky; the smells of drying meats, pungent herbs, simmering stews, and the stale mustiness of frequently used animal robes mixed with the odor of sweating human flesh. The walls were lined with bed spaces, stacked one on top of another to the ceiling. Cross-walls created compartments that two or more families could share.

Papineau could see a number of distinguished men and women gathered at the far end of the longhouse. He surmised that these were the elders, although some younger members of the tribe were present. The braves escorted them to the area where they waited to be acknowledged.

A furrow-faced warrior squatted at the center of the group. Several older women sat on either side of him. Papineau sensed an air of collegial governance, as they privately collaborated about the worth of the strangers. He eyeballed a prolific warrior standing behind the elders. He was as imposing in stature as the woodsman, an intimidating frown coursing over his painted face.

The warrior glared back at Papineau. He was clothed only in a loin cloth and leaned on a staff adorned with eagle feathers, wrapped together with a blue leather thong. Painted notches indicated the kills that the brave had committed by his own hand. He was flanked by a man that the woodsman suspected to be a shaman, decked out in ceremonial garb, and a young female sitting on a shimmering robe of silver wolves' skins. Her piercing eyes met his with the radiance of the sun. He was mesmerized by her presence. She recognized him immediately, but did not let on.

The chief greeted Papineau and Balmond in a soft, but firm voice, "She:kon, welcome!"

Papineau signed a greeting of peace he had learned from the Algonquin. "They have offered us a greeting and a meal, Balmond. Sit and partake of their generosity."

Balmond nodded, "Their kindness is universal. My feet are raw, my bones are chilled, and my stomach is howling for want of food. Whether they want me or not, they have me for a time."

The party sat in silence as they partook of a small meal and then graciously passed a pipe of peace, as a gesture of good faith. The tribesmen were wary of visitors who wandered into their isolated domain, so they probed the two men to ascertain their intentions. The two principals signed their conversation. Frustrated by this awkward process, Papineau finally spoke in Algonquin.

The mysterious woman in the bunk recognized the language of her foe. She was agitated, but coyly restrained herself until the warrior at her side lowered his lance. Tensions rose in the room. The squaw restrained him, speaking in a commanding voice, "Let the dead dog lie." She challenged the woodsman, "You are an intruder in our village. I ordered you on the trail above the great falls to leave our lands. Yet you have chosen to openly defy me. If I had known that you were in collusion with the Huron, I would have sent you to a swift grave. You have deceived me, Atiru':tak, (*Adirondack*—referring to him as a Barkeater for his perceived Algonquin allegiance)."

The woman's aggressive rebuke took Papineau by surprise. Women in his world did not command this type of authority, nor did they speak harshly to men. His mother was a perfect example of that. He saw the fierce passion in her dark eyes and suddenly remembered her. Her timely arrow had saved him from the Huron's cold blade. Now, she was commanding him on matters that were none of her concern. He coyly responded in a reassuring voice, "We have come from the Acadian Provinces to seek the headwaters of the great river that runs below this place. We pass through your village in peace and seek solace in your hospitality."

The maiden saw right through Papineau's facade. "Algonquin warriors have pillaged our villages, robbed our traps, raped our women, and decimated our tribe with war. Your presence here, Atiru':tak, is an evil omen. You have hoodwinked us into believing that you are trustworthy when I know that you are in collusion with our enemies. Therefore, we shall have no choice but to kill you, as we have recently done to so many of your brothers and sisters."

Papineau was incensed, but showed remarkable restraint. "It is true that I have lived among the Algonquin, but my allegiance is to no tribe. I am Acadian by birth, a trapper by trade, and I offer my deepest respect. You have saved me from a certain death at the hand of the Huron. I wish to repay that debt. I am called Papineau and my comrade lives by the name, Balmond."

Papineau sensed a tenuous, but spiritual bond with the crafty woman, but could not quell his anger. His demeanor changed, like his father's. "The trader Graham tells me that warriors from this village have given no quarter to my Anishinabe brothers. I demand an explanation."

Balmond looked at him in disbelief, as he began to realize that the woodsman had withheld information from him and was deceiving this woman. He grabbed Papineau by the arm. "You need to explain to me what happened above the falls. Curb your enthusiasm or you will manage to stir their ire. We are no match for them on any level. Your foolish rage will surely get us killed."

The woodsman whispered firmly, "I can manage my own affairs, boatman. Be still or leave."

Balmond responded with unusual anger, "Since my affairs are forever linked to yours, I suggest that you manage them well. Contrary to what you suspect, your rash actions will be our demise. Make peace with your demons, for waging war with them will bring you to your knees."

The chief was becoming annoyed with the side conversation. "Whatever it is that you discuss in our house must be shared openly in front of all of its members."

Papineau responded, "Then I suggest that you honestly remove all doubt about this affair."

Two Suns berated him. "It is not your bidding how we settle our differences. You are guests in our village and shall not question our actions on any level while you remain here."

The chief challenged Papineau, "You walk among us, uninvited and dare to question how we live? I'll have you know that we have done nothing more than what we have been sanctioned to do. The depth of those truths can only be understood if you walk in our shoes."

Papineau realized that the chief would not lie, but he would also take great care not to reveal the tribe's secrets. He decided to stop his probing for the truth would soon be revealed. He was determined to live among these people and then win their trust to fully expose them.

The young woman awkwardly blurted out his name, like a young child, "Papineau!" He was stunned by her transformation from a threatening tribal leader to a mischievous, vulnerable woman. She had revealed her weakness, but the warrior in her soon returned. "You have accused us of heinous acts. I'll remind you that the French were as deceitful as the Atiru':tak. Now, they are subservient people who are beholden to our wishes. Why should we welcome you?"

Papineau tried to interject, "The Brits—"

"The Brit are our allies, but we command these lands and no one, not even the Brits, shall alter that." She took a deep breath. "Furthermore, what gifts do you offer in return for our tolerance?"

Wampum, a symbol of trust and solidarity among the Iroquois people, came in many forms. A presentation of a gift bonded relationships and formed alliances. It was an expected part of tribal negotiations and ceremonial protocols, although its use in recent years was diminishing.

Two Suns unknowingly gave Papineau an opportunity to win their favor. "We are humble men who possess few worldly goods." He rifled through his possessions to find an endowment, then leaned over to Balmond. "Do you have something of worth to offer as a token of our respect?" Balmond glared back in defiance. "Balmond, they are waiting. What will you part with so we may enter into their confidence? What about the watch or the French saber?"

The boatman half-heatedly rummaged through his gunny sack. "You dare to ask me to sacrifice my most cherished possessions so you can manipulate these savages? I shall never part with that timepiece. It is my most precious treasure. As for the saber, it suits me to keep it."

The warrior who stood behind the chief sensed the tension, "Have you nothing to offer us?"

Papineau stood up and removed his greatcoat. Raising his tunic, he exposed a piece of cloth wrapped about his waist. He cautiously removed it, as the members of the tribe craned their necks to see what he would reveal. He held up a red and indigo sash, adorned with intricate lattice work and embroidered symbols. The menacing image of a wolf with piercing yellow eyes commanded its center. He cradled it his hands, saying a silent prayer, and then approached the chief.

The chief responded with a smile, but raised his hand in a gesture toward his daughter and nodded to indicate to Papineau that he should place his generous gift in her hands.

Balmond questioned Papineau unorthodox behaviors, "You are giving up that waistcloth? You told me it was given to you by the great warrior Three-Legged-Wolf. Are you a madman?"

Papineau responded angrily in French, "Let it lie, Balmond. I will soon enough have my day of revenge and this cloth of spiritual life will be back in its rightful place around my waist."

Papineau purposely brushed the warrior aside, never letting his eyes stray from the woman as he presented the sash. He could smell the scent of wildflowers upon her skin. Her lowcut garment bore the embossed image of the Hiawatha Belt, the mark of the Iroquois alliance. A tattoo on her breast: the sun and the moon traversing the horizon of her form to tumble toward each other.

Two Suns fondled the sash to examine the weave of the cloth. Her gaze was drawn to the wolf whose eyes followed hers. It was a mesmerizing bauble, despite its suspicious origins.

Papineau wanted to explain the significance of the wrap, but thought better of it. It was a valuable symbol of his transformation. But among these people, the sharing of personal treasures was the ultimate sign of respect. He winked at Balmond who shook his head in disgust.

The ensuing weeks were a chaotic whirlwind as Papineau and Balmond mingled with the tribe. Their animated personalities and strong work ethic made it easy for the Mohawks to accept them. Spring was in the air and the tensions of being fugitives were waning. They enjoyed living with the Wolf Clan and had little inkling to move on, but Papineau secretly probed for information, as he plotted his coup. For now, all of the celestial bodies seemed to be favorably aligned for the alleged Bark-eaters in the land of the alleged Man-eaters.

Chapter 40

Conclave

Months had passed since the white men presented themselves to the Mohawks. The callous Adirondack winds whipped up storms and dropped heavy snows. The stark landscape bore harsh witness to an impending calamity that would alter life for the people of the Iroquois alliance.

Chief Ten Hands moved his clan away from the established villages, fashioning their destiny by isolating them in the wilderness. He shared a vision with his trusted advisors. "An ominous cloud will blanket the earth for eight turnings of the seasons. When the thunderous billows drift away, and the sun rises again, the Iroquois nation will have melted away like the winter snows."

Ten Hands' radical actions evoked concern among the tribal and colonial leaders. But his small clan was hardly a threat and tiny rebellious factions were not unusual. The chief chastised the Iroquois statesmen in an open conclave, "You have sold your souls to a traitorous race of people who do not honor our way of life. Their treaties are filled with hollow dreams and broken promises."

Ten Hands pointed to them one by one. "You no longer embrace the sanctity of an Iroquois lifestyle. You dress in white man's clothes, so I hardly recognize you. You abuse the white man's liquor, making you a feeble-minded pawn to his manipulation. You think like the white man and have capitulated to his frailties: greed, lust, and infidelity. You have embraced his false god, defaming the spirits that have resurrected our nation. You have all forgotten your kinship with our Mother, breaking the circle of our alliance, yet you fail to see it through your own self-indulgence."

The statesmen listened to the renegade, as protocol demanded, but most would submit to the changes. Before they could ostracize him, the chief pronounced, "The Iroquois were once a feared and respected people. Now, we stand alone in a vast wasteland of turmoil. Each of you has brought that plague down upon us. May the spirit of the Great Eagle fill your hearts with wisdom and bring our nation back into harmony with nature." He left the congress, never to return.

On an oppressively cold day, as storm clouds gathered over the mountains, Ten Hands called a gathering of his clan. "We must be the masters of our destiny, not the subservient slaves to a submissive European way of life. The white man has taken our sacred land and destroyed the sanctity of our hunting grounds. We negotiate away that which our Mother has provided for us."

Some Indians embraced the more cultured colonial lifestyle. The traditionalists lived like their ancestors. But there were some who raided and pillaged, believing that war and plunder would strike fear and stop the incursion. Hatred ran cold in their blood, as the divide between them grew.

The British sought to control Indian aggression and bring peace to the region. Policies like the Treaty of Easton in 1758 and the Royal Proclamations in 1763 established firm boundaries along the mountain ranges and rivers to try to preserve Iroquois Borderlands and limit areas open to European migration. To men like Ten Hands, these treaties served as shallow promises.

Kariwase's dissenting voice rose above the murmurs. "We are strong in the eyes of the spirits, but he leads us down a destructive path. You are all pawns to an ancient warrior's wild imagination. He plots our demise, yet you are so blinded by his ranting that you fail to see the truth."

Yellow Elk stifled him, "Know your place, young warrior. When you have mastered the art of respect, you can speak freely among us. Do not allow your heart to violently control your mind."

Two Suns restrained her brother. "He is merely a boy whose tongue is sharper than his mind."

A meek, pleading voice cut the tension. "We are tired of the migration, Ten Hands. We are tired of the wars and exhausted by the debate. We have become a feeble nation of old woman. If our existence is but a breath on the howling wind, then what courses are we left to take?"

"Willow Woman, you are wiser than the Deganawida, but your vision is clouded by your pain. Among us are men and women who can manipulate our destiny, but we must first make them see what we see. Feel what we feel. Experience what we experience. Live as we live."

She wiggled her finger in a gesture of contempt. "You have never led me astray, great chief. I will continue to follow you, for I am too old to do otherwise. Once our numbers were as great as the trees, but now we are a weak and feeble people following a fool's path."

Standing Waters, the soft-spoken warrior, called out, "If you are courting the whites that live among us to fulfill that promise, then you misunderstand the nature of those egotistical men. I fear that they are no better than their brothers, although they would have you think otherwise."

Standing Waters was painfully loyal to Ten Hands and Yellow Elk. He was a robust brave who enforced tribal law, a man not to be trifled with. He was not reflective, nor wise, often standing silent is the face of verbal confrontation, but he was respected for his imposing physical prowess.

Hateya questioned his motivation, "Why is it that you, the silent one lashes out in dissent? I fear that your selfish intentions mar your soul. Petty jealousy cannot be part of our coup."

The valiant warrior buckled under the pressure of the accusations. His secret affections for Two Suns drove his jealous tirade. Unable to confront her on the matter, he was embarrassed by the thought of having his innermost feelings revealed in front of the rest of the members of the clan.

Ten Hands interceded. "Standing Waters speaks the truth. We cannot be sure that we can trust anyone. I am only asking that you trust me." He turned to Kariwase, "You can side with the Brits, as Thayendenegea has done. They will welcome you, for they think as you think. Or, you can remain with us, understanding that you have committed yourself to the fulfillment of our dreams."

The chief let others openly discuss his challenge then spoke, "If you will join me, cross the expanse of this great house to stand with me. I harbor no ill will toward those who choose to take a different path. You must leave us, though, before the sun crests on the morrow."

Two Suns was the first to cross. "My father has never led us down a dark path without knowing that there is a light at its end. Who will stand with us?" She spoke to Standing Waters, "And what will you do, great warrior? Will you join us or wander off to a life of uncertainty?"

The warrior could not break his bond to the chief or the young squaw that he coveted. He took his position behind his chief, plunged his lance into the floor, and folded his arms across his chest.

Kariwase naively questioned, "You do not beckon me as you have the others. Am I to take this as a sacking or are you merely taxing my will?" He scoffed, "It is clear to me that you are weak, so I will remain here with my braves to fulfill our destiny. Our alliance will bring you power."

Kariwase, (translated: *a new way of doing things*) was a medium built teen. His face was drawn, making him look much older than he was. His hair was braided in a pigtail. He wore a British Venetian red frockcoat, left open to expose his chest. His legs were covered with tan breeches and a blue loin cloth. He was brash and manipulative. His renegade behaviors were creating a rift.

The next morning, when the coup was completed, Ten Hands spoke to his lifelong friend, He Who Runs Slowly, "Why is it that you abandon us in our most fateful hour, my friend?"

Deep emotions marked the aging warrior's words. "I am too feeble to fight, too old to care. In my younger days, I would have proudly waged a defiant battle until death took my soul. Let me live out the remainder of my life clinging to the glory that once defined our nation."

"And what shall be the fate of your daughter, Katarina Morning Star?"

"She has guided me with wisdom, but chosen a different path. I ask that you cradle her in your bosom. Two Suns' guidance will enable her to face the challenges of an uncertain life."

Ten Hands wept openly. "The river of my soul pours out its sadness upon the earth. I shall carry you upon my back, friend, for the remainder of my days, so that your dreams can be fulfilled."

The two friends parted ways, never to see one another again. On that fateful day, the clan's destiny began to unfurl, masked in a cloud of discord, hatred, and misgivings. The small band of people bound to Ten Hands treatises tread lightly down a new path of transformation.

Chapter 41

Games of Emotional Chance

Papineau sat alone and whittled the image of a bear into a small piece of pine. A rustle on the flap of his hut and the bluster of the inrushing wind aroused him from his solitude.

Ten Hands, clad in a large robe, greeted him. "May I enter, friend?"

"Please join me, sir. Why do you venture out when the biting cold cuts to the very quick?"

The aging chief entered slowly. "The noble bear holds a special place in my heart, for he is my namesake. I have noticed that one of his brothers has laid his mark upon your cheek, and yet, you have survived. You are indeed a special man if you have staved off the power of the virulent beast."

Papineau rubbed the lightning scar and smiled. "I was most fortunate to escape the thrusts of the beast's mighty claws so that I may speak with you today."

"Then I suspect that it was not your time to die."

Papineau held up the carving to let the chief examine it. "When I have completed it, I shall present it to you as a gift. It will be a reminder of the power that nature holds over all of us."

The chief nodded his satisfaction. "I would like you to walk with me through the storm. The harsh elements will clear our minds so that we can communicate freely."

Papineau did not question the chief's motivations, for he had developed an appreciation of the man's quirky wisdom. He pulled on his greatcoat as he and the aging warrior left the hut. They leaned into the wind, elongating their gait to manage the drifts. Driven snow blistered their faces, as they left the compound and climb on their hands and knees over a formidable snowbank to enter the forest. They walked in the powdery snow through a pine-laden hollow where they came upon a small wigwam. They knelt down to clear the snow away from the opening and then entered.

"Before the spring comes, my people need to unearth the path that leads toward our journey's end. Your presence among us has altered our thinking on which path to take and it troubles me."

Papineau was curious about the nature of the chief's statement, but did not speak.

"You and Balmond honor our way of life and work unselfishly, but I question your motivation. Why are you such a guarded and mysterious man, when those around you are so open and honest?"

Papineau found it difficult to answer. "It is not often in my life that I can say that I have been settled in the presence of other people. Balmond and I have had occasion to discuss this and we feel that we have found a profound purpose in our lives living with your clan."

The chief studied the man called the Wolf. He was not fooled by his aloof answer, for the woodsman's eyes revealed the truth. "You are an enigma to me, a man of mystical ambiguity. Yet you continue to pique my curiosity. There are great changes that lie just beyond the horizon. If you wish to be a part of our future, you need to help fulfill our vision, not yours."

Papineau objected to the chief's assessment, failing to see that his persona was fraught with frailties. His impervious ways were his undoing, yet he could not overcome his grievous faults.

The conversation with Papineau enabled the chief to forge ahead with his quest. He speculated that Papineau and Balmond could play an integral part in the tribe's transformation. Through the callous exterior of these questionable white men, he saw a glimmering ray of hope for his clan.

The snows cleared to a point where the trails were once again passable. Balmond and Papineau were out checking their traps and resupplying their depleted food coffers. They spoke about the changes in their lives, Balmond offering a parable. "Life presents to you a gift of treasures, my friend. I have discovered this wisdom living among the Mohawks. For each with box we find ourselves locked out of, there is a key to discovering the treasure that lies inside another. We simply need to find the key and open the box to reveal the truth and we shall reap infinite rewards."

Papineau was not convinced. "So, you now believe that we all hold the key to our dreams in the palm of our hand? And what of all the misery we are put through to find that key?"

Balmond was philosophical. "To obtain the golden ring, you must make sacrifices. You live your life fighting arbitrary battles over questionable dalliances. You must succumb to life's pleasures and the key will beckon you. When will you forego your pigheadedness and learn this?"

Papineau was crass. "I am a content to be just as I am, Balmond. I need nothing more and refuse to be drawn into playful games of emotional chance by a man who thinks too much."

Balmond sensed that the woodsman was absorbing some of his ephemeral wisdom. It was just a matter of time before his preaching and life's circumstances would light the lamp in his soul.

Nothing was stirring in the camp save for a stray dog or a baying goat. There was no guard posted in the tower, no women at work, and no children frolicking. Papineau laid his cache of pelts upon the ground and spoke, "Ready your weapon, Balmond. Something runs afoul of us today."

The two men cautiously moved across the compound. They were accosted at the gate of the stockade by a lone warrior. "Halt where you tread, white men. You are not welcome here on this auspicious day. You will be summoned before us when the elders will it to be so."

Papineau spoke guardedly, as they turned away. "I suspect that they have reconsidered their trust in us. Ten Hands challenged me with questions about our allegiance, during the great storm. Do you suspect that they have been informed about our sketchy past or question our intentions?"

Balmond was confident. "We have given them no cause for alarm, although I suspect that your motivation is still to the contrary. They seem to have forgotten about your tryst above the falls and your accusations about the Anishinabe massacre."

Papineau remained suspicious. "They do not forget anything, friend. Best be on your guard."

Chapter 42

Sacrificial Lamb

The tribe had suffered deeply from the brutal winter, hunkered down in the longhouse to conserve their meager supplies and shelter themselves from the unrelenting snows. But signs of an early spring gave them hope that their torment would soon be behind them.

After the admonishment by the sentry, Papineau and Balmond watched the clan from afar, only going to the longhouse when summoned. Neither man was party to the scheme that was destined to alter their future, as the tribe sorted out the particulars of Ten Hands' contrary plan.

Papineau would frequently steal away, preferring solitude over communal living. He was distracted, often thinking about Two Suns. He wrestled with the divergent emotions of hatred and respect as he tried to understand her. When she would venture forth from the confines of the longhouse, he would study her with piqued interest. He was not sure about her private relationship with Yellow Elk, since he seldom took the time to understand the personal side of other peoples' lives. He was so emotionally shallow that he did not know that the two companions were siblings.

The squaw ignored Papineau, but he would catch her shooting him a passing glance. He was intrigued by her beauty and guile, but put off by her arrogance. The many faces of the woman confused him: noble warrior, brash leader, wise sachem, and fickle teen who coveted frivolous baubles. He hoped to confront her on these matters, but there was always a warrior in her presence.

Papineau expressed his frustration to Balmond, "I have reluctantly agreed to stay among these people to appease your desires, but

I am ready to move on. I see no benefit from lingering in the festering confines of these deep hollows if these people continue to ostracize me. They refuse to reveal their secrets and I am losing the passion to pursue this cat and mouse game any longer."

He stoked the fire. "The Mohawk are a secretive people, so loyal to one another that I cannot extract a smidgeon of information from them about the massacre, their personal lives, or their dreams. Lingering here will only serve to frustrate me. I need to get on with my life, pursue other quests, and meet more vibrant people. I have thought about moving into the isolated territories beyond the great lakes. I could benefit from the solitude and the game is still plentiful there."

The reflective Balmond smiled. "You take too much stock in things that you cannot control. Open up to them and reveal your inner being. Only then will they trust you enough to answer your questions. Loyalty, honesty, trust, and devotion are important things to them. You have shown them nothing but disdain and disregard, only pursuing your own selfish desires."

Papineau threatened, "At the rising of the full moon, I will depart unless my needs are fulfilled."

Balmond gave up trying to appease the man. He would have to suffer life's trials on his own.

Ten Hands summoned Yellow Elk, Two Suns, and Standing Waters. "Sit with me upon the moss-covered ground as I reveal the truth about our future. A horrendous storm will soon sweep over the land and change the face of our nation. We must agree to take matters into our own hands."

The warriors were patient with the chief. He would often divulge a stunning revelation that would prove to be true to the mark of his word. "The two white men hold the key to our future. We have purposely kept them at bay to test their will and understand their soul. They are still not to be trusted, for I surmise that they harbor a grievous secret." He continued, "What I am about to ask of you requires your complete devotion to the clan and your unwavering trust in my vision. It may ultimately serve to sever the bound you have with your Iroquois brothers and sisters."

The chief gave his calumet to his son. "The elders have directed me to pass the baton of peace to you. You shall bear the burden of leading our warriors. I am too old to walk among them, but I shall continue to serve as their trailblazer. You, my son, will carry the torch that lights our way."

Yellow Elk embraced his father as he looked into his sad eyes. "I will not fail you, father."

The stoic leader turned to Standing Waters. "You have openly challenged my authority, for I spoke in parables and asked you to support a veiled cause. You, the silent one, recognized that I was coaxing all of you to venture down an unknown path and risk everything on a whim."

The chief spoke carefully. "I know that you have strong feelings for my daughter. You are like a son to me, but I am asking you to set those feelings aside, for the betterment of the tribe. You have until the turning of the moon to render a decision, for it should not be taken lightly. If you choose to honor my wishes, you will sit at my son's right hand in all matters of peace and war. Do not speak of this until you have fully considered what it is that I have ask you to sacrifice."

The warrior nodded in agreement, but powerful emotions tugged at his fluttering heart.

"You, my precious daughter, will have to make the greatest sacrifice. What I ask of you transcends all logic, but is cornerstone our bequest. If we are to be swallowed up by the tide of change, then we must control that change to serve our own terms. You, child, bear the weight of preserving our past and carrying the seed of our rich history into the future."

Two Suns whispered into Ten Hands' ear, "What is it that you ask of me, my father?"

"Your mother does not sit among us because she does not fully comprehend the magnitude of what I will ask you to do. She has taught you how to lay down the footprints in the sand that will lead to our future, but what I am about to tell you is not the way she would have envisioned it."

Pity consumed Two Suns' face. "How can I bear the weight of your burden, father?"

"I will be blunt with you, my daughter. I ask that you make the most precious of all sacrifices and consider taking the hand of the white man, Papineau, in a bond of marriage."

Two Suns straightened her back and raised her chin, as she had done as a precocious child. She looked into Standing Water's eyes. They met hers with a cold stare, the emotion gone from his soul. She skillfully quelled her anger and deep hatred. "I will do as you ask, out of love for you and mother and my pledge to my people. But know this: I will make this sacrifice on my own terms. This callous white man must respect my way of life and be willing to sacrifice anything to preserve it. I must know that he can be trusted beyond a shadow of a doubt, for he will bear the burden of our secrets and suffer the pain of our existence. He must embrace our heritage, without reservation, and pass it on to his children. I must know if he will love me, unconditionally, for I shall not bear the children of a man who knows no love. Only then will I agree to your terms."

She looked away from Standing Waters, satisfied that they had an understanding. "My hatred for that cold-hearted wolf, Papineau, knows no bounds. The three of you must test him with physical, mental, and emotional challenges. Fortify him with the resolve of our noblest warriors. Only then will he see his way toward the light of our genius or falter along its path." She grabbed a handful of dirt, letting it slowly sift through her fingers. "Only the passing of time will be our judge on these matters." She left abruptly, doubting that her demands could ever be fulfilled.

Chapter 43

Covering the Grave

In the secluded Falcon's Trace, the Wolf Clan pushed forward with their plan to secure their freedom. Spring was blossoming, putting aside the misery of a turbulent winter, allowing the tribe to revel in nature's rejuvenation. But outside of these secretive hollows, a shadow of conflict was descending over the land. Newly crowned British King, George III, issued the Royal Proclamation of 1763, tightening the noose of imperial administration over the American Colonies. Despotic measures like the Articles of Governance: The Sugar Act, Currency Act, Stamp Act, and Quartering Act, raised the ire of the Colonists, pushing them toward the brink of insurrection.

Two Suns' would not be easily swayed toward feeling affection for the bumbling woodsman. She baited him into respecting her as a confident, self-reliant woman, trying to remove his preconceived notions that females were nothing more than fodder for violence. If he took the bait, then the courtship could begin on her terms. If not, the fate of the tribe could be left in god's hands.

Papineau paid little attention to Two Suns, too caught up in his own troubles to care. He tolerated her out of necessity, but had not even made the effort to remember her name. He was physically attracted to her, but caring for a woman seemed like a burden to him. He failed to understand how his father's abuse influenced the canvas of history that was about to be painted.

The woodsman had just returned from a hunting expedition. He was exhausted, had not eaten, and a rank stench emanated from his person. His mood was foul, for it was becoming harder each day to reap the benefits of the wilderness larders. He greeted Balmond in anger, "The trapping gets tougher each spring as the wretched Colonists drive the game into their compounds or kill it for sport. I fear it will only be a matter of time before the land is laid barren by their greed."

The jovial boatman didn't seem to care. "Just in time for a bit of bear meat and stewed turnip, my pungent friend," Balmond waved his hand across his nose as he quipped about the woodsman's hygiene. "It seems to me that you always have an insatiable appetite. It takes me the better part of each day foraging for food to feed you. Am I nothing more than a squaw to you?"

Papineau grabbed a slab of meat and sat down outside of the hut, still grousing.

Balmond had a more pressing matter. "It seems that the tribal leaders have been conjuring up some tomfoolery. I have seen Oneida, Onondaga, and Seneca warriors come here to take part in secret deliberations, but they do not linger. Scouting parties have been numerous and Yellow Elk has spent less time with the princess and more time on the trail with his warriors."

Papineau concurred. "The unusual amount of activity in the forest makes me think that they are anticipating trouble. I have noticed that the trails are heavy with traffic, including a patrol of British Regulars from the lake forts. The trappers tell me that there is turmoil in the colonial cities and war is being waged with the Indians on the western frontier. The Brits thought that they could command these unruly backwoods bumpkins better than the French. I will try to find out what the commotion is, but I suspect that they will not divulge anything of substance to me."

Balmond took a sip of tea he had procured from a trapper who frequented the camp. "These Americans are fiercely independent, like you. They are not going to succumb to subservient rule. I'll bet that if things are as bad as I suspect, we will soon be in for a rousing row."

Papineau commented, "The politics of this region has always been fragile. The Iroquois ally with the British, but that relationship is flimsy. Rumor has it that some renegade braves are churning up a hornet's nest, pitting the Brits against the Colonials, who in turn blame the tribes. It is none of my affair, but I fear that it is about to explode into universal violence."

Balmond frowned. "This region has been home to a variety of people with diverse beliefs for centuries, a formula for trouble. Even before Europeans came here, the Indians had been engaged in territorial squabbles. They would just as well shoot you, as look at you, the way I figure it."

Papineau was amazed. "How is it that you know so many things, my friend?"

"Let's just say that I have had an exposure to an educated life that others may not have been blessed with. Did you think that I did nothing more than run that ferry with a blind eye?"

The woodsman was concerned. "Are we under scrutiny for the indiscretions of our checkered past? I don't suspect that the tribe is privy to that information, but they have often surprised me."

"There have been no signs that they have been tipped off. I suspect that the Brits have bigger fish to fry, keeping the rampaging Colonials at bay and settling Indian affairs on the frontier."

Papineau replied. "The Iroquois believe in a rite of retribution called Covering the Grave. It is a way of exacting a blood revenge for a crime, an eye for an eye. They could turn us over to be tried under Provincial law or they could negotiate a payment to take matters into their own hands. They loathe the notion of legal proceedings and corporal punishments: imprisonment, the gallows, or the firing squad. They would prefer clemency rather than commit more contracted violence. They feel that if a punishment is to be carried out, it should be enacted upon by the offended party."

"I am afraid that you misunderstand the motivations of these people. If my experience tells me anything, they are loyal to a fault. If you gain their trust, they will guard your darkest secrets." The boatman hesitated. "There is another bit of trivia you should would be best served to know."

"And what would that be, my informed mate?"

"The princess has been subtly inquiring about you. I told her that she needs to bring her affairs directly to you. I only succeeded in making her angry." Balmond laughed.

"That one is a mystery to me, my friend. I pay her no mind. She has more suitors than a raging rabbit and is as unpredictable as the wind." Papineau stood up. "I am going to the stream to cleanse myself. When I return, we can continue this conversation. The subject intrigues me."

"That is the most astute disclosure that you have made all day. The world will be a far better place after you have bathed." Balmond returned to the hut to sew some hides into a robe.

Papineau headed for the stream and after a short walk, parted the brush to find a secluded spot to bathe. He descended the steep bank, still partially covered with snow and knelt by the placid water. He brushed back his long, tangled locks and splashed the cool liquid on his disheveled face. He looked at his image in the pool. The raised lightning bolt scar made him look hideous, but he assumed that it frightened others. He decided that he would wear it as a badge of honor.

The woodsman stripped off his tunic and gingerly waded into the stream. The brisk air and cold water invigorated him as the light of the sun filtered through the trees. It shimmered on his moistened flesh and accentuated his muscular form, giving him the aura of a mystical being. He stood still like a blue heron and after a moment of quiet contemplation, dipped himself fully in the water. He enjoyed its cleansing power, as the mist of the morning hovered over the beck. The smell of the fir trees was strong and the serenity of the hushed forest lulled him into a sense of security.

An annoying deerfly invaded his privacy, causing him to notice a rustled in the water downstream. He squatted, not wanting to be caught off guard. Through the haze, he could make out the figure of a woman hovering at the water's edge. He slowly stalked closer, his movements silent, deliberate. A fallen tree spanned the creek. He peered over it, careful not to expose himself.

The young woman was oblivious to his presence. She rhythmically leaned over to submerge her cloth, swirled it in the current, and then turned toward the bank to rub it upon a rock.

Papineau's recognized the sash draped across the woman's chest. He decided to take advantage of the opportunity and approach her. The anger seethed within him. *You will return that sash to me with an apology, wench.* The woodsman worked his way back upstream to gather his belongings. His intentional splashing was sure to attract her attention. He was not adept in the ways of the womanly world, so he could not have anticipated her instincts or her next move.

Papineau rounded the bend in the stream and peered over the log to reveal his presence. Much to his chagrin, she had disappeared. He was sure that he had scared her off. The disappointment was evident upon his unkempt face, as he furrowed his brow and scratched his forming beard. He had longed for the chance to confront her, but in the blink of an eye, the opportunity was lost. He artfully sprung over the trunk and approached the spot where the squaw has been washing her clothes. Her freshly laundered garments lay upon the shore. He bent over to pick them up when a screeching war whoop cracked the eerie silence of the morn. Before he could right himself he was struck a blow to the back of his skull. It stunned him enough to cause him to fall into the water.

The waters of the stream boiled, as the two bodies violently thrashed about. Although the woodsman had been momentarily caught off guard, he quickly gained the upper-hand. He pressed a firm palm on the back of his assailant's head and pushed it under the water, but his opponent was strong, agile, and wiry. As the long hair of his victim flowed downstream, he caught a glimpse of a red and blue sash. The embroidered wolf stared up at him and he suddenly realized with whom he was wrestling. With a mighty thrust of his arm, he hauled the woman out of the water.

Two Suns emerged from the stream coughing and screaming a string of obscenities in her Native tongue. She pounded on Papineau's chest and gouged at his eyes, while he held her at bay with his long arms. When she recognized him, the obscenities were seamlessly converted to the Algonquin tongue. She realized that further struggle was fruitless, but continued to berate him.

Papineau deposited her upon the bank to drip dry in the morning sun. He tried to awkwardly apologize, "I dare to say that if you had been a warrior your blood would be spilling freely. It is a great happenstance that I recognized you for who you really are and released you from my grasp."

Two Suns glared at him with disdain. *Father underestimates the futility of this affair. This man shall never be tamed as he suspects.* She began to gather her belongings. "You are the most uncivilized man on Earth. Why I have agreed to have anything to do with you is beyond reason."

He exposed his vanity, "I do not know your name. At least you could offer me that courtesy."

Two Suns pushed him aside. *How could this buffoon live amongst us for so long and not know my name, even as I have spoken it to him on several occasions? It is surely the devil's fool that I am asked to court.* She yelled loudly, for all in earshot to hear, "I am the daughter of the confluence of the rising sun and the cresting of the waning moon. I am a warrior and a princess. I am the vessel of a new tribal order and will triumph resurrecting our heritage to one of greatness and prosperity."

The people stopped what they were doing to watch the awkward scene unfold.

She averted her gaze toward the heavens. "I am the seed of Ten Hands and Hateya, who have named me Tekeni Karahkwa, Two Suns!" She stalked back toward the stockade with her bundle of dripping garments. They masked the trail of tears she had laid upon the earth's dried mantle.

Papineau was stunned, but gathered himself emotionally and then noticed that Balmond was waving frantically and yelling. He yelled back, "What devil has possessed you, man?"

Balmond finally spoke intelligibly, "You, my misguided friend, have stirred up a hornets' nest! The chosen one claims that you have brutalized her. She wants to extract some sort of revenge upon you. I would not be surprised if half of the warriors will be ruthlessly hunting you down to avenge the honor of their tribal princess. What did you call it? Covering the Grave?"

He paused to catch his breath. "And furthermore, a column of the King's soldiers is approaching from the southeast. You have emerged unscathed for the moment, thanks to the King, but do not think for one second that the squaw will forget that you have violated her, sir. You will have to defend the honor of the princess, assuming you survive the onslaught of the King's guard."

Papineau, unmoved, declared. "I'd rather take my chances with the King's troops than suffer from the wrath of that deranged woman."

Chapter 44

Covenant Chain

Papineau entered the chaotic stockade where the air was thick with apprehension. Warriors prepared for battle and the elders, woman, and children secreted away to hide. He came upon Yellow Elk, instructing braves of the Iroquois Nation. The eyes of the two men met, understanding that there was a personal matter to be settled, but for now, there were more pressing affairs.

The war party struck out toward the east and ran along a well-established trail, carved out by the feet of a thousand travelers. It wound its way through boulder-strewn terrain and then coursed into a fern-filled hollow where the file of men split into two columns.

Yellow Elk's war party leapt into the creek off of an elevated bank. They splashed through the water at breakneck speed and followed it down the mountain. The other column, led by Standing Waters, disappeared into a thicket, moving along a high ridge. The men leaned into the run for what seemed like an eternity, determination and anger written upon their painted faces.

Papineau could hear the boatman wheezing, as he struggled to navigate the boulder-strewn streambed. "Ease your pace, Balmond. You can catch up when the mood suits you."

Balmond, his heart racing, responded between gasps of air, "If it were up to me…I would turn tail…We don't know what we are getting into… Do you want to die on this trail of uncertainty?"

"There is no time to contemplate these frivolous ideologies, Balmond. These warriors would not strike out unless it was absolutely necessary for them to do so."

Balmond answered, "Since when have you become a person to foster loyalty or trust toward others? For all you know, this could be a trap sprung to catch us in the Brit's lair."

Papineau was frustrated. "I am committed to this fight, no matter what the outcome may be. Are you with me? If you are not, head back to the escarpment to be with the squaws."

The column in the water arrived at a bluff overlooking a well-marked trail situated in the depths of a grotto. The creek abruptly cascaded over a cliff into a pristine pool at its base. The roar of the water masked other noises, as it crashed over the rocks and sent a fine mist into the towering trees.

Papineau exited the stream, climbing up the steep, mossy bank on all fours to make the grade. When he reached the bluff, he received a stern visual reprimand from Yellow Elk. He sensed that the chief disapproved of his unexpected absence, suspecting that he had committed a treasonous act. Papineau's eyes followed the warrior's pointed finger toward the grotto floor. He could see the blazing red coats of a column of Regulars snaking their way toward them.

Yellow Elk whispered, "We will lure the Brits into a trap and then subdue them with a pincer movement. My warriors will let the column pass, marching directly into the path of Standing Waters' hidden men. They will engage them from the front while I bring my warriors in from the flank and rear. The confines of the grotto's rock walls are perfect for triggering such a snare."

The British regimental commander halted the column to reconnoiter. He sent out flankers on either side of the meadow situated at the head of the grotto. A company of Fusiliers proceeded into the defile to scout the path. A mishmash of militia was commanded to face south to cover their path of retreat. After a few minutes, a lone soldier from the scouting party returned to the column on a dead run. After an animated conversation, an order was given for the flankers to come in. The column advanced, disappearing among the boulders strewn upon the dark grotto floor.

Yellow Elk motioned for his warriors to spread out along the heights. He selected a handpicked band of men, including Papineau, to accompany him toward the meadow.

Balmond, out of breath, caught up with the war party. Not able to muster the strength to fight, he stayed on the bluff, watching the Indians vanish over a rise and reappeared in the meadow.

A chorus of musket fire and the blood-curdling cries of attacking warriors rose up from the grotto floor. The firefight escalated as the warriors forced the embattled Brits to slowly retreat. They tried to reach the meadow where they could use their traditional lines of battle to bring their superior weapons and concentrated fire to bear. But the inexperienced militia failed to hold the ground against Yellow Elk's vicious assaults. They were trapped like rats in the hold of a ship.

The Covenant Chain, a pact of reason and compromise, was being tested. Vengeance, in its shadowy, sadistic form cast a pall on the land and struck at the heart of trust.

Chapter 45

Chaos and Carnage

As the British troops fell back, their path was blocked by Yellow Elk's warriors. The Indian's field of fire created a deadly killing zone; a hail of lead ricocheted off of the boulders and canyon walls, splintering into shrapnel that cut through flesh. The soldiers tried to keep up counter-fire, but soon the raging battle fizzled down to a few sporadic shots. As their blood was spilled and their cries of agony echoed off of the grotto stone, the outcome of the battle was never in doubt.

The warriors crept forward to prey upon the wounded or engage in hand-to-hand combat with soldiers who had been left in isolated pockets. The inexperienced militia men suffered the most, as the braves committed unspeakable acts of depredation upon them as they begged for quarter.

High above the slaughter pen, the remaining warriors watched the melee through the smoke and mist. The soldiers red coats stood out in the filtered light, making them easy targets. Volley after volley was thrown into them from the bluff. Escape was virtually impossible.

Balmond focused his gaze on an officer who knelt behind a dead horse. He confidently barked out commands, carried upward by the wind over the din of the battle. There was something very familiar about the Captain's precise articulation of the words. An errant ball suddenly removed his cap. Through the parting smoke, Balmond could see that he had no left ear. A sense of horror suddenly consumed him. It was Cameron James. He was sure that he was not mistaken.

Cradling his firelock tightly to his breast, Balmond flashed back to that fateful day on the landing. Now, in an obscure grotto hundreds of miles away, he was reliving the uncertainty of that tragedy and his deathly fear of the hangman's noose. He mustered the courage to peer out from behind the tree to make sure that he had not imagined things. Cameron James was the only man alive that could identify him for his part in the slaughter. *What in God's name should I do?*

The boatman primed his firelock and set the ball. He looked for James, but could not make out his form through the haze. He aimed the musket and slowly moved it about in the hope that the officer would carelessly expose himself. Much to his surprise, a sturdy foot was placed upon the barrel of the gun. Kariwase, the young, impetuous brave he did not trust, loomed over him.

Kariwase held out his hand. "Our time will come to kill the British dogs."

Balmond nodded to the slapdash warrior, but was frustrated that an opportunity had been lost. He turned back toward the battle and continued to observe its progress.

Yellow Elk, frustrated by the stalemate, considered a charge into the abyss to end the savagery. Fortunately, Papineau, who had been the catalyst of similar rash behavior, dissuaded him. The young chief finally put an end to the hostilities with a blood-curdling war cry. A few more bursts of gunfire cracked the morning air before everything became disconcertingly silent.

Chapter 46

Exposed

A tall soldier emerged from the swirling smoke, a white flag of truce waved defiantly on the tip of his sword. "Give us quarter, good sir. We no longer wish to prolong this senseless killing."

The odor of trampled moss, blood, and black powder mixed with the waterfall's mist to waft through the heavy air. The officer's fair complexion was masked by pain and grime. His left ear was gone, replaced by a grotesque scar. Blood trickled out of a bullet hole in his shoulder.

Yellow Elk, musket resting on his hip, fought the urge to massacre the remaining men. He understood that more soldiers would come to wipe out his race. A resolution of peace must be sought to restore the balance of nature. In the future, he would find a way for all men to live in harmony. For now, his warriors had proven their superiority and the threat had been suppressed.

Papineau caught a glimpse of Balmond, pointing frantically toward the officer carrying the flag. He ignored him as he stepped over the body of a decapitated militia man. The officer immediately recognized him, a face he swore he would never forget. They glared menacingly at each other.

Yellow Elk demanded, "How do you know this man, Papineau?"

Papineau replied, "We have had our differences in the past. They do not concern you."

James attempted to thrust the blade of his flag-draped sword into the woodsman's abdomen. Papineau anticipated the parry and avoided the attack. As the officer stumbled, he disabled him with a blow to the side of his head. He planted the officer in the mud with his foot and spit on him.

Yellow Elk interceded. "Stop this madness. There has been enough killing on this day."

Balmond decided to take matters into his own hands. He picked up his weapon, but a blow across his arms caused him to drop it. A second blow to his abdomen buckled him, gasping for air.

"Who do you serve, Frenchman?"

Balmond was puzzled by the question and too overcome by physical distress to respond.

"I asked you, Frenchman, who do you serve?" Kariwase smiled. "All things are not as they seem. In due time, I will make it known who rules the Borderlands. You and your friend stay out of my way or you will pay dearly." The warrior kicked Balmond's weapon over the cliff. He struck him again with his war club, then walked away to get a better view of the parley below.

James had recovered enough to berate Papineau. "This man is a traitor and a murderer. If you have placed your trust in him, then he will betray you. He cares little about the lives of others and will unwittingly take yours, if the notion possesses him."

Standing Waters unexpectedly came to Papineau's defense, "Do you think that these lies will succeed in swaying our opinions? We have just defeated you in battle. Nothing that you can say or do will change the fact that this woodsman has fought beside us with honor."

"The Frenchman is protecting his own interests. He has lived among the Algonquin, your sworn enemies. He has recklessly killed three of the King's officers. He has maimed me, the scars of his felonious acts resting upon my mutilated brow. He is a bloody scoundrel, a coward, and a cad."

Yellow Elk tugged on James' hair to lift his head, "Did you do this, woodsman?"

"I did, sir, and I would do it again. Ask him why he has provoked you. Do you not have binding treaties with his King? Has he not defamed his government by breaking the sworn oath of the Covenant Chain? He speaks thusly so that you will show him mercy."

Kariwase yelled to Yellow Elk, "Kill the lot of them and take their scalps, including the two Frenchmen. There is no place in our world for white cowards."

Yellow Elk conferred with Standing Waters. "How should we settle this quandary?"

Standing Waters spoke honestly. "This woodsman lives his life in a shadow of distrust. Let the Brits cover the grave so that we do not have his blood or the blood of others on our hands."

Yellow Elk replied, "The air is foul with conspiracy. We cannot be baited by these fools nor let them command the day. The woodsman and his friend are suspicious men, but before we do something rash, we must look deeper into their past. We are bound by my father's visions to fulfill a prophecy, but if we find that they are living a lie, we shall strike them down with just cause."

Standing Waters put his finger on the middle of Yellow Elk's chest. "The vision be damned! I do not trust this woodsman, nor do I trust the Brits. You stand alone on this decision, my friend. Decide wisely, for your actions will have grave consequences."

"I respect your words, brother, but for now I must act alone. Ten Hands would not have entrusted us with his prophecy had he not seen promise in these men." He placed a hand on Standing Water's shoulder. "Go to the bluff and put yourself in the presence of Kariwase. I fear that he has cast his lot with the Brits. The fires of his hatred have brought today's raid down upon us. But until I have proof of his duplicity, we will watch him from afar. Will you do this for me?"

Standing Waters, seething with anger, quickly disappeared into the forest.

Yellow Elk spoke to James, "Lead your rampaging band of marauders away from our home. Your treaties are no longer binding here." He looked up toward the bluff to see Standing Waters posturing behind Kariwase. "I do not know what alliances you have forged, but take heed, for the tribes of the Iroquois Nation will come down upon you like a plague if you persist with these fruitless forays. Settle your quarrels with me in a congress of peace, not at the tip of a sword."

James countered, "Do not harbor the Frenchman. Turn him over to me to stand trial for treason and murder. This vagabond, who pretends to be your ally, deserves to die by the noose."

Yellow Elk answered sternly, "When you set forth from your fortress to attack us, you vacated the laws that have bound us together in accords of mutual understanding. You still fail to recognize that we are a sovereign people, governed by our own principles, not by yours."

James' blood boiled as he surrendered to Yellow Elk, tossing his sword away in submission.

The warrior chief allowed the soldiers to care for their dead and wounded. He decided to let them return to His Majesty's Fort at Crown Point, unmolested. "The Borderland is our home and shall remain so as long as I am able to defend it. Notify your commanders, political leaders, and land-grabbing squatters that we will fight to the death to preserve our sovereignty."

As the sun began to set, Balmond caught up to the woodsman on the trail back to camp. "What causes you to tread so slowly, woodsman? You should be reveling in a glorious victory."

Papineau was incensed. "I thought we were rid of that hearty fool, James. I left him for dead in your hovel. How could he have survived the inferno? Now he conspires with that wag, Kariwase, to bring on today's battle. I do not trust any of them for they are all impetuous rogues."

The guilt riddled Balmond avoided the telling question about James' survival, for he had saved him from the blaze. "Kariwase has convinced me of his treachery. He attempts to profit from our demise and the downfall of his clan. That one is foolish and rash, in relentless pursuit of power."

Papineau was concerned. "Yellow Elk has saved us from a heinous fate, but the braves think that we have defamed them. I do not know how much longer we can remain in their confidence."

Balmond winced. "The Mohawks have given you a chit for fighting fearlessly because they honor trust and loyalty. But that fool James is hell-bent on avenging the deaths of his brothers-in-arms. He will not rest until he hunts us down like dogs and strings us up from the Dule Tree."

Papineau showed remorse. "I fear that we have brought a plague down upon these people. If we remain with them, they will suffer unspeakable depredation and we will meet a heinous fate."

Papineau and Balmond retired to their hut where Standing Waters met them. "Yellow Elk will move the clan deep into the mountains at sunrise. Your valor today has given him cause to put aside our differences and allow you to accompany us." He left abruptly, not wanting to linger.

Balmond challenged Papineau, "I go where the clan goes, but which path will you take?"

Papineau was terse. "For now, Monsieur Balmond, I go where my heart leads me."

The woodsman sat outside of the hut in a foul state and watched Two Suns lead her people back into the compound. The incident with her at the creek replayed in his mind. He still chafed as the flamboyant words of his father echoed in his head. *Do not pretend that you are my equal, wench.* He was not sure how to crack the mysterious shell of this aloof woman. He had vowed that he would be different, but for now he was shadowed by his own self-doubt and anxious fears.

Brisk air settled over the village bathed in moonlight, as a harrowing day came to a peaceful end. It was quiet, save for the screech of an owl or the incessant chirp of the tree frogs. Unable to sleep, Papineau walked with no purpose other than to go somewhere else. He was soon greeted by the rising sun, offering up a new day and a new twist of fate for the man known as The Wolf.

Chapter 47

Fateful Rendezvous

As promised, Jon made the side trip back to Gettysburg to see Gretchen. The war was nearly over, as the battalions mopped up operations in the South and secured the peace. The country suffered from the depredation of the conflict and the untimely death of the President, but there was hope that things might soon return to a sense of normalcy.

The day was sunny, with spring in full bloom, as Jon left the train. He began to walk up Carlisle Street. The sleepy little village was still ravaged by the occupation of the two massive armies. He noticed the bullet-riddled building walls and the remnants of waste piled high in the streets.

Soldiers lingered in the squares or taverns, questioning Jon about the action at the front. He took the time to speak to each until they had their fill of stories. It was almost noon, so he excused himself from a conversation and limped up Baltimore Street. He remembered his first journey up this quaint thoroughfare, lined on both sides with colonial era row houses and churches. As the battle raged, Federal soldiers swarmed toward the rear, desperately throwing up barricades or fighting house-to-house to check the Rebel advance. He was ashamed about getting caught up in the panic. He shook his head in disgust and moved off toward Cemetery Ridge.

After a short walk, Jon found himself on the Emmitsburg Road, its stalwart fences standing as they had during the battle. He passed the Dobbin House Tavern and thought about Josias Weed. He ended his road to freedom at the place where Jon's struggles to free himself began. He thought it to be poignant that two men from diverse backgrounds could be thrust together by a twist of fate.

Cemetery Ridge loomed in the near distance, eerily silent and coldly barren. The copse of trees stood as a symbol of defiance against the azure sky. It marked the spot where it all came to an abrupt end. Jon could hear the cries of the soldiers, the boom of the artillery, and the crack of the small arms fire. He shuddered at the thought of men defiantly charging toward certain death. His reflection was interrupted by a nasal voice calling to him from just down the road.

"Hey, Yank, what are you cogitating about?"

Jon turned to see a grey-clad soldier sitting on a rail just a few paces to the south. "I was just mulling over the battle. No man should be subjected to that kind of horror." Jon suddenly realized that he was talking to a Southerner. "Why on earth are you still in Gettysburg, Reb?"

The scrawny, dirty soldier spit his tobacco onto the downtrodden road. "It struck me, why should I fester in Elmira Prison when I could stay right here? The Yanks were most obliging after I signed that durned oath of allegiance. It is America, ain't it and I am free to live where I please?"

Jon half-smiled as he walked toward the Reb. He rested his musket against the fence and shook the man's hand. "First Lieutenant Jon Holland, Army of the Potomac, at your service."

The man vigorously shook Jon's hand. "Pleased to make your acquaintance. Waya Applewhite, sir, formerly of the 26th North Carolina Regiment. We planted our flag on that angle." He squinted. "I swear that I seen you before, for I never forget a face. It's a blessing and a curse you know."

Jon interrupted him. "Waya is a mighty peculiar name. What is its origin?"

"I am a half-breed, but that is of no mind to me. Mum was Cherokee and pap was English, three generations back. They hitched up during the Removal. Folks in these parts call it the Trail of Tears." Waya put a chaw in his cheek. "My pap was detailed to the military escort that guided the Cherokee to the Oklahoma reservations. Mum was a young squaw, barely able to survive the rigors of that perverse extrication. Somehow they overcame all of that prejudice to make a go of it."

He wiped his mouth on the soiled sleeve of his faded uniform. "Look at me, a child of oppression, fighting myself to suppress the darkies. It is quite contrary if you ask me, but I had three squares a day and a warm bed in the army. It was a far site better than that ramshackle hovel in the Smokies. You know, Yank, I think that is why I was drawn to stay here. I owe somebody a debt, but I have not quite figured out who I might be beholden to or how that may come about."

Jon was quite amused by the quirks of this countrified Reb. "What does Waya mean?"

"Mum says that I have the piercing eyes of a wolf, cold and grey like my soul. See here, this left one is blue and the tother one is yeller. It's the dearndest thing, so they named me wolf."

Jon looked into Waya's eyes to see the peculiar anomaly. He was taken aback by what he saw.

Waya chuckled, "My mum thought I was possessed by the spirit of the Shadow Self. She told me that the wolf was the teacher, you know, your conscience. Don't feel much like a shaman, but mum insists that somewhere within me is the power to provide wisdom and strength to others. Durned Indians are always preaching about something mystical or other-worldly. Hell, I don't need that kind of responsibility. I am simple folk like me Pap. Cat taken your tongue, Yank?"

Jon was startled by the Reb's revelations. "We live worlds apart, but we are alike in many ways, Reb. My ancestors went through the same suffering as yours did. Here we stand without a care on a beautiful spring day when just a few months ago, we were aiming to gun each other down."

The Reb's eyes opened wide with astonishment as he began to realize where he had seen Jon. "Where were you posted during the charge on the last day of the fight, Yank?"

"Why do you ask?"

"Well, I have the vision of an eagle and can pluck the eye out of a needle with my shootin. When the boys were running back to Uncle Bobby, I stopped right cheer, set my squirrel gun on this here rail, and plunked a Yank off of that wall by them trees. Durned if he didn't look like you."

This Carolinian, who symbolized the Shadow Self, the creature that had manifested itself in many forms to haunt Jon and was the one who had struck him down. If this carefree Reb had not shot him, he would have never met Gretchen, wrestled with his demons, or found his resolve.

"Yup, that Yank aimed right at me. And then, as if God willed it, he pointed his musket toward the sky. Well, I wasn't going to look a gift horse in the mouth, so I shot him before he could change his mind. He spun around like a top and fell dead away behind that-there angled wall." Waya removed his hat. "See that spot where a stone is misplaced? That is where he stood, jeering like he was some kind of hero. I couldn't let him mock us in our most dire hour, so I finished him."

Waya jumped off of the fence. "Shoot, I was so proud of myself that I forgot to run. Lickety-split, those Yanks posted on the left rounded me up like a stray calf. I spent a month as a prisoner of war in that stanking barn before I signed the oath." He squatted and grabbed a handful of soil. "I've been digging graves, but I have a hankering to fetch me up some land and start a farm."

Jon was stunned by the turn of events. "It is as if the saints have delivered you to me, Reb. My ancestor from long ago was named Wolf. It was the wolf that guided him and it is the wolf that guides me. How is it that you appear before me to haunt me as he has?"

The Reb looked up at Jon with curiosity. "I'd say that you are a bit balmy, Yank. Have you had too much to drink at Dobbins or are you crazed in the head from ills of the war?"

"Let's just say that I have received some advice from peculiar places, trying to set me straight on life. I speculate that there is more to divine intervention than meets the eye."

"Shoot, don't go making a mountain out of an anthill. I only happen to be here 'cause them cranks insist that I go through that mass grave bone by bone and sort the fellers out. They are going to send the Rebs home so they can be buried proper. I ain't sure whether I am sorting a Reb from a Yank. The bones lie to me, 'cause they all appear to be the same once the devil has had his due."

Waya continued to yammer. "Yup, I don't think my recollection of the shooting is that good. The fella I plucked was a sergeant major and you are a first lieuie. The mind plays tricks on you in the heat of battle. Nope, you ain't the fella I knocked off of the wall. I am quite sure of that."

Jon took Waya's hand and hauled him up off of the ground. "Let me tell you a macabre tale over a pint at Dobbin's, Reb. It is a fable you cannot believe would be true on your best day."

The two markedly different soldiers headed toward the tavern, blue walking next to grey. As they sat in the dim light of Dobbin's front room, Jon reminisced about the harrowing experience at the wall. It was a three-pint story, something Grandpa Michael would have been proud of.

Waya sipped his ale, mesmerized by the breadth of Jon's tale. He was not sure that either of them possessed shaman-like powers. He was all about living life in the moment. Jon, he surmised, was working toward something greater. It was a surprisingly familiar theme to Waya, but he was not sure that his bullet or divine intervention was the cause of their chance encounter. "Shoot, let's go back to that spot where you fell, Yank. Maybe we can find some resolve to the whole mess."

The two men exited the tavern, crossed the road, and walked up the ridge. "That little filly sitting there on the wall by the copse of trees, she wouldn't be waiting for you now, would she, Yank?"

Jon looked up and knew right away that it was Gretchen. "That remarkable woman nursed me be back to health. It seems fitting that you meet her." Jon could sense the Cherokee's reluctance. "She won't bite your head off. She is as gentle as a newborn lamb and as forgiving as the Lord. I suspect that she has a little wolf blood in her as well."

Waya laughed and then relented, helping Jon manage on his wounded leg.

Gretchen greeted Jon with a smile. "I am so glad to see that you are alive, Jon. I have been sitting here a spell, thinking that you may not come." She hugged him tightly about the waist.

Jon finally stepped away. "There is someone I would like you to meet."

Waya wiped his soiled hands on his pants and then removed his slouch hat. He spoke in a heavy drawl, "Waya Applewhite, ma'am. It is a pleasure to make your acquaintance."

"Charmed, sir."

Waya smiled sheepishly. "Are you going to tell her, or am I?"

Jon hesitated. "Gretchen, this Reb was defending a cause he thought to be righteous. Well, he was only doing what he thought was right and on three July he was the one who shot me."

Gretchen studied the two men. "Have you gentlemen resolved your differences?"

The two soldiers looked at each other and then both nodded, simultaneously.

"Then it seems to me that we should forget past transgressions and start life anew. All men brave and true are sometimes forced into unspeakable acts due to contrary opinions or the convictions of war. God has blessed both of your souls to come together so you can forgive and forget. What more can we expect from civilized men and the will of merciful Lord?"

The two soldiers were relieved as Gretchen balanced their curious lives. She invited the men to her home in York for a meal. The two lonesome soldiers spent the evening with her family, despite Reverend Jung's contrary opinions toward Jon's spirituality or Waya's Rebel convictions.

Waya took to the road as the sunlight faded. "I'll look you up, Yank, when things get settled."

Gretchen and Jon spent the next few days getting reacquainted before he boarded the train for home. He wanted to stay at Gretchen's side, but he felt a strong obligation to return to his family.

For the time being, their romance would be put on hold while Jon continue to sort out his life.

Chapter 48

Wolf Trap

Before the sun had crested the horizon, the camp in the Lower Trace was abandoned. The longhouse and wigwams were left to let nature run its course over them. The horses and dogs were packed with caches of supplies and the tribe moved to a summer retreat in a remote region high among the mountain peaks. It would be an arduous journey to a place of peaceful obscurity.

Papineau stood on a bluff that overlooked a beautiful valley nestled at the base of the mountains. For the most part, it was still untouched by civilization, pristine and serene. He could barely make out the snake-like appearance of the river as it coursed through the bottomland. Wisps of smoke marked the sites of a few scattered homesteads or villages nestled quietly along its shores.

The woodsman barely noticed the valley's natural brilliance, for he was too caught up in his own affairs. *If only Three-Legged-Wolf could see me now. I stand above the trees commanding nature. I have fulfilled my childhood prophecy. I am an island casting no burden on man or country.* He wondered if the vaunted warrior was really dead. He needed to resolve this matter, for it ate away at him like a cancer. He glanced up at the majestic peaks that towered above him. *Maybe Graham was right, the answer to the questions that haunt my life lie up there.* Without contemplating it further, he carefully descended the cliff and headed back toward the camp.

Sitting on a blanket outside of the hut was the indomitable Balmond. "The way I figure it, you would simply be lost without me. So, I decided to sit a spell and see if you would have the gumption to return. That firelock leaning against yon post convinced me that it was likely."

Papineau spoke, "There is no time for that muddle. We need to catch up with the tribe."

"There is no need to hurry. They were moving like a turtle when they left here at sunup. They can't be more than a league or so ahead of us. They are heading up the Wolf Trap Trail." He stood up and grabbed his pack. "I did have the sense to inquire where they were going."

Papineau was quite relieved, "You have done well, Balmond. I commend you."

The two men lit out toward the northwest on a well-marked trail. The fresh imprints of overloaded horses, meandering pack dogs, and many moccasins made it easy to follow. Balmond probed, "Why have you chosen to rejoin the tribe when your heart still battles with your mind?"

"I have inquiries to make and scores to settle. They eat at me like the buzzards eat the carrion."

"I hope your motivations are honorable. I, for one, will not be a party to any misguided plots."

"The answers I receive will guide my course. You can be party to it or not, as you so choose."

"Here's the way I see it," Balmond said. "You are disoriented. Today, you run toward the sun and tomorrow you will run way. Until you choose to follow one path and hold a determined course, you will be doomed to wander aimlessly through life. What is it that you seek?"

Papineau quickened his pace to move away from the annoying man who challenged his convictions. He caught up with the tribe and found Yellow Elk at the head of the column. He would seek the truth about the Algonquin and challenge the chief about his relationship with Two Suns.

The chief was playing with young Joseph Grey Fox. "You fought well, woodsman."

Papineau responded, "I fought for my own preservation, sir, nothing more, but why did we have to engage the Regulars when parlay would have accomplished the same thing."

"We know that rogue warriors from the Confederation raided a remote village and massacred many people. The Colonials wanted revenge, assuming that we had masterminded the raid, so they sent the Regulars to confront us. False alliances and traitorous people seek to break the Covenant."

The chief was baiting Papineau. He hoped that he would divulge information about the accusations of murder and treason, or reveal some information that would implicate him in the plot, but the woodsman did not take the bait. "The Confederation offered to cover the grave. But the Brits would not stand for compromise and stepped in where they do not belong. I suspect that the Colonial protests and uprisings fueled the raid, but we suffer at their hand because of it."

Balmond, having just joined them, interrupted. "What will you do with that turncoat, Kariwase? He plots to overthrow you. He laid bruises upon me for trying to shoot the British officer."

Yellow Elk's spoke honestly, "He has aroused our suspicions. Should he play his hand, we will act swiftly." He sighed, "We won a hollow victory yesterday, but I fear that the Brits will return in great numbers to avenge their loss. We are forced to migrate from our homes, while the defeated soldiers wallow in the comfort of theirs. We will never concede to their demands and reprisals."

Papineau was frustrated. "So where will you go so that you can live as you please in peace?"

"There is a most holy place high up in the deepest recesses of the mountains. We only go there during a time of celebration or a time of healing. It is suitable for living only during the summer, so we will have to move again as the leaves begin to turn and the cold begins to fall."

Papineau inquired, "What is this place called?"

Yellow Elk replied with reverence, "Tear of the Clouds."

The Mohawks lived a simple life, but had an intricate hierarchy of beliefs to guide them. A woman's role in that order was complex. The woodsman, not understanding those convolutions, awkwardly tried to explain the details of his confrontation with Two Suns. He got through it, to the amazement of the chief, who was thoroughly amused by his clumsiness.

The warrior eased the tension, "That one has a bit of the devil in her. I have learned not antagonize her for she is capable of humiliating the bravest men." Yellow Elk jested, "You, my friend, are fortunate to come away from the fracas unscathed. Others have not been so lucky."

Papineau was relieved by Yellow Elk's humor. The conversation unexpectedly moved on to inter-tribal marriage which sustained the order of power, while fortifying the strength of the Iroquois Alliance. Women held a prominent role in that order, particularly with regard to the sustenance of the clan and the carrying on of the clan name. It was complicated and the minute details began to bore Papineau. The conversation was not traversing the path that he had hoped. He surprisingly asked Yellow Elk about his personal intentions for the hand of Two Suns.

The warrior stopped abruptly in the path. He burst into a fit of guttural laughter, "Have you not lived among us long enough to know that Two Suns is my sister?" He shook his head in utter amazement. "It is not my motivations that you need to concern yourself with, woodsman."

Papineau was so self-centered that he failed to recognize how things stood among the people he had been living with. Twice, over a two-day period, he had been humiliated.

As the column coursed its way through pine barrens, over swiftly flowing streams, and through meadows dotted with the spoils of winter, Yellow Elk confided in Papineau, "As you are so vaguely aware, my sister is unwed. Although Standing Waters fancies her, I do not believe she will be swayed by his attempts to win her favor. It is an opening that you should contemplate, my friend." He glanced over at Papineau and smirked. The trap to snare the wolf had been sprung.

Chapter 49

Eyes of the Storm

The tribe's exodus from the valley took them into the deep recesses of the snow-covered mountains. The horses struggled with the undulating terrain that coursed through the Wolf Trap and then the Upper Falcon's Trace. An extensive tract of virgin forest blanketed the earth with a lush canopy. The vernal, aromatic air smelled of wildflowers, sweet berries, and savory pines, intermingled with the smoky essence of moss covered bottoms. Vibrant streams crashed swiftly over the boulder strewn landscape, as runoff from the melting snows filled them with new life.

At midday, Yellow Elk halted the column in a high peaks meadow. It had been burned off by another tribe to clear it of unwanted brush. Sprouts of lush, green grass began to appear amongst the char. These burnt hills were a common sight in the lands occupied by the People of the Flint, a contrast of light and dark upon the land, reminiscent of their precarious existence.

Balmond, who had a tendency to linger, caught up with the clan. He milled about looking for Papineau, who was preparing a meal at the forest edge. He fell out next to him in the grass. "What demon has possessed me to stay with this tribe? My old bones are not used to adventurous living."

Papineau handed the boatman a piece of dried meat and a cup of herbal soup. He stared unconsciously across the meadow, not paying much attention to his weary friend.

Balmond rolled to his side. "I think that squaw has made you feebleminded. You are moon struck or is it Two Suns struck? When will you speak to her about your intentions?"

"You speak far too much nonsense for an old man. What makes you such an expert on the fairer sex? Surely, that ferry service could not have provided you with the experience you believe you have acquired on this matter? So, keep your primal thoughts to yourself."

As the woodsman left in disgust, Balmond rolled back in the grass and laughed. He sipped his soup and thoroughly enjoyed his revelry at his bumbling friend's expense.

At the far corner of the meadow, Two Suns tended to a male child. She was patient and gentle, not at all like the woman who had attacked Papineau or challenged him at the lodge. She caressed the child's cheek and fed him cornmeal. She tickled his stomach and then chortled with him as he reacted. Her laugh was like sweet music singing on the wind, calling to the woodsman.

The Indian princess heard Papineau's feet part the brittle grass. She brushed her dark hair from her face. She had secretly wanted to speak with him. His overpowering guile and relentless spirit intrigued her, despite his independent, selfish, and emotionally hamstrung ways.

Standing Waters watched the event unfold from the wood line. The stoic warrior had continued to pursue Two Suns' affections despite his reluctant agreement to support Ten Hands' plan, but his efforts had been foiled by the tumultuous circumstances of their lives. He was jealous, but his loyalty to the tribe was unquestioned, as he struggled with deep emotions.

Papineau squatted next to the child and patted him on the head. He summoned some courage and touched the back of her hand as Two Suns raised another bit of meal to the child's mouth. She hesitated and then brushed his hand aside. Their eyes met. The ice had been broken.

Yellow Elk yelled across the meadow to gather the clan for the final leg of the journey. His commands interrupted the brief interlude between the two suitors. Papineau stood up and hoisted the child over his head. The young brave gurgled and then expectorated cornmeal onto his tunic. He jumped backward and held the boy as far away from him as his arms would allow.

Two Suns giggled and chastised Papineau for his abrupt behavior. She took the child from him, picked up her belongings, and started toward the trailhead with the child gathered about her waist.

Discomfited, Papineau doffed his cap and reluctantly let her walk away. He brushed the child's waste from his shirt, wrinkling his nose at its sour smell, and then returned to Balmond.

"This seems like a lovely place to set up shop," Balmond stated as Papineau approached.

"I think we need to stay with the tribe," Papineau bent over to pick up his satchel and musket.

"Do you think that your sudden motivation to stay may be influenced by that shapely squaw?"

Papineau gave Balmond a shove. "My intentions are honorable and you should be so lucky to be in the presence of a woman who is as fine as she is."

The two men sauntered across the meadow and ventured upon Ten Hands, who sat by himself under a tree. His head was down; eyes closed and chin upon his chest. "I need to speak to you privately, Papineau, about a matter of grave importance. Sit here before me, if it pleases you."

Papineau replied, "What you have to say to me, Ten Hands, can also be said to my friend Balmond. We harbor no secrets from one another. What is it you that wish to share with me?"

The chief chose his words carefully. "I answered your questions about the Anishinabe in riddles. I see in your eyes that it still troubles you. I will speak with candor about their fate."

Papineau's body tensed, his fists clenched in his lap. The chief grabbed his wrists so tightly that he could not pull away. He felt the old man's remarkable strength, but anger commanded him.

"Our search for the men who raped our women and stole our livestock led us toward the New France provinces of the Acadians where some Algonquin clans resided along the river the French call the Chaudière. We approached a village from the west and attacked as the sun blinded them. It is a nightmare that festers in my soul to this day." The chief swallowed hard. "The carnage was horrific, for I could not control the pent-up fury of my warriors. I, too, was caught up in the hatred."

Papineau could not hold back his rage. "You heartlessly killed them all?"

The chief put his head down in shame. "The Anishinabe were no match for us, but three of their men fought heroically. Yellow Elk killed Stanley Two Toes with his lance. An adopted Frenchman, Pierre Dumont, was shot by Standing Waters. Their deaths were swift."

Papineau's lunged at the chief, grabbing him about the throat with both of his hands. The chief gasped for air as the woodsman's powerful grip tightened. He let his body go limp in submission. Balmond interceded, stopping Papineau from killing the ancient one in a matter of seconds.

"Get off of him, Papineau. Do you want to live your entire life as a murderer and a fugitive?"

Papineau's mother's words echoed in his head. *You will be no better than he is.* The image of his father's face flitted for an instant through his muddled brain. Then, the fiery, painted face of Three-Legged-Wolf, basked in the light of a morning sun. *The better man walks away.*

The woodsman released his grip and rolled back upon the meadow grass, regaining his composure as the chief struggled to breathe. He spoke lucidly, "Did you encounter a man whose face was painted with the fire of the devil's mask? Did you kill Three-Legged-Wolf?"

Ten Hands struggled to raise himself up on his elbows. The fatal words came out in a gargled whisper, "He confronted me with the rage of a rabid dog. I easily subdued him, for his strength had been sapped away. While he knelt before me, he spoke with clarity and wisdom, eradicating my anger, while bringing me to a state of inner peace and euphoria. I admired him, for he was a man of conviction and spiritual sanctity. He mesmerized me with the precision of his mind and the lucid reasoning of his speech. Even though my warriors called for his death, I lowered my weapon, intending to spare him. He was a man of integrity, not one to rape and pillage, but one to heal."

Papineau openly wept, placing his massive hands over his face to cover the trail of his tears.

"I let down my guard, but sensed that he would die a martyr when the thrust of his lance pierced my side." The chief raised his tunic to expose a broad scar in the fleshy part of his abdomen. The image of Christian cross marked the place where the lance had been extracted. "I swung my belt axe and instantly removed his head. His eyes glared at me as it rolled across the dried river bed."

Papineau looked into Ten Hand's eyes, glazed over with remorseful tears. A calming voice eased him. "Leave it lie, woodsman. What's done is done and no act of man or God can undo it. Three-Legged-Wolf died valiantly. We all have our crosses to bear. You can choose to carry another one or you can choose to burn one. What course shall it be, my friend?" It was Balmond.

Papineau knew all along that the people of the Wolf Clan had committed this atrocity, but he had to hear it first hand to believe it. He had imagined when he heard it from Graham that he would kill them all when the truth had been revealed, but now he suffered from a quandary, for the will to forgive was haunting him. He spoke to Balmond, "Although our time together has been short, I have grown to admire and respect you. You have taught me many things. For that, I am grateful. I will hold each moment of our acquaintance reverently in my heart until the day we meet again."

Ten Hands handed a tarnished Christian cross dangling from a bloodstained chain to the woodsman. "Take this as a token of my shame and a reminder that good can come from evil."

The woodsman snatched his childhood cross from the chief's hand and ran off across the meadow. As he distanced himself from the tribe, he felt alone, hurt, and bewildered by the complexities of his life and the pain of his embattled soul.

Chapter 50

Celestial Twins

Balmond took Ten Hands by the arm and they walked slowly toward the trailhead, cloaked in a mystifying darkness. They could feel the cool air rush from the sheltered spaces when suddenly, Standing Waters appeared, startling Balmond. "Are you ready to rejoin the tribe, my chief?"

"Help me to mount, brave warrior. I am too feeble to walk another step on this troubling day."

Standing Waters hoisted the chief onto the pony and covered him with a robe. Ten Hands surveyed the meadow for any signs of Papineau. He hoped that he had a change of heart. Disappointed by this turn of events, he frowned and kicked at the flanks of his horse trying to reach his son at the head of the column. As he passed by Two Suns he yelled to her to follow. She tugged at the reins of her horse to ease it out of line and nearly ran the beast over a cliff in pursuit.

Ten Hands talked to Yellow Elk. "I have told him everything and he has reacted, but not as you would have expected. Yet I fear that he is no longer affable toward our way of thinking."

"Have you banished him, father?" was Two Suns' admonishment when she arrived.

"No child, he has chosen flight. He thinks that escape will remedy his woes. I fear that he has been running all of his life and will continue to do so unless the spirits settle his soul."

Yellow Elk interceded, "Then I shall go after him and coax him to return. We need to console him and bring him around to our way of thinking if the prophecy is to be fulfilled."

"We have killed his friends. He suppresses his fears rather than confront them. His anger fuels his courage so he cannot or will not see reason on any matters of the heart."

Yellow Elk spoke. "Do you not believe that I can transform him and alter his thinking? I am of the mind that if he is in the state that you suggest, then we should just let him go astray."

Ten Hands answered his son, "I have seen the light of goodness in his eyes, but he has yet to discover how to release the demons that cast a shadow over the light. He needs someone to reach into the deepest recesses of his soul without fear of retribution. You pose a threat to him so he will lash out at you in defiance. We need a soft hand, not a violent hand to sway his thinking."

Two Suns had already anticipated Ten Hands' request. "I will find him and bring him back. He will listen to me, but he is so strong willed that he may not understand me or our intentions."

"You are the only one who can alter his thinking, but take care, for he is a dangerous man. Take Standing Waters and three warriors of his choosing to protect you from afar."

"Do you think that prudent father? Standing Waters' harbors ill will toward the woodsman."

"It is the wisest thing, daughter, for it will be a solemn test of loyalty, an affirmation of your leadership, and a verification of their ability to sacrifice for others. Leave him with wise choices so that he can follow his heart. Only then will we know which path leads to the truth. Only then will we know if loyalty or revenge marks the trail of his existence and the fate of our future."

Two Suns turned her horse about and stopped long enough to converse with Standing Waters. He immediately summoned three young braves and retraced his path back toward the meadow.

The search for Papineau took several days. But his trail was hot, for he had been careless. He was distraught; his emotions masking his keen judgment. On the third day out, as the sun was setting over the ridges that outlined a narrow, barren valley, Two Suns saw Papineau standing in an open defile below her. He was speaking in an animated way to someone, but from this distance, she could not determine who it might be. She summoned a brave to go forward to get a closer look.

It took a great deal of time, but the warrior finally returned. "He speaks to the Scotsman, Graham. They are haggling over the price of pelts. They have no idea that we are watching."

Two Suns smiled. *Two false suitors brought together by the fate of the gods.* She turned to Standing Waters. "I am going down to talk to him. Keep your distance, but be vigilant. I am unsure how he; or Graham for that matter, will take to this chance encounter."

Standing Waters asked, "Why is it that you bother yourself with those fools?"

Two Suns was not going to be drawn into a debate. She dismounted her horse and carefully made her way down the steep grade to the bottom of the defile. She cautiously approached the two men and called out, "Woodsman, can I speak to you without fear of retribution?" She waited for an answer, concealed in the brush with an arrow knocked on her drawn bow.

Both men turned abruptly toward her, startled by the voice coming from the blind. "Who is it that hides there? Show yourself or suffer the consequences." Graham readied his weapon.

Two Suns emerged from the brush, keeping her bow at the ready. "It is Papineau I wish to speak to, Caleb. He feels that he has been wronged by my brothers and we need to set a new course."

Graham looked up at the woodsman. "So, you have been beguiled by this wily harpy? Did I not warn you on the night that we navigated the great lake that she would steal your heart away?"

Papineau seethed, "She and her cowardly brothers mean nothing to me, Graham. They have taken my soul and fed it to the devil. Stay out of my business, if you know what is good for you."

"Quell your anger, woodsman. I am not the one to take issue with. You can be assured that I, for one, am finished with her. What do you want for the pelts, Papineau?"

"Take the lot, Graham, as a gift. I have no further use for them."

Graham was surprised, considering Papineau had been fiercely negotiating. "I will leave you to the whims of the woman. If you need me, I'll be at Ticonderoga. It seems that the Brits are in need of my services." He tipped his tam and headed off through the swale that led toward the lake.

Papineau turned his attention to Two Suns. "What do you want from me, wench? I have no use for you. As far as I am concerned, you are all scoundrels, murderers, and thieves."

Two Suns wanted to call his suspect character into question, but the crafty woman appealed to his sympathies instead. "I have come to humbly petition you to return to us. After you have heard what I have to say, then you can choose your fate. Will you give me an audience?"

Papineau's remembered the touch of her hand. That brief, innocent gesture had drawn him closer to her. "Where have you hidden your warriors? I know they linger in the blind."

She withdrew her bow and quivered the arrow. "We have all done things that have brought shame to our house. We have killed, rather than be killed. We have scorned rather than be scorned. We have suffered a thousand heartaches. No one is immune to the frailties of the human spirit. We instinctively do things against our will because the wisdom to do otherwise has escaped us."

Papineau's eyes ran cold with hatred, the features of his scarred face skewed with the pain that coursed through his heart. His fists were clenched in anger upon the stock and barrel of his musket.

Two Suns tried to sway his emotions. "I have a legend to tell you, one that may help you to see another side of life and quell the beasts that reside within your heart."

Papineau found it demeaning to sit before her, so he stood, arms folded across his weapon. His rage blinded his sharp intellect, so he failed to see the value of parables. The tales marked the lives of people that had shared the same pain, lived through the same challenges, and overcome the same adversity. He refused to embrace the human resolve and divinity that the stories alluded to.

"In the Native world, there exists a set of twins, both unique, but both necessary to maintain the balance of life. The Right-Handed Twin rules the world under the blazing sun. The Left-Handed Twin commands the Underworld that resides beneath the mantle of the rising moon. As long as we are centered as a people, the equilibrium between good and evil will never be broken."

Her emotions seared in her passionate eyes. "I was born at the confluence of time when the sun and the moon crossed each other's path. At that moment, the Twins wrestled for control of the land and upset the stability of life. As they came together to battle for our souls, everything was bathed in a dark shadow of doubt. But slowly, triumphantly the light returned. It is during that time that the balance of all things in nature is at its fullest. My name, Two Suns, represents the stability between the darkness and the light. I am forever bound to the cause of preserving good over evil."

She deliberately paused. "If the balance between the light and dark is broken, then nature as we know it will cease to exist. This equilibrium is fragile and must be handled delicately."

Papineau interrupted, "So why should this story concern me?"

She looked into the woodsman's dark eyes. "You harbor evil in your soul, hardened I suspect by a violent life. It is commanded by the Left-Handed Twin. But, I sense that deep within you lay a man of integrity, a brother to the Right-Handed Twin. Although you have upset the balance of life in our world, your presence among us could reveal the truth that will help to lead us away from our strife. If you could find a way to center yourself, the weight on your soul will be lifted."

The woodsman sensed sincerity in her placid voice. *Two Suns is a creature of vast intellect with a deep conviction to preserve nature and her way of life. Under the false mask of her harsh exterior there resides a loving, loyal, and acutely sensitive woman. Is her motivation to woo me filled with personal convictions; or is she offering me a straightforward gesture of love? How can I give her people a sense of hope in an evolving world that may not include them?* He lashed out like his father would to his mother, "So what is it that you will have me do, you foolish wench?"

"Forgive us of our wrongdoings, as we have forgiven you. Forget the darkness of your past. Embrace the challenges of living among my people, building generations of hope for those who walk in our footprints." She looked into his eyes. "We all want to love and be loved. We all want to be treated with respect and dignity. We all want to live freely. Can't you understand that?"

Papineau believed that Two Suns was asking him to lay down his life for people who had aggrieved him to a point of hatred. *Why am I afraid? What do I run from? Why do I covet her?* The hollow void in his soul gnawed at him like a festering wound.

The persistent woman continued, "You and I are very different, much like the Twins, but it is those differences that will help us to restore the balance. If we join together in a circle of friendship, then we both can overcome the challenges to our existence and fulfill a legacy of promise."

The woodsman was intrigued by the thought-provoking essence of her words. She understood things that he never could begin to comprehend, yet she was reaching out to him, of all people, to bring fulfillment to her life and the lives of her people.

"You must decide your own fate, but before you do, consider this. You have no circle to attach yourself to. You will drift aimlessly until you die of a broken heart. On that day, the man known as Papineau will bear no legacy, swallowed up by the shadows of the Underworld." Two Suns lost her desire to coax the pigheaded man posturing over her. She removed the sash draped over her shoulder and handed it to him. "This sash is a reminder of the man you mourn and the lessons he tried to teach you." She stood up, kissed him on his scarred cheek, and walked away.

Papineau watched the squaw struggle up the slope of the defile. When she reached the top, Standing Waters greeted her with an extended hand and an embrace. The hamstrung woodsman chastised himself, feeling that he may have lost her, but was he unable to bring himself to follow.

The moon passed behind the cover of lingering clouds and blackened the sky. Nightfall embraced the woodsman as he mulled over the day's events. He wrapped the sash around his waist, the eyes of the embroidered wolf staring out at him. He had seen this penetrating glance before in the eyes of his mentor, when he reprimanded him as a child or cajoled him as a young man. He was consumed with doubt, sensing that the Left-Handed Twin was engulfing him in the mantel of evil. He longed for the guidance of the Right-Handed Twin. Rubbing the scar emblazoned on his cheek. The pain of the wound returned as the Celestial Twins wrestled for his embattled soul.

Chapter 51

Back to Beverwijck

The train to Albany, formerly the outpost of Beverwijck or Beaver District, tested Jon's fragile will. It stopped frequently to take on wood and water or allow somber troopers to unload the coffins of the dead. Exhausted and alone, he spent the last night of the journey in Poughkeepsie before making the final few miles upriver to his home.

The war, in all of its misery, drove the contemplative farmer to right the sinking ship of an uncertain life. He had discovered his inner fortitude. His instincts were keen, but a void still lingered within his soul. He was coddled by a conviction to do something of such magnitude that it would alter his life and the lives of others. He thought about Gretchen. She was the spark that ignited his revival, but he did not understand the depth of their relationship. Her goodness was overwhelming and her ability to decipher the complex codes of his dreams was uncanny. He hoped that he could find the answers to all of his questions by returning to the farm where he would probe the deepest secrets of his ancestry for the one message that would finalize his quest.

The weary Lieutenant debarked from the train in East Albany. Across the river, the capital of New York was small by most standards, but influential. The locals felt that the seeds for democracy were planted here when the Iroquois and colonial fathers crafted a collegial approach to governance. It bustled with activity, especially around the river and railhead where trade and commerce were heavy. It carried on government, business, and life as the Indians, Dutch, and British had done for centuries.

Overwhelmed by his return to civilian life, Jon melded into the seething city, one of the oldest in America. It was more than a day's ride to his farm and he had arrived late, so he decided to stay the night. He roamed the narrow streets reflecting on the war, preparing himself for the onslaught of questions that he was sure to endure.

He listened to the whispers in the crowds as they discussed the assassination of the President. While serving as a provost guard, Jon had met the Mr. Lincoln at City Landing. He was impressed by his intellect, backwoods humor, and sincere kindness. The mark of an assassin's bullet made people appreciate the magnitude of his political and personal genius. His passing would be a great loss to the country under the pending reconstruction, for his benevolent leadership would have helped to ease the reunion of a bitterly divided nation. Jon hoped that he could find the courage to be as munificent and humble as the President. He was inspired by Lincoln's ability to move people to do extraordinary things and hoped to do the same. He found it to be ironic that Lincoln was pressed by haunting dreams, yet could overcome debilitating hardships and uncertainty to flourish.

The weary war veteran happened upon a tavern by the river called The King's Arms, a familiar place from his grandfather's stories. He refused offers of free ale and solicitations from the local ladies of the night to hole up at a table in the corner. The dark room with a low ceiling of exposed beams was smoky and noisy. It smelled of stale beer and the stench of human flesh as people pressed in upon one another. He ordered a pint of brew and a plate of beef and beans from a stout matron. His palate was tainted by years of eating army food, but he quickly devoured the fresh beer. He soaked up the remains of the beef and beans with a swath of soda bread and closed his eyes.

A riotous commotion aroused Jon, as street urchins chided two men to fight. Jon paid them no mind, but the deep Irish brogue of one of the men piqued his curiosity. He thought that the drink and the lack of sleep were playing tricks with his mind, so he did not perseverate over it.

The second man in the argument bellowed, "I don't care if you are a wounded vet with only one leg, you ugly Mick. If you touch my lady again, I will beat you silly."

Jon sighed heavily and then reluctantly rose out of his chair.

Damn! O'Reilly! He paused briefly to contemplate his options and then parted the crowd to limp across the room.

The barkeep cajoled the two men by inviting them to belly up for a drink. The local man had his posterior resting precariously on the bar, propped up by his cronies. His imposing opponent leaned unsteadily on a homespun crutch. Dressed in a soiled uniform, light blue sergeant's stripes displayed on both sleeves, the soldier threw down a beer, tossed the mug aside, and spat into a spittoon at his feet. He raised his fists, an aggressive move Jon was very familiar with.

Jon tapped O'Reilly on the shoulder, which prompted him to turn and swing. He instinctively ducked. "Well, Shannon, me boy, fancy meeting you here in jolly 'ole Beverwijck."

Shannon put his face close to Jon's, breathing foul breath upon him. "Is that you, Jonny?"

Jon placed Shannon's arm over his shoulder and the two invalids limped back to the corner. "I'm going to the bar to get us a few pints. Sit tight and keep yourself out of mischief, Shannon."

Jon confronted the boisterous local. "It seems to me that I have just saved your life."

The man stopped his litany of bragging to turn toward the uniformed vet standing at his side. "Who might you be, boy? Those bars on your shoulders carry no weight here, mate."

Jon stared at the mirror at the back of the bar that reflected his own worn image. His boyhood features were now replaced by a battle-hardened, weatherworn figure he did not recognize. He was shaken back into reality by a painful brush on his wounded shoulder.

"Hey, boy, I am talking to you."

His Irish blood was boiling, but he did not react. Elbows resting on the bar, Jon turned to look up at the man, a hint of his youthful brogue reemerging as he spoke, "I am a little hard of hearing from exposure to the shot and shell. Would you mind repeating yourself?"

Enunciating his words, the brash brawler yelled, "I said that your friend is a bloody coward."

"That wounded hero has killed more Rebs than any man I know." The barkeep brought the two pints and Jon paid him with a few greenbacks. He began to walk away, but turned to confront the obnoxious local. "You should be thanking him for fighting in your place and for saving the country that keeps you and your sorry friends free. You, sir, who may be the only coward in this room."

The local lunged at Jon. He nimbly stepped aside as if he was avoiding a Rebel bayonet and struck the man on both sides of his head with the mugs. The glasses shattered, spewing beer everywhere. The man fell to the barroom floor and lay groaning in the spittle. Jon stood over him and quoted Irish scripture, *"May ye be in heaven forty years before the devil knew you be dead."*

With the two new beers safely in tow, Jon returned to Shannon. "I am getting a wee bit tired of saving your lardy arse. It pained me to do it, but I bought you a pint for old time's sake."

Shannon slurred his words. "Jonny Holland, how are you me boy? It is a lovely day when you cross my path, laddie. The lads traveling through here last week said you were cut down at Five Forks by some scattered Reb shot, but here you sit in front of me like a ghostly apparition."

Jon responded. "It will take a lot more than a Rebel ball to bring me down. How's the leg?"

"It is aching and festering all of the time. I hope I get the army pension they promised, so I can at least eat regular. The barkeep lets me clean-up for food and ale, but I have to sleep in the street."

"I smell the ills of the alley all over you! Don't you ever bathe?" The mulish man had lost his stubborn Irish will. Jon had never seen him waver in combat, but now he was a withering shell of a man, eaten up by the savagery of the war that beckoned him. "Come on. We're going home."

The unsavory sounds and smells of the city accompanied the two friends as they began to walk north. Black coal dust fouled the air, open sewers reeked of waste, and public houses belched out human revelry. Steamboats plied the river and the shrill train whistles cracked the cool night air.

To the two battle-hardened soldiers, these carefree civilians could not begin to comprehend the suffering they had and continued to endure. They took their freedom for granted, while others sacrificed in their stead. Jon and Shannon settled back into civilian life, hardened men, with disfigured their bodies from a war that toyed with their minds and ravaged their disparate souls.

Chapter 52

Tear of the Clouds

Trees, marred and misshapen by the elements, cast an eerie pall as the band of nomads wandered further into the clouds and ventured onto hallowed ground. The trail that led to it meandered beside a rushing beck, plunging over waterfalls or coursing secretively between rock outcroppings to become the great river. Its roar, at times was so deafening that the birds could not be heard, nor voices understood. The column exited the trail to stand beside a small tarn. Its shoreline resembled a teardrop nestled in the bosom of the mountain peaks that loomed over it.

Legend told of an almighty being, raised up from the bowels of the earth on the day that the mountains rose from the sea. He climbed on the back of the turtle that was his Mother. He stood alone upon her peaks and cried a single tear of joy. It fell into the crest of her bosom, forming the pool that marked the birthplace of the river that coursed over her surface to return the water to the sea. And so, the circle of a natural order of life was completed for the Mohawk people.

The elevation at which the pool rested melded the warmth of the sun and coolness of the waters into a mist that pranced on its surface like a mystical fairy. The scene was incorporeal, humbling the virulent warriors. A droplet of water slid down Ten Hand's cheek as he led his people in a song that gave thanks to the elements of earth, wind, fire, and water and renewed hope for peace.

Papineau remained alone in the hidden valley after his encounter with Two Suns. He missed Balmond's cajoling. The boatman was mysterious, with a checkered past, but Papineau understood that the quirky fellow settled his soul. He removed the sash from about his waist and laid it upon the ground to study its cryptogram. The wolf represented The Shadow Self, a simple but telling depiction of the human soul. Symbols surrounding it portrayed a stark message about people and life. The experience where Three-Legged-Wolf forced him to examine the minute details of that symbiosis suddenly rang true in his mind. All of nature's creatures are dependent upon one another.

Papineau focused on the wolf, persistently staring up at him. It is an evocative creature, the spiritual teacher who would guide him along the path of life. It is reliable and devoted: personal skills that he could not objectify. The wolf is a pack animal by nature, fiercely dependent on others and loyal to a fault. It is the bridge between two diverse worlds, providing symbiotic balance.

Papineau combed his hair back off of his face. *My God, I am the wolf.* He paced uncontrollably, analyzing the significance of his revelation. Then he had an epiphany. *I have been sent here to restore the balance to a fractured landscape. I must build a bridge between many diverse cultures. It is my destiny to subdue my vanity by serving others. It is my destiny to heal, not to destroy.*

Speaking out loud, he assessed his life, "The people that I dishonor have been the ones who have taught me the most profound lessons. Instead of shunning them, I should have embraced them. My Algonquin name, Pashkwadjash; the aura of my teacher, Three-Legged-Wolf; the masked wolf who saved my life and nursed me back to health; the sash; and the clandestine meeting with the Wolf Clan all represent a part of an unbroken circle coaxing me into its fold."

He breathed hard with anxiety. "Two Suns is not the evil spirited princess of the forest. She is the balance between the dark and light, the center between the rising of the sun and the setting of the moon. She is the shaman that closes the circle of life and binds all wounds." He put his hands over his face, fraught with apprehension. *These people have revealed to me who I really am, but I was too simple minded to see it. They have guided me to the path of enlightenment.*

The woodsman secured the sash around his waist, gathered his belongings, and walked confidently out of the defile. As he reached the top of the bluff, he shouted, his deep voice echoing over the hills, "It is my solemn vow to right the wrong of my past. I am the Shadow Self and the fortune of the known world is there for my taking. When doubt clouds the earth, I shall become the great compromiser, bringing harmony where there is chaos and peace where there is discord."

Chapter 53

Recompense

After days of searching, Papineau's found the Mohawk camp, but his return was not as triumphant as he had hoped. He tried to reassure himself that minor setbacks were not going to deter him. He loped into the clearing by the longhouse, pausing momentarily to take in the sights.

The high peaks meadow by the tarn was abuzz. The great lodge was the focal point of the communal village. Wooded areas had been leveled to furnish clear sight lines, build a stockade, and open up fields for crops. Since the growing season was short at this elevation, the women were actively sowing seed, carefully stored throughout the winter. Children ran about and warriors prepared for a hunt.

The woodsman felt invigorated by the commotion. His unexpected presence momentarily put a halt to the hubbub, as the residents gazed upon him with curiosity or disregard.

Standing Waters ran across the compound to aggressively confront him. "You are not welcome here, woodsman. Go back to your own people, if you think they will take you."

"I have come here a changed man ready to make amends. You can stand with me, step aside to let me pass, or do your best to challenge me. I will persevere and finish what I have come to do."

Yellow Elk stepped between the two men. "Leave your quarrels for another day. We have far greater needs to serve than your petty jealousies. Join us in the longhouse where we will settle our differences in the privacy of our home, not in the public eye."

The interior of the longhouse was dark, a stark contrast to the bright glow of the day. The essence of the freshly cut cedar permeated the space. The fire pits were cold and the dirt floor was dank and musty, like the mood of the warriors. Papineau approached the gathering of elders confidently, ready to make his case for his triumphant return. Hateya was the first to speak to him.

"Why have you returned to us, woodsman? Is it to disrupt our lives and further our misery?"

Papineau was humbled. "I have come to pay homage to you. Although I am deeply bruised by the death of my Anishinabe brothers, at your hand, I have put that pain behind me. I too have committed heinous acts, yet you have shown me mercy. You called me back to your arms when you could have easily cast me off, teaching me compassion and humility."

Willow Woman took a puff on her pipe and drew the smoke deep into her lungs. She held it there before blowing the smoke in Papineau's direction to show her disrespect for him. He spoke directly to her, "Making amends for my past transgressions will not be something that I can fulfill in one day. I have erred in my ways for most of my life. I am a changed man, but I am still haunted by the demons of my sketchy past. I come to ask you to help resolve the conflicts deep within me."

The conversation went on for a long time. It was painful to watch, as this towering man cowered at the reprisals of the women. He demonstrated great restraint, patiently answering all of their questions with honesty and conviction. In the end, they reluctantly agreed to allow him to stay, under the condition that he could pass some grueling tests of his loyalty, trust, and devotion.

Papineau left the longhouse and tried to befriend some warriors. He grew tired of the rebukes and set out to find Balmond. He happened upon a small hut situated by the edge of the lake. He recognized it immediately, for it was similar the cabin that Balmond had constructed by his ferry.

Balmond was marveling at the straightforwardness of Indian life. Despite his incessant complaints about the lack of creature comforts, he reveled in his rejuvenation. He continued to dabble in different trades, but had plenty of time to indulge in moments of leisure. He applauded the less rigorous lifestyle of the Mohawks, which placed a high value on people and community. He even took up reading again, procuring a rather bulky book on religion from a passerby. The trader demanded a hefty price, but Balmond convinced him that carrying such a large volume through the forest was intolerable. The man ended up giving up the book for a plug of tobacco.

Many of the Colonials misinterpreted the tribal lifestyle as one of savagery and sloth. Balmond discovered that the Natives looked at life through a different lens. That which was perceived to be wanton was actually orderly, spiritual, and tranquil. Life on the fickle river made Balmond's personality course and abrasive. It did not afford him the time to contemplate things, as he had loved to do as a child. Life in the mountains helped him to rediscover inquiry, including a devout spirituality and a rabid sense of humor. No one was immune to his notorious pranks.

While Ten Hands and Yellow Elk carefully manipulated Papineau through a series of exacting trials, Two Suns was left to her own devices. She tried to tame the stubborn Standing Waters and woo the emotionless woodsman. Standing Waters proved to be the easier mark. She appealed to his loyalty to the tribe and coaxed him to finally give up his pursuit of her affections. She goaded him into seeking the company of Katarina Morning Star, who secretly loved the reticent warrior.

Two Suns had seen a dramatic transformation in Papineau. But he would often transgress, wearing a shadowy mask of doubt while remaining fiercely independent. She set about to crack his emotions and release the anger pent up inside of him. Without being too bold, she made an effort to tutor him about the nuances of tribal life. The conversations soon became more personal, as she tried to unmask the inner soul of the man with one name. He would give her bits and pieces of his private thoughts, but would never expose the intimate details. He gradually became more relaxed around her and she began to fall in love with this awkward, but virulent man. True to her promise to her father, she would not enter a sacred covenant until he honored and respected her.

As Papineau labored intensely to make amends, Two Suns continued to dance her way into his heart. But it would take more than guile to spark the fire of a passionate love between them.

Chapter 54

The Origins of the American Clan

Balmond carefully scrutinized the blossoming relationship between Two Suns and Papineau. He surmised that their fragile courtship needed a shot in the arm if anything was to come of it. It also provided him with fodder for his droll schemes and serendipitous plots.

The warriors had just returned from a bountiful hunt and were preparing the meat for storage in the caches. It had rained for the better part of three days and the ground was saturated. Weeds seemed to spring to life overnight and threaten to take over the thriving gardens. Mosquitoes and other pests swarmed unmercifully over the compound. Tensions were running high, as the besieged people of the Wolf Clan tried to cope with the deluge of misery provided to them by nature.

Papineau was skinning a large buck under a rough shelter. He was distracted by the memory of his mother when a din by the longhouse roused his attention. It subsided quickly, so he went back to work, not giving it a second thought. He was abruptly accosted by a rain-bedraggled Two Suns.

"You have scorned my advances once too often, Pap," as she often called him. "How can you be so shallow as to dismiss my true feelings for you and brazenly court another woman?"

He was surprisingly pleased by her gesture of jealousy, the first true indication that his feeble advances had made an impression upon her. He was puzzled, however, that she would accuse him of making overtures toward other women when he had been on the hunt for more than a fortnight. He put down his skinning knife, realizing that he was suddenly devoted to winning her affections. Resting precariously on one knee, he raised his bloodied hands and tried to plead his case.

Two Suns berated him, "You are the most stubborn, independent man that our Mother has ever brought upon her back. If you would think about someone other than yourself, you may see that I am here standing before you for the taking." Two Suns' raving turned to sullen tears and she fled.

Papineau decided that he had to articulate his intentions toward the spirited woman or lose her to Standing Waters. As he walked across the compound, he suddenly realized that he may have been duped by Balmond who had inquired about his relationship with Two Suns. *Perhaps the boatman had set him up for another one of his frequent ruses.* He contemplated the situation for a moment and then made an abrupt about-face. He decided to confront the boatman on the matter.

The rain rolled off of his slouch hat as he squatted in the opening of the hut and raised the deer skin flap. His eyes adjusted to the darkness and his nose to the abrupt smell of human perspiration. The infusion of light from the outside illuminated the dour space. He scanned the small room. The smoldering remains of a petty blaze filled the fire pit. At the far side, the woodsman noticed some movement under a large bear skin robe. *Balmond, you scoundrel!*

Before the woodsman could speak, his wily friend raised his head from under the cloak. His sinister grin was an indication that he was up to no good. Another head soon emerged. Much to Papineau's surprise, it was the old woman who had tormented Balmond since his arrival in the camp. She ignored his presence and pulled the boatman back under the covers to finish their tryst.

Papineau withdrew from the hut and sat on the wet ground in the pelting rain. The boatman soon joined him, hiking his leggings up over his long-johns. Papineau chastised him, "Someday you will find those putrid garments in the throes of a fire and we will all be better served." He grabbed Balmond by the nape of the neck and dragged him toward the longhouse.

The boatman protested, but he knew that this time he had gone too far with his pranks. Papineau squeezed harder on his neck the more he jawed about it. The power of Papineau's grip finally caused him to endure the rest of the journey in miserable silence.

As the two men crossed the rain-soaked compound, they were closely pursued by the old woman, She Saved Me, dressed only in a buffalo robe. The rain did not deter her from berating Papineau with a string of obscenities for interrupting her interlude with Balmond. He ignored her, as most people did, for she was an unpleasant, crotchety woman. But she served the important role of tribal mid-wife. Her unique name was acquired as a young squaw when her swift action helped to save a future chief from strangling on an umbilical cord. He later changed her name to from Kahente, Before Her Time, to She Saved Me to honor her odd place in tribal history.

Papineau entered the longhouse, dragging Balmond along the earthen floor. He parted the bystanders and approached a sulking Two Suns. "Go on and reveal to her what you have done."

Balmond stuttered, "The rumor I spread about Papineau taking a fancy to Katarina Morning Star is not true. I made it all up to bring the two of you closer together, so—"

Two Suns sat up straight, ire pasted vividly across her bronze face. "So, you deceived us?"

"It was a harmless prank," Balmond stammered. "I thought that my deception would get the two of you to set forth some honest emotion and commit to a matrimonial bond. It is as inevitable as the rising of the sun, so why do you continue to play these trivial games of the heart?"

"You forget your place, Mr. Balmond. This time, you have taken your foolish pranks too far." She summoned a warrior. "This foolish man will be made to run the warrior's gauntlet. Let us challenge his bravery and teach him the truth about the Mohawk way of life. He will not be so quick to tamper with the hearts of others, if he survives the challenge of the gauntlet's hell."

Balmond begged, "I meant no harm. You can clearly see that the gauntlet will kill me."

Two Suns replied, "Then so be it. Death will be your calling and hell your penance."

Papineau tried to mollify her. "He meant us no harm. Surely you can understand that? Let me cover the grave as your law prescribes and run the gauntlet in Balmond's stead. I am the one to blame for all of the mystery. Balmond is simply a pawn to my inability to expose my feelings."

A twinkle could be detected in Two Suns' eyes, but she did not fall prey to his challenge.

Balmond's hands were bound and he was escorted out into the rain. He stood in a puddle, like a bedraggled dog and awaited his fate. The braves lined up on either side of him. They carried an array of clubs, switches, and leather thongs to test the mettle of the Frenchman. If he survived the legendary test of Indian virility, he would be honored for his good medicine. If his courage faltered, he would be scornfully and disgracefully banished; if he did not die along its vaunted path.

Yellow Elk stripped the boatman of his garments, much to the delight of the female members of the tribe. They mocked him for his less-than-virile body and bedraggled manhood.

The gauntlet was invoked as a part of the rite of passage for warriors or as a way to punish an intruder. The means of torture were unique for each person. The warriors prepared for Balmond's run by cracking whips or pounding clubs, while they hurled obscenities at him. They openly mocked him, knowing full well that he was no match for the grueling nature of the maze's torment.

Balmond made a quick coup d'oeil and blessed himself with the sign of the cross. Yellow Elk nudged him with his lance on the fat of his buttocks, drawing blood, but the Frenchman dug in his heals to try to stave off the inevitable. His feet came out from under him and he fell into a puddle. The entire community laughed, as Yellow Elk raised him up by his armpits, covered from head to toe with mud. He cringed, arms folded across his body for protection as he was thrust into the maze. The first brave in line slapped him briskly on his hindquarter. Balmond yelped and sped forward at a dead run, but the braves descended upon him, shoving him to and fro like a ragdoll.

After a few moments, the circle of exuberant braves parted to expose line of women who held willow switches. The warriors propelled Balmond into their midst. The women happily finished the rite, vigorously whipping him about the head and neck, behind the knees, and on the buttocks. He escaped out of the other side running headlong toward the lake. He was immediately collared by Standing Waters. The warrior held a bowl of blue liquid made from the berries which grew prodigiously around the shoreline of the lake. Balmond struggled to free himself, but was wrestled to the ground by the stocky warrior, a firm knee placed upon his chest. Standing Waters painted blue heart-shaped symbols on each of his cheeks. The sullen Frenchman, defeated and disgraced, was dragged in front of the chief. He was forced to kneel in the mud, while he covered his exposed manhood, (now painted a beet red). He brooded, the gauntlet sapping the brazen spirit from him.

"You have survived the gauntlet and achieved an honor that only our bravest men can boast about. Your medicine in strong, for each day it fills us with laughter and brings joy to our hearts." He held back a smile. "Your head is often filled with the foolish notions of a bumbling jester, but you test us with your erudite wisdom. You have brought harmony to our fragile souls." He raised his eyes to the heavens. "Today we honor you with a new name. Until the time that your dust is scattered upon the winds, you shall be known as Fool's Heart, brave and glorious warrior."

The rain began to soften as the chief dismissed Balmond with a wave of his hand. The tribal members hoisted him high onto their shoulders. He bounced up and down as they carried him about the camp, his stark nakedness contrasting against the dark sky. He suffered greatly from his wounds, but he was glad that he was not dead, nor banished. Although his ego was bruised and his persona slightly altered, he had survived a most grueling ordeal and was a little wiser for it.

Two Suns had used Balmond's own misguided ruse to fill each tribal member's heart with a moment of joy and a little sunshine on an otherwise gloomy day. The young woman unconsciously embraced Pap, who had stood at her side throughout the ordeal. As their eyes met, the harmony of the moment fortified the passionate, but divisive bond between them. The woodsman hugged her back, as new emotions coursed through his veins. Neither broke the embrace, feeling comfort in each other's warmth. Their bond to one another was finally sealed, just as Balmond had planned.

Chapter 55

The Mountain of the Gods

The summer in the clouds was tranquil. It transformed the Wolf Clan, leaving them free from want and far removed from the threat of retaliation from their adversaries. For a time, they could revel in nature's wonders, as the exquisite weather with soft rains and warm sunshine quantified a peaceful life. But the signs in the forest were a deceiving prelude that hardships were not far off.

Papineau was emboldened, actively seeking Two Suns' company. They walked among the virgin trees to climb higher into the peaks. Through reflective conversation they began to realize that their lives were intertwined in ways they could not have imagined. They reveled in their shared interests and embraced their differences, painstakingly trying to meld their hearts into one.

The two unique beings from vastly different worlds were both deeply spiritual. The teachings that guided them were similar, despite their diverse origins. Papineau struggled with the concepts of a supreme being, even though he had a strict religious upbringing when he was a child. He could not define a single moment in his life where he had felt the presence of celestial spirits. There were rare occasions when other forces intervened, but he was satisfied that what happened in the here and now was guided by nature's course, not orchestrated by a divine sovereign.

Two Suns clung to her strong heritage. She believed that fate was orchestrated by higher powers and man could do little to alter its course. She would expertly point out incidents in her life, as an Iroquois woman, that would authenticate her ideologies. The woodsman would politely listen and then relate the symbolic meaning of the stories to the development of his own life. He would question her endlessly, trying to reveal something of mystery that had escaped his understanding. Their spirituality was becoming the energy that bound them in a closed circle of trust.

There was no physical relationship between them except for an innocent touch or a furtive glance. When they were in the public eye, they remained aloof. The women taunted her and the braves poked fun at him. But both realized that their relationship went well beyond physical passion, dependent on sustaining kindred ideologies. Each would fight to the death to protect those beliefs, but preferred to translate those virtues into terms everyone could live by. Their respect for the sanctity of life and their lust for freedom fueled the fires of a profound and ardent love.

Balmond coaxed his friend to make his intentions known. "If you do not snatch up that girl, she will quietly slip away from you. She is the finest women I have ever known and if you do not covet her, I will take her for my own. I ran the gauntlet as her chosen champion," he chided.

Papineau cuffed Balmond on the back of his balding head. "You cannot, for one moment, manage She Saved Me. Do you think that Two Suns would even pass you a blind eye?" He left the hut, irate with his partner, but more frustrated with his own inability to act out his intentions.

As the summer waned, Ten Hands purposely probed Papineau for his feelings on everything from politics to the meaning of life. He spoke about their bond to nature, the history of the tribe, and the state of the Iroquois nation, now pressed by invaders. He never once mentioned Two Suns.

The woodsman discussed his life with the Anishinabe and forgave Ten Hands for the massacre. Retribution could not be a part of his evolving story. "I realize that I have selfishly misjudged you. You are like Three-Legged-Wolf, for whom I harbor deep respect and love. I regret that I have not had the opportunity to tell him so, for I had misjudged him as well. It is my hope that I can make amends so that he who resides in the afterlife can forgive me, as you have forgiven me."

Ten Hands was pleased that the surprisingly humble woodsman was moving away from his self-centered ambitions and had accepted the Mohawk culture. He had begun to transform into the person he suspected he could be and surmised it was time to move ahead with his plan.

On a gloomy summer's day, the chief announced to the clan that he would leave for a full turning of the moon. He intended to head for the sacred hollow in the Eagle's Nest known as the Mountains of the Gods. Once there, he would be commune with the spirits and seek guidance for the governance of the tribe. He would be accompanied on his journey by three noble braves.

Yellow Elk and Standing Waters were natural selections, for they were second only to Ten Hands in tribal authority. The third choice, Papineau, was scorned by Kariwase and some of the more vocal members of the warrior order. "Ten Hands, you have chosen a stranger to accompany you on this the most sacred of journeys, insulting me and dishonoring my brothers. As you have taught me, white men are not to take part in our most holy ceremonies, nor permitted to desecrate our most sacred places. You have blatantly assumed that we will agree to this madness."

Ten Hands knew he had taken a risk, possibly dividing the clan. So, at the rising of the full moon, he shunned the admonishments and the stalwart men set out toward the looming peaks. They traveled lightly on foot, the spry chief easily managing the grade. He talked incessantly, enlightening the braves with quips about life. They were eager to hear the lore firsthand, even though they had heard it from the women, who were the most prolific storytellers.

Papineau found that the tales were very similar to those told by the Anishinabe. Since these tribes were at odds with one another, he surmised that one embellished what the other loathed.

Ten Hands studied the three warriors intently. He was pleased by their growth, but was still concerned about their ability to lead the clan in a world that demanded assimilation. Despite his reservations, he forged ahead with his mission. These men had values, unselfish motivations, and balanced each other. The tribe's future depended on their strong, burgeoning relationship.

As the little band approached the summit of the great peak, they were halted by a sudden stillness. They marveled at the passing of a bald eagle. As the great bird lifted himself upon the thermals, the chief began his ascent of the path that led toward the Eagle's Nest. He had walked this trail before, seeking guidance from the gods, complete a rite of passage, or find personal solitude. He enjoyed these moments for he would always return with a new outlook on life.

From the isolated peak, he looked down upon the valley that sprawled below him. He scanned the horizon in search of the sign of acceptance that would allow him to enter the cloistered chapel. The cloud cover parted to reveal the brilliant, streaming rays of the sun, filtering through a vibrant rainbow. The light caused the small tarn nestled in the bosom of the mountain peaks to twinkle. Ten Hands chanted his appreciation and then climbed into the beatified haven of his ancestors.

The sanctuary was covered with relics and tokens of appreciation to the spirits. Pictographs depicting fierce battles, glorious hunts, and tribal lore adorned the smoke-blackened, grey walls of the hollowed-out stone fortress. Trinkets to commemorate each warrior's passage into manhood hung from an ornate arbor constructed to honor their personal medicine.

Ten Hands gathered some sticks and started a fire in the ancient pit. He spread his robe upon the ground, exposed his aging chest to the crisp air, and prostrated upon it in deep reverence. He lit his pipe, taking a long drag on its stem, as he admired the eagle's head carved upon its bowl. He absorbed the smoke into his lungs and held it there, eyes closed. He savored its warmth as the herbs brought on a sense of euphoria and his mind reeled to enter a meditative trance. He chanted tribal songs and a litany of unearthly incantations for the better part of two days. When it was over, he was physically weak, but spiritually enlightened. His mind was lucent and he clearly understood what he had to do to fulfill his dreams. He collapsed into a deep slumber.

Papineau quizzed the braves about the Eagle's Nest. They only spoke in generalities and inferences. It was not their place to reveal its dark secrets. It was difficult for him to speak truthfully, but he felt that the honest sharing of the annals of his life would establish trust. He embellished extraordinary feats, but they revealed the horrible truth about his checkered past. He began to talk openly about his father, reveal his most private thoughts about his mother, and share his impressions about a shattered life. As he did so, he began to feel a weight lift from his shoulders.

Yellow Elk had more pressing concerns. "You have helped us to see into your soul, but tell us what other secrets you harbor. Why do the Brits relentlessly pursue you? Enlighten us about your hatred for Captain James. Do we need to fear reprisals for your sketchy affiliations?"

Papineau hesitated, for he knew that the truth may cause the warriors to ostracize him, or worse, kill him. He decided to accept whatever fate would offer. He told the entire story about the encounter at the Inn, the deadly struggle on the landing, and the ensuing manhunt.

Yellow Elk understood his frustrations, for his personal dealings with the Brits had been tenuous at times. But he had also seen that they could be men of great vision and generosity. If it were not for the most recent concerns about false alliances and tribal sovereignty, he might have been at odds with the woodsman on this matter. "So, tell me, Papineau, how does your deep seeded hatred affect our relationship? Will it cloud your judgment in times of peace or war?"

Papineau answered honestly, "I cannot say what I will do should I have to choose between my allegiance to you or open defiance against the Brits, for the circumstances will dictate my actions. For now, I stand with you. But know this, I will not ask you to be dragged into any of my affairs."

Standing Waters believed that the recent events with the Brits were engineered by Papineau as a way of escaping the noose. "We have taken a risk by taking you into our confidence, while you have exposed us to retribution from men who were once our brothers. How can I be sure that the officer James or the Anishinabe, for that matter, will not bring further suffering to our people?"

Papineau answered quickly, "On that matter you can never be sure, but I can tell you that I will never consciously put you or your loved ones in harm's way, even if it means severing our relationship. I will fight my own battles with Cameron James. I cannot, in good conscience, drag you into that affair for he is a relentless madman who will pursue me into my grave."

Yellow Elk tried to expose the woodsman's fragile emotions. "If you cross me or my loved ones, I will kill you. How can I be sure that you will not strike us down in our sleep? Will you suddenly turn on us like a rabid wolf, as you did against the Brits or the Huron?"

Papineau realized that he was being tested, but suppressed the urge to act violently. "I am the one who should ask that question of you. Were you not the ones who hunted down and massacred my Algonquin brothers?" He challenged Standing Waters. "I saw you ruthlessly slit the throat of a Huron above the falls. Yet you dare to question me about killing. What say you to this charge, brave warrior? I have put these incidents aside out of respect for the dead, for the better man walks away. So, is it not I who should be the one who sleeps with one eye open?"

Standing Waters was outraged. "You, of all people, should understand the complexities of life in the wilderness. Every tree harbors a fugitive who will take your scalp for a price. In our world, it is kill or be killed. So, each day we live and die by the sword, or we are branded a coward."

Yellow Elk sensed that the rising tension could explode into violence. "I give you my word that what was done in the past will stay in the past. Standing Waters, although he defies you, will honor this pact out of respect for me. My word on this is my trusted bond, never to be broken.

Papineau knew that he had to make concessions. The peaceful circle of life would not be broken if he made wise choices, reasonable compromises, and embraced forgiveness.

Standing Waters purposely insulted Papineau. "The code of a Mohawk warrior is that he does not hide behind the skirts of a squaw or openly reveal his frailties. That scar you bear is a testament to your weakness. You cowered under the weight of the bear and survived by chance because of the bravery of the wolf. Do you see this hand painted across my mouth? It tells a thousand tales about my courage. I do my talking with these." He raised his fists. "I spit on your bravado, for it carries no weight in our world. An honorable warrior marks his words with courageous actions."

Papineau rose to his feet, as quick as a cat, and lunged at Standing Waters. The brave anticipated his attack and easily pushed him aside. Papineau recovered quickly and swiped the legs out from under the warrior. They rolled around on the forest floor in heated hand to hand combat.

Yellow Elk leaned casually against a tree and chewed on berries as the two men thrashed each other. *If they fight to the finish, then so be it. It will resolve many questions and end many doubts.*

Fatigue soon mastered the two venomous men and Papineau started to get the upper hand. Standing Waters yelled at him, "You have taken from me the only thing that matters in my life and you shall die at my hand because of it." The woodsman immediately stopped fighting, allowing Standing Waters to turn the tables. The brave drew his knife and raised it over his head, only to have it swiftly removed from his grasp by Yellow Elk.

"Both of you stand down and end this affair."

Standing Waters stood up. "What are your intentions towards Two Suns? Will you marry her, as it has been decided or will you leave us so I can take her as my woman? Choose wisely for I will not allow any man to toy with her emotions. Answer now, so this affair can be put to rest."

Papineau brushed his hair off of his face. He had deep feelings for the woman, but never in his wildest dreams had he considered marriage. He understood that Standing Water's affections for Two Suns were boundless, but assumed that he had set them aside to court Katarina Morningstar.

Standing Waters reiterated, "I have asked you a question and demand an answer."

Finally, Yellow Elk intervened. "What are your intentions, Papineau? Are they honorable?"

Papineau recovered enough to speak, "I have a deep regard for her, but I am not a man who has ever considered a bond of marriage nor am I sure that I am capable of fulfilling its promise."

Yellow Elk moved directly to the point. "Your fate on this matter has been decided for you. Assuming that you pass one final test, you shall be married at the turning of the moon."

Papineau asked, "What test? Who arranged this? Why was I chosen?"

"You will understand all of this in due time. For now, you need to embrace Standing Waters. He has stepped aside out of loyalty to his brothers so that a legacy can be realized. The future of our clan now rests in your hands. Do not disappoint us, woodsman."

Papineau's shoulders slumped from the weight of the burden. Standing Waters, calmed by the abrupt resolution of matters, looked into his puzzled eyes. Nothing more needed to be said.

At sunrise on the third day of the vigil, the warriors were aroused by a rustle in the undergrowth. Ten Hands, his face gaunt and pale, emerged from the brush. He approached the men with small deliberate steps then struggled to sit down. He relived his visions and then spoke to Papineau, "If you are patient, you will comprehend the magnitude of our vision and how it could change the fate of our nation." He cleared his raspy throat. "Your medicine is remarkably potent. You have proven to be as brave as the wolverine, pure of heart like the dove, and wise like the owl. Your conviction to humanity is the strength of your resolve, despite the demons you have battled. You will have an honored place in our history if you pass a test to measure the fortitude of your spirit and resolve."

Papineau had no idea that this journey was designed to examine his worth. Questions raced through his chaotic mind. *What do they have to gain and how shall I benefit? Why was I chosen and not Balmond or Graham? Why was one of them asked to step aside so that an outsider could step in? What was the ultimate goal of this union of people from two distinct and diverse cultures?*

Ten Hands continued, "You will be escorted by Yellow Elk to the Mountain of the Gods and remain there for two risings of the sun. The spirits of our fathers will guide you through the maze of uncertainty. On the dawn of the second day, you will be asked to determine your own fate and ultimately seal ours. A powerful sign will be given to you and the decision will be clear."

The chief grabbed the woodsman by the shoulders, his grip firm and powerful. "Many have ventured into that sacred place, only to return as broken men. You will wrestle with your innermost demons. If you succumb to their evil, there will be nothing we can do to save you from the insanity that will follow. If you defy them and strike them down, you will be a renewed man."

The chief revealed some of his vision. "Many races have come to our shores, only to prove that they do not wish to live in harmony.

They gobble up our land, defile our way of life, and riddle us with disease and false promises. We seek to preserve our rich heritage and strike out anew toward a reawakening of our nation. You will help to plant the seed of that glorious future."

Papineau was struck with fear, like a punch to his jaw. *How could he possibly manage the fickle woman, Two Suns, or help dictate the future for their offspring and the clan?*

Ten Hands spoke, "There is anxiety in your heart. The providers will transform you with their powerful medicine and give you the answers that you seek or strike you down where you stand."

Papineau placed a brawny hand on the chief's shoulder and then followed Yellow Elk up the mountain path that led from the Upper Falcon's Trace to the Eagle's Nest.

The chief spoke to Standing Waters, "Your personal sacrifice moves me to tears. I have nothing of value to give you except my respect and devotion. You have proven to be a better man than I."

Chapter 56

New Medicine

The cavernous shell formed by the granite walls of the Eagle's Nest was dark. It was a cold place, damp and musty like a subterranean cave. Nothing grew there save for some black sphagnum moss and yellow-green lichen clinging to the face of the stark, grey walls of the cliff.

Papineau was overcome by the ordeal he had endured in the Eagle's Nest, a place where boys became men. His head pounded and his body ached. He flirted with insanity during the ritual, traveling deeper into his soul than he had ever done before. When he was a boy, Three-Legged-Wolf had described the power of the torment. The Anishinabe shaman refused to allow him to complete it, for he felt that he was too fragile to survive it. Now he understood why. As he began to regain his senses, he felt wholly cleansed and the demons deep within him had been released.

Yellow Elk had endured the rite and understood the overwhelming power of the experience. He appreciated the perseverance it took to complete it. Not every brave left the grotto with their sanity and the good medicine that defined their virility. He knew that the woodsman possessed all of the physical qualities that the Mohawk demanded of their warriors. But Papineau had succumbed to personal frailties, struggling with his emotions and wallowing in self-pity. Through the guidance of other people, he began to remove the shadow of doubt that shrouded his soul.

The woodsman was reminded about the story of the serpent that Two Suns had told him. The evil beast of the Underworld had blocked his path to understanding. She had recognized that the flight of the eagle would whisk the serpent away, opening up a new path of reason to him and revealing the light of hope. The ceremony had completed that rite. *How could I not see it? Was I so blinded by my own greed, rage, and ambition that I was too selfish to overcome my afflictions?*

A violent strike of lightning rattled the hollow. Yellow Elk saw this as the sign that Ten Hands had alluded to, but Papineau sloughed it off, "This is nothing more than a fickle storm, as so often happens in the deep recesses of these mountains." The raised scar on the woodsman's cheek surface burned liked never before. He passed it off as a coincidence.

Yellow Elk grinned, "Assume what you will, but you have awakened the gods who reside here. The lightning did not kill you, so I suspect that they have other challenges for you to face."

As the warriors walked to the clearing, Papineau inquired, "It is the custom of your people to take a name that represents the essence of their being. So how has the chief come by his moniker?"

"His birth name was Great Bear, Ohkwari, a tribute to the spectacular beast that roamed these forests during the time of his awakening." He swept his hand in an arch over his head. "Now he runs across the night sky, chased by three relentless warriors."

Papineau found this odd. "How does the beast who resides in the forest roam the sky?"

"The legend tells of a Great Bear that ravaged the land during the famine. He left our ancestors destitute and starving. The soldiers of the forest could not subdue this mighty creature. Our bravest men were struck down as they battled the bear for control of the land. Then, when all seemed lost, three brothers dreamed the same dream on three successive nights. They believed that they could track the bear and render him helpless, to restore wealth to the land and health to our people. So, they stalked him to the end of the world. But the beast leapt into the sky and followed the seasons across the heavens. The three warriors pursued him. They would catch up to him in the fall and shoot their arrows into his flesh, but they never could bring him down. He bleeds upon the earth and colors the trees before he goes into his winter hibernation. When the stars are full on a clear night, you can see that they still hunt him doggedly."

"I can see how the chief has come by such an illustrious name, for his spirit resembles that of the Great Bear, but you have not told me how that name has changed to Ten Hands over time."

Yellow Elk stopped walking. "During a furious battle with the Wyandot, who were our brothers in ancient times, our warriors were overrun. Great Bear became enraged by the prospect of dying at the hands of people he did not respect. He was propelled into a fighting frenzy. His war club flew at unimaginable speed and he quickly killed ten Wyandot. Our foe surmised that Great Bear was a demon with ten hands, single-handedly mowing them down as a razor-sharpened scythe mows the summer wheat. On that day, my father became known as Ten Hands, Oyeri Ohsnonhse."

Papineau could not imagine that this genteel, wise chief was a heartless warrior. But he was the man who had easily subdued the fiery Three-Legged-Wolf. He was beginning to realize how Two Suns and Yellow Elk had acquired their extraordinary skills.

As the men reached the clearing, Ten Hands immediately questioned Papineau, "Have the spirits transformed you and are you ready to decide your fate?"

"I have been enlightened by the circumstances of my life and the unrelenting kindness of your people. I am not sure that I can fulfill the promise that you have placed upon me, but I will accept the burden. I ask you to be patient. You can trust that I will be loyal, embrace your way of life, and be a devoted husband to your daughter, even when she tests my patience."

"She will be your supreme test." Ten Hands quipped, "What shall you be called?"

Papineau had anticipated this question after his inquiry about Ten Hands. "The Anishinabe warrior, Three-Legged-Wolf, called me Pashkwadjash, the Wolf. I quite fancy the allusion."

"It is a fitting name, for the wolf is a noble, wise, and fearsome beast. Three-Legged-Wolf was a brave and righteous man. It is proper that you should honor him by taking his name. From this day forward you shall be known in our circles as the Wolf, Okwaho."

The four warriors immediately began their arduous journey back to the clan. When they entered the camp, they were welcomed with a great celebration. The tribute lasted for two days. A feast was prepared, the drums echoed throughout the high peaks, and the warriors danced into the night.

Papineau's harsh demeanor softened and his relationship with Two Suns blossomed. He carved little trinkets or would coyly offer her a bouquet of wildflowers. Each simple measure of devotion solidified a much stronger bond of affection than she could have imagined.

Ten Hands called the two of them to his private hut in the forest on a blustery fall day. As they entered the small, isolated shelter they were greeted by Hateya and a party of elders gathered around a fire. "Sit with us and revel in the solitude provided by nature, our Mother."

The two lovers meditated until Hateya broke the awkward silence. "The Celestial Twins will soon cross each other's path as they did on the day of your birth. On that fateful morn, your trail in life was set ablaze by the spirits that rule the Twins." Hateya smiled. "It is fitting, as they cross their paths again, that we honor that providence and set in motion events that will alter history."

Two Suns was relieved that her mother was about to reveal the true nature of her calling. She could feel the weight of the responsibility descend upon her as Hateya chastised the woodsman. "You are the Left-Handed Twin. You must accept your fate or the legacy will be lost."

Papineau was offended, for the Left-Handed Twin represented evil. He had made amends for his egregious transgressions to appease these people whom he hardly knew, but respected.

"Take no offense, for your fortuitous arrival has provided balance to my daughter's life. Without that stability, her destiny could not be realized. Your darkness has revealed her light and set in motion events that will lead to the fulfillment of a prophecy. In turn, her light controls your darkness and subdues your evil. Together, you balance the forces of nature and bring us a lasting equilibrium that will be carried on through your offspring. They will hold the key to the preservation of our way of life, but it is your balance that will guide them along the way."

Ten Hands spoke, "Within the dancing flames I see a horrific struggle that will transform the land and alter our existence. When the circle of the seasons has closed one hundred times, a man of prominence will walk the earth. He transcends the time that lies between us."

Neither Two Suns nor Papineau could fathom how their relationship could change the volatile world around them. They looked deeply into the flames, but were unable to see what the chief saw. He recognized their angst. "The vision is revealed to those who believe in the power of human resolve. You must trust your instincts and in time you will find the truth."

The wise chief spit some water onto the flames. "The flames balk at the presence of the water, for it seeks to quell their resolve, just as the white man has sought to subdue ours. But as the flames revive, they tell a story about a young man who comes to our land from far across the great sea. He is the seed of your loins, a prophet from the distant future who will fulfill the promise of our race. Blown by the winds to our land from an outlying shore, he will have to endure the anger of many turbulent storms to satisfy a legacy that the two of you will forge. He will bear the strength and cunning of his ancient father and the wisdom and foresight of his ancestral mother. He will be the catalyst for unprecedented change in a turbulent world ravaged by oppression and strife. He will fulfill the bequest of your dreams by harboring others."

Two Suns pressed her father like a child, "Who is this prophet, father, and how will we provide for him when you say he will arrive long after we have gone?"

"You will bear a child who is destined to carry on the name of the clan. She will test your will, question your principles, divide you and your husband, and challenge your way of life. She will understand, however, better than any of us, how to bind wounds and mend hearts. You will plant within her the seed of our legacy, but generations will pass before it bears fruit."

The chief sighed. "A horrific war that pits brother against brother will consume the land. A son will rise from its ashes to renew people's optimism. He will not appear to us like the Great Eagle or the revered Peacemaker. He will appear to be an ordinary man, a face in the crowd like so many others, guided by the haunting of the past. Each of you, from the shallow depths of your grave, will resurrect a fire within him that will drive his fate and seal our destiny."

The two young lovers were overwhelmed by the magnitude of the chief's vision. Two months later, when the moon passed across the face of the sun and they were of one mind in their resolve, the seed to the prophecy was planted. The circle of life that Ten Hands had alluded to was finally closing and the melding of the hearts of two people, one with pure Mohawk blood and one with deep foreign roots were finally consummated under nature's painted canopy.

As prescribed by tribal law, the couple exercised their right to choose who presided over the ceremony. They selected Ten Hands. Normally, marriages were complicated affairs, expounding upon the lives of the couple through oration, but the chief chose to let the spiritual power speak for him. He bound the couple's hands with the red sash and chanted a short vow.

Two Suns, dressed in her ceremonial gypsum-colored garb, adorned with rabbit fur, was radiant as the moon began to pass in front of the sun. The colorfully beaded tunic shimmered, as if an ethereal force emanated from it. The young woman's raven-colored hair streamed down her back. It posed a stark contrast to the white tunic draped over her bronze skin.

Papineau breathed slowly as he concentrated on the words of the chief. He quietly twitched his leg in rhythm with the chant. He felt Two Suns squeeze his hand in confident reassurance as the two celestial bodies merged, blanketing the earth in darkness.

When the sun began to command the moon and the light reemerged, Hateya whispered in her daughter's ear, "You will provide me with a strong and healthy grandchild who will carry on the hope of a new generation of our people. That child, conceived under the influence of the rising of the sun and the waning of the moon, will be the soul for a brighter future for all people."

Two Suns kissed her mother and was lifted onto the Arabian draped in alabaster ceremonial coverings adorned with iridescent baubles, ribbons, and feathers. Papineau escorted her, pulling gently on the tether. It reminded him of the days when he drew the oxcart to the city for his mother. He secretly hoped that she had observed this event from her place in the heavens. He was sure that she would be proud of his transformation and admire his new wife.

The couple headed toward an isolated hut on the outskirts of the compound. Papineau lifted his bride from the horse and embraced her affectionately. She looked down at him longingly, as Hateya and other tribal members coaxed them playfully to enter. Papineau ducked into the opening, but glanced back, spying Yellow Elk, who had placed himself in front of the entry. The flap was closed, the crowd dispersed, and the two lovers were left to their own devices.

The marriage was consummated that evening as the moon slowly obliterated the sun before giving way to the light of a new day. As the Celestial Twins wrestled with fate, a new chapter was about to unfold in the lives of the young couple and their child of destiny.

Just beyond the confines of the camp, a small group of warriors secretly huddled against the cold around a small fire. Kariwase, decked out in full battle regalia, preached to the braves, "On this evening, our fate has been sealed by the cowardly actions of a feeble-minded chief. The time has come for us to command the Borderlands."

Chapter 57

Aristocrat

By horse or carriage, the trip to the Holland farm was just a few days' ride. Jon and Shannon had marched farther in one day during the war, but in their current physical condition, it would be an arduous journey. So, they decided to hole up in a guest house for the night.

The brick, Dutch-style hostel sat along the river on the north side of the city. It was a quaint two story, but derelict dwelling. After living in tents and ramshackle huts for the better part of four years, the lads did not much care about the condition of the place. The thought of a warm bed and a good night's sleep was all that mattered to them.

Jon had a few dollars left from his $105 a month First Lieutenant's pay. He gave the matron four bits and then helped Shannon up the narrow stairs to a cramped space in the rafters. As was the custom of the times, two men often shared a bed. Jon, however, could not stand the stench of his vermin riddled friend, so he opened the window to let the warm spring breeze into the space. He curled up in the corner of the dusty room, wrapped in a skimpy wool blanket, and fell asleep.

As morning sun peeked over the horizon, the lads began their journey towards the greener pastures of home. The walk was pleasant as the two hobbled men passed through small villages and over open farmland. The new leaves on the trees lining the roadside rustled in the warm air, blowing briskly off of the commerce-laden Hudson River. At midday, they stopped to rest on an isolated spit of land that jutted out into the river. They ate a meal of bread and dried fish that Jon had procured from a peddler and drank from the cool waters of a spring.

Jon insisted that they bathe and wash their clothes. Shannon resisted, but Jon forced the issue, no longer able to tolerate his odoriferous friend. The sergeant felt rejuvenated as he picked the lice from his body, but what he really needed was a week of salt baths to rid himself of the pests.

The weary veterans hung their wet clothes on a fence rail and sat half-naked in the medicinal sun. They took time to reminiscence about their youth until their war worn-garments were tolerably dry. "So, what will you do, Shannon, when you get back to the village?"

"I guess I'll take up with me Pap at the smithy. But I don't know if I can tolerate his violence. The man is insufferable and I am too weak to cope. He will beat me silly at the simplest mistake. I'd rather be fighting the Rebs than face the wrath of that intolerable man."

Jon deflected, "You will always have a place with us, Shannon."

"I appreciate that, laddie, but don't you fret about me. I'll make my own way." The mask of death cloaked Shannon's face. The war and his abusive life had transformed the monolithic warrior into a sniveling drunkard. "What will you do, Jonny?"

"I will return to the farm and help out my family. I am sure the place will need rebuilding."

"No, Jonny, what will you really do with your life? Surely, after all you have been through; the visions, the wounds, and a fine lady friend, you can't consider going back to farming?"

Shannon had struck a nerve in Jon's soul. "When you come face-to-face with death, you discover that life should not be frittered away. I have decided to live mine with more vigor." Jon tossed a stone into the river; the rolling hills beyond, emerald green from the spring growth, reminded him of the Irish highlands. "Have you ever considered going back to Cork?"

"I gave it a hankering, but I don't think that I could stomach the voyage. They say it is better in the steam vessels, but I about lost my lunch on every swell and don't want to risk it again."

Jon reflected. "Every vision I had during the war and every unique person I met, called out to me to leave the darkness and step into the light, you know, to find a new calling. It has eluded me to distraction, for the obligation of my heritage still summons me back to the land."

"You owe no allegiance to that land, Jonny, but you will always owe a debt to your family. That debt can be repaid however you see fit. If it is working the land, then so be it, but if it means that you must do something else, then your family will accept it, without reservation. That is what your heritage dictates. You have a remarkable gift for healing, Jonny, embrace it."

Jon surmised that Shannon would be the last person who would understand the complexities of his heritage. O'Reilly's family was loyal, but they were muddled in a life of violence and turmoil. They were the antithesis of Jon's family in many ways, yet they had always stood by each other, through thick and thin. The two families balanced each other.

"Allegiance to my family is allegiance to the land, Shannon. Since the dawn of time, it is all we have stood for. We have fought throughout the ages to hold on to our share of it. For now, I am the last generation of Holland men to work that land. If I leave it, the legacy will die."

"No one said anything about leaving it. Look to your calling, laddie. You have the grace of two legs and a settled soul to fall back on. I am sick to death of your whining. There are one hundred thousand men like me who could only pray to be as lucky as you. Get over it, Jon, and move on." Shannon pressed his back against the tree and adeptly stood up. He was frustrated by Jon's over analysis of every aspect of his life. "Hand me my crutch. I am going home, with or without you."

Jon helped his friend prop the crutch under his arm. The two men donned their damp uniforms and then continued their trek up the riverside wagon path. Jon could not get over Shannon's brash berating, but understood how frank his analysis of the situation was.

By nightfall, the two men had reached the outskirts of Schuylerville, a small village on the west bank of the Hudson. They hunkered down in a hollow by the river below the bluffs of Bemis Heights on land owned by Jon's great uncle. This farm was procured by the Holland men just after the Revolution. As they melded their blood with the Natives who secreted in the defiles of the deep mountains, the Holland family set in motion the legacy of life that Jon wrestled with.

Jon looked up into the starry night, trying to catch a glimpse of the ground above them. His ancestors had fought there at the Battles of Saratoga nearly ninety years before, during the Revolution. American victories on those heights proved to be the crowning moment in the fight for freedom; a freedom Jon and Shannon had fought to desperately maintain during the Civil War.

The new day emerged under a blanket of misty rain. The soldiers hiked the remaining few miles to the village where they stopped to purchase some civilian attire. It seemed fitting that their lives should start over with a new set of garments, but they decided not to wear them until they had rid themselves of the battle camp lice, chiggers, and fleas.

Jon dissuaded Shannon from visiting the local tavern. The timely whistle of the ferry caused them to stop their argument. They hobbled to the landing and arrived just as the boat was docking. They attempted to pay for their passage. "War veterans ride free. Your service to our nation is appreciated by everyone in the Valley. My name is Louis Papineau Balmond."

Jon, in his haste to get home, failed to comprehend the significance of this chance meeting. He and Shannon boarded the little steamer and passed to the east side of the rapid river in peaceful silence. They headed north along the River Road and after a mile or so they could see the Holland farm sprawled out on the flats. It was a meager one hundred and twenty-five acres of fertile river bottom land. On the northern fringe, a red barn stood perpendicular to the road. The clapboard house sat next to the barn and faced the river. A large herd of horses was corralled on the edge of the corn plot behind the homestead. They were the prize of the Holland legacy.

Jon could see a woman on the porch, rocking in a chair. Across the Champlain Canal, he could see a small gaggle of men tending to a herd of young cattle. He felt an urge to run, but his wounds and the gait of his invalid comrade precluded rash behavior.

"Looking pretty fine, hey Jonny?"

"I haven't seen anything so sweet in all of my life, Shannon."

The weather-hardened Irish woman on the porch glanced up from her needle-point and saw the lads coming. She stood up, thinking that her eyes had deceived her. She hesitated and then bounded spryly down the steps. She yelled loudly to the party across the canal, as she had been known to do on many occasions, especially at the dinner bell, "Papa, it's Jon! My God, come quickly."

The man laboring across the way put his hand to his brow and then ran swiftly to his horse. He mounted nimbly and rode across the footbridge over the canal. Before the horse stopped, he dismounted and embraced his wife. The two elated farmers ran toward their son.

"Go on ahead, Jonny," Shannon encouraged. "I can make it on my own."

Jon helped Shannon secure the crutch. "I'll be right back to get you."

"No need to hurry. I've been waiting this long to get home. I can wait a wee bit longer."

Jon hobbled down the road. He shed his pack and rifle, the two objects, so long a part of him, tumbled into the tall grass and rested beside the peaceful river. His youthful exuberance had returned and he soon reached his weeping parents. They all fell to the ground in a deep embrace.

Draighean's maternal instincts soon got the better of her. "Jon, you are injured."

"It is nothing mama, just the waste of a miserable war. I'll be fine in due course."

"Mother and I have not heard from you in quite some time," Jon's father scolded.

Jon had not told them about his wounds for fear it would devastate them. They had other things to worry about and he could barely write, so news from the front was sparse.

"We were worried sick, Jon, not knowing where you were or even if you were alive. We would check the casualty lists posted on the church door every day, but your name never appeared. Sylvester, Addie, Seamus, Jedidiah, Samuel, Ezra, dear Ezra...so many vibrant young men are now gone." His virulent father melted under the weight of the sorrow and wept.

Jon tried to change the mood. "They fought valiantly, Papa, but it's over and I am grateful to be home. I'll just need a little time to get back on my feet and things will be like I never left." He knew that things were not the same. He had changed dramatically during the war and would find it difficult to assimilate back into civilian life. His body was wasted and his soul was scarred.

After a little small talk, the happy couple began to escort the veteran back toward the house. "Are you hungry, Jon?" his mother inquired. "You are nothing but skin and bones."

"Army food is rather repulsive to eat. It ain't anything like your good home cooking, Mama."

"Come on, Jon," his father said as he embraced him about his shoulders with one arm and wiped away his tears with the other. "Let's go to the house so you can rest."

Jon had almost forgotten about Shannon. "I have to tend to Shannon. I'll be along in a piece."

His father inquired, "Is that Shannon O'Reilly? I hardly recognize him."

Draighean gasped, "He's lost his leg. Oh, for land sakes! How will he ever get by in the world? Go and fetch him, Jon and be smart about it. Papa, you should help."

The two men sauntered down the road to retrieve Shannon. He was all smiles, but had a colossal headache from his alcoholic withdrawal. "You're looking mighty spry, Mr. Holland."

"Why thank you, Shannon. I am sorry about the leg. War is a God-awful thing. Young men should not be made to suffer so, with their whole life ahead of them and all."

"I forgot to jump at North Anna and that cannonball lopped off my leg like a sharp scythe, sir. I'll get by, I'm sure, especially with Jonny's help."

Jon boasted, "Shannon never relinquished his grip on the flag as he lay bleeding in the mud. Those Rebs tried to take it from him, but we drove them Grey-backs right out of their trenches."

Riordán put his arm around Shannon's waist to help him walk. "Come on boys. I have a new batch of honey liquor and I am sure your mother will cook us up a robust country feast."

Jon tried to keep his dad from contributing to Shannon's ailments, "The last thing Shannon needs is some of your home brew, Papa. A little cold cider will do."

"Nonsense, son, it will help him forget about that leg and everything else that ails him."

Jon was sure that drink would be the cause of Shannon's demise. His silence on the matter, out of respect for his father, would come back to haunt him on another day.

Jon slowly settled back into farm life. With time, he was able to resume his duties, content to be back in the peaceful fields. It was a far sight better than the ravages of war. To ease his mind, he worked vigorously with the horses. He took an immediate liking to a rambunctious new foal. His father said he had a gift, like his ancestors, to listen to the beasts and will them to do extraordinary things. Before the war, he had not taken that seriously, mostly in defiance of his grandfather, who pushed him toward that aspect of farm life. The feisty Irishman backed off, realizing that the boy would find out on his own that he had the flair for the equestrian trade.

Jon had discovered the gift on a cold and rainy day when he was about eight years old. He was trying to right a grievous wrong when he had a chance encounter with the wealthy entrepreneur Cornelius Vanderbilt in New York City's Hell's Kitchen. The *robber-baron's* carriage was drawn by a distinguished breed of Belgian Brabant Heavy Draft horses. Jon subdued one of the feisty giants, Satan, to a whimper. Mr. Vanderbilt was so impressed with his gift that he offered him a job as a stable boy. Jon had to refuse the work when his family moved north to the homestead.

The horses, even the strongest willed, seemed to respond to Jon. Managing them brought him peace of mind as he sorted through his troubled existence and tried to find a way to overcome the miseries of war. He devoted his attention to the obstinate Arabian foal he named Aristocrat. The Blood-Horse stallion challenged his patience. Jon worked hard to temper him, while he built up his strength and stamina. He saw something special in this foal that made him press on with the rigorous training. This young horse would soon leave an indelible mark on his uncertain future.

Chapter 58

Adirondack Autumn

It was a peaceful Adirondack autumn under the multihued confines of the wilderness canopy. The fall had rushed into the fragrant hollows of the dark woods, dotting the landscape canvas with the colors of orange and umber, posed subtlety against the evergreens. The azure air was crisp, tainted with the essence of the wood smoke that lingered in the bottoms and harbored the sweet aromas of hemlock and pine. It was a quiet morn, save for the endless trickle of the meandering beck that flowed amongst the dells or the chirp of a hovering bird that flittered in the brush.

Papineau, the French Acadian boslooper, had vivid memories of the vexing chronicles of a misshapen life. He reflected on the whirlwind of events that led him to this precipitous moment. He glanced up at his bride, who was squatting by the fire tending to their first formal repast. She was radiant in the sachet of light. She did not notice his stare, as she diligently nursed the rabbit roasting on the spit. He inwardly smiled, as he recalled the fate that had brought him to her side.

Two Suns reached across the smoky void to touch him. He responded with a caress of her cheek and a wisp of a kiss on her forehead. Her smile brightened the dim space, as she reveled in the joy of love. Her solvent prayers to Skennenrahawi, the Great Peacemaker, had been fulfilled.

A rustle on the deerskin flap of their lodge shook them back to the reality of the not-so-private tribal life. A raspy voice called in. "I saw the smoke and assumed that you had been awakened from your lover's lethargy!" It was Balmond. "May I enter?"

A long silence greeted him, as Two Suns gathered robes about her naked, supple body. A nod from her assured Papineau she was ready to resume her complicated life. Papineau squeezed her hand. "Please join us, friend. We have a bit of catching up to do."

Balmond greeted them with his irrepressible smile, the sparse elf-locks on his balding head scattered to all points of the compass. "So, will we be birthing a new warrior prince this spring?"

Papineau quickly changed the subject, "What mischief have you been up to, good fellow?"

"The braves are recovering from too much celebration. That God-awful firewater that they got in trade, Dutch Genever, has given them a fierce infirmity of the head." Balmond grabbed the hare from the spit, as he nestled his body between his friends. "Mind if I lop off a leg?"

Two Suns waved off the offer of the first bite and took a drink from a gourd. The boatman's gregarious nature repulsed her, but she could not mask a smile as she intently watched this waggish specimen of a man go about the routines of his life. He forever brought a spot of joy to the tribe and occasionally a wee bit of felonious backwoods wisdom, when the mood suited him.

Papineau intervened, "I am going on the hunt today. Do you care to join me?"

"Well, you see, my dear friend, I have an appointment with King George, followed by tea with Lord Fairfax." He took a deep puff on his pipe. "And, oh yes, my attendance is requested at a grand ball hosted by the Queen. I am not quite sure if I can fit you into my rigorous schedule."

Papineau nudged him. "Are you coming or do I have to tame the wilderness by myself?"

Balmond mocked a British accent, "I suppose I can rearrange a few things to play a little fox and hound on this glorious autumn day." He rubbed the fur of the luxurious ermine robes wrapped about Two Suns' shoulders. "I see that you have been saving the best of our catch for your woman. You will live to regret your selfishness. At what hour, should I be expected to loose the hounds?"

Papineau had learned by now that half of what the boatman said was done simply out of a desire to arouse curiosity or stimulate someone's ire, so he ignored him.

"I almost forgot why I had originally come." Balmond removed his grandfather's watch from around his neck. He caressed it for a moment like a newborn child and then carefully wound it. "I can always rely on this piece to keep me on a straight and narrow course, for the boat trade requires precise schedules. I thought I would be lost without it, but now, out here in the deepest recesses of the wilderness, it has simply become a burden to me."

He rubbed his fingers over the etching inscribed on the cover, *JPB*. "I got it from my father when I went off to war. He said I should carry it as a token of whom I am and who I am destined to become. This watch harbors the birthright of the bearer's future. I guess Papa thought he could rewrite history, but he underestimated the challenges thrust upon us by the uncertainties of life."

Tears welled in the unflappable boatman's eyes. "On this day, I have decided to unburden myself to my two most trusted friends. For years, I have carried an affliction of immeasurable horror, a heinous crime so unthinkable that it is almost a sin to speak of it." He lingered on the thought. "I was mustered into the Compiegne's de la Marine, as an officer. The military was my legacy. All of the Balmonds were high ranking officers in the French Legions. They were aristocrats trained in the finest schools, by handpicked tutors. It was a life I could not ignore."

Papineau interjected a question, "Then how is it that you have become a boatman?"

"I must not be interrupted, for the pain of this tale is too great and I fear that I may not get through it." He sighed, "The military was my life until that fateful day in '53. We were marching south towards the Ohio Valley, trying to uphold our claim on the land and remove threats from that quarter. We came upon an isolated Native village nestled along the river. I questioned the feeble band of peaceful people and seeing no menace, I ordered my men to move on."

He balked, but pressed on. "My directives to move off were rescinded by Captain Fournier. He ordered me to confiscate anything of value so he could line his own pockets with wealth. He was a rogue, so naturally, I refused, but it soon became evident that it was to be their heads or mine. Treason is punishable by the firing squad or hanging, both of which I loathe to this day. I reluctantly carried out the order with great disgust, so as not to tarnish my family name."

Fear coursed over the boatman's face. "Then it happened. A young brave, not more than ten years of age, attacked me with his lance. I instinctively cut him down with my sword before I realized what had happened. The pain on his face as he passed still lingers in my soul. Fournier, to save his own skin, had me tried for murder in a backwoods kangaroo court. They attempted to hang me, but bungled the whole affair so miserably that they only succeeded in leaving this gruesome scar on my neck." He removed his ever-present kerchief to expose the twisted skin.

"I convinced Fournier that if I resigned my commission and did not expose him for the cad that he was, he would set me free, never to speak of the affair again. The shame of the resignation caused my family to disowned me. I became a destitute, impoverished, and broken man after that."

Two Suns sighed, disgusted by the greed and lack of conscious of men like Fournier.

"I murdered that boy, but it was Fournier who was marked by racial hatred. I have never been able to unburden myself of that lie. I wallowed in disgrace and moved away from my family. I worked the river as a hired hand, and then, with my earnings, I purchased the raft from the tired owner. I built up the trade and became a respected business man. But I was alone until I met you."

The boatman put his head in his hands. "At first I hated you, but now you are my most endearing friend. You have helped me to resolve the indifference in my life. You have brought me to a place of peace. I can finally relieve myself of my burdens. You have given me the family I have never had. Although I had resisted your coaxing to move here, I am now grateful that I did."

He spoke to Two Suns in a soft voice, "You are the most resilient woman I have ever met. Each day you teach me about the spirit of living and the sanctity of nature. You have unselfishly given yourself to others so that they may endure the hardships of an uncertain life. You have made me realize that we are all bound to one another, despite our many differences. I now recognize that we should cherish the fleeting moments that we have in one another's company."

Balmond offered Two Suns the timepiece. "Please take this as a token of my love and respect. The watch is a reminder of the friend-ship that we hold and the bond of trust we have forged. It can be the legacy of a new life for you, as I close the door of that horrible chap-ter in my life. Within that watch lay the spiritual resolve to carry on when things seem to be the darkest."

Two Suns was moved to tears. "We cannot accept this gift from you, Jean-Pierre. It is too precious." (She had never called him Jean-Pierre before. It was always boatman or Balmond.)

"It is those values that make it so unique. It is a reminder about all of the good that can come out of trusting and loyal relationships. It is a reflection of the past and a hope for the future. It is a legacy that can be passed on for generations, as a symbol of freedom, sovereignty, and the power of human resolve. It has been altered by the flowing sands of my life, changing from a stark reminder of hatred to a cherished reminder of love. The two of you have made the same sacrifices by putting aside your differences to forge a new life together. Do not let that legacy die."

Two Suns understood. "We shall cherish this gift as we do our lives, Jean-Pierre."

One brisk day, as Two Suns tended to her horse, she had a rev-elation. She rushed across the compound to find her husband, who was busy repairing their shelter. She pulled him away from his work to accompany her back to the russet mare that she was grooming.

"The legacy of our family shall be symbolized through the power of the horse. The beast represents freedom, love, devotion, and loy-alty, as told through ancient Indian lore. We shall build the birthright of our children upon those principles. We will carry the burdens of others, like the horse. We will become the symbol of for-titude that others can rely on. It will be a reminder that we can set aside our differences and become conjoined as one under the umbrella of freedom."

Papineau was pleased. "I am confident that our children, and our children's children, will live by that legacy. They will know the power of love and the strength of their birthright. They will be guided by spiritual fortitude. Their survival, at the hands of life's trials, will be measured by enduring hope. They will pass that hope on to others who are stricken, as you have to me."

Two Suns was overjoyed. "We shall represent our covenant by engraving the image of a horse on the inner face of the watch. You shall reside there too, for you have made the greatest transformation and the most devoted sacrifices so that the legacy may endure."

"And how shall that be, my dear wife?"

She reached up and rubbed his cheek affectionately. "The horse shall be emblazoned with bolts of lightning prominently displayed across his neck and torso. We shall ride upon the horse, through time, influencing others who carry it. It will be a faithful reminder of what we stand for and how we have transformed ourselves, the lives of others, and history itself."

With painstaking, intricate detail, the mystical horse was emblazoned on the inside of the cover of the fateful watch. It became a bold symbol of the power of the human spirit and a lasting tribute to freedom, personal resolve, and the heritage of a great people. But as war lingered on the horizon, the fate of that powerful bond was about to be tested.

Chapter 59

Revelations

The summer of 1865 passed rapidly as Jon re-acclimated himself to civilian life. His physical wounds made day-to-day life taxing, but it was his mental duress that pressed him. He would secrete off to the Trace for days at a time to seek solitude and find inner strength. Rather than be consumed by the memories of the carnage, he used them to fortify his resolve. Like a preacher, or perhaps a shaman, he sometimes found himself comforting those around him who could not cope. This burden never seemed too great as he set out to right the wrong of a misbegotten war.

The calling to pacify and guide other people was strong in Jon's heart. During a church picnic, he tried to comfort his cousin Ezra's grieving wife. Lottie had been persuaded by her mother to attend, but was reluctant to stay. Jon's soothing words helped her to get through the day, but it was evident that she would never be the same vivacious women. Jon had hoped that he could infuse some verve into her mundane life, so he solicited her services as a teacher to perfect his reading. Despite Jon's encouragement, the young lady's spirit continued to deteriorate. Melancholy soon consumed her and she leapt off the widow's walk of her home to an early grave.

Shannon became a teamster for a time and lived off of his meager army pension. He refused to work for his father, despising the violence and verbal abuse. The Holland's tried to help him, but he was too proud to accept their charity. He soon began to succumb to his festering wound and battle with the bottle, falling into a disheartening state of post-war malaise. His father took him in, but the two men battled one another, as they had since Shannon was a child.

He hopelessly wallowed in a state of self-pity and anger, teetering on the edge of insanity and death.

Jon could not stand to see his lifelong friend suffer. As he had done so often, he set aside his own affairs to tend to Shannon so that his strapping comrade would not self-destruct. He managed the feisty Irishman as best he could and tried desperately to help him turn his life around. For every bit of progress they made, there was always a setback of the same magnitude. He refused to give up, but he was hard pressed to find an answer to Shannon's trifling woes.

Jon had passing acquaintances with the few young men left in the Valley, like the siblings of Addie Jones and Jedidiah Johnson. Instead, he spent most of his idle time traveling to the mountain retreats of his ancestors, where he hunted, fished, or communed with nature. He found peace in these serene places and began to understand the complexities of life as he had never done before.

Jon attended church on the insistence of his mother, but the congregation did not understand what the carnage and depredation of the war had done to his soul. He found the most satisfaction in the cloistered forest, not in the confines of the House of the Lord. He abhorred the Reformed minister's arduous sermons that focused on generalities and abstract philosophies rather than substantive, meaningful life experiences. He wondered how a preacher, who had lived such a sheltered life, could guide others about matters he had never experienced himself.

During the services, he daydreamed about the war, Gretchen, or the spiritual stories that had been such an important part of his life. He found meaningful messages in his ancestors' tales: ones of perseverance and hope that were based on the reality of life's challenges. They were not some fabricated gesture of good will. They were genuine, heartfelt, emotional treatises about experiential living. He soon stopped going to church and turned toward a more natural approach to reflection.

Jon despised war and loathed oppression. His encounters with people like Josias Weed and Waya Applewhite impressed upon him that human suffering was reprehensible. He surmised that peoples' lives were intricately interwoven, like the threads of a finely crafted tapestry. Suppressing others rights upset the balance of life and broke the circle of harmony for all of mankind.

While he put up the grain in the barn one fall day, Jon came upon an old, domed travel trunk in the haymow. He settled into the straw and examined the oversized chest covered with dust. The container was made of blackened tin held together by brass rivets. He fondled the handcrafted oak straps that bound it, darkened with age and smooth to the touch. The palm prints of two delicate hands in the filth on the lid revealed that it had been recently opened. He unhinged the clasped latches and coaxed open the stubborn lock. He lifted the heavy cover which creaked on its worn, brass hinges to unveil a musty, dark space beneath. He squinted, but found the light of the barn too dim to see inside. He retrieved the oil lantern that hung in the rafters and lit it, careful to replace the glass over the flame, so as not to set the barn afire. He held it over the trunk to get a better look at the contents. The excitement of a child welled up in him as if it were a Christmas morning.

A multicolored horsehair blanket covered the treasures hidden beneath it. He breathed hard, hung the lantern in the rafters, and carefully lifted the blanket to reveal a treasure trove of memorabilia he had often heard about, but had never seen. His army blouse, marked by bullet holes and the blood of battle, was carefully folded on top. It laid there as a memorial to the most recent events in the treasured history of his family. He understood why his mother secretly hid the blouse, despite his pleas to burn it. She was the wiser and he was glad she had saved it.

Jon removed the watch from the uniform pocket where he had left it. He had to touch it again and look at the image that was painstakingly engraved inside. He popped open the vessel and then quickly closed it as an intermittent light flashed like a tiny lightning bolt. He was dumbfounded and thought that he had imagined it. He slowly opened the cover again to a bathing glow of light. He closed the cover abruptly and set it aside, fearful that he was losing his mind.

Underneath the frockcoat were other treasures: his promotion letter from General Grant, Sergeant Gilhooly's locket that he had meant to return to his family, and his kepi. He found his gunny sack, full of wartime reminders, including some moldy hardtack left there from the lean years. As he carefully removed these items, he noticed his worn rifled musket and attached bayonet leaning precariously against the wall. He prayed for those who had been struck down by its ball.

As he dug deeper, he uncovered a comical daguerreotype of his mother and father posed stoically in their Sunday go-to-meeting clothes. A fading tintype presented him in his new uniform, going off to war. A stained leather satchel concealed letters of love, lockets of hair, Revolutionary war brocades, and relevant historical and legal papers.

The depths of the trunk seemed endless. He found a large, ancient bible, the name Holland emblazoned in fading gold inlay on the cover. The first few pages were scribed with the names of many of his ancestors. He recognized them from the stories his grandfather had told. After a long while, he grew tired of his efforts to piece the roots of his family tree together and soon settled in for a short nap amongst the hay. He dreamed about ancient people, as if he lived among them. They spoke to him in parables, which ran together in a confusing maze of information and advice.

Jon unknowingly cried out, "Stop!"

The scurrying of doves in the rafters and the braying of a goat in the stall below awakened him. Sweat ran down his brow to sting his eyes. He rubbed them and soon found himself bent over the trunk, driven by the dreams to exact the truth from these riches. When he reached the bottom of the hollow space, he was disappointed. He had not found the tangible link that would connect him to those who had tread the path before him and make his grandfather's stories plausible.

As he had done as a child, he closed his eyes, trying to imagine life in another time. He could hear his grandfather's voice, strong and firm. In a never-ending riddle, he teased him with puzzles to force him to uncloak the mystery and hone his mind into a keen tool.

Jon picked up the Bible, looking for more clues in its ancient pages. He combed the scriptures and perused the names, trying to weave them into a solution. Fully consumed by the task, he soon became frustrated and heaved the book back into the trunk with a thud and a crack. He felt guilty and worried that he had damaged the precious book. He looked over the trunk wall. The book lay precariously on its side, having unearthed a loose board in the trunk's bottom. *Many travel trunks of this kind had false bottoms for securing valuables, secreting treasures, or hiding contraband.*

Jon removed the Bible and placed it on the floor. He lifted the loose board to reveal a bleached leather tunic, pure as a new fallen snow. It was meticulously beaded with symbols of the confluence of a rising sun and a setting moon traversing across its chest in bright gold and blue. Its lining was a shimmering dyed red cloth, the color of freshly spewed blood. It mesmerized him and transfixed his gaze. A few precious other trinkets were under it: a small needle-pointed cloth with the initials N and C Holland embossed on it, a faded yellow, satin ribbon, and a large woven quilt with the symbols of Irish and Indian lore emblazoned upon it. A small, leather pouch was drawn tightly closed at the end with a sinewy string. Its heft caused Jon to shake it. *Coins?* He opened the pouch and peaked inside. *Gold sovereigns and a lock of jet black hair.* He was elated.

A fine, Algonquin mocotaugan rested quietly in its sheath at the bottom of the trunk. Blood stained the hilt, a memory of another trying time and another struggle.

A blue, beaded bracelet was found in a gunny sack along with a small clay pipe, an embroidered Glengarry cap, and a fur-lined slouch cap, each revealing a piece of history he could cling to.

He drew a French saber from its scabbard. It tingled as it was extracted and glimmered in the soft lantern light. He cut his finger while wiping the dust from its finely-honed edge. He sucked the blood from the wound, careful not to let it drip onto any of the artifacts. The simple treasures of life were magically connecting to the knowledge he possessed from the stories. He was overcome by the spiritual power of the moment, exultant at the historical panorama it began to paint. He continued his search, but the greatest treasure of them all was not there. It was the essence of the story. It was the focal point of all the lives that were influenced by it. *Where could it be? Grandfather had talked about it in great detail as if it had some magical powers.* A mystical voice called out to him. *Step out of the shadow into the sun.*

The light was waning in the barn so he got up and threw open the large doors to the mow. The low afternoon sun filtered its way through the great oaks that lined the watercourse and reflected off of the water to transform the room. Suddenly, an eagle appeared, hovered for a moment, and then with a flap of its giant wings swooped down toward him. It climbed sharply upward on the thermals and disappeared over the barn roof. *Let the eagle guide you on a path to a new life.*

He dove into the trunk. *Damn it. It has to be here.* A voice from behind startled him. "It's under the lid, Jon." His father peered up at him, perched on the ladder, his eyes revealing his excitement.

At first, Jon saw nothing under the lid, but then, as clear as day, it was there. The black cloth lining had been peeled away to reveal another secret hiding place. Wrapped in a faded and tattered red shawl, was the treasure he sought. He shivered as he took it from its resting place.

"Go ahead, Jon. Open it. I think you will be pleased."

A women's voice whispered softly in his ear. *Immrama! Life is a circle, no beginning, no end; only finite moments in that continuum bring fear to your soul.* Jon acknowledged his father's words and then took the precious article from the shawl, itself a priceless treasure.

The wolf's piercing yellow eyes followed his as he examined the red sash. It was fragile. He could smell the scent of pine, human flesh, and wood smoke embedded in the cloth. He fondled the tarnished and bloodstained Christian cross sewn into the wolf's image. The cloth closed the circle of trust and connected the dots of his lineage. It was the symbolic, transforming piece to all of the lives vividly portrayed in the stories. It was the home of the infamous Shadow Self.

"So, Jon, have you exacted the truth from the emblematic treasures you have unearthed?"

Jon discussed his revelations, battlefield dreams, and struggles with survival with his father in great detail. They mulled over his transformation until only the lantern cast its light upon them.

"You have suffered greatly, Jon, but now you recognize that our family history is complex, one where people of diverse races and divergent ideologies have melded together. It is fraught with misfortune, discord, and persecution, yet somehow, we have overcome it all. That bond between us has helped us to survive war, famine, and the humiliation and desecration of our races. It has helped us to find the resolve to guide others toward inner peace, as they seek to find the truth."

"I understand it now, Papa. From the shared circle of life, we draw our courage to persevere. We are guided by powers we do not fully understand, yet cling to with conviction and hope. It is our bond to one another that fortifies our relationships and moral persuasions. It is our devotion that keeps us on a straight course when others try to dissuade us or simply fail themselves."

"You have come to an understanding about the fundamental aspects of our chosen way of life. The inherent freedoms we value, the bond to a sovereign land, and the devotion to the nature that is our Mother are all a part of that rich heritage. I fear that you have failed to grasp the most important aspects of the lore, the ones that drive the human spirit to do extraordinary things. You are a symbol of that, my boy. What is it that fortifies you?"

Jon was disappointed that he had failed the most crucial test. He was sure that he had interpreted the symbols for their spiritual truth. He closed his eyes to rework the scenarios of his life through his lucent mind. The hunger and abject poverty of the famine, the harrowing voyage to America on an ancient wooden ship, his fight for survival in the slums of New York, his struggles to remain good when evil tempted him, and the desperate struggle to outlive the war. They all tested the limits of his will. Somehow, he had overcome them, sometimes with the help of others, but most often by his own tenacity. He picked up the sash and fondled the cross as the symbols of the two diverse worlds collided within his mind. His puzzled look caused his father to intercede.

"You are looking in the wrong place. The sash is a powerful symbol of the light and dark our lives, but it does not reveal the wisdom you seek to unravel the message of your calling."

"Why must you and grandpa always talk in riddles, pile mystery upon mystery, truth upon falsehood?" Jon was becoming angry and frustrated, so he stood up to leave.

"When have I ever known you to give up, lad? The answer is within your grasp. It has been there all of the time. Think, boy. What is the one thing that has always been true and resolute? What is the eternal linchpin to our legacy, the capsule connecting the past to the present?"

A frown coursed across Jon's furrowed brow, as the circumstances of the day began to weigh upon him. He put his head in his hands, the throbbing in his temples consuming him, as it had done in the field hospital. *Why do I have to bear this burden? Why am I now the keeper of the legacy? Why has time thrust this responsibility upon me when I seek only to break away?*

"Reach out son for the answer rests in the palm of your hand or is cradled next to your heart."

I am sick to death of stories about the balance of life and the circle of our fate. "What time is it, Papa? The cows' udders will burst if we do not start the milking." Jon rummaged through the straw to find the timepiece. He opened the cover, forgetting that the watch had not been wound.

His father interrupted, "Carefully describe to me what you have learned, not what you see."

Do not look for the answers you seek in that which you see. Seek answers to those elusive riddles in that which you don't see. Jon eyes widened. "The wolf is the teacher and the pathfinder. He balances my loyalty with my independence. He provides subtle guidance or leads me to the wisdom of others. Gretchen, Waya, Pritchard, Josias, McGuilicutty, Shannon, you, mama, and grandpa... The spirit of the wolf lies within you." *Let your eyes be the window to your soul.*

Riordán patted his son on the leg and spoke to him, "What else have you discovered?"

"I have not told you, Papa, but during the most desperate times of the war I was haunted by the images of mysterious ancestral people who spoke to me in foreign tongues. I began to understand them as if they had raised me. They each challenged me to expose the truth."

"The legends provide a chain of truth that should never be altered or broken, Jon."

"Pashkwadjash urged me to overcome adversity and put aside selfish pride so that I could help others, as he had done. Two Suns, our clan matriarch, spoke to me about the precious circle of our existence. She encouraged me to balance life so that circle is never broken. I was commanded to pass the truth on to others. I was encouraged to become the healer when it was others who were healing me." *The Twins balance our lives, helping us to understand the complexities that define good and evil. As long as we are centered as a people, that balance will never be broken.*

"A fiery devil appeared, his face painted with the flames of hell. I thought he had come to take my soul, so I resisted him as I lay on my deathbed in Gettysburg. He really came to test my resolve. I discovered that his wisdom was all encompassing. Under his fearsome face lingered the gentle soul of a wise Indian shaman. This two-faced man called himself Three-Legged-Wolf." *I fear my son that you have not recognized that life has many paths. You only have sought to venture down one of those paths. If you wander off of that path to take another, you will see that life will twist and turn, then lead you toward new understanding, a truer vision of your destiny.*

Riordán smiled. "Go on boy. What else have you learned?"

There is more? I have revealed the depths of my soul and he is not satisfied? Does he intentionally drive me toward insanity and to what purpose? "What is it that you seek, father, for I am at a loss to bring more substance to the legends than I have already given you?" Jon looked down at the watch that mysteriously ticked away the time. "What about the needs of the cows?"

"The cattle can wait, Jon. You need to sort through this dilemma you are burdened with before we leave the barn, even if it takes all night. Your future depends on it and the legacy depends on it. If you allow it to fester, it will consume you with hatred and regret. Then, all will be lost."

A revelation struck Jon like a Reb bullet. He fingered the image of the horse. The stallion seemed to be in endless motion, galloping across the face of the legendary timepiece with its tail and mane trailing behind as if driven by the wind. The iridescent lightning bolts across his neck and torso emanated an ethereal light that drew Jon's eyes to them, revealing the truth.

Live within the Sacred Space. Walk in balance between the light and the dark. "It's the watch, isn't it? It is the key to my quest?"

"It is more than the watch, although that is the vessel that represents the devotion, loyalty, and loves that binds us together and secures the circle of our fate. It is what lies within the watch that is the force behind your renewed life. The power of your future lies with the horse, Yakohsa:tens. What have the stories told you about the mainstay of our family trade for over a century?"

Jon reworked the stories in his head until he had defined their meaning. The legacy of the powerful and influential men and woman that came before him was transforming his lucid soul.

Papineau had overcome human frailty to become the great compromiser. His quest for the truth fostered the assimilation of the clan into an evolving world. His unflappable wife, Two Suns, had conquered oppression to become a strong matriarchal leader and masterful horse whisperer. She was the soul of the legacy, placing women on a pedestal of high regard with her vision and straightforward approach to life. Their kin closed the circle, faced the challenges of an unresolved life, and uncloaked the mask of false hope to foster and fulfill an American dream.

Jon suddenly put the final pieces of the puzzle together. *Shallow roots will cause the mightiest of oaks to topple, uncontested to the ground in a stiff breeze. Spread your roots and nurture them so that their fingers may touch many lives and alter many fates.*

"Legend tells that the horse, Yakohsa:tens, represents the power of human resolve. It carries the medicine that purifies our soul, bears the weighted burdens of others, and binds us together. It strengthens our will to remain independent and free." He looked to his father for affirmation.

"The horse gives me the courage to be myself, seek my own balance, and bear the strain of complex challenges. In the ancient world, the horse came to our family as a gift from the Pathfinder, to show us the way toward enlightenment and to bind us together under common experiences and personal triumphs. When Two Suns and Papineau memorialized that bond in the watch, they forged our legacy." He fell back into the hay and looked up toward the rafters. A dove flew over him and he smiled as the weight lifted from him as if an angel had cast it away.

"You have always been free to seek your own path in life, Jon. Your calling is of your own choosing, as it is willed to you by the course of nature and your personal motivations. The horse will convey you through this journey. Aristocrat will fulfill your dreams and open up a new and exciting chapter to your life. Remember this. The calling of our clan has always been to serve the greater good of mankind. It is the horse that will carry you there."

The horse shall be emblazoned with bolts of lightning prominently displayed across his neck and torso. We shall ride upon the horse, through time, influencing others who carry it. It will be a faithful reminder of what we will forever stand for, how we have transformed ourselves, the lives of others, and history itself.

The lantern flickered as its oil began to run out. A breeze blew off of the river and whispered, *I am Pashkwadjash, the Shadow Self. Live unto thy true self and you shall be free, for you now carry the legacy of my name.* For the first time in his life, Jon understood the mystery behind his birthright. He was finally free of doubt and filled with the conviction to forge ahead, confident that he had the courage and wisdom to reconcile life's trials.

Riordán helped his son return the precious heirlooms to the trunk, save for the mystical watch. Other things of value were added to the deep confines of the chest over time. There they rested in relative obscurity, preserved for posterity for the next Holland generation to discover. As the antediluvian tales were passed from one mouth to another, other young men and woman would open the trunk's heavy casing to unveil the cloak of mystery it obscured in its dark hollows.

Jon slept for two days after the ordeal. He dreamed of a new awakening and communed with those who had created it for him. He arose from his slumber, refreshed, enlightened, and ready to carry on the traditions that defined him. But now, he was eager to venture out into new frontiers, just as his ancestors had done before him. He was the Shadow Self, carrying the burden of others and fulfilling the promise of an ancient woodsman, a tribal princess, and a sagacious chief.

Man, cannot discover new oceans, unless he has the courage to leave the shore…

Soon, the saga of the American nation would turn to another page and reveal a new chronicle of intrigue for the family that had descended from the woodsman, Papineau and his Indian bride, Two Suns.

When you are troubled, be still and wait. When your doubt has been lifted from you, then go forward with courage. So long as the mists encircle you, be still. When the sunlight pours through your soul and dispels the mists, as it surely will, then act with conviction, for your true calling has yet to reveal itself to you.